THE FIRE PIT

THE FIRE PIT

A FAROES NOVEL

CHRIS OULD

TITAN BOOKS

The Fire Pit
Print edition ISBN: 9781783297085
E-book edition ISBN: 9781783297092

Published by Titan Books
A division of Titan Publishing Group Ltd
144 Southwark Street, London SE1 0UP

First edition: February 2018
10 9 8 7 6 5 4 3 2 1

A CIP catalogue record for this title is available from the British Library.

Printed in the USA.

For Jens Jensen,
Per Skov Christensen
and Henning Munk Plum,
without whom these books would be much poorer.
Stora takk fyri, og tak.

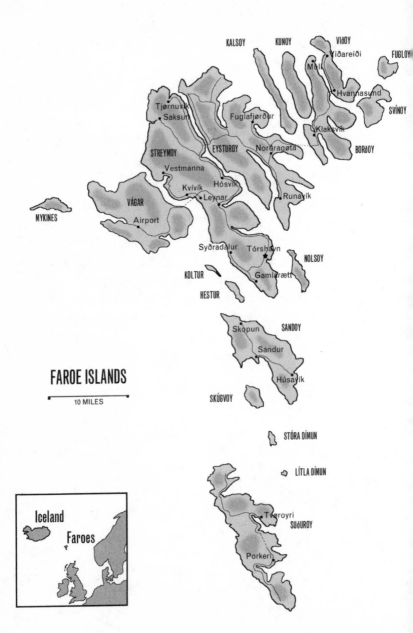

KALSOY   KUNOY   VIðOY

FUGLOY

Viðareiði

Múli

Hvannasund

SVÍNOY

Tjørnuvík

Saksun

Fuglafjørður

Klaksvík

STREYMOY

EYSTUROY

Norðragøta

BORðOY

Vestmanna

Hósvík

Kvívík

Leynar

Runavík

VÁGAR

MYKINES

Airport

Syðradalur

Tórshavn

NOLSOY

KOLTUR

Gamlarætt

HESTUR

Skopun

SANDOY

Sandur

FAROE ISLANDS

Húsavík

10 MILES

SKÚGVOY

STÓRA DÍMUN

LÍTLA DÍMUN

Iceland

Faroes

Tvøroyri

SUðUROY

Porkeri

FAROESE PRONUNCIATION

THE FAROESE LANGUAGE IS RELATED TO OLD NORSE AND Icelandic and is spoken by fewer than eighty thousand people worldwide. Its grammar is complicated and many words are pronounced far differently to the way they appear.

Ø is a "ur" sound, and the Ð or ð is usually silent, so Fríða would be pronounced Free-a. V is pronounced as a w, and j as a y, so Hjalti is pronounced "Yalti".

PRELUDE

Denmark, August

IN THE SUMMER HEAT OF MID JUTLAND, THOMAS FRIIS DROVE IN his shirtsleeves, his suit jacket hanging from the hook in the back of his Volvo estate. Rather than put on the air conditioning he preferred to travel with the window down, enjoying the warm, buffeting air. He had a day's leave, although he hadn't told this to his wife, whom he'd left at home in Aarhus with their two sons. If the boys had known about his day off the only destination on the cards would have been Legoland, which was definitely not on Friis's agenda.

Thomas Friis was thirty-four, a *kriminalassistent* grade 2 with Aarhus CID. In the department he knew he was regarded as something of an oddity; not in an especially bad way – he was a decent detective, after all – but mostly because he was someone who chose not to try to fit in. He was a *book man*, people said: always investigating by the book, by the numbers; always in a good suit, shoes polished daily, clean-shaven every morning. In other words, *dry*, *intellectual*, *dull*.

As the GPS showed he was nearing his destination Friis

checked his rear-view mirror and slowed on the quiet country lane. As far as the eye could see on either side of the road there were fields of tanned wheat, gracefully following the soft undulating contours of the low hills, occasionally scarred by twin tracks of a tractor's passage.

On the verge up ahead he saw the small wooden sign beside the mailbox – "Karensminde" – and at the entrance to the farm track he pulled in and brought the Volvo to a stop. In front of him the track went down a slight incline, unbounded by fences between it and the wheat fields, and after five or six hundred metres it ended at a solitary house out of sight of the road. It was bordered on two sides by tall, dark-green poplars, perhaps planted as a windbreak or to give shade.

Friis took all this in for a moment then reached for the thin manila file on the passenger seat. Inside it was Niels Jesper Kruse's three-page statement, and although Friis had exactly the same document on the laptop beside him he preferred the portability and ease of reading from paper.

> I got to the house at about eleven thirty in the morning and as I turned in at the top of the track I saw a white van down by the house, next to Helene's car. It was facing towards me and I didn't recognise it. I couldn't tell if there was anyone in it so I waited for a few seconds to see if it was going to move and come up the track, but when it didn't I drove on. I went fairly slowly because there had been ice on the roads that morning.

Looking at the track now, Friis had the same view that

Niels Kruse had had seven months ago. In January the fields would have been empty, of course, and the poplars would have been leafless, but neither of those factors would have affected the view of a white van parked beside the house. Okay then, Friis could move on. He let the Volvo roll forward, and stopped in the gravelled turning area in front of the house.

There was a stillness in the warm air when Friis got out of the car. Off to his right there were two small, wooden outbuildings, both black tarred, while the house itself was clad in white boards with yellow paint on the window frames. It looked well kept and neat, despite the fact it had been unoccupied since the winter.

I parked near the van. It had a sign on the side, something like Sørensen Cleaning; I think that was it. I thought Helene must have called someone in to do the carpets or something so I didn't think it was odd. I went to the house and in through the front door and I called out because I didn't see anyone.

There was no answer and I couldn't hear anything so I went to see if Helene was in the kitchen. She wasn't there, but there was a broken bowl on the floor and while I was looking at that I heard the van starting up outside. I went back to the hall and saw the van driving off very quickly and that was when I began to think something wasn't right. So I looked in the sitting room for Helene and Maja – I looked in all the downstairs rooms, calling out – and then I went upstairs. That's when I found them.

There hadn't been a problem getting the keys from the real-estate agent and Friis used them now, opening the white-painted front door as Niels Kruse had done.

Inside, the trapped air was warm and smelled vaguely of wood and of dust. The hall, like the rest of the house, was now empty of furniture and personal possessions. Only the carpets, curtains and blinds remained in place, doing something to stifle the sound of Friis's footsteps in the otherwise echoing space.

Holding his laptop before him, Friis visited each room on the ground floor, looking from the photographs of the house as it had been found by the technical team to the rooms as they were now. In a few places marks in the carpets showed where a piece of furniture had been, but beyond that the house had been returned to a blank canvas, awaiting the imprints of a new owner.

Having examined the ground floor, Friis took the curved staircase upwards. Upstairs the rooms had also been stripped bare, and in the master bedroom there was new, untrodden carpet, still smelling of lint. The original carpet had been disposed of, along with its blood stains. Helene Kruse had bled for some time before she died from the knife wound to her stomach.

I found Helene first. She was on the floor beside the bed in our— in the main bedroom. There was… There was a pool of blood and… I knew she was dead. I just stood there in shock. I couldn't move. Then I remembered Maja and I went to her room and that's where I found her. She was on her bed, lying very straight – you know, not like she was asleep but stiff, like a doll. She didn't have any clothes on and at first I thought she was dead, too. But then I realised she was breathing. I could just see her chest moving, so I went to her and tried to wake her up but she wouldn't respond. She was unconscious and nothing I did made any difference so that's when I called for an ambulance and the police. That was the first time I thought that was what I should do. I don't know why I didn't think it straight away, when I saw Helene, but I didn't.

The daughter's room – Maja's – was across the landing from the master bedroom. There were still traces to show where the posters of pop stars and Maja's drawings had been stuck to the walls, and from the window seat in the dormer there was a pleasant view across the fields. The room would have been a nice one for a young teenage girl to have as her own, but as he looked round Friis became certain that it was also the place where the second murder would have occurred – the one the killer had set out to commit from the start.

Maja had still been unconscious when she had arrived in the emergency department and the general consensus was that she had been drugged. Blood samples were taken and a thorough examination showed no physical injuries and no indications of rape or sexual assault. After two hours she started to come round and within six she was fully coherent and aware, although confused and very distressed when told what had happened to her mother.

Helene Kruse was confirmed dead at the scene and the

next day the results of the post-mortem showed that she had been stabbed once without signs of resistance. The cause of her death was blood loss and the technical analysis of the scene showed she had not moved or been moved after incurring the wound. This led to the conclusion that Helene, like Maja, might also have been drugged, but subsequent lab analysis could find little evidence to show what sort of drug had been used. Either the compound had been metabolised in the bodies of the two victims or had naturally broken down in a short space of time.

And exactly how the drug had been administered was another puzzle. There were no puncture wounds on Helene or Maja's bodies to indicate injection and Maja had no memory of events from that morning. However, both she and Helene had had milk with their breakfasts and both had recently drunk orange juice, which led to the suspicion that one of these liquids might have been spiked.

Tests on the cartons and other food in the refrigerator eventually came back negative, but as someone who might have induced his wife and daughter to unwittingly ingest a drug, Niels Kruse became the prime suspect in the hours immediately after the killing. The fact that he'd been separated from Helene for six months – albeit on apparently good terms – also brought him under suspicion until witness statements and data from his cellphone established beyond doubt that he could not have been at the house for more than five minutes before calling for help.

And that conclusion left the Billund CID with precisely no other viable leads. Technical could find no useful trace evidence of anyone else in the house; the white van marked *Sørensen Cleaning* couldn't be identified, and no matter how deeply the investigating officers dug into the private lives of Helene and Maja they could find no one with even a tenuous motive to do them harm. After six months, the best they could come up with was the theory that this attack had been the work of a stranger who had somehow talked his way into the house, overpowered and/or drugged mother and daughter and then been disturbed by the arrival of Niels Kruse. It was a conclusion that satisfied no one, but unless a witness or informant came forward with new information it was all they had.

After about five minutes in Maja's room, Thomas Friis closed his laptop and went back downstairs. He didn't believe anyone *would* come out of the woodwork to help Billund CID solve the case. What he did believe – what he was practically certain of now – was that there was nothing at all unprepared about the crimes at the Kruse house. They hadn't happened by chance, the acts hadn't been hurried and whoever had committed them had been forensically aware to the point of obsession. This, Friis was convinced, all went to show that the crimes at the house had been meticulously planned over weeks and probably months.

And this planning and forethought wasn't the only element that fitted the patterns in the cases Friis had been collecting over the last eight years. Maja Kruse was thirteen at the time of the attack, which placed her at the lower end of the age range of victims he was interested in, but even so she fitted all the other criteria. She was physically adolescent, slim, tall, had blond hair and didn't wear glasses or have dental braces. She also had a familiar pattern to her family background: one absent parent, a relatively isolated home and a quiet, somewhat introverted social life. In other words, Maja Kruse came from a predictable household and had a largely predictable life. If Friis was correct, then all this meant that – had she died – Maja Kruse would have been the eleventh murder victim of one man.

Outside in the heat and warm breeze, Friis walked round the house to the sound of the poplars. He looked at a copse of trees perhaps half a kilometre away on a small hillock and he examined the view from the house towards the road, going back inside and looking again from the master bedroom window. In all he spent about forty minutes in this manner before he got back in the Volvo and left.

Once he'd dropped off the house keys with the real-estate agent he set off back towards Aarhus. On the main road there was a sign for Billund, and beneath it to Legoland. It made him feel guilty for letting his obsession win out over his children and he made up his mind that next time – on his next day of leave – he'd take them somewhere to make up for it. But not Legoland.

1

Faroe Islands, September
Saturday/leygardagur

ON THE HILLSIDE BELOW THE LAST REMAINING HOUSE AT MÚLI, Hjalti Hentze waited. There was a light rain in the air, not yet heavy enough to make a noise as it landed on the various pieces of plastic sheeting around the stone wall of the sheepfold.

"You people have to stop killing each other," Sophie Krogh said, somewhat muffled.

"Yeh, you keep saying that," Hentze told her.

"Well, you keep on finding bodies."

"This one's hardly anything to do with us, though, is it?" Hentze said. "I mean, it's not recent. Jan Reyná thinks it's been there for a decade at least."

"And he's an expert is he?" Sophie asked, somewhat drily.

Hentze didn't say anything. It was hard to have a conversation with someone's backside, which was effectively what he was doing. Sophie Krogh was on her knees, her head down by the hole in the base of the wall, peering in with the aid of a torch.

Finally she wriggled backwards on the plastic sheet, then stood up.

"So what do you think?" Hentze asked, glad to finally be face to face again.

Sophie assessed the circular wall. "There are definitely remains in there still. We'll assume that they're human, given the skull was found nearby, so we'll have to dismantle the wall by hand. There's always a chance that something else is in the stones above the body – or below it, come to that."

"So you'll call in a team?"

Sophie shook her head. "We're busy enough as it is. No, I'll do the extraction myself if you can find me some muscle to help move the stones."

"How many people?"

"A couple should do. More than that and you risk missing something or just get in each other's way."

"Okay, I'll find a couple of guys who don't mind labouring on Sunday. Any idea how long it'll take?"

She looked at the wall, then the sky. "A day – probably. Depends what I find. It's too late to start now, though, and she's not going anywhere, so I'll record things as they are, then we can start first thing tomorrow."

"So you agree with Reyná that it's a female?"

"Based on the skull, yeh, I'll give him that. But you'll need to have Elisabet Hovgaard confirm it when we have all the bones. Do you have any sort of tent we can put up while we work?"

"I'll find something."

"Okay, *tak*. And you never know, if you're lucky she'll turn out to be a hundred years old and then you can forget it."

Hentze shook his head. "I'm never that lucky," he said, then looked away as a waterproof-clad figure strode up the hillside towards them. She was a young woman in her twenties, red hair spilling out from her hood and her face flushed with the exertion.

"*Hi, hi,*" she said, panting.

"This is my friend Katrina," Sophie said. "She wanted to see the islands so she flew out with me for a couple of days."

"It can't be much of a holiday for you if Sophie's working," Hentze said. "Aren't you bored?"

"Actually, I think it's really interesting," Katrina replied. "I mean, I get to see what Sophie does all day. I think that's exciting."

"Exciting? Oh, well, yes, I suppose so," Hentze said, but he saw Sophie roll her eyes slightly as she turned to take a camera from a flight case on the ground.

"Is it okay to look at the burned-out house?" Katrina asked then. "It's not a crime scene or something?"

"No, you can look," Hentze said, "but don't go too close. The whole thing's unstable."

"I'll be careful," Katrina said. And to Sophie, "Meet you at the car?"

"Yeh, give me five minutes."

Katrina set off up the hill at an enthusiastic pace and Hentze turned to Sophie with a questioning look.

"What?" Sophie said.

"I was just thinking that you know how to show your girlfriend a good time."

Sophie drew a sigh. "To be honest, I wish she'd stayed in Tórshavn to look at the shops or something."

"Oh? I thought this was a new and exciting romance. Isn't that what you said the other day?"

"Yeh, well, that was then and this is now," Sophie said gloomily. "I barely get to go for a piss on my own. It's claustrophobic."

"Ah, well, there's no one as enthusiastic as a new convert," Hentze said drily. "Didn't you say *that*, too?"

"Okay, go ahead and make fun," Sophie said. "I probably deserve it."

"Yeh, I think so," Hentze said. "For five minutes, at least."

Sophie gave him a look, then lifted her camera to take some photographs of the site. "So what's the story behind all this?" she asked, changing the subject. "There was a fire and a guy was found dead, is that right?"

"Yeh, his name was Justesen," Hentze told her. "He owned this land. He was also an alcoholic and terminally ill, so it looks like he hanged himself and his final cigarette burned the place down."

"And this?" Sophie asked, gesturing at the hole in the partly dismantled wall.

"We're only guessing, but at the moment I think Justesen uncovered the body – well, the skull anyway – before he died. Maybe it was some sort of act of contrition; not wanting to kill himself and leave her in an unknown grave. We don't know."

"Well he might have had the decency to do the job properly and take down the whole wall," Sophie said, snapping a last photo of the hole. "Some people have no consideration."

"No, no, that's true," Hentze said seriously. "But still, I expect if you give her the chance, Katrina will be only too glad to lend you a hand. Shall I ask her?"

"Don't you bloody dare," Sophie said. "Otherwise you might find yourself under your own pile of rocks."

An hour later Hentze drove without hurry along Yviri við Strond, past the heliport and a new care home for the elderly that was nearing completion. The traffic wasn't heavy and over the waters of Nólsoyarfjørður it was a flat, grey afternoon.

Remi Syderbø's car was in the parking lot at the back of the police station and as he pulled in beside it Hentze was glad to see that the extra vans – shipped in from Denmark to deal with the anti-whaling protests – had gone. Good.

Inside, the ground floor and stairwell were quiet. It would be busier later for the night shift, but Hentze's days of policing Tórshavn on a Saturday night were long gone. It wasn't something he missed.

Reaching the third floor he found the CID corridor practically deserted; a subdued stillness that reminded him of the atmosphere after last year's big storm had finally passed. Thirty-six hours of almost hurricane-force winds and heavy rain had stretched everyone to the limit, responding to emergencies as they arose, never certain what was going to happen next. It wasn't until the winds slackened and the phones gradually stopped ringing that they had finally started to believe that the worst might be over.

Hentze hoped that they were experiencing a similar, slow

return to normality now. It was almost two days since the explosion at the harbour and the arrests across the islands, and one day since the Danish security service had finally confirmed that the emergency was over and there was no further threat. Although there was still some dispute about jurisdiction in the case, the terrorists – a term Hentze disliked – had been transported to Denmark to be held on remand in a high-security facility. The Danes were citing national security as a reason to indict the suspects in Copenhagen, while the Faroe Islands' Prosecutor argued that the group should face a judge in Tórshavn.

It came down to politics, really, and unless he missed his guess, Hentze believed that having stood on principle for a while, the Faroese Prosecutor would "reluctantly" cede jurisdiction to Denmark. Better that than have the brouhaha of a large and complex prosecution eating up resources, followed by a trial dragging on for weeks or months. None of the accused were Faroese, so what did it matter where they were tried?

The one exception would be Lukas Drescher, who would undoubtedly be returned to stand trial for the murder of Erla Sivertsen. That was as it should be, but it wouldn't be for six months at least, and more likely closer to a year.

Hentze didn't bother to go to his own office but instead went along to Remi Syderbø's door where he knocked perfunctorily before going in. He was expected.

The only light in the room was from the reading lamp on Remi's desk. He was casually dressed and had his head on his hand as he read through a sheaf of papers, but he put them aside when Hentze walked in and waved him to a chair.

"So what does Sophie think?" Remi asked, standing up to come round the desk and take the second leather armchair.

"She agrees that it isn't a recent death," Hentze told him. "Which we could tell, so…"

"So there's no rush to find answers."

Hentze shook his head. "I don't think so. Sophie reckons it'll take a day to extract the remains so I'll talk to Hans and get a couple of his people to help shift the stones, starting tomorrow. Then it'll just be a matter of waiting for forensic results and going from there."

"You still think there's a link between the body being disturbed and the man – what was his name? Justesen? – who hanged himself in the house?"

"It's only a theory," Hentze said. "But it seems very coincidental if there isn't *some* link. It was Justesen's land after all."

"So you're still happy to oversee the case?"

"Sure, of course. At least until Ári comes back."

"Yes, well, I need to talk to you about that," Remi said. He took a moment, seemingly to try to formulate a diplomatic way to frame what he wanted to say next. In the end, though, the task seemed either too difficult, or perhaps just unnecessary. He pushed his glasses back on his nose. "This is strictly between us," he said.

"If you say so," Hentze agreed.

"Okay. Then you should know I've extended Ári's sick leave. He was signed off for a week because of his injury but I've added another week's leave. It hasn't been fully worked out yet because there needs to be some reshuffling, but when he does come back he'll be moving to the Prosecutor's office with responsibility for liaison with Denmark over the terrorism cases. To fill the gap, I'd like you to move up a grade."

Hentze made to speak, but Remi held up a hand. "Yeh, yeh, I know. Temporarily. I know you don't want the job, but someone has to step in or I can't do this. And you'd be doing Ári a favour as much as anything else. If he comes back here, I think— Well, let's just say things might be difficult. But the move to the Prosecutor's office allows him to save face."

"I suppose so," Hentze said: acknowledgement and acceptance. It was possibly the worst kept secret in CID that Ári Niclasen had lost the confidence and support of most of those working under him. To be fair, the events of the last few weeks could hardly have been anticipated, but even so Ári hadn't reacted well when the tensions around the whaling protests had been exacerbated by Erla Sivertsen's murder and the subsequent bombing conspiracy. After responding in the way that Ári had to all that, it was hard to see how he could simply return to his job as if nothing had happened.

"Would I have to change offices?" Hentze asked.

"Would you want to?"

"Probably not, given that it's only a temporary move."

"Okay, stay in your broom cupboard then," Remi said. "I don't care as long as we get back to some kind of normality as quickly as possible. So, you'll step up?"

"If that's what you want."

"Thank you. I think it's best all round."

Remi shifted then, as if he'd finally put something distasteful aside. "So, as acting inspector you should also know that I've been in discussion with Petra Langley from the Alliance. It's been agreed that there will be no more anti-whaling protests."

"She agreed or was told?"

Remi blurred the distinction with a gesture. "The Prosecutor is willing to acknowledge that the people being held on terrorism charges were not representative of the Atlantic Wildlife Conservation Alliance. In exchange, Petra Langley accepts that any further protest action by AWCA could be unnecessarily provocative. They planned to leave in a couple of weeks anyway so they'll wind up their operation early, leaving a few observers for any *grinds* that take place."

Another way to save face, Hentze thought. Still, it was all for the best. Perhaps now they *could* get back to normality, as Remi wanted.

"Okay then," Hentze said. "So, if that's all sorted out, do you have any objection if I bring Annika Mortensen on to the CID team?"

"Annika? Isn't she on sick leave because of her injuries from the explosion?"

"Yes, but I'd like to give her the opportunity to come back if she wants to. And since we seem to be playing musical chairs at the moment anyway…"

"Okay, whatever you think," Remi said with an air of finality. "I'll leave it to you." He stood up and went back to his desk.

"Are you staying?" Hentze asked, getting to his feet.

Remi nodded and glanced at his watch. "Rosa invited the grandkids over for the afternoon."

"But unfortunately Grandpa got called in to work?"

"Just for another hour or so, until they've worn themselves out."

"No wonder we have a bad name with our wives," Hentze said. "Even the weekends aren't safe any more."

2

Monday/mánadagur

I AWOKE, TENSED UNTIL I KNEW WHERE I WAS AND THEN LAY still for a while, until my pulse slowed. When I looked at the time on my phone it was 4:50 but I knew I was too awake to sleep again now.

Downstairs my packed bag was on the floor of the sitting room. I went to make coffee and some toast from the last of the bread. Outside it was still very dark and there was the faint noise of rain on the windows. Beyond that – perhaps – I thought I could pick out the sound of the waves on Leynar's black beach. It was high tide, I knew without thinking.

I'd grown very used to this place and thought I might miss it, although maybe what I'd miss most was the fact that living in Fríða's guesthouse gave me the feeling of being detached from real life; from the need for decisions or action. It couldn't last, but maybe that was as it should be. We might be cousins, but I couldn't live off Fríða's hospitality forever. She'd done enough over the last few weeks; it was time to go back.

After eating I had a shower and dressed. By the time I'd

done that I noticed that there were lights on in Fríða's place. She was a naturally early riser – usually coming back from a run just as I raised the blinds – but today I'd beaten her to it, albeit not out of choice.

At the table I sipped another coffee and opened my iPad to a magazine article Tove Hald had translated from Danish. I'd read a couple of paragraphs when there was a knock on the door and when I called out Fríða came in. She was in running gear, her blonde hair tied up and back to accommodate a head torch on a sweatband.

"I saw the light was on," she said, with a touch of concern. "You know we don't need to leave for more than an hour?"

"Yeah, I know, but I was awake so…" I shrugged and then, to deflect the subject, I gestured to the iPad. "I was just catching up on my reading. Tove sent me an article from a Danish magazine called *Provokation*. It's about Rasmus Matzen and the commune movement. He talks a bit about the Colony commune at Múli and why it didn't succeed. Apparently it was hard to grow food there and the weather wasn't what they expected."

"It never is," Fríða said drily. "But you have to come here to know that. Are you still thinking you'll go to Denmark to see him, to ask if he remembers your mother?"

I put the iPad aside. "I think so. Maybe at the end of the week. And Hjalti Hentze has asked a colleague in Copenhagen if she'll let me look at the police report on Lýdia's suicide."

"So you've talked to Hjalti about Lýdia?"

"A little."

"Good," she said with a nod.

"Why *good*?"

"Because he reads people well," Fríða said matter-of-factly. Then, "And it won't be a problem for you to go?"

"Not for me, no."

From her expression I could tell that she thought I'd dodged the question – which I had – but my interview with the Directorate of Professional Standards was set for tomorrow and once it was done the cards could fall as they liked. I wasn't sure how much I cared about the outcome any more – not enough to talk about it, anyway – so I picked up my mug and stood up.

"Coffee?" I asked.

Fríða shook her head and straightened up. "*Nej, takk. I* still want to run – just a short one," she added. "Twenty minutes, then a shower and we can go."

"It's still dark," I pointed out. "Listen, why don't you run later? I'll call a taxi instead. I don't want to mess up your day."

"The dark doesn't matter," she said, as pragmatic as ever. "I have my torch and the road's very smooth. No, I'll go now and we can leave for Vágar in an hour, okay?"

I knew better than to argue, so I didn't and later we drove to the airport as the sky started to pink up and the rain slackened off to a drizzle.

In the car park Fríða hugged me and kissed my cheek before getting back in her car, pulling away as I towed my bag across the wet tarmac to the terminal building. From then on whatever mixed feelings I had about leaving this place were gradually subsumed by the practicalities of travel, and then by the slow widening of distance – both real and imagined.

3

UNDER THE STARK MORTUARY LIGHTS ELISABET HOVGAARD surveyed the bones from the sheepfold at Múli, now laid out in skeletal order. They had been cleaned and the accreted dirt had been collected, filtered and sampled for lab analysis in Denmark. What was left was only human, and all the more naked for that, Hentze thought.

"It's a long time since I had to do this," Elisabet said, assessing the layout of the bones as if Hentze was responsible for setting her an unwelcome test of anatomical knowledge. "But for our purposes I don't suppose it matters so much whether I've got metacarpals and metatarsals in the wrong place. What's most to the point is that we seem to have everything accounted for." She looked towards Sophie. "You did a good job."

At the end of the stainless-steel table Sophie Krogh took a final photograph of the skeleton's clavicle, then lowered the camera to look at its screen.

"It was easier because she hadn't been buried," Sophie said. "At least not by much; the ground's pretty stony. My guess is they tried to dig a grave but then thought it would be easier – maybe quicker – just to dump rocks on top."

"And then build a sheep shelter?" Hentze asked, with only the slightest hint of scepticism.

"Well, it would be one way to make it less obvious that it was a grave site," Sophie said. "Also less chance of it being disturbed later on."

"True," Hentze agreed. "So, what do we know?"

Elisabet peeled off her gloves and crossed to a worktop where she picked up an iPad and an e-cigarette. She tapped the first and sucked on the other, making the light in the end of it glow.

"I'm trying to quit," she said when she saw Hentze's vaguely quizzical look. She exhaled vapour. "Don't say anything, all right?"

"Not a word," Hentze agreed.

"Good." Elisabet glanced at the iPad. "What I can tell you is that she was female, as we already thought. Approximately 170 centimetres tall, aged between thirty and forty. As far as it's possible to tell I'd say she was in good general health – no signs of osteoporosis, arthritis or disease, although she had an *ante mortem* break to the right-hand side of her clavicle: her collarbone. It was healing, though," she added, anticipating Hentze's question. "I'd say it happened between a month and six weeks before she died."

"Is it suspicious?" Hentze asked.

"No, not in my book," Elisabet said. "It could easily have been caused by a fall. Most are, unless you count contact sports. She'd probably have been wearing a sling, but maybe not."

"Could it help to identify her?"

"It's possible. If it happened here and if she was treated in the hospital there might be a record. The problem is, we don't know how far back to go."

"Between 1973 and 1975 might be a good starting point," Hentze said. "That's when the commune was active."

"I'll get someone to take a look," Elisabet said. "We have a new intern who shouldn't be let loose on the living *or* the dead yet."

"Thanks." Hentze looked back at the skeleton. "So is there anything to say how she might have died?"

Elisabet took another pull on her e-cigarette. "There's nothing as obvious as a fractured skull or multiple unhealed breaks, if that's what you mean. But Sophie thinks she may have found something else."

"It was only because I was cleaning the bones," Sophie said, as if she didn't want to accept any credit for extraordinary perception. She picked up one of the higher vertebrae and Hentze followed her across to an illuminated magnifier on the worktop. Holding the bone under the lens, Sophie turned it and then used the end of a wooden spatula to point out a thin mark about a centimetre long.

"Can you see it?" she asked.

Hentze squinted and leaned in closer to the lens. "I think so. The straight line?"

"Yeh. Nothing in nature is straight. I think it may be some kind of tool mark."

"What kind of tool?"

"My guess is a knife or blade," Sophie said. "It needs to be properly examined, though. I'm not an expert, but Per

Olesen and his team at Roskilde could tell you."

Hentze stood back. "And if it *is* a cut mark, what would that say? What would it mean?"

"It's on C4, a cervical vertebra, here," Elisabet said. She pointed to her neck just to the rear of her jaw. "Which could be consistent with her throat being cut, the same way you can kill a sheep."

For a second Hentze had to remind himself that the dumpy, often good-hearted woman before him was as unfazed by discussions of death and its causes as he was by a break-in or a domestic dispute.

"So we must suspect murder," he said. "Not just from the possible cut mark, but also from the way she was buried."

"Sorry, Hjalti," Elisabet said.

Hentze gave a resigned shrug. "Never mind. I'm sure one day I'll ask a question and someone will tell me I don't need to worry, everything's fine."

Sophie laughed drily. "You'd better not come and work in Denmark," she said.

From the hospital Hentze drove the short distance to Tvørgøta, which lay halfway up the slope of land that enfolded Tórshavn in the crook of the bay. Officer Annika Mortensen's flat was in the top half of a house, accessed around the back and up a flight of grey metal steps. By the door there was a solitary pot containing a lemon tree about a metre tall. It didn't have any fruit.

Hentze knocked on the door and waited. After half a

minute he knocked again, calling out, "Annika, it's Hjalti."

This time he was answered by an indistinct call from inside. It sounded like, "Hold on."

A minute or so later Annika Mortensen opened the door. She was dressed in pair of sweatpants and an oversized cardigan and was wearing her hair down. It also seemed a little more swept forward than usual, although this did little to hide the dressings on her forehead, right cheek and on her neck. Her left hand was bandaged as well, all the result of a burning mixture of petrol, diesel and oil. The same stuff had so badly injured the girl carrying the explosive device that she'd died twelve hours later; if Annika had been closer in her pursuit it was possible she would have been severely injured or killed, too.

"Are you hiding?" Hentze asked when Annika glanced warily at the steps behind him, as if she suspected he might be the scout for a larger raiding party.

"Yeh." Annika nodded.

"From who?"

"Start with my mother and go on till you get to Heri," Annika said. She stood back and held the door wider. "Come in. I'll make tea."

"I'd prefer coffee," Hentze said, following her inside. He knew about Annika's herbal teas.

"Sorry, I don't think I have any."

"Well it'll have to be tea then, I suppose. Thanks."

Annika made tea while Hentze prowled the sitting room. He felt slightly remiss for not coming before, although he had visited Annika in hospital the day after the incident. Since then, though, there had been an almost constant procession of paperwork to be dealt with, which had only increased now that he was covering Ári Niclasen's job.

"So, how are you feeling?" he asked when Annika carried two mugs in from the kitchen. The aroma they gave off was reminiscent of Chinese herbal medicine and when Hentze took a tentative sip it tasted like it, too. He put it discreetly aside.

"In myself, fine," Annika said. "I'm going to see Hans Lassen tomorrow about coming back to work."

"Are you sure?"

"Yeh I am," Annika said, sounding a touch jaded. "I mean, it's not like I'm *ill*. Apart from this" – she gestured with her bandaged left hand – "I'm perfectly well, and I'd rather be doing something than sitting around here. I don't suppose Hans will want me out on patrol while I still look like an extra from *The Curse of the Mummy's Tomb* but I could man the control room."

It was one of the things Hentze liked about Annika: she wasn't one for self-pity, and if she said she'd do something you knew that she would. That same attitude was at least partly responsible for the burns she'd sustained a few nights ago.

"Well, if you're set on coming back you *could* come in to CID," he told her. "We're one short at the moment, so there's a gap."

"You mean because of Ári?"

"Mm, sort of," Hentze said. "It hasn't been generally announced yet, but he's moving over to the Prosecutor's office, so I'm standing in until Remi sorts out a permanent replacement. Anyway, that leaves an opening – if you want it."

"Yes, yeh, of course," Annika said. "But you do know I've already applied to Copenhagen CID, right?"

"Sure, yes, I know. Have you heard back yet?"

"No, I think it'll be at least another couple of weeks."

"So you could think of this as a dry run until then. And if you want it I've got a case you can look after."

"Which case? I mean, not that I'm being picky."

"It's the woman's remains from Múli. Has Heri told you about it?" Heri Kalsø was her boyfriend and another uniform officer at the station.

"Yeh, a bit," Annika said. "Do you know who she was yet?"

"No, still unidentified, but it looks pretty certain she was murdered – not just because the body was concealed, but because she was buried face down and naked. Her throat may also have been cut."

"Seriously?"

"Unfortunately, yes." He considered Annika for a second. "So that's what you'd be working on: finding out who she was and how she came to be there."

"Who else is on the team?"

"Just you. Because of the age of the skeleton and the death of the most likely suspect, Remi's not keen to expend a lot of manpower on it. People are busy enough after last week, so that's understandable, I suppose, but this woman has already been forgotten for years, so I think the least we can do is give her what attention we can."

"Yeh, of course," Annika agreed. "But if it *is* murder, shouldn't you give it to someone more experienced?"

"Of course, but beggars can't be choosers, can they?"

Hentze said, his tone light. "So, what do you think – are you interested? You can do all the legwork and then I'll take the credit."

"Sure, of course. I wouldn't expect anything else." Annika grinned. "Thanks, Hjalti."

Hentze waved it away, then dug in his pocket for a flash drive which he tossed across to her. "This has what we know at the moment, so you'll be able to do your homework before tomorrow. We'll talk it through then." He glanced at his watch and stood up. "I have to go. Ári scheduled about a dozen meetings this week and I haven't been able to cancel them all yet, so…"

"So you have to grin and bear them?"

"Well, I have to bear them at least," Hentze said.

Annika followed him to the back door and held it as he went out of the flat. "By the way," she said, "I meant to ask you before, is Jan Reyná still around? I haven't seen him since the explosion."

"No, he had to go home."

"Oh. Right. But he was okay?"

"Better than he would have been if he'd drunk your tea," Hentze said, pursing his lips in distaste. "If you bring it into CID I'll have to send you back to uniform. Detectives only drink coffee. That's the first rule."

Annika laughed. "Thanks for the tip. I'll remember."

"Good. I'll see you tomorrow, then," Hentze said. "Eight o'clock."

4

IT WAS MID-AFTERNOON WHEN I OPENED THE DOOR OF THE flat and pulled my holdall awkwardly after me, letting the door close itself. The air inside was suspended and stale and there was the sweet scent of a browning apple in the fruit bowl. The light from the windows seemed grey and worn out, as if it, too, had been trapped. You see it a lot as a copper, places where time has been stopped and where nothing has been touched for days, weeks or months. Even so, it was odd to view the place more like a crime scene than a home, although it had never really been that. It had been intended to be temporary after the divorce, but somehow I was still there after eight years.

I dropped three weeks' worth of mail on the counter that divided the kitchen from the living room, and left the holdall where it was. I went to the bathroom, then the bedroom, then back to the living room. I opened a window a couple of inches, then checked the answerphone display but didn't pick up the handset despite sixteen messages blinking at me.

I was home, but I wasn't. I looked out of the window over the stepped skyline of roofs and block buildings. The first thing I'd noticed outside the airport was that the landscape was constrained wherever I looked: everything parcelled, divided, confined. The once-known had become foreign and I didn't feel that I fitted here or anywhere now.

I turned and looked round the flat. I could still feel the momentum of travel and when I considered all the dull practicalities of restarting my interaction with this place I knew the black dog was stirring. It was too soon to come to a rest so I picked up my car keys and let the door slam again as I went out.

The car had a thin coating of dust, which I took to show there hadn't been much rain while I'd been gone. The water jets and windscreen wipers created a double arc through the grime and I left it at that, adjusting to driving on the left again as I navigated the side streets as far as the ring road and headed west to the leafier suburbs where the sprawl of the city hadn't entirely subsumed older, smaller villages into its red brick and greyness.

The traffic hadn't reached rush-hour proportions yet and muscle memory took me out to Wingfield without major hold-ups. Off the main road this was a place of avenues and closes: the place where I'd been brought up; not much changed and not a bad place for that. At the end of Peter and Ketty's road I used the turning circle, then I came back and stopped beside the drive of the house.

Peter, my uncle and adoptive father, answered the door and we hugged on the step before he stood back, appraising me. Even in retirement he still managed to look as if he was only on a day off and tomorrow he'd be back to solicitor's business. Only the slight Parkinson's tremor in his left hand gave the lie to it.

"So, how are you?" he asked, as if his own appraisal wasn't enough without my own verdict, too.

"Okay," I told him. "Fine."

He nodded and ushered me inside. In the kitchen Ketty was preparing a meal, dressed in jeans and a sweatshirt that might have looked unnaturally optimistic on a woman ten years her junior, but with her well-cut grey hair and Faroese looks they just seemed effortlessly stylish. She was my mother's sister so it had always been tempting to think there would be some similarity between them if Lýdia had still been alive, but from what I knew about Lýdia now I doubted that would be true.

Ketty and Peter always ate early so Ketty's first order of business was to ascertain that I would stay, that I'd eat, and that I should know she had to go out to her knitting group later. After that she kissed my cheek and put her arm around me for a few seconds. She'd never been an overly tactile or expressive woman: too practical and down-to-earth for that. Childhood grazes and cuts warranted antiseptic and plasters, and sympathy for as long as they took to apply; adult wounds like divorce were self-inflicted and she wanted no part. *Sum tú reiðir, skalt tú liggja*: as you make your bed, so you can lie.

In reality she wasn't quite as chilly as that made her sound, but she was tough and to the point – maybe more so the older she'd got – so I was prepared for an interrogation as she tended to the cooking. But for once she was uncharacteristically forbearing, perhaps because she believed it was only her insistence that had made me go back to the Faroes: a last chance to make peace with Signar, my father. She'd got her way, even if the outcome hadn't been what she might have wanted. Perhaps she thought she should give me a break now.

There was still one question that couldn't be avoided, though.

"Did you speak to Signar in the hospital?" she asked, lifting the lid of the casserole dish to stir it.

"A little." I didn't say it had been barely six words. "It was the right thing to do," I added. "You were right about that." I could give her that much, even if it was less than the truth.

"Good. I'm glad if you think so," she said with a short nod. "These things, they should be done."

She covered the pot again and gestured to the cutlery drawer. "Set a place for yourself at the table, then we can eat."

We ate in front of the window that overlooked the garden and I was glad of the distraction that eating provided. It let me space out or divert the questions Ketty still had: who had I met, where had I been and what had I done? Peter, perhaps wisely, didn't say a great deal.

What I told them was heavily redacted, in part because to go into detail would have taken too long, and partly because I knew Ketty's main interest was in people, not events. So I talked about the people and places she'd know or know of. She hadn't been back to the Faroes for more than twenty years – the last time for her father's funeral – but she still had an expatriate's bond to the place. She tutted when something I said made her realise that something had changed in Tórshavn, as if the place had obviously gone to hell in a handcart because of her absence. I was almost prepared for her to announce that she'd have to go back and tell them the error of their ways, so she surprised me when she rose from the table at the end of the meal and said flatly, "Well, I won't see it again."

"Why not?" I asked.

She made a pragmatic shrug. "Why would I want to? Just to sit around talking to people and saying how things have changed for the worse? No. It's not my business any more." She picked up a plate, as if that put an end to the matter, and then turned to Peter. "You can get Jan to help wash the dishes. I need to change."

Peter and I decamped to the kitchen as bidden and a few minutes later Ketty came in wearing a jacket and looking Scandinavian smart. She was carrying a cloth bag full of knitting. "I won't be late," she told Peter, then touched my arm briefly. "Come back again soon."

I told her I would and she was gone. Ketty was like that – the sort of person who goes away to figure things out.

After we'd finished the dishes Peter took two beers from the fridge, and we carried them outside because it was still fairly warm and I had a pack of duty-free Prince in my hand. We sat at a wrought-iron table on the patio amongst the pot plants Ketty favoured for their neatness. I struck a light to the first cigarette from the pack and leaned back, finally beginning to relax.

"When did you start smoking again?" Peter asked.

"I haven't, not seriously."

For a moment he seemed to debate whether to challenge me about it, but then said instead, "So, you survived the family reunion."

"More or less."

"Ketty was glad you went. You know how she is. She might not show it, but she was worried that you'd regret it later if you didn't."

"Well it wasn't much of a reconciliation," I said. "I don't think he knew who I was."

"Oh. I see. I'm sorry."

I dismissed it with a gesture. "It doesn't matter. In some ways it might even have been better that way."

I drew smoke and flicked ash towards a plant pot. "Listen, can you tell me something? How well did you know Lýdia?"

Peter accepted the change in the subject without apparent reservation and considered it for a moment. "Not well," he said in the end. "I met her for the first time when Ketty and I got engaged. And she came to the wedding, of course. She would have been about fifteen then, I suppose. After that I don't think I saw her again until she left Signar and brought you to England."

"In '75?"

"Yes."

"Did you ever find out what was behind that – her leaving Signar, I mean?"

He thought about that, as if deciding on the best way to sum it up. "I think your father wanted a traditional wife," he said in the end. "And Lýdia didn't like the constraints."

"Was he abusive?"

"I don't think so; not physically, as far as I know. *Domineering* might be a better word, but that's only my impression. Lýdia's English wasn't as good as Ketty's and she never really talked about what had happened – not to me."

I took a pull on my beer. "While I was in the Faroes I saw Lýdia's medical records," I told him. "And I talked to a couple of people who knew her before we left the islands. From the sound of it her behaviour was pretty erratic. I think she might have been suffering from bipolar disorder, or something like it."

He thought about that, and I could tell that the solicitor's habit of not passing judgement hadn't left him even after three years of retirement. "I don't know enough about that sort of thing," he said in the end. "She was certainly... *impulsive*. When she came here she didn't seem to have any plan: she just arrived and then you were only here for a few months before you went off to Denmark. That was the last time I saw her before she died."

"Did you know she'd tried to kill herself before, on the Faroes?"

"No."

Which meant Ketty didn't know either, I assumed.

"So you had no warning when she died in Copenhagen," I said.

"No, nothing. The first thing we knew about it was a phone call from the police there. They said Lýdia was dead and they were calling because Ketty was listed as her next of kin."

"Not Signar?"

"No. I don't know where they got the information from – maybe her passport – but Signar wasn't mentioned. You were in a foster home and they said they needed a blood relation to take responsibility for you, so we flew out late the following day. It was harder to arrange things like that in those days."

I knew most of the rest: not from memory but from what I'd been told in the few instances when I'd asked Ketty about it. They hadn't been many because I'd always instinctively known it wasn't something either Ketty or Peter felt comfortable with, perhaps because they thought I should be protected from it. But I was as close now as I'd ever been to the subject, so in the end I trod out the cigarette I'd almost forgotten and sat forward a little.

"Did you have to make a formal identification?" I asked.

Peter nodded. "Ketty, not me. After that we were taken to see you. I think they were concerned because you wouldn't speak. To be honest, I had the impression they just wanted to pass on the responsibility for you as quickly as possible. It took a few days to sort out the papers, but after that – because Ketty was a Danish-Faroese citizen and Lýdia's next of kin – they let us take you away."

"Did they tell you anything else about how Lýdia died – I mean beyond the fact that she took an overdose?"

A look of concern crossed Peter's face and he'd started to shake his head before he thought better of it.

"What?" I asked.

He shook his head, more clearly this time. "It wasn't an overdose," he said, then took a moment. "She cut her wrists."

It wasn't what I'd expected – known. "No. Ketty told me… She definitely said it was pills."

"When?"

I frowned. "I don't know. Years ago, when I was a teenager, I suppose."

Peter nodded, as if that explained it. "She told me," he said. "You'd never asked before and when you did she thought it would be better – less upsetting – if she said it was tablets. I'm sorry."

The shift in perspective – in reality – threw me off kilter. It felt like *déjà vu* in reverse: not the feeling that I'd seen it before, but instead that what I'd always taken for real was an illusion. I'd pictured it, of course, and in that sense maybe Ketty had been right. It had been easier – less upsetting – to simply imagine someone going to sleep and not waking up. The setting may have varied in my imagination over the years, but always at the centre of it were a bed and a bedroom and a still, peaceful figure. I'd managed to hold on to that illusion – to protect it, I suppose – even after I'd learned the truth: that deaths by overdose aren't necessarily any more comfortable or clean than any others. But in my illusion there was no vomit or spasm, no voiding of bowels and bladder, only peace and repose. An easy death. Too easy. Too easy to do. Too easy to leave.

To leave me.

I knew that's what the various child psychologists had thought: that I resented Lýdia for abandoning me, and that I blamed Signar for failing, as my father, to make it all right afterwards. That was why I'd been troubled, they thought.

That was why I'd been disruptive, resentful and reckless and given Ketty and Peter a dozen years of various shit: some of it worse than the rest, but all shit just the same.

Truth was, you didn't need to be a psychologist to figure out any of that. I could have told them myself at any point between the ages of ten and eighteen – I just chose not to. Fuck them. I knew what I knew and it was my business, not theirs. They could all just fuck off and leave me alone.

"Jan?"

It came to me that Peter was speaking again and when I looked up I saw he was watching me with a frown of concern.

"It's getting chilly," he said again. "Let's go inside. Yes?"

He stood up but I stayed where I was. "Do you have any documents?" I asked. "Her death certificate? Anything official?"

"Yes, there were some things. I'd have to find them, though. I'm not sure where they'll be."

I was pretty sure he wasn't telling the truth. Peter was an organised man, and if I'd pressed him I think it might have taken him five minutes at most. But I knew what he was trying to do, and that it was well meant, so I didn't press him. Besides, his instinct to hold back might have been better than my own at that moment. I stood up and followed him inside, to the kitchen.

I was more tired from the day's continual movement than I'd realised, and probably not at my best, all things considered. I ought to go home, take a shower, go to bed in good time. I ought to think about tomorrow.

"I'll get off and leave you in peace," I told Peter, putting my not-quite-empty bottle down by the sink. "I've still got a few things to catch up on."

47

"Sure, of course."

"You'll look for that stuff, though? Anything you have. I'd like to see it."

He nodded. "I'll look in the morning and give you a call. I can bring it over to you; I'm thinking of Ketty."

Which I already knew. Peter Sherland was a good, decent man. He had to be to have put up with me for all the years that he had.

"Okay. *Takk*," I said.

He chuckled, a lighter note, and I realised what I'd said without thinking.

"*Takk fyri*," I said, and meant it this time.

5

IT WAS DARK BY THE TIME I GOT BACK TO THE FLAT, CARRYING a pint of petrol-station milk and a bottle of tonic I'd picked up on the way. The mundane action of buying the things had finally reconnected me to being here, despite the foreign notes in my wallet. It had also served to refocus my head on the here and now – or, more precisely, on tomorrow. Like it or not it demanded attention – if only until the interview was over – and as if to reinforce that fact I heard a call when I was a few yards away from the entrance door to the flats.

"Jan."

In the light from a street lamp I saw a woman in her early thirties, dressed in jeans and short jacket. Donna Scott moved briskly to be sure she'd reach me before I got to the door. Out of instinct I glanced round, checking the other cars I'd passed in the parking area, realising even as I did it that it was a waste of time.

"Have you got a minute?" Donna asked as she stopped in front of me.

"You shouldn't be here," I said.

"I need to talk to you. About tomorrow."

That went without saying, and for a moment I was tempted to tell her that *I* didn't need to talk. Instead, though, I turned and moved towards the building again. Donna came alongside me and after a couple of steps I said, "How did you know I was back?"

She gestured upward towards the flat. "Your window. It wasn't open before. And your car wasn't here."

That was the sort of copper she was.

"I was sorry to hear about your dad," she said.

I wondered how she *had* heard about that, but not enough to let it lead to a further discussion that I didn't want.

"Thanks," I said, unlocking the door. "You'd better come in."

We went up to the flat in silence and I opened the door, switched on the lights and took the milk and the tonic to the fridge while Donna went into the living room.

"When did you get back?" she asked across the breakfast counter. My bag was still in the centre of the living-room floor.

"A few hours ago."

"You cut it fine."

It was hard to tell from her tone whether she thought that showed confidence or that I'd made a mistake. "Did you hear about Paul Carney?" she asked, changing the subject.

I left the kitchen and went into the living room. "I haven't heard anything," I said. "What about him?"

"DNA's matched him to another rape in Doncaster eight months ago. They got a positive match from our arrest sample: hair and fibre, the whole lot. The girl took a chunk out of his cheek with her nails so he beat her to a pulp.

Fifteen," she added. "He took her from a bus stop, just like Claire Tilman, so it's a no-brainer: he obviously did both."

It was a simplistic interpretation, based more on hope than on logic. The Directorate of Professional Standards' questions tomorrow wouldn't be based on whether Carney had, in fact, raped Claire Tilman three times in the space of thirteen hours; or whether he'd kept her terrified and gagged in a garage during that time.

Donna Scott and I both knew that Paul Carney *had* done all that, leaving Claire so traumatised that she wouldn't leave the house unaccompanied even now, but it still wasn't the point. What the DPS were interested in – *all* they were interested in – was the allegation that Claire had been coached in her identification of Carney; prepared to the extent that she'd been shown his photo as a possible suspect several hours before she'd been asked to make a formal identification of her attacker. In The Job or out of it, coaching a witness was perverting the course of justice and it was a criminal offence; it was also what Donna and I would be facing if the DPS decided she'd done that and I'd let it go when I found out.

I went to the desk by the window, turned the chair and sat down. "So what did you tell the DPS when they asked why you had Carney's mugshot on your phone?" I said.

She shrugged. "The same as before. I said I had it because Carney matched a description we'd been given and I'd been looking for him that afternoon."

"*Before* Claire made the ID of Carney from the video line-up?"

"I had to," she said. "They examined my phone, so they

knew when the picture went on. But I told them I left the phone in the car while we were at Claire's, so she couldn't have seen his photo. I said you could verify that."

"So how did you account for Claire saying that she *did* see Carney's picture on your phone?" I asked.

Donna stiffened a little, the way some people do when they're on the stand. Her voice became neutral, matter-of-fact. "I said I'd done several interviews with her and during some of them she was very upset, so she must have got the sequence of events mixed up. I told them I'd only shown her the photo the day *after* Carney was charged, to prove to her that he was in custody and couldn't hurt her again."

"What about Matt Callaghan?" I said. "Will he back that up?" Callaghan had been partnered with Donna on the day she claimed to have shown the picture to Claire.

Donna shook her head. "He bottled it," she said with more than a touch of disdain. "He said he didn't see it because he'd stepped out to talk to Claire's parents."

So it came back to me, which was what Kirkland, my superintendent, had wanted. If the DPS believed that Donna had coached Claire to identify Carney, then at the very least I'd be seen as guilty of inadequate supervision for letting it happen. At worst I'd be deemed to have helped or encouraged her to pervert the course of justice.

Like I said, it didn't matter that Paul Carney *was* Claire Tilman's attacker and that everyone knew it. That wasn't the sort of justice DPS investigations were concerned with.

"So, what do you think?" Donna asked.

I knew what she wanted. She'd been in limbo for over

three weeks, not knowing how to prepare herself, or for what. But I'd been out of it, too, and I still wasn't fully back yet. I needed a drink and a shower and to unpack my bag and open the mail, and unless I was prepared to commit myself now there was nothing left to say. Donna had given her statement to the DPS and there was no changing that. *Sum tú reiðir, skalt tú liggja.*

I stood up. "Let's see how it goes in the morning," I told her. "I need to unpack."

She hesitated for a moment, then nodded stiffly. "I've been told to make myself available after they've seen you."

"Yeah, well, they'll want to make a decision without dragging it out."

"I suppose. Got your suit pressed?" She almost managed to make it offhand.

"Nah, sod it," I said, matching her tone. "I'll turn up like this. What can they do?"

6

Tuesday/týsdagur

ANNIKA HAD SET THE ALARM EARLY AND IN THE BATHROOM mirror she assessed the patches of pinkly blistered skin on her forehead, cheek and neck. She unfocused her eyes and tried to discern how obvious they were, then moved away from the mirror and tried again. At a distance of a couple of metres did they stand out?

Annika wasn't particularly vain about her appearance and she knew that she was only hypernaturally aware of it now because of the burns. It was impossible to be objective, though. She knew they were there, so her gaze sought them out.

The question she was trying to answer was whether or not she should cover them up with dressings. Her hand needed protection, but apart from while she was in bed at night, the doctor had said the facial dressings weren't necessary: it was up to her. She wasn't to apply any form of make-up to the blisters, however: not for at least two weeks. So, which drew – or would draw – most attention: unnatural dressings or unnatural scarring?

She looked at her watch and the time pressed her decision. She would go "naked".

Naturally enough there was some surprise and concern from the people she encountered as she entered the police station and went to her locker. She did a lot of smiling and nodding and repeating that yes, she was fine thanks; no, she didn't want to stay at home any longer, and yes it was true she was going to work in CID for a while.

The interest was all well meant, of course, but Annika could see people surreptitiously evaluating her blisters and wondering whether they would scar. She consoled herself with the knowledge that people only notice changes for a short time until the different becomes normal. All the same, by the time she went to Ári Niclasen's office to find Hentze she had the start of a headache.

The office was empty and dark and a vaguely irascible note was taped to the door: "*I am working from my own office, H.H.*"

"I thought you'd have moved into Ári's room just for the espresso machine," Annika said when she located Hentze in the small office Remi Syderbø referred to – not wholly inaccurately – as the broom cupboard. It was barely large enough to accommodate one other person besides Hentze himself.

Hentze shook his head, as if Annika's comment warranted serious consideration. "I know the way Remi's mind works," he said. "If he thinks I'm getting comfortable and settling in to the job he'll try to lumber me with it for good. The more people complain about having to come here to see me the sooner he'll find a permanent replacement for Ári." He stood up from his chair. "Come on, I need coffee," he said.

The CID lunchroom was empty and Hentze boiled the kettle and made strong instant coffee. Annika saw how many teaspoons of the stuff he used and said she'd make her own, then they sat down at the nearest table.

"You've looked at the files I gave you?" Hentze asked.

"Yeh, of course."

"Good. So, tell me your thoughts."

Annika opened her spiral-bound notebook. The first page was filled with neat, well-spaced handwriting. "Actually, I have more questions than conclusions," she said. "To start with, how certain can we be that Boas Justesen was the person who dug up Eve's skeleton?"

"*Eve?*" Hentze queried.

Annika felt momentarily embarrassed. "Oh, sorry, yeh. I thought it was easier to give her a name than keep saying *her* or *the victim*. I just thought…"

"No, it's a good thought," Hentze said. "And as to Justesen digging her up, I think it's the most likely scenario. I found cigarette butts and a vodka bottle near the sheepfold and sent them to the lab for a DNA comparison but I haven't heard back yet. You could chase it up."

"Okay." Annika turned a couple of pages to make a note. "So, if he *did* uncover her, he must have had something to do with her death."

"Logically, yes," Hentze acknowledged. "But it doesn't have to mean that he killed her. It would be easy to lay it at his door, but we shouldn't overlook the possibility that he was only a witness – possibly involved in the burial – and that someone else was responsible for her murder."

"And they could still be alive," Annika said. "They could still be here."

"Yeh, well, I wouldn't get too excited about that idea," Hentze cautioned. "I still think Justesen's the most likely suspect, all things considered, but I don't want to take the easy conclusion until we've explored every possibility. The main thing is to find out who Eve was. If we know that, we may be able to establish a motive for her killing."

"And you're sure she wasn't from the islands?"

"As sure as I can be. There are no outstanding reports from the 1970s of missing Faroese women matching her age and physical description."

"Well that's the other thing I was going to ask you," Annika said. "How do you know that's when she died?"

"I don't, not for certain," Hentze said. "Until we get a full analysis of the bones it's only a guess, but I think there are a couple of things that point us that way. For a start, that's when the Colony commune occupied the buildings at Múli – between 1973 and 1974 – and by all accounts there were people of several nationalities there. You saw the photos of the beads from Eve's bracelet?"

"Yeh. They do look pretty hippy-ish."

"The other indicator is this," Hentze said, opening his folder and taking out two large-scale maps, both folded back on themselves to show the same area. One was older and more visibly worn than the other. He turned them both so Annika could see.

"Here's Múli as it was in 1964," he said, indicating on the older map. "Now, compare it to this one from 1984. See the difference?" He pointed to a black *C*-shaped mark on the later map. "That's the sheepfold where the skeleton was found. It wasn't there in 1964, so it must have been built in the twenty years between the two surveys being done."

"Only you would have two maps of the same place, Hjalti."

"I have a modern one, too," he admitted. "But these were my father's. He was a man who liked to know where he was. Anyway, that's why I think Eve could have been killed at the time of the commune. The place was abandoned after they left and the peace symbol bracelet I found with her body could mean she was one of that group. If she was also a foreigner her disappearance might not have been noticed or reported."

"Well if she *was* there I suppose it's possible she could have met Justesen, too," Annika allowed. "Maybe he went out there to make sure they weren't wrecking the place. So I guess I should talk to his friends, relatives and neighbours and find out what he was doing during the seventies."

"I think it would be a good start," Hentze said. "Any background on his history and lifestyle may be useful, and you'll also need to keep track of the various lab reports I've asked for. It's too soon for any results to be in yet, but don't let them drag their feet just because she's been dead for a long time."

"No, I won't."

"Good." He pushed back his chair. "Find Oddur or Dánjal and tell them you need a desk. I have a planning and strategy meeting with Remi and the drugs team."

"*Planning and strategy?* You're starting to sound like an inspector already."

Hentze gave her a pained look and stood up. "Don't say that, even as a joke. I'm doing this for a couple of months at the most."

7

WE SAT IN AN INTERVIEW ROOM, LIKE TWO OLD FRIENDS OVER coffee. But there was no coffee, we weren't friends and everything we said was being recorded. As these things go it was relaxed enough, though. We all do our job.

"Detective Inspector Reyna, I'm DCI Jane Shannon attached to the Directorate of Professional Standards at Warwick Road police station. I am conducting an internal inquiry in relation to the arrest and charge of Paul Edward Carney for the rape and assault of Claire Victoria Tilman in April this year. You are not under arrest and you are free to leave if you wish. You may also seek free independent legal advice and have a solicitor or legal representative present during this interview if you'd like to. Do you wish to obtain legal advice?"

"No. Thank you."

"In that case I must tell you that you don't have to say anything, but it may harm your defence if you do not mention when questioned something you later rely on in court. Anything you do say may be given in evidence. Do you understand the caution?"

"Yes."

And so it began.

Fifty minutes later it was over and I didn't linger. There was no point.

Outside the nick I picked up a message on my mobile from Peter and called him back from the car. He was in town running errands, he said, and he'd brought Lýdia's things with him. If I'd be at home he could drop them off in an hour or so. I told him I'd see him then.

Now that I'd said my piece to DCI Shannon there was nothing else to do, so I took stock while I waited for Peter. I put clothes in the washing machine, cleared out expired food from the fridge and applied myself to the utility bills that had come in while I was away. I spent twenty minutes on the phone to the bank, shuffling money, paying off my credit-card balance and getting stung by the exchange rate with the Danish krone. It wasn't quite as bad as I'd feared, but not as good as I'd hoped. The one saving grace was that I was still being paid. Kirkland hadn't been able to stop that while I was suspended.

None of these tasks was enough, though. I still felt the urge to clear away even more crap, so I opened my laptop and went through my emails, deleting ninety per cent until I came to a message, sent an hour ago, with a *Københavns Politi* logo at the bottom. It was from Vicekriminalkommissær Christine Lynge, who said in stiff English that she was responding to my request via Hjalti Hentze to look at documents. These were now in her hands and if I would contact her by email or phone she would make them available to me at Station City, Halmtorvet.

I wasn't surprised that Hentze had been as good as his word, only that it had yielded a result so quickly. Even in Denmark I didn't believe it was normal for detective chief inspectors to bother themselves with requests like that, so I just hoped that Christine Lynge's stiff email tone was more to do with language translation than a general indication that she resented Hentze asking for a favour. Whatever the case, I sent a reply thanking her and saying I'd be in touch again within the next couple of days. I'd just finished typing when Peter buzzed the intercom.

He came in carrying a brown filing box and took stock of the place while I made us coffee. "Have you been in to work yet?" he asked. I'd changed back into jeans and a sweater, but the fact that I'd shaved might have prompted the question.

"Briefly," I said. "Just to sort out a few things."

I hadn't told him about the suspension, mostly so he wouldn't have to keep it from Ketty, but also because he'd be concerned.

To change the subject I looked at the box he'd brought in. It was taped closed and wasn't particularly large. Typical of Peter, there was a label on one side: *Lýdia Reyná*.

"You found her things."

Peter nodded. "We weren't able to bring much back to England. I just took the things from the flat that I thought might have sentimental value."

I resisted the impulse to draw the box closer and open it. Instead I said, "You did that on your own – collecting her belongings?"

"We thought it was better that Ketty spent as much time as possible with you and I'd look after the formalities: the funeral, her possessions, travel arrangements."

"So run me through what happened," I said. Since the previous evening I'd been able to gain some objectivity. "Last night you said that the Copenhagen police called to say Lýdia was dead and you went out there. Then what?"

He sipped his coffee and I could sense his reluctance. But he knew me and in the end he didn't bother to voice whatever reservations he had.

"We had a meeting with two police officers the morning after we arrived," he told me then. "They took us to the hospital and Ketty made a formal identification of Lýdia's body. Later, we went to see you at the foster home. You wouldn't speak at all. A Danish doctor we talked to afterwards said he thought it was elective mutism, but I don't think he was sure. No one knew how much Danish or English you understood, so Ketty talked to you in Faroese. It was better, but not much."

I had no recollection of any of this: never had. I was only three when Lýdia and I left the Faroes and my memories went no further back than the age of six, maybe seven. It was as if I'd wiped the slate clean of everything that had happened before I'd started living with Ketty and Peter and had only allowed myself to begin storing memories away once I was sure that I wouldn't be going anywhere else. Sometimes I thought the dark, formless things that woke me in the night might come from further back in my childhood because they seemed instinctive and primal, but I had no way to tell.

"Where were we living in Copenhagen?" I asked, to bring myself back to more neutral ground.

Peter couldn't quite prevent a look of distaste crossing his face. "It was a flat in the Christiania area. I remember I never felt very safe when I went there. It wasn't the sort of place you wanted to go after dark."

"So it was rough?"

He nodded. "I don't think you'd been living there – in the flat – very long. I collected up your clothes and toys and Lýdia's personal possessions but there wasn't very much." He nodded at the box. "Well, you can see. There was no point in taking away clothes and so on, so I told the girl who was sharing the flat to keep them herself or give them to charity. I don't know how much she understood, though: her English wasn't very good."

"Who was she, do you know?" The idea that someone else could have been around before Lýdia's death opened up a new possibility.

"I don't remember her name. I'm not sure she even told me. She was Danish, I think, but I only saw her once. I was sorting some things out for you at the flat and she let herself in and got a surprise when she saw me. I don't think she expected anyone else to be there."

"But she was definitely living in the flat?" I asked to confirm it.

"Yes, she had her own room. There were two I think. I remember the whole place was pretty makeshift: it was probably a squat."

"Do you know the address?"

"No. Sorry, I don't remember. It might be in the official documents, though. Everything we were given at the time is in there."

I looked at the box but knew I wouldn't open it until later. Instead I stood up and went as far as the window, looking out but not really seeing. Peter said nothing.

"So what about Signar?" I said in the end, turning away from the window. "Where was he in all this? Did anyone speak to him – I mean, as my father?"

Peter drew a breath. "Yes, I did."

"And?"

He looked as ill at ease as I had ever seen him; as if this, more than any other, was a subject he'd hoped not to revisit. "It was complicated – difficult," he said. "Ketty sent him a telegram when we arrived in Copenhagen, but he was working at sea and didn't get the message until three or four days later. Eventually he called the hotel and I spoke to him and told him what had happened. The funeral was already arranged for the next day – a cremation – and I'm not sure if he'd have come even if we'd delayed it, so we went ahead."

"And he didn't have anything to say about me going to England with you? He had no problem with that?"

"Like I said, it was difficult over the phone. There were several calls. In the end Ketty told him that unless he could come to Copenhagen before we left, we were going to take you home with us and we could sort things out from there."

I could imagine Ketty making that decision and then standing steadfastly by it. Even Signar, the bull of a man, wouldn't have been able to shake her once she'd made up her mind.

"And he didn't come."

I made it a statement, because it was, but maybe the fact that I said it so bluntly stirred Peter's instinct that every case has two sides.

"To be fair, I don't think it could have been an easy situation for him," Peter said. "He was out fishing for days at a time and to bring up a child on his own... Maybe he thought—" He broke off. "I don't know. I can't speak for him."

"No, of course not," I said, because it was true. He couldn't, and neither could I.

But it was no resolution, and now that Signar was dead there would never be one. I was free to choose how I interpreted his actions: as indifference to his son, or as a decision forced on him by circumstances he couldn't change.

Peter put his coffee mug aside. "I should be going."

"Yeah, of course. Thanks," I said.

I saw him to the door and when he'd gone I moved the box of Lýdia's things to the desk and opened it up.

The contents didn't fill it. A leather purse, handsewn and empty; a marbled fountain pen; a carved jewellery box holding inexpensive necklaces and earrings; and a small, gilt-framed, black-and-white photograph of a family group, stiffly posed in traditional costume. Flanking the two central figures in the picture I recognised Lýdia and Ketty, both smiling. Lýdia looked no more than thirteen, I thought, and I studied her closely for a few seconds before putting the frame to one side and picking up a couple of notebooks that had lain beneath it.

The first of these was a sketchbook and in it Lýdia had drawn things as disparate as flowers and plants, buildings, and a few landscapes. It seemed to me that she'd had a deft hand and a good eye, but none of the sketches looked finished, as if she'd only wanted to capture a moment and had simply stopped drawing when it had passed.

The other notebook was less well filled and from the way the handwritten entries were laid out I guessed they were poems, with crossings out and adjustments. As far as I could tell they were all in Faroese, which made them impenetrable to me, so I put them aside and picked up the last thing in the box: a solid, black camera.

It was a Leica, I saw from its embossed logo, but given that there were no photographs with it – no album or packet or envelope of loose snapshots – it struck me as odd. I couldn't imagine that Peter would have overlooked any photos when he collected Lýdia's possessions, so it seemed a strange thing for her to have owned if she didn't use it.

I turned it in my hand and when I looked at the counter on the top I saw it had reached twenty-one, so it looked as if there was film still inside. I didn't know much about film cameras – only that failing to rewind or open them properly would ruin the pictures – but after a moment of thinking I dug out my phone and pulled up the number for a guy called Ben Skinner who worked in the analysis branch.

"Listen, who do you know who could get a film out of a forty-year-old camera?" I said when he answered.

"What sort of camera?"

"It says Leicaflex SL2 on the front."

"Car boot?"

"No. Family heirloom. I only just found it and if there

is a film in it I'd like to get it out and have it processed. Is that possible?"

"It's possible," Ben said. "Depends how well the film's kept. Are you working?"

"No. Day off."

"Okay. Bring it down if you want then. I'll have a look."

"Now?"

"Yeah, I'm not busy. I can get the film out, at least, but if it is forty years old it may not be up to much."

"Thanks, Ben. I'll see you in a bit."

It was a distraction, I knew that. But better than being reduced to cleaning the flat, or just sitting and listening to the washing machine going round.

I drove the twenty miles down the motorway, turning off after four junctions and navigating my way round the anonymous industrial estate a mile further on until I came to an equally anonymous grey steel building. The analysis branch did various jobs and kept sensitive material of different types in this place, none of which were accessible or on view to the general public. To make sure of that the only windows were on the first floor and the gated reception desk was manned by a burly ex-copper called Dave, who knew me but still made me sign in while he called Ben Skinner to confirm that I was expected.

Ben met me at the head of the stairs to the first floor and led me the short distance to his office. He was a large man about my own age, with a rugby player's broken nose and the look of someone who wasn't afraid of a scrum: an odd type to be confined in a small, high-tech office. A sign over his desk summed him up: *Inefficiency on your part doesn't constitute an emergency on mine.*

"Decent camera," he said when I was seated and passed it over to him. "Expensive when they were made."

"Very?"

"I don't know how much, but more than the Japanese jobs like Pentax and Minolta. Leica's German," he added, just so I'd know.

He handled the camera with the facility of someone who was familiar with that sort of equipment, checking it over, then flipping out a little crank handle I hadn't been aware of.

"Thing is, if it's been like this for forty years like you said, the film'll probably break as soon as I try and rewind it."

"So it'll be screwed?" I asked.

"No, not necessarily, but you might lose the last couple of frames. Still want me to try?"

"What's the alternative?"

"You could just put it on your mantelpiece."

"Go ahead," I told him.

Ben applied a gentle pressure to the crank, increasing it slowly until it started to turn and I could hear something moving inside. He kept on going, his large fingers incongruous against the delicate mechanism, until finally the handle spun more rapidly without any tension.

"That's it," he said, glancing at the counter. "Better than I thought."

He sprang a catch and the back plate popped open. He

prised out a yellow roll of Kodak film and looked it over.

"Colour stock," he said.

"So I can take it to Boots?"

He gave me a withering look. "Leave it with me."

"Sure?"

He nodded. "You won't get prints, but if there's anything on the negative I'll scan it and you can print it off from a flash drive."

"Okay, thanks," I told him. "What's your poison?"

"Single malt. Glenfiddich for preference."

"Done."

"I'll call you," he said, looking at the roll of film again with a speculative expression that said it might be the most interesting part of his day. If so I was happy to share my distractions.

8

ACCORDING TO HENTZE'S NOTES, BOAS JUSTESEN HAD ONLY one known relative: a great-niece from Eiði called Selma Lützen, so Annika started there.

"I hardly knew him," the woman said, pegging clothes to the drying lines in the undercroft. She had a put-upon air, Annika thought, as if – what with the daily chores and everything else – talking to a police officer was yet another trial.

"I don't know anything about him, not really," Selma Lützen went on. "Only what I've heard, and I can't say that was good. Drank a lot, lived like a pig – so I'm told."

"Do you know if he had any close friends? I'm specifically interested in anyone who might have known him in the 1970s."

"No, I've no idea."

"Did he have any other relatives?" Annika asked. She picked up the peg basket and held it out, which earned her a faint warming.

"Well, now that you mention it, yes," Frú Lützen said. "I never knew till all this. There's a cousin – his name's Mikkjal Tausen. He's lived away for years – in America," she added as if that explained a lot. "But he's here now, on a visit. He's renting a house at Rituvík – a new one on Rituvíkarvegur. It's very nice." She lowered her voice confidentially. "He's done very well for himself."

Annika nodded to show she understood she was being trusted with this information. "How old is he?"

"Oh, I'm not sure," Selma Lützen said. "No youngster. Mid-sixties, maybe. About the same age as Boas."

She hung up the last shirt from the laundry basket and then she and Annika moved out of the undercroft to stand on the concrete path while Annika made a couple of notes.

"So apart from Mikkjal Tausen, is there anyone else you can think of who might be able to tell me about Boas?" Annika asked.

"No. I hadn't seen him since I was little and I hadn't given him a thought till that other officer rang me to say he was dead. I'll go to the funeral, though. You have to, don't you?"

"Yes, I suppose so," Annika said. "When is it?"

"Tomorrow at two in Fuglafjørður. Mikkjal's dealt with it all. That was a relief."

"You weren't expecting him to do it?"

"Well, I didn't know, did I? I mean, I thought it might fall on me. But as it turns out Mikkjal is – was – the closest relative, so I don't have that worry."

"Right, I see," Annika said. She recapped her pen and put it away. "Well, thanks for your help."

She was ready to leave but before she could do so Selma Lützen said, "If you don't mind me asking, what did you do to your face?"

Annika started to raise a self-conscious hand before she

caught herself. "It was the explosion at the harbour," she said. "Last week."

"Oh, that was a terrible business," Frú Lützen said. "I couldn't believe that would happen here. Well, it wouldn't, would it, if it wasn't for foreigners. It must've been horrible."

"I've had better experiences, yes."

"Well I'm glad you're all right."

It struck Annika as an odd expression of compassion from the otherwise indifferent woman.

"Thank you," she said and headed back to the car.

From Eiði, Annika drove the forty kilometres to Fuglafjørður, first south through the steep, brown-sided valley of Millum Fjarða as far as Undir Gøtueiði, then doubling back northwards to Justesen's home. There was no shorter or quicker way, although start and destination were only about twelve kilometres apart on a straight line.

At Justesen's house she interviewed the young couple who rented the upper part of the building, Aron and Kirstin Hallur. They had a newborn baby, four days old, and were understandably concerned that Justesen's death could mean they would have to find somewhere else to live.

The couple were well placed to be aware of Boas Justesen's lifestyle and they quickly confirmed Annika's impression that the man had been a barely functioning alcoholic whose days had been spent in a depressing cycle of drinking beer at Tóki's café bar by the harbour and weekly trips to the *rúsan* in Klaksvík to stock up on vodka. Boas didn't usually have visitors, Aron Hallur said, but uncharacteristically there had been two in the last couple of weeks. The most recent was an Englishman called Reyná who'd asked Boas about the commune at Múli; the other was an older man whom Aron Hallur didn't recognise: not a local, though, that was for sure.

After this, and for the sake of thoroughness, Annika also went to speak to Justesen's nearest neighbours along the road towards Fuglafjørður. She approached the house as a car pulled up on the drive and a middle-aged couple got out – the man in a sports jacket, his wife wearing a coat over her supermarket overall.

Once Annika explained why she was there, the man – whose name was Debes – cast a disapproving look at Boas Justesen's house, as if he was well used to doing so. They'd lived next to Justesen for twelve years, he told Annika, but apart from exchanging the occasional nod they'd had nothing to do with him. Nor had they wanted to.

"He should have been locked up years ago," Debes said. "Or had his car confiscated. He was a menace on the road. I don't think he ever drove when he was sober, and with kids wandering around… To be honest, I'm not sorry we won't have to put up with it any more."

"Did you ever report your concerns?" Annika asked mildly.

"No, but if the police did their job properly… It shouldn't be necessary for people to tell tales, should it?"

It was a fairly typical attitude. No one wanted to be accused of being a busybody, but at the same time they wanted their problems sorted out. All that was lacking was telepathic police officers, Annika thought.

Having said his piece, Debes went inside, but his wife lingered, which Annika took as an indication that she wanted to say more.

"You wouldn't know any of Boas's friends, I suppose?" Annika asked.

"We barely saw him," Frú Debes said. "Sometimes in the garden in summer, but that was years ago now. You can tell." She nodded towards the unkempt, overgrown patch of "garden" round Justesen's house. "He kept himself to himself and when our girls were small I used to tell them not to go bothering him – you know, just to stay away."

"Oh?" Annika said. "Didn't he like kids?"

"No, it wasn't that," Frú Debes said, glancing away for a moment. "I just didn't want them near him. Do you know what I mean?" She looked to see if Annika had picked up the inference.

"I think so," Annika said. "But did you have any reason to think—"

"No, no, nothing like that," Frú Debes cut in quickly. "I'm not saying he *would* have done anything. It was just… I don't know. *Something* about him, you know? As women, we have a sense for those things, don't we?"

"Yes, I suppose so," Annika said.

The acknowledgement seemed to satisfy Frú Debes, and now she gathered her bag. "Well, I'd better get on," she said.

Annika nodded. "Thanks for your time."

Her phone chimed in her pocket as she walked back towards her car. It was Dánjal Michelsen.

"Elisabet Hovgaard just rang from the hospital," he said.

"She says she's found some information about the body from Múli. Records, I think."

After only a day and a half as acting inspector – he still chose *not* to think of it as filling Ári's shoes – Hentze had come to a new understanding and perhaps even a grudging admiration of Ári Niclasen's talents. The greatest of these, as far as Hentze could work out, must have been one for typing. There was no other way Ári could have responded to the seemingly continuous stream of emails, reports, agendas and documents that seemed to be the sole function of an inspector.

And then there were the meetings. It was one thing to meet and discuss something specific like a theft or fraud case – even a murder. Those cases had a clear goal and the decisions you made could be acted upon. But rather than casework, most of the meetings Ári had scheduled seemed to be about things like "out-sourcing" and "productivity" or "maximising internal resources", all subjects about which Hentze knew almost nothing and cared even less.

No, there was no doubt about it, he decided; he just wasn't cut out for the role of inspector. He had been rowing his own boat for too long to suddenly be confined to the harbour and told to count masts.

"Is Ári a touch typist, do you know?" he asked Annika when she interrupted yet more laboured work at the keyboard.

"I don't know," Annika said with a frown. "Why?"

"Because it's the only thing I can think of that would account for him always leaving the office by five," Hentze said. He gave a sigh and pushed the keyboard away. "So, how did you get on with Justesen's friends and neighbours? Anything useful?"

"No, not so much. I did get the name of another relative, a Mikkjal Tausen, but I haven't found anyone who knew Justesen back in the seventies yet. I was thinking I might go to one or two of the bars he hung out in. If I can find someone about his age who knew him at school or worked with him…"

Hentze nodded. "When you find one you'll find the rest. Did you get the message from Elisabet by the way?"

"Yeh, I called in to see her on my way back," Annika said. She took a photocopy of a hospital record from the folder in her hand. "On 16 August 1974 a woman called Astrid Hege Dam was treated for a broken collarbone – the right-hand side – at the hospital emergency department. The cause of the injury is given as *fall from steps*. From her date of birth she was thirty-three and her address was just put down as *Norway*."

She handed the paper to Hentze, who took it and put on his reading glasses while Annika manoeuvred the spare chair into a position where she could sit down.

The hospital form had been filled out by hand, Hentze saw; and cursorily by the look of it. In places the handwriting was barely legible and simply stated the nature of the injury and the treatment given.

"Does this injury prove Astrid Dam is our skeleton, Eve?" he asked, looking up.

Annika shook her head. "Elisabet says they can't be certain without the X-rays from the time to make a direct comparison and the hospital can't find them. But I thought if Astrid was – is – our victim she might have been listed as missing, so I called the Missing Persons department in Oslo. She *is* on their database and they emailed her file across."

She opened her folder again and handed a poorly printed photograph to Hentze who took it and frowned. It was a studio portrait of a smiling, pleasant-faced woman in her early thirties, with brown, wavy hair down to her shoulders. It was cut in a noticeably 1970s style, as was the round-collared blouse she was wearing.

"According to the Norwegian information, Astrid was a teacher from a town called Voss," Annika said. "She'd taken a year out to travel but was reported missing on 4 November 1974 by her parents. The last contact they'd had with her was a series of postcards and a letter from the Faroes. In it she said she was living with some friends at Múli."

"The Colony commune?" Hentze asked.

"She doesn't say that specifically," Annika said, handing him a scanned copy of the handwritten letter. "But it must have been. The commune had the whole place, didn't they?"

"Yeh, I think so." He looked at the letter where Annika had highlighted the word Múli. "Do you read Norwegian?" The language was quite similar to Faroese in some ways.

"No, but I got the Norwegian officer to run through the basics," Annika said. "And I've been using online translation for the details."

"Okay, go on."

"Well, when Astrid's parents didn't hear from her again for a month they became concerned and went to their local police who contacted the station here. Apparently someone went out to Múli and asked about Astrid but was told she'd left a few weeks before. That was when she was listed as missing by the Norwegians."

Hentze absorbed all that for a moment, then said, "Well, we'll need dental records to confirm an identification, but from everything you've said I don't think there's any doubt, do you?"

"No, I don't think so," Annika said. "The Norwegians collect dental records as a matter of course once someone's been missing for more than a year so I've asked for Astrid's to be emailed across. Unfortunately that's not the only thing they're sending, though. Astrid wasn't travelling alone when she disappeared. She had her daughter with her: Else Elisabeth Dam, aged ten. She's also listed as missing."

"Oh, bloody hell," Hentze said.

"Yeh, that's what I thought. And there's one other thing, too. When I talked to Boas Justesen's neighbour, she implied that she didn't trust him near her children – her daughters. She said she wouldn't let them play near his house."

Hentze frowned. "Did she have anything to justify her suspicions?"

"No, not as far as I could tell. Just that he was a drunk. But with the little girl, Else, also missing…"

"Yeh, I see," Hentze said. "Bloody hell."

9

IN THE TIME IT HAD TAKEN FOR SOPHIE KROGH TO ARRIVE AT the station on Yviri við Strond there had been confirmation that the dental records held in Astrid Dam's Norwegian missing persons file matched those of the skeletal remains from Múli. The identification was unambiguous.

Armed with that information and the missing persons file on Astrid's daughter, Hentze had cancelled a meeting with HR about intranet protocols or something like that and called a case conference: something *worth* doing. Remi Syderbø joined him, Annika and Sophie in Ári's office. There was no question of meeting in the broom cupboard for this.

"Do we know when Astrid died?" Remi asked, leaning on Ári's desk.

"Not precisely," Annika said. "We know she was alive in September 1974 because of her hospital record and because she wrote home. In November it was said that she'd left the islands a few weeks ago, which would make it some time in October. Of course, she didn't leave at all, so we could suspect that October was when she died."

"And the daughter, Else?"

"We don't know," Annika said simply. "All we know is that she was with Astrid when she came here and was listed as missing at the same time."

Remi looked at the photograph of Else Dam stuck to the whiteboard. It might well have been taken at the same sitting as the portrait of her mother beside it; the background and lighting were the same. The little girl was blonde and blue-eyed, and she had a bright, slightly mischievous look, as if she had just been privy to a joke.

Remi looked at Sophie Krogh. "You're sure there was no other body under the sheepfold where Astrid was found?"

"As sure as I can be," Sophie said. "Your guys looked like they needed the exercise so I got them to take the whole structure down. There was no evidence of a second body: no soil staining or disturbance beyond the base of the wall. The ground's very stony, so digging a grave would have been difficult and there would have been traces."

Remi turned to Hentze. "So we have no way of knowing what really happened to Else."

"No," Hentze allowed. "But now we know that the body we have *is* that of Astrid Hege Dam I think we have to assume that Else is probably dead, too. It's hard to see any other likely possibility. In which case, the question is what happened to her body?"

"Well, there's no way to know, is there?" Remi said. "She could be anywhere, even in the sea."

"I don't think the sea's very likely," Hentze said. "There'd always be a chance that she would wash up, and anyone local would know that. Also, to me it doesn't make sense that the killer would go to the trouble of burying Astrid's body and carefully covering it up, but not do the same for Else's."

"Then why not put them *both* in the same place?" Remi asked.

Hentze shook his head. "I don't know, unless there was some delay between the crimes."

"Well, without evidence either way it's all still guesswork," Remi said. "So, as I said, Else's body could be anywhere. After all this time it's probably gone forever."

"If you wanted to check the immediate area around the settlement you could use ground-penetrating radar," Sophie said. "That would show up any potential grave sites and it would be fairly easy to bring in: just one person – the operator – and the equipment, that's all."

"And it's expensive, I expect," Remi said. "Plus flights, accommodation, subsistence allowance – all on an off chance."

"It would be an off chance," Hentze agreed. "But even if nothing came of it we'd be able to say we've put our best efforts into the search. I'm thinking of the Dam family," he added. "I'm sure they'd want that."

Remi gave him a sharp look but it was impossible to tell if Hentze's reasoning had swayed him. He turned back to Sophie instead. "How many days would it take?"

"Probably two, to cover the immediate area."

Remi chewed that over for a couple of seconds, but he was never one for much prevarication. "All right," he said in the end. "Two days, but no more. Will you be staying as well?"

"Well, with such warm hospitality how could I not?"

Sophie said, dipping her head in mock deference. "Although technically I'm on leave, so today was a freebie. Speaking of which, I'd better go and find Katrina. If I'm not getting paid at least I want to have sex." She stood up. "I'll call Copenhagen and see who can come out with the GPR rig."

"*Takk*," Hentze said.

"Okay, but tomorrow I'm back on the clock." And with that she made for the door.

"Was she serious?" Remi asked, once Sophie had left. He had switched back to Faroese now.

"About the sex? I expect so," Hentze said. "And probably about working for nothing today. I think she was glad of the distraction. Her girlfriend's a little... demanding, I think."

Remi was clearly reluctant to hear any more personal details. "So, apart from looking for a second grave, what's our strategy now?" he asked. "We know approximately when Astrid was killed, so are we still thinking Boas Justesen is the most likely suspect?"

"Well, he certainly knew about the grave," Hentze said, his tone measured. "And there's an implication that he might have taken an interest in young girls like Else, although there's nothing to show it's true. We can look into it, of course, but given that Astrid and Else were living at the commune I think we should concentrate on the people who were there at the time. Any one of them could have been a witness to Astrid's death – or her killer."

"And how easy is it going to be to find them after forty-odd years, do you think?" Remi asked a tad drily.

"Well, that's hard to tell until we start looking," Hentze

acknowledged. "But I think there *are* a couple of leads we could follow up."

When I got the call I didn't bother to put the suit on again, although I did exchange my sweatshirt for a jacket before I left the flat.

Outside Kirkland's office, I waited. But not long. When he opened the door his expression was serious but unreadable, which was the intention, of course.

"Come in, Jan."

I closed the door after me without being asked. I wasn't asked to sit down either, but that was all right with me.

"I can tell you now that the DPS won't be taking it further," Kirkland said as he moved round his desk. "DCI Shannon's satisfied that Claire Tilman could have confused the times when she was shown Carney's photo, so there's no case to answer. Your suspension, and DC Scott's, are lifted, although the facts of the inquiry may still come out at Carney's trial, if there is one. The CPS is in the process of reviewing the case."

I didn't have anything worth saying about that, and anything I did say wouldn't make any difference, so I just nodded. In the end it had been my word and Donna Scott's against a statement from a traumatised young girl who could easily have been mistaken, even if she wasn't. My silence wasn't enough for Kirkland, though. He thought he deserved some reaction.

"Do you have anything to say?" he asked, sitting down behind his desk.

"No, sir, not really," I said, keeping it formally stiff. "I'm just glad it's finally been sorted. I think Claire Tilman's been put through enough."

"Yes, well, maybe you should look to your own actions – and those of DC Scott – regarding that. Whatever the DPS says, I'm not happy with the way this was handled. At best you've dodged a bullet, so I think you need to seriously consider how you handled your team in this instance and whether lessons can be learned."

Kirkland had a streak of the vicar about him – a predisposition to sanctimony when an opportunity presented itself – but in a way I was glad he'd chosen to take to the pulpit now.

"And you'll do the same?" I asked flatly.

He looked genuinely surprised, as if I'd contradicted his sermon from the pews. "Excuse me?"

"You'll be considering whether lessons can be learned about how you handled things, too?" I said.

I'd put it in front of him, gift wrapped, but for a moment I could almost see him trying to make up his mind whether it was too easy. He wanted it, of course, but he was also suspicious. He was afraid it might explode in his face.

"I think you'd better explain what you mean," he said in the end. "When there's an allegation of misconduct—"

"Bullshit," I said. "There *wasn't* an allegation until you went to Matt Callaghan looking for dirt, and when he gave you a sniff of what *might* have happened you jumped on it." I shook my head. "You knew the DPS would have to interview Claire, even in her state, but you were so keen to get something on me that you didn't care. So after everything else she'd been through, Claire's left thinking no one believes her and runs away from home, making herself even more vulnerable."

Kirkland made to speak, but I didn't give him the space. "I reckon if anyone dodged a bullet it was you," I told him. "And that was only because she was found before anything else happened to her."

To give him his due, Kirkland knew when there was no purpose in arguing a moot point. Besides, I'd just changed the agenda, but before he could formulate a response to that I went on. "I'd like to request a leave of absence," I said. "Starting now, for a month."

I could tell he hadn't seen that one coming, but he was nothing if not quick to adapt. "On what grounds?"

"It's a personal matter."

He thought for a second or two and I knew what the calculation was. If it was something I wanted and something he could deny, then he would. Besides, he'd want me where he could see me while he worked out his next move. He shook his head. "I can't grant leaves of absence with the current workload, and obviously there are other issues we need to address here."

He looked for my response so I shrugged. "Okay then."

I took the ID lanyard from around my neck and my warrant card out of my pocket. In the time it took me to do that he'd already figured it out.

"I won't accept this," he said.

I put the IDs on the desk. "You'll get it in writing," I told him. "I'll take holiday entitlement to cover notice, or put in a sick note. Whichever you want."

I'd hoped for a better reaction. Of course I had. That's the point of making a dramatic gesture. But Kirkland was too good for that. It was the last thing he could withhold so he did, although it must have cost him to give up the satisfaction of a parting shot as I walked out. That was something, at least.

On the way out of the station I passed Donna Scott, smoking by the handrail of the disabled ramp. I barely stopped, but it was long enough. "They can't touch you," I said.

"Are you sure?"

"Yeah. In the clear."

She looked relieved. "Thanks, boss."

I waved it away, already moving again.

By the time I got to Ben Skinner's office – in response to his phone call as I'd started back to the flat – it was past five o'clock. I hadn't expected to hear from him for another day or so at least, but given what I'd just done it was probably better that it was now, before word had got out.

"I haven't had time to get the whisky," I said when he met me on the stairs once again.

"Doesn't matter. Come through."

It struck me that most of his previous bonhomie was gone, but some days are like that, especially in his job, so I followed him back to his office and Ben closed the door. "Where did the Leica come from?" he asked.

"Like I said: it's a family heirloom. It was one of the

things my mother had when she died in 1976. I hadn't seen it until today. Why?"

He'd moved round his desk and now he sat down and shifted his weight in his chair. He gave me a brief appraisal. "You'd better look at the pictures."

He turned to his monitor screen and I moved forward so I could see it as well. "It's not pleasant," he said. "Just to warn you, okay?"

"Okay."

He double-clicked a window and opened a photo viewer.

It took me a couple of seconds to fully adjust to what I was seeing. Whatever I'd expected, this wasn't it, and as my eye ran from one frame to the next I already knew it was one of those things you can't ever unsee. You get hardened to various things as a copper, and to some you become more sensitised. This wasn't one of the latter, but even so the cruelty of the images was shocking.

The girl was naked, pale-skinned, dark-haired, aged between fourteen and sixteen. She lay on some kind of bench or rough table above a flagstoned floor. Her head was inclined to one side on the boards, her eyes open but vacant. The only hint that she was alive were slight shifts in her unfocused pupils between one photo and another, and in one shot a blink or a closing of her eyelids had been caught part way through.

In each frame she seemed to have no reaction to the way she had been brutalised. The pictures became more specific, more intimate, more obsessed with the detail as they went on. They had a quality that seemed to reflect a desire to leave nothing to the imagination; to leave no possibility of doubt about what had been done. They celebrated it.

I'd seen enough. I moved away from Ben's desk and heard him clicking the computer mouse a couple of times, closing the file.

"These are level-one images," he told me then. "You don't get much worse, but I've never seen anything at that level from before the mid-nineties when the web really got going; nothing ever from the seventies."

"Maybe some things never change," I said flatly.

"Yeah – only the way they're distributed and the number of people who see them."

"So what do you need to do?" I asked.

He thought about that. "I don't know," he said in the end. "I could put them into the system, on to the database, but you know how many thousand images we get every week – I mean, new stuff, some of it only a few hours old? If your pictures were made forty years ago there's no chance of linking them to any paedophile networks active now. And the film stock *is* at least thirty years old, I checked."

"So?"

"Have you *any* idea where they were taken, or who by?"

I shook my head. "I can't start to guess," I said. "All I know is what I told you, except that the camera was in Denmark. That's where my mother died."

He thought about that for a moment, then made a decision. "Okay, I'm going to log them as recovered images from an unknown source and that'll probably be it."

"Fine," I said. "But can you put them on a flash drive for me as well?"

He gave me a sharp look and shook his head. "No."

"Ben—"

"Listen, if this isn't a case and they aren't evidence, you could be on very dodgy ground if you were found with them. Technically it could be taken as possessing, making or distributing indecent images of a child. Besides, why *would* you want them?"

"I don't," I said. "But they are evidence if I try to find out where they came from."

He frowned. "In Denmark?"

I could see how it didn't fit together from the outside, so I said, "It's a long story. My mother died when I was a kid, so I don't know why she'd have had that film or where it came from. But if I try to find out – if I got a chance to identify the girl or who did that to her – I'd need something to compare."

Ben didn't like it and there was no reason he would. It went against his instinct and probably a whole page of regulations, too. "So it'd stay off the books?"

"Unless I find something. And you said yourself, no one else will bother."

He still didn't like it, but he rummaged wordlessly in a desk drawer and took out a flash drive, which he plugged into his computer. He didn't say anything as he did what was necessary, then pulled the data stick from its slot. He held it out.

"It's just one picture," he said. "And you didn't get it from me."

I nodded. "You want me to sign anything – a disclaimer?"

"Fuck off. Just don't copy it on to a computer."

"I won't. Thanks."

He didn't want thanks. I didn't *want* the images that were now in my head, so that left two of us unhappy.

I didn't stay any longer than necessary when I got back to the flat: just long enough to go online, then write an email and make a couple of phone calls before I re-packed my bag. By midnight I was in a hotel at Heathrow. The first flight to Copenhagen was at six thirty.

10

Wednesday/mikudagur

THERE WERE THREE MISSED CALLS WHEN I SWITCHED ON MY phone as I walked down the ramp from the plane. Two of them deserved to be ignored, so I did, but I tapped the screen to call Hentze back without bothering to see if he'd left a message.

"Hey," I said when he answered. "You called me?"

"Yeh. Are you busy?"

"No. What's up?"

"I need to ask you a favour," he said. "The other day you told me you had the name of the man who was the leader of the Colony commune at Múli."

"Yeah, Rasmus Matzen."

"Do you have an address for him, too?"

"It's a place called Dannemare," I said. "I'm going to see him this afternoon to ask him about Lýdia."

That seemed to throw him. "Where are you?" he asked.

"Copenhagen," I said. "Kastrup. My flight just landed."

"Have you— You've been back to the UK?"

"Yeah, it's all sorted. No further action."

"So you're no longer suspended?"

"No, but I wanted to finish this now," I said, leaving it deliberately opaque. "I got an email from Christine Lynge as well, so I'm hoping to see her later today or tomorrow. Thanks for arranging that, by the way."

"*Nei*, it wasn't much," he said. I could still hear him recalibrating. "But if you're intending to speak to Rasmus Matzen in any case, would you do me a favour in return? Do you think you could ask him some questions for me?"

There weren't many reasons why Hentze would ask that, so I chose the most obvious one. "You've got an ID on the body from Múli?"

"Yeh, from a missing persons report in 1974. She was a Norwegian woman called Astrid Hege Dam."

"And you can connect her to the commune?"

"Yeh, I think so," Hentze said. "According to the Norwegian report she wrote letters home to say she was at Múli, but we don't have them so we don't know why she was there or for how long. Of course, I could call Rasmus Matzen to ask him, but if you're going to see him…"

"I could ask face to face?"

"It might be more… constructive. If you feel comfortable to do it."

"Sure, I'll ask him," I said. "I owe you that much for Christine Lynge. Hold on."

By now I'd emerged on to a wooden-floored mezzanine level with tall windows and benches. I took the nearest seat and fished in my bag for a notebook and pen. "Okay, tell me what you've got."

Hentze knew what I'd need and I wrote down the information he gave me without stopping him to ask questions. I filled a page with names, dates and what he wanted to know from Matzen. Some of it was questions I'd have asked anyway.

"So are you thinking her daughter's buried at Múli as well?" I asked when Hentze had finished.

"It has to be a possibility, yeh," he said flatly. "Sophie Krogh is looking for a second grave now."

I sensed that he wouldn't be happy whatever the outcome, and I knew why. Finding something would be just as bad as finding nothing at all.

Him and me both, then, although I didn't say it.

At the east harbour in Tórshavn, Annika boarded the ferry to Nólsoy with a few minutes to spare. The regular car ferry was in dock for repairs, so its place had been taken by the *Jósup*, which only carried foot passengers but was faster once it had nosed out of the harbour and into the strait of Nólsoyarfjørður.

The journey took just over ten minutes and it was choppy, the wind casting droplets of spray on the salted windows of the cabin where Annika sat and looked out. There was a freezer ship in the sound, its white hull stained by rust and showing no sign of life. Behind it, broken sunlight played across the hump of Eggjaklettur, rising to the south of the island's only village. It was a good day to be out on the water.

When the *Jósup* docked at the old quay Annika was the first to hop off, keen to do what she needed and not to miss the return sailing in an hour. A light rain blew in through the sunshine as she walked briskly around the harbour, then up the hill through the village, following the directions Gunnar Berthelsen's wife had given her when she'd rung to make sure the ex-superintendent would be at home. Hildur Berthelsen had sounded like a good-natured, obliging woman, which seemed a little at odds with her husband's reputation as an authoritarian. Although he'd retired well before Annika had joined the force, Gunnar Berthelsen was still quoted as a benchmark for any uncompromising attitude.

On the crest of the road Annika found the yellow, four-square house and her knock on the door was answered almost immediately by Hildur Berthelsen, as if she'd been waiting. She was a slight, withered woman with arthritic hands, and she greeted Annika warmly, inviting her in. The house smelled of dog and cigarette smoke.

"I'll tell Gunnar you're here. Please, go through to the sitting room."

An old Labrador greeted Annika with a twitch of its eyebrow but didn't rise from its bed beside the fireplace. The sitting room wasn't large and it was made to feel smaller by the dozens of paintings on the walls. The largest of these hung over the fireplace and on first glance Annika thought that the picture had been in some sort of accident. Painted in bright oils, it showed a naïve-style view of a Faroese village encircling a harbour. It would have been pleasant enough, like many in the Tórshavn galleries, except that on top of this scene the picture was scarred by gouges in its surface, harsh strokes of paint, which looked as if they'd been applied with a stick. When Annika looked closer there was no doubt about it: the slashes and defacement were intentional and something about the violence of that made her vaguely uneasy.

She was still looking at the painting when Hildur Berthelsen returned.

"That's Gunnar's favourite," she said, coming to stand beside Annika to appreciate the picture. "A collector in Los Angeles offered him half a million króna for it but he wouldn't let it go."

"Really?" Annika said, glad her surprise wouldn't necessarily be taken as disbelief that anyone would want to buy such a thing, let alone at that price.

"Oh yes," Hildur Berthelsen said proudly. "Gunnar has quite a following and he's entirely self-taught."

"You mean your husband painted that?"

"Yes, of course." Hildur Berthelsen chuckled. "And the thing of it is that he'd never even picked up a paintbrush until he retired from the police, and now it's a second career. He works all the time. I say to him – only in joke – that if he'd got on to it sooner we could be living in Paris or New York now. Of course, he'd hate that. We both would."

She cast a last, admiring look at the picture, then gestured Annika towards the door. "You can go over to the studio now. He's waiting for you."

Outside Annika followed a short path through untidy grass to a single-storey building – perhaps once a small cottage – of whitewashed stone under a red corrugated-iron roof. Beyond that there was a view over Nólsoy's rooftops to the rocky shore and then the wide expanse of open sea to the east.

She knocked on the worn wooden door of the studio and when she heard a voice from inside she worked the latch and went in. The place was a single, open room but cluttered by old tables strewn with tubes of paint, brushes, bottles, and the accoutrements of painting. The only clear area was one where a large canvas was supported by two easels side by side; an idealised picture of somewhere like Bøur or Gjógv, with grass-roofed houses and weatherboards rendered in yellows and blacks.

"Come in. Close the door," Gunnar Berthelsen said from in front of the picture. He must have been about eighty years old by Annika's reckoning, but he gave little sign that his age was a limiting factor in anything he did. He was a heavy-set man of medium height who moved with determination rather than ease. His white hair was severely cut and he was dressed in green overalls which bore the marks of hand-wiping and accidental rubbing on wet paint.

"Harra Berthelsen, I'm Annika Mortensen," Annika said after closing the door. "Thank you for seeing me."

"I can't give you long," Berthelsen said. "I've work to do."

"Yes, of course. I'll try to be as brief as I can, but I wanted to ask you about a missing persons enquiry from November 1974."

Berthelsen gave a dry laugh. "Are you joking?"

"I know it's a long time ago," Annika acknowledged. "But a couple of things might make it stand out."

"All right, sit down," Berthelsen said, gesturing to a scuffed leather armchair. For himself he dragged a tall wooden stool over the flagstone floor then leaned his weight against it, more as a prop than a seat. "So why would I remember a missing person from that long ago?" he asked.

"Well, for a start the enquiry came from the Norwegian police," Annika said. "And it concerned a mother and daughter, Astrid Hege Dam, aged thirty-three, and Else Elisabeth Dam, aged ten. They were believed to have been living at the Colony commune at Múli."

Gunnar Berthelsen gave her a slow, calculating look. "Which body did you find?"

"Well, I can't—"

Berthelsen cut her off with a wave of his hand. "Yes, you can. I heard about the skeleton being dug up, and it must be one of them or you wouldn't be here. So you might as well tell me – or do you think I'll go blabbing to the newspapers?"

"No, of course not," Annika said. "I didn't mean to—"

"So, who is it?"

"Astrid, the mother," Annika said, although the moment she did so she felt that she'd given up any kind of control over the way this conversation would go from now on.

Berthelsen straightened up off the stool and crossed to the large canvas. With his back turned towards Annika he stood still for a few seconds, then picked up a brush and used the point of the handle to make several harsh, angled scratches through the shapes of the houses.

"Do you remember any enquiries from the Norwegians?" Annika asked, attempting to gain traction again.

Berthelsen was weighing up the scratches he'd made and didn't reply. He added some more.

Annika tried again. "As an ex-police officer yourself I'm sure you—"

"I don't remember any enquiry," Berthelsen said. "But that shouldn't be a surprise. In 1974 I was Superintendent. An enquiry like that wouldn't have gone higher than the duty sergeant, or perhaps the inspector. Someone would have been sent out to see if the mother and daughter could be located and if not, that would've been that."

"Can you tell me who the inspectors were at that time?"

"Jørgensen, I think. But he's dead. And probably Karl Weihe."

Annika took out her notebook and wrote down the names. Berthelsen didn't look away from his canvas except to pick up a palette knife, which he used to slice through the oils.

"What about the sergeants at the time?" Annika asked.

"I don't remember. Look in the records," Berthelsen said, his back still towards her.

Annika could read all the signs, but what she couldn't work out was why the ex-superintendent had chosen to take this uncooperative attitude. It might be that he was just naturally obdurate, or that, given the opportunity, he felt like asserting his old authority again. Whatever the case, Annika knew he wanted to put an end to the interview, and for that reason alone she chose not to. She could be stubborn, as well.

"So what can you tell me about the commune at Múli?" she said, standing up and going across to position herself by Berthelsen's painting.

The old man glanced at her briefly then reached high on the canvas and carved a broad stroke from top right to bottom left. "They were foreigners," he said. "Outsiders. As bad as those anti-whaling protesters you've had to deal with."

"You mean they caused trouble?"

"No, I mean they came here without knowing anything about us or how we live. They just think they can come and inflict their views on to us."

Annika wasn't certain whether he was referring to the AWCA protesters now, or to the commune, but she didn't want to get sidetracked. "*Was* there any trouble at the commune?" she asked.

"Not as such, no." Berthelsen made a last slash at the canvas, then tossed the palette knife onto the nearest table. "Most of the time they kept themselves to themselves, but there were some complaints. The Hvannasund tunnel was still fairly new then, so you could get to the north side of the Borðoy more easily than in the past. Some people from Klaksvík said the commune was a bad influence on young people and attracted them away from the town."

"But there was nothing more serious than that?"

"Not that I recall."

Berthelsen wiped his hand on his overalls and crossed to the windowsill where a single cigarette lay beside a disposable lighter. He lit the cigarette, staring out at the sea, then turned back. "This is ancient history. Whoever you talk to, their memory isn't going to be any better than mine, not after more than forty years. In my opinion the best thing you could do is give the woman you found a decent burial and leave it at that."

"Even if we suspect a crime was committed?" Annika said.

"Of course a crime was committed," Berthelsen snorted. "How else would her body be there? But you've no chance of proving who did it any more than I'd expect your commander, Andrias Berg, to come here and ask me about it himself. He's got more sense. All he'll want is to be able to say that he's conducted an inquiry and no further action can be taken."

"Is that what you'd have done in your day: just given up?" Annika asked.

She'd intended to sting him, but instead Berthelsen just chuckled humourlessly as if he was wise to that trick. He drew on his cigarette then waved it towards the door.

"You'd better be on your way, Officer Mortensen. I can't help you," he said.

11

IT WAS A TWO-HOUR DRIVE FROM THE AIRPORT TO DANNEMARE and the satnav that came with the rental car – a Suzuki – didn't speak much: there was no need. The dual carriageway undulated its way more or less due south in bright sunshine that made me reach for sunglasses for the first time in weeks.

In the Faroes you're overshadowed by mountains wherever you go, and now – in their absence – I realised I'd got used to their overbearing presence, like a stern father, always looking on disapprovingly. The Danish countryside was gentler and more forgiving, though: rounded hills and sculpted, ploughed fields; trees still greenly in leaf despite a loose fall of orange and brown on the verges. There was blue, open sky and white clouds and I savoured the warmth as if it was something foreign. I had a strange feeling of release, too: I couldn't think of a better word for it. Perhaps it was just because I was a stranger in a strange land again; or perhaps it was simply that I could drive for close to a hundred miles without turns, without mountains or tunnels. Whatever it was, for the first time in several days the sunlight and space chased the grey pall from the edge of my thoughts and I felt better for it: focused on what I wanted to know.

A productive interview starts with good planning. The more you know before you question a suspect, the more you'll get when you interview them. Rasmus Matzen wasn't a suspect, though, so I knew I'd have to be tactful and that talking about the body under the sheepfold would not be a good starting point. I didn't mind asking Hentze's questions, but it wasn't my primary interest. Matzen was the only person I'd been able to locate who might have some direct memory of Lýdia from just before she abandoned the Faroes and what I wanted was anything he could tell me about the time she – and presumably I – had spent at his commune at Múli.

Most of what I knew about the place came from the newspaper clippings Tove Hald had found in the library in Tórshavn and translated for me. It was those I'd read again on the flight out, starting with the first mention of the Colony commune in an edition of *Sosialurin* from May 1973. In less than two column inches the news report said simply that land and houses at Múli had been rented by a group of young people from Denmark who wished to live close to nature as a commune. Their leader, as the report called him, was a man called Rasmus Matzen from Flensburg in Denmark whose age was given as twenty-six.

After that there was nothing more until August 1973, when a series of letters in the islands' two newspapers were published, voicing concern that the commune was attracting unsavoury elements from Denmark.

What followed was an article with the headline "A Visit To Múli", written by a journalist from *Dimmalætting* who appeared to have been sent to investigate what he referred to as "the recent questions and concerns about the Colony community at Múli". There was no direct reference to what those concerns might have been, so I could only assume that they were so familiar to the locals that they didn't need explaining.

The article spread to a generous page, with a photo of half a dozen hippyish men and women in their twenties standing against the backdrop of the houses and hillside. What it said, by and large, was what you might expect from any feature article even today. It seemed fairly well disposed towards the "Colonists" who, the reporter said, were young men and women who had come to the Faroes as an escape from the city life. They hoped to build a self-sufficient and peaceful community where artists would want to live and work in a cooperative and inspirational atmosphere.

It was all good, flower-power stuff: wholesome, wholegrained, vegetarian and woolly, but it didn't appear to appease the locals very much because the following week the article had prompted another flurry of letters questioning why the Faroes should play host to Denmark's drop-outs, whether there was drug use and criticising the newspaper for making the commune seem like a viable alternative to hard work and a God-fearing life.

It was difficult to tell how much this was all a "storm in a glass", as the Faroese would say. In close-knit communities small things take on larger significance than they would anywhere else, but all the same there were sporadic complaints via the letters page for several more weeks. Then there was nothing until the following November, 1974. This time it wasn't a letter but a short news report, as brief as the first, saying simply that the last residents of the commune at Múli had left earlier that week and gone back to Denmark. It also noted that fifty sheep, owned by the residents, had been bought back by the man who originally sold them. He said they were in poor condition. The commune had lasted seventeen months.

I suppose I'd expected Rasmus Matzen's house to be rustic and old. Instead it looked as if it had been built in the fifties: red brick, square and angular, with dormers in the roof. It sat in isolation about quarter of a mile from its nearest neighbour on a bend in the road, surrounded by a gravelled area at the front with a rack of vegetables for sale beside a sign, *Lokale Økologiske Grøntsager*. There was a dilapidated Volvo estate on the gravel and after a pause to assess the place, I pulled off the road and parked next to it.

Getting out of the car, I stretched my legs and looked the house over again. Closer to, it was tatty and clearly needed attention. There was flaking paint around the windows, loose mortar between bricks and the old panelled door had a crack in its glass.

There was no reply when I knocked so after waiting a minute or so I went around the house to the back where a wire fence marked out a square patch of land. It was planted with geometric precision and a woman in her sixties was raking one of the herb beds. She was about average height, dressed in work clothes, and when she sensed my arrival she looked up. I raised a hand in greeting.

"*Hi*," she said and her face moved to an easy smile, as if she was used to greeting strangers.

"*Hi, goddag*," I said, matching her smile. "*Taler de engelsk?*"

"Yes, sure, of course." She nodded. "How can I help you?"

"I'm looking for Rasmus Matzen. Does he live here?"

"Yes, he's my husband, but he isn't here at the moment."

"Oh, okay," I said. "Do you know when he'll be back? My name's Jan Reyna. My mother was—"

"Lýdia."

As she said it she seemed momentarily surprised at herself for making the connection, but then the frown was gone and in its place there was a look somewhere between incredulity and incomprehension as she looked me over again. "*Min Gud…* I can't believe this. You are Jan. I'm Elna, Elna Eskildsen." For a second she looked to see if my recognition matched her own. "But of course, you won't know me."

"No, I'm sorry."

She waved it away. "No, it's not important. You were too small: only four years the last time I saw you. How are you here?"

"Well, I'm trying to find out about Lýdia," I said. "I wanted to talk to people who knew her."

She shook her head, perhaps still getting to grips with my appearance out of the blue. "I can't believe it is you," she said again. "You must come in. Please." She gestured to the house. "Would you like to have coffee?"

"Sure, *tak*," I said, not to pass up the opportunity. "Coffee would be great, as long as I'm not interrupting anything."

"*Nej, nej.* Come in. Please. Come."

* * *

Inside the house the kitchen was very warm, the heat coming from a wood-burning range and despite the north-facing gloom Elna didn't switch on any lights. A long table sat at the centre, piled with papers, a basket of potatoes and two oil lamps.

"We live off the grid," Elna told me, as if anticipating a question. "No oil or gas, and just solar power for a few things. But we always have hot water for coffee." She tapped an enamel kettle on the stove plate. "Please, sit down anywhere."

I took a chair near a clear area of the table, and she talked almost without pause as she made coffee. By the time she brought two mugs to the table I knew that she lived here with Rasmus Matzen, that they ran an organic smallholding and that sometimes Rasmus ran courses for people who wanted to start their own self-sufficient plots. Elna herself taught people weaving so when I'd arrived she'd thought I might have come to enquire about that, but of course not, she said now, "You don't look like a man who likes plants or makes things."

"Not really," I admitted. "Only mistakes."

She laughed. "But not today, to find me," she said. "That is so good."

Given her unreserved pleasure that I was there, it wasn't surprising that I found myself liking her. But now that she'd settled across the table from me it was my turn to talk, answering her questions about where I lived and what I did with a potted history of my life since she'd last seen me.

'My father, Signar, died in the Faroes a couple of weeks

ago," I told her. "And while I was there I talked to a few people about Lýdia, too. I don't remember anything very much from when I was small – when Lýdia died – but when I was told that she'd been involved with Rasmus and the Colony commune at Múli I thought I'd see what else I could find out about her."

Elna nodded, as if to acknowledge that I'd brought us back to the nub of the thing. "I met Lýdia for the first time at the Colony, in 1973," she said. "It was also where I met Rasmus. I was there for six months and Lýdia stayed with us often at Múli: for a few days – sometimes longer. And you were with her, of course."

"What did she do there?" I asked. "I mean, was she just a visitor or did she get involved?"

"Oh, *ja*, she was involved," Elna said. "She was very, er... *enthusiastic* about what we were trying to do. And because she was Faroese she could sometimes help when we talked to local people for work or to buy things. To some of the group she gave lessons in Faroese, and she also helped with the cooking and garden and animals, too. Whatever was needed. That was just how it was there: we lived as a group and all did a fair share."

"Do you think she would have liked to be there all the time?" I asked.

Elna considered for a moment, then nodded. "I think maybe so. At Múli she always seemed joyful, you know? But at home with your father I don't think so much."

"Oh? Why not?"

She shrugged, perhaps reluctant to pass judgement. "I

can't say for sure. I never met your father, but I don't think it can have been so good for Lýdia or why would she want to come somewhere else – to the Colony – so much?"

"Were you at Múli until the commune closed down?"

She shook her head. "*Nej*, for only six months. My father was ill, so I had to come home to Denmark. The next year, when the Colony ended, I met Rasmus again and we have been together ever since. I didn't see Lýdia again until she came to stay with us in Christiania, the freetown in Copenhagen."

The jump forward caught me by surprise. "We stayed with you? When was that?"

She thought about that, working it out. "It was 1976," she said then. "Maybe *januar* – January or February. I'm not so sure, but one day there is a knock on the door of our apartment and there is Lýdia with you holding her hand. You are both looking very tired and cold, I remember that very well. So, of course, we took you inside and gave you some food and Lýdia told us you had left the Faroe Islands for good. She wants to live in the freetown, she says: to find a place to stay and to work. And because we have space in our house we all had a meeting and we gave you a room."

The place – more of an old warehouse than apartments, Elna said – was shared between half a dozen people: a communal squat, just like all the other buildings in the abandoned military base that made up Christiania. And from the way Elna described it, the house operated in a kind of organised chaos. No one was in charge and decisions were made by the inhabitants who also cooperated with day-to-day chores like cooking, cleaning and childcare. They shared basic necessities and a communal fund to which everyone contributed either in cash or in kind. They didn't reject the idea of paid work and earning a living, Elna said; they just chose to live as a group – *a family*, she called it – and be stronger together.

The whole set-up sounded impossibly idealistic and naïve to my cynical ear, but I reminded myself that those were different times, and maybe shouldn't be judged by what had come afterwards, which had hardly been better. Whatever the case, in order to contribute to the household Lýdia got a job in a city restaurant and I was left in the care of either Elna or anyone else who happened to be around, which led me to ask another question.

"While we were living in the house with you, what was Lýdia like?" I said. "I mean, was there anything odd – strange – about the way she behaved?"

Elna looked at her empty mug. "No, I don't think so," she said.

It was the first time I'd sensed anything other than the straight truth so I said, "Are you sure? I'd like to know because I think she may have been suffering from bipolar disorder – manic depression? I'm trying to understand what led up to her killing herself."

The reference to suicide made Elna shift and she turned it into pouring more coffee from the pot. We were drinking it black. "It's hard," she said. "To think of her now. Even in a short time she was in Christiania we became very close. Lýdia was my true friend, but I think maybe it was the first time she can do what *she* wants to do, so she did everything at once: always going from one place to another to see people and do lots of things."

"It doesn't sound like she had much time for childcare," I said.

"*Nej, nej,*" Elna said to negate the idea. "She was a *good* mother. Always. She loved you. I know that."

"But while she was working or off being busy, I was with you?" I asked. It wasn't hard to guess.

"*Ja*, nearly all of the time."

"And you didn't mind?" I asked. I felt vaguely guilty that I couldn't remember her from that age.

She laughed, as if the idea was absurd. "No, of course not. It was what I liked the best. To go with you out to the river or in the trees, or to do cooking: all sorts of things. Like my own. And if I sat down for a moment to rest you would straight away run to find a book and then you would say, 'Elna, Elna, read me a story in Denmark!' That was always the way you would say it. That I loved."

She laughed again, until a more serious look crossed her face. "But sometimes I think I should have told Lýdia what she is missing, you know? Perhaps I should have said to her to slow down. Perhaps if I had…" She trailed off. "I feel wrong for that." To punctuate the thought she reached for a tobacco tin on the oil cloth and sprang its lid.

"If she was manic I don't think it would have made any difference," I told her. "But thank you."

She looked up. "For what?"

"For being honest," I said. And then, because it sounded too solemn to my ear, I added, "And also for reading me stories."

"You are very welcome," she said with a faux-serious nod, then laughed and pulled a cigarette paper from its packet.

"So how long did we stay with you in Christiania?" I asked.

"A few months, maybe six. I thought you would stay for longer, but Lýdia had been told of a place in the country where there was a large house – a clinic of some sort – and a job for someone to clean and to cook. There were places to live for people who worked there, she said. And she didn't like the city so much any more because there were drugs in the freetown, and some trouble, too. It wasn't always so safe in those days, so she decided to go."

"Do you remember where this place was – the clinic?"

She frowned. "No, I don't remember the name," she said. "But I may be able to find it. After you left we wrote letters to each other – Lýdia and me. I think I still have them somewhere. I can look."

"*Tak*, that would be great," I said.

"There aren't so many," Elna said, as if she didn't want to get my hopes up. There was a distant, unhappy look in her eyes. "Afterwards it was a hard thing to hear what had happened. I wish I had known sooner where you were, who you were with. But it was not until a long time that I knew, and then it was too late. But I have thought often what happened to you. And if— If things could have been made different, I…"

She shook her head and turned away. I realised that she was fighting off tears.

"Hey, it's okay," I said, caught off guard.

She raised a hand to her face so I wouldn't see, but I thought I understood. There's no way to know – either as a child or an adult – what emotional roots you plant just by sharing time with someone. But I realised now that my four-year-old self must have planted them deep in Elna Eskildsen while she looked after me in Lýdia's absence. *Like my own*, she'd said. Not a figure of speech. I kept quiet for a while.

Finally Elna won herself back, stiffening her shoulders. "When you left Christiania I cried for a week," she said. "But you were Lýdia's boy. I knew this. So."

Then we heard the sound of a car engine outside. "That will be Rasmus," she said.

12

IT HAD ALWAYS SEEMED UNLIKELY TO HENTZE THAT BOAS Justesen's funeral service would be a well-attended affair, and so it proved. Apart from the hearse and the funeral car there were just two other vehicles in the Fuglafjørður church car park. The coffin and mourners were already inside and Hentze entered the church just before the service started.

The woman Hentze took to be Justesen's great-niece, Selma Lützen, and her husband sat in the front row of pews. They were accompanied by a distinguished-looking man in a dark suit, and by a tall, elegant woman, her blond hair in a plait. Behind them were a handful of people, amongst them the young man Aron Hallur who rented the upper part of Justesen's house, and the proprietor of Toki's café bar, who might well have been mourning the loss of his best patron.

Hentze himself sat to one side and several rows back and did no more than look solemn and thoughtful. He did not join in the prayers and, wisely, there were no hymns. In the high-vaulted modernist interior of the church any singing by the small group, however lusty, would have been lost.

The sunshine falling on the light wood of the church's

interior did nothing to make the small turn-out a less depressing reflection of Boas Justesen's passing and it was clearly a struggle for the pastor to find anything very uplifting about his life. She chose to focus on his early years working on the sea, and then on the courage with which he had faced illness and the challenges of his last months, naturally failing to mention that the main source of this courage had been found at the bottom of a bottle. No one seemed to mind that the service was short, and once it was concluded the undertakers returned to the coffin to carry it out. Hentze didn't join the small party at the graveside, instead seeking out a grey-haired man from the small congregation who had stayed by the church for a smoke.

"Did you know Boas well?" Hentze asked, declining the proffered pack of red Prince.

"Since school," the man said. "Tell the truth, I never liked him that much. You're not supposed to say these things, I know, but he was an arsehole so I never had a lot to do with him if I could help it."

"So why come to his funeral?" Hentze asked, genuinely curious.

The man shrugged. "Not sure, really. I've been to two others in the last year: both blokes I grew up with. Seems like we're all suddenly dying off. And it's not like we're old – I mean, not *old* old – but all the same it makes you think. Maybe that's why I came: to focus my mind on the fact I might be the next one. That's something we should all think about, eh?"

"I suppose so," Hentze concurred.

The man took a last drag on his cigarette and trod it out. "Well, have a good day," he said, moving off.

Hentze did not attempt to detain him with any more questions.

* * *

In the basement of the church a small meeting room was set out for a wake that was clearly over-catered. There were enough cakes and pastries for at least thirty people, and all of them had obviously been made by a baker rather than put together in somebody's kitchen.

Without the cover of numbers or the background noise of multiple conversations, Hentze knew it was unlikely that anyone would be particularly candid about the man they had just buried, so after paying his respects to Selma Lützen and her husband, he approached the prosperous-looking man who'd been with them during the service. This was Mikkjal Tausen. And he was in his early sixties, Hentze guessed, about the same age as Boas Justesen.

They shook hands and Hentze noticed that although his Faroese was still fluent, Tausen's accent and pronunciation occasionally showed signs that he had spent a long time speaking American English.

"This is Sigi – Sigrun Ludvig," Tausen said, introducing the woman beside him. She was at least twenty years his junior; good-looking and wearing a black designer dress.

The woman smiled easily at Hentze but then her gaze drifted past him, to the people hovering near the food.

"We're going to have nearly as many cakes as we started with," she told Tausen with some concern. "I'll try to get people to eat more."

"Okay, thanks, love," Tausen said.

"Your wife?" Hentze enquired lightly as Sigrun moved away.

"No, at the moment we're just dating," Tausen said. "I've been married twice – both times in the US, both a mistake for one reason or another. So after the last time I thought that was it: no more romance. But I met Sigi the day I arrived here. She works for Müller's, the letting agency, and when she showed me the house I'm renting in Rituvík we hit it off immediately. To tell you the truth, she's the main reason I decided to stay for longer than I originally planned."

"I see," Hentze said. "So you're only on a visit?"

"At the moment. But if things go well... You never know, do you?"

"Do you mind if I ask what you do in America?"

"I'm retired now – well, semi-retired. I trained as a chemist, but in the States I got into manufacturing polymers – plastics – and specialist mouldings. I've done well, I'll make no bones about that, enough that I can step back a little and make the most of life. If I'd known Sigi was here I would've come back years ago."

He glanced appreciatively at Sigrun, then looked back at Hentze as if remembering his manners. "Listen, I should thank you for coming," he said. "I appreciate it, especially as I gather that Boas didn't always have the best of relationships with the police."

"No, well, that's water under the bridge," Hentze said. "And in the circumstances..."

"Yeh, yeh, of course."

"And as well as paying the department's respects, I was hoping to find out a little more about Boas," Hentze said. "Although I realise this might not be the best time."

Tausen looked around the barely occupied room, as if it made his point for him. "Please, ask away," he said. "I don't know how much I can tell you, though. I hadn't seen Boas for forty-odd years until just recently."

"You were cousins, is that right?"

"Yeh, on my father's side. But we weren't close. I didn't see much of him, even before I left for America."

"But you knew him in the 1970s?"

"Yeh, I'd see him in Klaksvík on Saturday nights. He liked a drink even then."

Hentze nodded to acknowledge the fact that Boas Justesen had set his path early. "So would that have been around the same time that the Colony commune was renting his land out at Múli?" he asked.

"Yeh, I suppose so," Tausen said.

"Do you know if he had much to do with the people there?"

Tausen gave Hentze a slightly reappraising look. "Are you asking because of the grave they found there?"

"Yes, in part," Hentze admitted. "We still can't be sure when the person was buried or how they died, but it seems possible that it might have been while the commune was there."

"And you think Boas might have been involved in some way?" Tausen sounded sceptical.

"Well, it's too early in the investigation to have any theories," Hentze said. "We don't have enough information, which is why I was asking about it."

"Well Boas did go there," Tausen said. "In fact, I went with him once myself. I was on a visit home from Denmark and there was a party of some sort – a birthday, maybe. As I remember,

Boas seemed to know the people pretty well. I think the – what would you call it? – the free spirit of the place appealed to him. It was certainly very different to the rest of the islands at the time."

"Oh, in what way?"

Mikkjal Tausen hesitated for a second, as if debating the wisdom of being candid. "Well, everything was very relaxed there – *laid back* as the Americans would say. And I don't suppose it hurts now to say there was some hash and home brew. So, with a few pretty foreign girls, too…"

"Yeh, I see," Hentze said. "So do you think Boas was a regular visitor to the commune?"

"No, I don't know," Tausen said. "He certainly could have been – he was the landowner, after all – but he wasn't the sort to be involved in someone's death, I know that. Like I said, he was more interested in the free and easy lifestyle."

"I don't suppose you remember the names of anyone who was living there, do you?"

Tausen shook his head hopelessly. "No, not after this long. I think most of the people were Danish, maybe a few other nationalities, but I really can't remember any more than that. Like I said, I was living in Denmark and then I went to the States. I didn't see Boas again until a few weeks ago, when I came back. It was quite a shock."

"Oh? In what way?"

"Well, just the state he was in, what with the drink and the cancer. To be honest, I felt sorry for him. He'd done nothing with his life, he had no one to care about him and he was obviously afraid of dying alone and in pain. I think that's why he chose to kill himself when he did, rather than go on to the end."

"Did he ever say anything that struck you as odd? Anything about Múli or the commune?"

"No, nothing like that. He just seemed depressed and very bitter about life."

They were interrupted by the owner of Tóki's approaching to take his leave, and once that precedent had been set it didn't take long for the few other people in the room to start doing the same thing: a welcome relief.

Hentze left Mikkjal Tausen to his duty, but at the door Sigrun Ludvig intercepted him with a pair of cakes in confectioner's boxes.

"Please, take these back for your colleagues," she said.

"That's kind of you, but…"

"No, please. I insist. They shouldn't go to waste."

"Okay, well, thanks. I'm sure they'll be appreciated," Hentze said.

He accepted the boxes, but back at his car he found there was no way to secure them, so he placed them in the footwell hoping he wouldn't have to make any emergency stops as he set off back to Tórshavn.

Apart from the cakes it hadn't been an entirely fruitless expedition. The confirmation that Boas Justesen had indeed spent time at the commune made the link between him and Astrid Dam stronger, but it wasn't enough to show any connection to her death. For that, even as a hypothesis, he'd need to find someone who had lived at the commune and could give a first-hand account of Astrid Dam's time there. It was asking a lot after all this time, but without it Hentze couldn't see many other routes forward.

13

FOR SOME REASON RASMUS MATZEN PUT ME IN MIND OF A
preacher: dark hair with wings of grey at the side; tall and
rangy and with a slightly uncompromising bearing. Elna took
me outside to make introductions as her husband unloaded
trays of plants from the back of an old Citröen van and he
broke off from the work to shake my hand. However, in
contrast to the warmth of Elna's recollections, Matzen was
distinctly reserved when Elna prompted him to think back
forty years. I got the impression that he was the sort of man
who didn't like things sprung on him out of the blue and
preferred time to consider what he would say.

"I need to take the rest of these things to the tunnels,"
he said once Elna had paraphrased our own conversation. He
turned to me. "You can come if you wish. We can talk at the
same time."

His tone was still slightly reserved and I wasn't sure
how much he'd be able to add to what Elna had told me
already, but I remembered Hentze's request, so I accepted. I
climbed into the van for the short drive down a rutted track
away from the house. We passed several subdivided plots of

land growing cabbage and pumpkins and I asked a couple of questions about the crops, but neither one engaged Matzen beyond two or three words so I decided to let him make the running in his own time.

At the end of the track, about two hundred yards from the house, there were two large polytunnels. He backed the van up to the entrance of the first one and we got out. I thought he might start unloading immediately once he'd opened the back doors of the van, but instead he put his foot up on the bumper and took out a tobacco tin to roll a cigarette.

"So Elna has told you all about Christiania?" he asked, as if to establish the parameters of what he needed to say.

"Yeah, I think so," I said. "But I'm interested in the Colony, too. Elna said she wasn't there very long, so I wondered what you could tell me about it. Why was it that you chose to set up a commune in the Faroes in the first place?"

He gave a dry laugh. "That was easy. It was Danish but a long way from Denmark: in the middle of nowhere. That was what we wanted. We were going to start a new way of life." He lit his cigarette and now that he'd found a foothold on the past he appeared to relax a little. He rested against the back of the van and described how the group of idealistic young people had left Denmark and sought a fairer and simpler life on the Faroes; how the commune had operated; their attempts to grow crops and projects like building a greenhouse and keeping sheep and a cow.

It was the good life, as he described it, and – if you believed him – the days had been idyllic. Twenty-odd people living together, sharing a dream; putting their backs into honest and simple labour without thought for the self, but only for the good of them all.

But I'd been out to Múli when the sun wasn't shining and my knowledge of the reality tempered the rosy-hued picture Rasmus Matzen was painting. And because of that a warning bell rang: the instinct for when the person in front of you thinks that the more they keep talking the more you'll buy into their vision. It's what they want.

"So why did it fail?" I asked, not so much to puncture his balloon, but because I was interested to know.

Rasmus Matzen shook his head, not accepting the premise. "I wouldn't say it was a failure. Many things were successful, but there were also things we didn't know: like how difficult it was to grow anything except potatoes, and that it was hard to find the jobs we had hoped for."

"The locals didn't play ball? They were hostile?"

"*Ja*. Not in the beginning, but later there were stories and fairy tales about what we did. That made it harder."

"What sort of stories?"

"Oh, the usual things: sex and drugs."

"And they weren't true?"

"That we had sex? Of course we did. And some of us smoked pot; we were normal people. We didn't walk around naked or have orgies as some people said, but people believe what they want to believe – and what they're told by others, like your father."

"Signar?"

"*Ja*, he came to the Colony one time. He came to find Lýdia and you and take you away. That was not such a good situation. He made a lot of noise, saying Lýdia was forgetting her duty at home. I remember there was almost a fight when one of our people told him it was a free country and your mother is not a slave and can do what she wants. Your father didn't like that, but he was there on his own so after some hard words he went away."

"Did Lýdia and I go with him?"

"In the end, yes. But after that there was bad feeling with the other Faroese people and some of our group said it was because your father had been making lies about us."

I could imagine Signar's reaction to being told that his "rights" as a husband and father didn't hold any sway in the commune, and also to the fact that Lýdia chose to spend time there, perhaps taking advantage of his absence when he was at sea.

"Do you know if Lýdia had any sort of relationship while she was there?" I asked, because it was an obvious question and perhaps an obvious reason for her to have kept going back.

"No," Matzen said, thinking it over. "No, I don't think so. Not that I know. I think one or two men would have liked it; she was very pretty. But no." He said this matter-of-factly and when he tossed his cigarette aside I got the impression that this was a signal he was nearing the end of the road. But before he could completely disengage I still wanted to ask the questions Hentze was interested in.

"Just out of interest, do you remember the man who owned the buildings and land at Múli?" I asked. "His name was Boas Justesen."

Matzen pursed his lips in thought. "Yeh, I remember.

He came out to see us quite often. I think it was because he was curious about us, and also to see that we did no damage."

"Did he do any work on the place while you were there – build anything, like a shelter for the sheep?"

He frowned. "No, I don't think so. Why?"

"I just wondered," I said, keeping it light. "But if I wanted to get in touch with the other people from the commune, would you be able to give me their names? Do you keep in touch?"

"*Nej*, not for many years."

"But you remember their names?"

"Some, maybe. But it was a long time ago. People came and went. Some stayed for a long time and there were others who didn't like it after being there for a few weeks, so they went home."

"Do you remember a woman called Astrid? Astrid Dam. She was Norwegian and she had a daughter called Else, about ten years old."

He frowned. "Yes, I think so. She wasn't with us very long, I think."

"Do you know where she went when she left the commune?"

"No, I don't know." He shifted and I could tell he was becoming suspicious. "Why are you asking about her? How is she to do with your mother?"

I knew I couldn't push it much further without coming clean so I said, "I'm asking because a woman's body was found buried at Múli a few days ago. The police think she was Astrid Dam."

Matzen's whole attitude stiffened. "I don't understand. If this— If it is a police matter…"

"It is," I told him. "An officer in the Faroes police department asked me to talk to you about it because I was coming to see you."

His expression darkened. "Are *you* a police officer?"

I made an indefinite gesture. "British police," I said, not to go into the detail. "But—"

"So you say you want to know about Lýdia but instead you come to make an investigation about Astrid?" He shook his head. "No, I don't think this is honest."

"Listen, if you'd like to talk to the officer in the Faroes he'll be happy to explain," I said. "His name is Hentze. He can tell you what he needs to know."

But Rasmus Matzen was already shifting away. "No, I think I have talked enough," he said. "I think you should leave now. I have work to do."

He turned and heaved a hessian sack out of the back of the van and up on to one shoulder before heading towards the polytunnel.

I left him to it and walked back along the track to the house. It could have gone better, but I didn't necessarily read anything into his reaction beyond my previous feeling that Matzen wasn't a man who liked to be taken off guard. Without any authority to press him further I'd hit a dead end, but even so I wished I'd been able to get something a little more concrete for Hentze.

When I got back to the house I went to the back door and Elna called me in. She had an old biscuit tin open on the table, obviously a receptacle for memorabilia, and in front of her there was a small bundle of envelopes.

"I found some letters," she said. "And some photographs."

She opened the topmost envelope and handed me half a dozen snapshots. One showed a smiling Lýdia and me, aged about four, in a park of some sort; another was in the same setting but instead of Lýdia it was a twenty-something Elna beside me, her hair long and straight.

The rest of the pictures had obviously been taken at different times and were only of me. In the photos I was still the same age: at a table with a drawing; sitting on a wall; and one where I looked very seriously down the lens of the camera. By and large, I seemed like a fairly happy young boy.

"Did you take these?" I asked when I'd looked at them all.

"Yes, while you were with us in Christiania."

"Did Lýdia own a camera, do you know?" I was thinking of the Leica.

"I'm not sure. I don't remember so." She picked up the rest of the envelopes and held them out. "I kept Lýdia's letters together," she said.

I took them and lifted the top one from the bundle. It was addressed to Elna at an apartment on Gasværksvej in Copenhagen and the handwriting was the same, flowing style that I'd seen in Lýdia's notebooks, written with a fountain pen by the look of it, the ink light blue but still clear. I didn't take out the letter because that seemed too personal and I wouldn't have been able to read it in Danish anyway.

"The place it came from – the clinic – is on the back," Elna said.

I turned the envelope and saw the address on the flap: *Personale Indkvartering, Vesborggård Hus, Skovbakkevej, Skanderborg*.

"Do you know what sort of clinic this place was – Vesborggård House?" I asked, finding my notebook and copying out the address.

"*Nej*, I'm not sure. Before you went there, Lýdia told me it was a place for young people." She frowned and searched for the word. "They had a behaviour problem. Is that right? Troubled people. They were there to get help, I think – to be in control."

I nodded. "You said before that she got the job there because she met someone she knew. Do you know who that was?"

"No, I don't remember. I think it was someone she knew from her home in the Faroe Islands, but I didn't meet him. I don't know his name."

"But it was a man."

"Yeh, I think so."

"So how long did Lýdia work there – at Vesborggård House – do you know?"

"Maybe six months." She shrugged uncertainly. "I'm not sure. While you were there Rasmus and I also moved out of Christiania. We had a flat on Gasværksvej, here," she touched the address on the letter. "But Lýdia and I still wrote to each other – perhaps two times every month – until October, I think. And then for a time I had no reply. I thought maybe Lýdia was busy, you know? But one day I saw her in Copenhagen: on Prinsessegade, near Christiania. You were with her, and a teenage girl about sixteen years old who I didn't know. Of course, I was very surprised. I didn't know you were in Copenhagen, so I called out and ran after you, but I had to get right up to Lýdia's side before she would stop."

She paused for a moment, as if trying to find the right words to sum up the situation. "Right away I knew something was strange," she said then. "Lýdia pretended that she hadn't heard me calling to her, but I knew that wasn't true. And when I asked when you had arrived, where you were living and all those kinds of things, she made all her answers very short – as if she was in a hurry and didn't want to talk."

Elna shook her head, as if it still didn't make sense. "Of course, I asked where you were living but she said she couldn't remember the address. She said she would come and see me as soon as she could, but now she had to go and then she walked quickly away and you were gone. It was... I didn't understand why she had acted like that and my feelings were hurt. I still hoped she would bring you to see me, but it never happened, and then, maybe a month afterwards, I heard from some friends that Lýdia was dead and you had gone away."

She drew a breath, then she looked up. "So, now you know," she said with a finality I knew she didn't feel. Then she stirred herself and I knew she wanted to put it away so, to help her, I reached for my notebook again.

"Can you tell me what you remember about the girl? The one you saw us with? Do you remember her name?"

"No, I don't know," Elna said. "I don't think she spoke at all. It's in my mind that Lýdia said you had all come to Christiania together, but I don't know for sure."

"We'd all come there from Vesborggård House?"

"Yeh, I think so. I think that's what she said." Elna looked vaguely troubled. "You want to find her?" she asked. "Is that why you want to know?"

I made a half shrug. "I don't know. It's probably not possible, but apart from you, no one else I know of saw Lýdia just before she died."

Elna's expression suggested she doubted it was a good idea, but instead of saying so she gathered the photographs and letters up from the table between us. "Would you like to keep these?" she asked.

I shook my head. "*Nej, tak*. They're yours."

For a moment she seemed about to press them on me anyway, but in the end she nodded. "Okay. But I will keep them in case you change your mind."

"Thank you."

She put them back in the tin and, from the way she closed it, I knew I should leave now. Sometimes people just need to seal up the lid on what might have been, to preserve it.

14

"ARE THESE TO CELEBRATE YOUR PROMOTION?" ANNIKA ASKED Hentze, looking at the cakes on a low filing cabinet in the CID office.

"Help yourself if you're hungry," he said. "The funeral was a little over-catered. If Boas Justesen had any close friends they must be atheists or Jehovah's Witnesses because they stayed away."

"Pity to let it go to waste," Annika said, putting a slice of Victoria sponge on a napkin. "How many were there?"

"Seven or eight, including family," Hentze said, resisting the urge to take a second piece of cake. Instead he followed Annika to her desk and pulled a chair round so he could sit down. While she ate he gave her a summary of what Mikkjal Tausen had told him. It wasn't much more than they'd already assumed: confirmation that Justesen *had* spent time at the Colony commune, and had seemed familiar with the people there.

"So now tell me how you got on with Gunnar Berthelsen," Hentze said as Annika wiped her lips with a tissue.

She shook her head. "I didn't," she said. "He made it

clear I was interrupting his work and when I told him why I was there he got very tetchy. He said he didn't remember any enquiry about Astrid and Else and that he wouldn't have dealt with it anyway."

"That could be true," Hentze allowed.

"Yeh, but he still didn't need to be so hostile about it."

"Well, maybe it's not surprising," Hentze said thoughtfully. "I mean, if there was a murder while he was in charge and we start looking into it now, Gunnar may think it will reflect badly on him or his reputation."

"How could it? If no one knew what had happened…"

"I don't know," Hentze said with a shrug. "Gunnar's a difficult devil at the best of times. Did he say anything else?"

"No, not really. I asked him if there'd been any incidents involving the people from the commune and he said not. I had to push him to get even that much, though. He clearly didn't want to talk about it, which struck me as strange."

"Oh? In what way?"

"Well more often than not old people can't wait to tell you their war stories, or how it was better back in the old days, can they? Usually you have trouble getting them to stop. But not Berthelsen. He couldn't get rid of me fast enough."

Hentze thought about that, weighing it up. "How long were you with him?" he asked in the end.

"Maybe five minutes. He was painting – if you can call it that. More like doing violence with brushes."

"Apparently it sells well."

"Yeh, so his wife said. She was sweet. What the hell she's doing with him…"

"Just be glad you didn't have to work for him," Hentze said.

"Did you?"

Hentze nodded. "Only for a short time. We overlapped by a couple of years when I was first out of the academy." For a moment he was thoughtful again and then he stood up. "Well, since Gunnar was a dead end, let's go at this from the other direction. See if you can find out whether Astrid has any family still alive and what they know about the time she went missing. Can you do that? I'll be back in an hour."

"Sure, of course," Annika said. "Where are you going?"

"To see Elisabet. The toxicology results on Boas Justesen came in but I want her to interpret them for me."

For once they met away from the mortuary, in the hospital café where they sat with coffees by one of the tall windows overlooking the hillside and away from the other patrons of the place. Making precise cuts with a fork, Elisabet Hovgaard dissected the large slice of funeral cake Hentze had brought along as a gift.

"From the medications he'd been prescribed for his cancer, and the fact he was an alcoholic, the results were what I'd expect," she told Hentze. "Morphine, heparin, paracetamol and alcohol. Nothing else worth speaking of. The level of morphine was pretty high, but given the level of alcohol in his blood it's quite possible that he took an accidental overdose."

"When you say *overdose*, do you mean he just took more

than he should, or that it was the morphine that killed him?" Hentze asked.

"No, no, he died as a result of asphyxiation from the hanging. There's no doubt about that." She paused and gave him a quizzical look. "Are you treating this death as suspicious?"

"Well I wasn't until you asked me that," Hentze said. "Why? What's on your mind?"

Elisabet cut another cube of cake, but then put the fork aside. "I suppose it's just that if Justesen had simply died in the fire I'd believe that he simply passed out and left a cigarette burning. But it's the hanging that bothers me. The morphine in his system probably wouldn't have impaired him, but he had a blood alcohol content of 0.36 which is enough to floor the majority of people."

"Isn't the effect of alcohol relative, though?" Hentze asked. "We all know that one person can drink several beers and show no effect, while another will be practically under the table. And Justesen had been a hard drinker for years, so isn't it possible he had a much higher tolerance than you or I?"

For a moment Elisabet looked as if she was reconsidering, but then her resolve seemed to harden. "Hjalti, listen. Even if the man *could* have stood up – which I doubt – he probably wouldn't have remembered why he'd done it, never mind thinking clearly enough to stand on a chair and put a noose round his neck."

"But there's nothing to prove that he couldn't have done that, is there?" Hentze asked reasonably.

"Prove? No. But I'm telling you what my experience

says about what he'd have been capable of with that level of alcohol in his blood."

"Right," Hentze said. "So, if I understand it correctly, you must think that someone else was involved in his death, even though there's no evidence of that."

"I don't know," Elisabet said, and he could tell from her expression that she hadn't expected him to press her quite so hard on the matter. "But I just don't believe he would have been capable of killing himself in the way he's supposed to have done."

"Good," Hentze said with a nod. "I'm glad you're so sure."

Elisabet looked puzzled. "What? Why?"

"Because when I tell Remi that we need to open a second murder case I might have to call you in to shoulder the blame."

"Are you— So you *agree* it's suspicious?"

"From what you've said, sure, of course," Hentze said. "And if Justesen wasn't capable of killing himself then it can only mean he was murdered. I just wanted to see how certain you were. Sorry."

"You're a rat."

"Yeh, I know. But I did bring you cake."

Elisabet gave him a look. "So, *will* you change the enquiry?"

Hentze weighed it up. "I'm already walking on thin ice by pursuing the Astrid Dam case so Remi will probably have apoplexy when I tell him, but I don't think I've got any choice."

"Well if the facts support it…" Elisabet said, but then waved it away. "But what really concerns me is that if Boas Justesen *was* murdered, then the person who did it is still walking around. They could do it again."

Hentze shook his head. "I don't think you need to be concerned about someone going on a killing spree. I think Justesen may have been killed for a very specific reason."

"You mean because he knew about Astrid Dam?"

"Yeh," Hentze said. "I can't see any other reason to kill a man with terminal cancer, can you? Only to keep him from telling his secrets before he dies."

Which also meant that the neat possibility of Boas Justesen being solely responsible for Astrid Dam's death had just come unravelled, he realised. Someone else must have been involved: there was no other way to explain it.

15

I MADE GOOD TIME RETRACING THE ROUTE BACK TO Copenhagen. The roads were dry, it was still sunny and there was just enough traffic to keep me focused on driving rather than becoming absorbed in what Elna and Rasmus Matzen had told me. That needed time to settle anyway, so in the interim I called Hentze, hands-free with the phone wedged into a cup holder on the dash.

"I thought you'd want to know what Rasmus Matzen said about the Colony," I told him when he answered.

"Yeh, *takk*. How did it go?"

"Well, the useful bit was that he was pretty open about the commune in general. He says he remembers the names of some of the people who were there, and he also confirmed that Boas Justesen came out to see them. It sounded like he was a fairly regular visitor."

"Good, okay, that is useful to know," Hentze said. "What about Astrid Dam?"

"Yeah, Rasmus remembered her, too, but not very well. The trouble was, when I told him why I was asking about her he became pretty defensive and didn't want to say any more."

"In a suspicious way, do you think?" Hentze asked.

"I've been wondering about that, but my feeling is not. I think it was more that finding out she was dead and had been buried at Múli took him by surprise. After that I think he was worried that he could be dragged into something serious and didn't want to say any more in case it might be misinterpreted."

"But you think there might be more that he *could* say?"

"I think so, yeah," I said. "I tried to get him to go into more detail – to give me names of other people who were there – but without any authority I couldn't push it any further once he clammed up. I think you'd have to talk to him yourself now if you really want to get any more. Sorry."

"No, that's okay. At least it confirms that Astrid *was* a member of the commune. That was something we couldn't be sure of before, so *takk* for your help. I'll see how things go here before making a decision whether to talk to Matzen myself."

"Okay, well let me know if there's anything else I can do," I said, although I doubted there would be anything more I could contribute, and when we'd exchanged farewells I let the phone switch itself off.

In Copenhagen I left the rental car in a parking garage and hauled my bag a few streets to the hotel near the central train station. I'd made good time so once I'd checked in and found my room I still had forty minutes in hand before my appointment with Christine Lynge; enough to make coffee and write a couple of brief emails. There were only a few people back in the UK I wanted to tell personally that I wouldn't be working with them any more. The others would get the information from Kirkland, along with whatever spin he decided to put on it, but I didn't care. The people who knew me – or knew Kirkland – wouldn't take him at his word anyway. Besides, I was out now, so what difference did it make?

When I'd finished I set out to navigate my way to Halmtorvet, a ten-minute walk west. Beyond the tattoo parlours, transit hotels and sex shops closest to the railway station the five- and six-storey buildings gained a more gentrified air. The side streets I cut down were relatively quiet: apartment blocks mainly, in pastel-shaded brick and as lean as the people going in or coming out.

I emerged from one of these shaded streets on to Halmtorvet, where the brick-paved road was edged by trees still in leaf and any number of bicycles lined up neatly below them. On the far side of the road there was what looked like a rejuvenated collection of semi-industrial buildings, but the bold green-and-yellow *Politi* sign on the pavement stood outside a charmlessly modern eight-storey building.

The glass entrance door bore a sign in several languages telling people to wait outside and stand at least two metres away from the building. This instruction was reinforced by a uniformed officer who was manning the entry, overseeing a line of four or five people already waiting to be admitted. Given that I had an appointment I wasn't sure if I had a case for jumping the queue, but I knew the Danes generally liked things done properly and in order so I decided not to upset the system and to wait. I was early enough and the afternoon sunshine was bright and unfamiliarly, pleasantly warm.

Five minutes later I reached the head of the line and when the uniformed officer asked my business I gave Vicekriminalkommissær Lynge's name and said she was expecting me. He stepped away to use his radio and after a minute or so he escorted me inside to a long reception area. There were three or four officers at booths in a counter, all dealing with forms and enquiries from the people who'd preceded me, but I was led to one side and asked to wait.

Christine Lynge emerged from a door and cast a look along the reception area. She was a tall, athletic-looking woman in her early fifties, I guessed: dressed in a well-tailored jacket and trousers. She had a file under her arm.

"Detective Inspector Reyná?" she asked when she saw me, but it was barely a question. "I'm Christine Lynge."

We shook hands as I thanked her for seeing me at short notice, but she didn't seem inclined towards pleasantries or small talk. "We can go upstairs to talk," she told me and handed me a visitor's pass on a lanyard before leading the way briskly back towards the door from which she'd emerged.

Beyond it we went up a flight of stairs and on the next floor Lynge led the way along a corridor for a short distance before opening a door and inviting me in. I'd thought she might have been taking me to her own office, but that clearly wasn't the case. The room was simply a general purpose office with a couple of empty desks and windows looking out over the cobbled street below. Lynge gave the view a brief glance, then turned away.

"I appreciate you taking the time for this," I said, to break the ice.

"As a favour for a colleague it's not a problem," she said, leaving me unsure whether she meant Hentze or myself. "As I said in my email, I have the file you requested." She gestured me to a chair at a desk and took the other one, facing me. She placed the file on the desk, opened it and looked over the first page, as if refamiliarising herself with the details. "Lýdia Tove Reyná. Is that correct?"

"Yes, that's right," I said.

"And you're a Danish citizen?"

It wasn't a question I'd anticipated. "Well, Faroese, yes. At least, that's where I was born."

"Which is the same thing."

"Yeah, I suppose so," I said, unsure where this was going, but hoping that any claim I might have to Danish citizenship would help rather than hinder things.

"And this is a private enquiry, not related to any British police case?"

"No, not at all," I said. "It's entirely personal."

"Okay, I understand," she said, as if finally reassured. She leafed past a couple of sheets, then took out two or three pieces of paper stapled together. The front page bore a crest and official markings. "This is a copy of the coroner's verdict on your mother's death," she said. "You know the facts?"

She gave me a look that I recognised: the one that weighs up how someone will react to what you're going to say.

"She killed herself," I said flatly. "I was told she cut her wrists."

It was enough to convince her that what she told me wasn't going to be a shock.

"*Ja*, I'm sorry to say," she acknowledged. "Can you read Danish?"

"Not so much, no."

"Okay." She turned to the second page of the document. "In summary, it says Lýdia Tove Reyná died 13 November 1976 at apartment 3, Nordrområdet 37, Christianshavn, Copenhagen. The cause of death was loss of blood from self-inflicted injuries. The verdict was suicide." She passed me the papers. "You may keep those," she said. "They are public documents."

"*Tak*."

She nodded and sat back, as if the next move was mine. I indicated the other papers in the file. "Is that the incident report?"

For a moment Lynge seemed to be in two minds, but then she sat forward again. "Yes. My colleague was able to find the file that was sent from the police department to the coroner's office in 1976. There is a police report with some statements and also a post-mortem summary. I have only looked at it briefly, but as far as I can see there was no doubt what had happened."

"May I look?"

"Yes, you can see it, but it's also in Danish, of course. It is the official police record so it cannot be taken away. Or copied," she added with a significant look. Then she stood up and moved the file closer to me. "I can leave you to look for a few minutes. Is that okay?"

"Sure, of course. *Tak*."

"Okay, then," she said. "I'll be back shortly."

I waited until she'd left the room with a firm click of

the door, then drew the file to me and leafed through the uppermost sheets. There were about a dozen pages of statements and forms, all typewritten. I had little or no idea what they said but that didn't matter for the moment. I took out my phone and tapped the camera app.

When Christine Lynge came back about ten minutes later I was standing by the window with a view of the waiting queue of people outside the station. I'd been there for a while because photographing the papers hadn't taken very long. The only thing that had brought me up short was one sheet with the pre-printed outlines of a female body on it: the anterior and posterior views. It was annotated by hand: two notes, one on either side of the outline with arrows pointing to single lines drawn on each wrist. I didn't need a translation for that.

"You've finished?" Lynge asked as I turned.

"*Ja. Tak.* I appreciate it."

She made an expression that indicated she wasn't sure whether appreciation was really the issue. She picked up the file from the desk and I half expected her to check it, but she didn't.

"I was curious about one thing," I said. "There aren't any photos of the scene. Were any taken, do you know?"

"No, I don't think so. At that time they would only take photographs if the case was suspicious."

"And if I wanted to see the full post-mortem report?"

"The pathologist's report will be at the Forensic Institute, but I think you would have to apply in writing to see it. As a police officer you know what it will say, though. And for a family member…" Her expression made her reservation clear.

"Yeah." I nodded to show I understood.

She looked at her watch. "I have to give a briefing in a few minutes," she said. "So if there is nothing else I can show you…"

"No. Thanks."

"Okay. Then I'll find someone to take you out."

16

DESPITE THE NEW INFLUX OF EMAILS THAT HAD ARRIVED during his absence, Hentze's mind was still on his conversation with Elisabet Hovgaard when he got back to the office. There was no word from Sophie Krogh about the GPR survey at Múli, however, so he assumed there was nothing to report, which was both good and bad.

Most people were starting to pack up for the day but Remi was still at his desk when Hentze went to find him.

"I thought you'd want an update," he said, taking a seat on the sofa.

"Are we any further forward?"

"Yeh, a little," Hentze said. "Annika got the technical report back on the vodka bottle and cigarette butts I found near Astrid's grave. They all had Boas Justesen's fingerprints or DNA, which means he's definitely linked to Astrid's grave and therefore to her death."

"Right," Remi said. "So we can say we believe he killed Astrid, and probably Else, in 1974, then uncovered Astrid's body in a fit of remorse a few days ago before hanging himself."

"We could say it, but I don't think it's true," Hentze said.

"I believe Justesen was involved in the killings, but I don't think he was alone."

Remi scratched the top of his head in a dispirited way, then leaned back in his chair. "Go on, then," he said. "Tell me why not."

Briefly Hentze went through his conversation with Elisabet Hovgaard, which really came down to the one issue: whether or not Boas Justesen had been capable of killing himself.

"So, can Elisabet say with absolute certainty that he wasn't?" Remi asked.

"Absolutely? No," Hentze said. "But she firmly believes he was too intoxicated, and weighing up everything else, I agree. I think somebody knew Boas might talk about the killing of Astrid and didn't want that. So Boas was killed before he could talk and it was made to look like a suicide."

"And you think the motive for killing Justesen was self-protection – because the killer, whoever he is, was an accomplice in the death of Astrid Dam."

"Basically, yeh."

"And there's no other reason he might have been killed, I suppose? I don't know – a disagreement with someone; a debt?"

"There's no sign of anything like that, no."

Remi sighed disconsolately. "So you want to open a second case; a new murder inquiry on top of Astrid Dam."

"I don't think we have any choice," Hentze said. "Justesen's death is clearly suspicious now."

"Well, that's going to go down like a rat sandwich upstairs – you do know that, right? The budget's blown, people are still dealing with the fallout from last week…" Remi shook his head. "I could justify the search for Else's body as a matter of decency and for the family, but it was still neatly contained in the past. Now you want to drag the whole thing into the present with a new, unknown suspect: someone we have to find."

"We *could* run the two investigations in tandem," Hentze said. "After all, they are linked."

"And you'll want a team?"

Hentze had worked with Remi Syderbø long enough to recognise that this was now a tacit negotiation: an attempt to find a compromise between what he would want and what Remi could justify upstairs. In response, he gave a slight shrug. "Not necessarily. Annika and I could probably manage, although it would be easier if I didn't have to spend half my day in meetings and answering emails about staff training and welfare…"

"Well, that's an inspector's lot," Remi said flatly.

"Yes, I know. Which is why it's not really the job for me," Hentze said. "Maybe not even temporarily."

"And who else is going to do it?"

Sensing that Remi was on the cusp of making a decision, Hentze decided to leave it as a rhetorical question.

"All right, listen," Remi said in the end. "I know you think the inspector's job is a pain and you'd rather be out doing" – he made air quotes – "*real police work*. So I'll make you a deal. You can handle this inquiry with Annika *if* you remain as acting inspector and look after the day-to-day supervision of the department. *But* you can ignore the management and housekeeping stuff."

"No meetings?"

"No meetings. Is that fair?"

"Of course. Whatever you think."

"All right," Remi said, relatively gratified. "Don't take anyone off their current caseload and don't run up any more costs than you have to. No DNA tests or facial reconstruction or anything fancy like that – at least not without asking me first."

"Of course not."

Remi nodded, seeming satisfied with the deal. "Maybe it's for the best," he said. "People were starting to comment on how bored you looked in the last conference."

"Sorry. I have an expressive face, so I'm told."

"Only when you choose," Remi said drily. "I think I may have created a monster. You were much easier to keep in your place before you were an acting inspector."

"You don't know the half of it," Hentze said standing up.

"No, and I don't want to," Remi said. He turned back to his computer. "Go away and reply to *some* of your emails at least."

Outside Remi's office Hentze closed the door and felt reasonably pleased to have cleared a small path through the forest. And in the spirit of compromise he decided he *would* deal with some of his outstanding emails before he went home, but as he started along the corridor, his phone rang.

"Hjalti, this is Kass Haraldsen."

"Hey, Kass. How are you?" Hentze said. Kass lived on Sandoy and had been retired from the police for more than a decade. Although they'd never worked closely together, Hentze had always found the man amenable and friendly whenever they crossed paths.

"I'm pissed off with being old, but that's nothing new," Kass said. "But that wasn't why I called. You've been poking Gunnar Berthelsen with a stick, so I hear."

"Not me personally, but yes, I suppose you could say that," Hentze admitted, letting himself into his office. "How did you know?"

"Because the old bastard called me just after lunch," Kass said. "He told me there might be someone asking questions about a missing Norwegian woman from the seventies, but no one could be expected to remember details from that long ago, could they? An enquiry about a missing person? What was that? Nothing."

Hentze kept his voice neutral. "Gunnar said that?" he asked, sitting down at his desk.

"Word for word, more or less. He said it was nothing anyone with any sense would remember, not even if they had found her body now."

"Well obviously, Gunnar remembered the report that she was missing," Hentze said.

"Course he did," Kass said without any doubt. "Well enough to know it was me who was duty sergeant, too, which I wouldn't normally have been. I was living on Suðuroy at the time and I'd only come over to Streymoy to cover somebody's holiday leave. I don't remember whose."

"But you *do* remember an enquiry about Astrid and Else Dam from the Norwegians?" Hentze asked.

"Well, to be honest, no, I didn't," Kass said. "If you'd come to me yesterday and asked if I remembered a missing persons report from 1974, I would have laughed. But when

Gunnar said they were Norwegian and had been out at Múli, that rang a bell."

"So what can you tell me about it?"

"Not much," Kass said. "I mean, as far as I recall it *was* just routine. There must have been an enquiry from Norwegian police I suppose, so I sent someone to Múli to see if they were still there."

"And they weren't."

"I suppose not," Kass said. "I mean, I don't remember who I sent or what they said when they came back. But *because* I don't remember anything happening, I'm pretty sure Astrid Dam and her daughter can't have been there."

"And that was it?" Hentze asked. "Nothing else happened?"

"Not as far as I know. Sorry. Like I said, if old Gunnar hadn't jogged my memory I wouldn't even have been able to tell you that much, but I thought you might want to know that he's covering his back, or at least trying to."

Hentze thought about that for a second or two. "Did he say *why* he thought it was a bad idea for anyone to talk about the missing woman and her daughter?"

"No, he just said that with hindsight it's easy to criticise and point out things that could have been done differently," Kass said. "He tried to make it sound as if he was concerned for the good of everyone who was on the force at the time, but I reckon he's just worried that something will come up and show he wasn't the great superintendent he always claimed to be. You remember what he was like to work for."

"Yeh, I remember," Hentze said. "As a matter of interest, did you ever have anything to do with the commune at Múli?"

"No, not really," Kass said. "I heard gossip about it, of course, but like I said, I was living on Suðuroy then, so what they really got up to out there I don't know."

"Right," Hentze said. "Okay, well thanks for tipping me off about Gunnar. It's useful to know."

"You're welcome," Kass said. "I don't see why the old sod should think he can still hand down orders from on high. But listen, if you want to talk to someone about the commune you should try Uni Per Heinesen. He's my brother-in-law, married to Noomi's sister. He was a reporter before he retired: worked for *Dimmalætting* and never threw anything away, if his office is anything to go by. Papers and files up to the ceiling."

"You think he'd remember the commune?"

"Sure. He wrote about it, I think, went out there a few times."

"Do you have his phone number?" Hentze asked, reaching for a pen.

17

"I OWE YOU SOME MONEY," I SAID WHEN TOVE HALD ANSWERED her phone. "And there's something I'd like to talk about. I'm in Copenhagen, so could we meet? This evening if you can."

"Sure, okay. Where are you?"

I told her.

"I can be there at seven thirty."

"*Takk*. I'll be in the bar."

I nursed a bottle of Tuborg in the library bar of the hotel, listening – because it was impossible not to – as three American guys at an adjacent table bickered about how long it took to fly to Cancún from various places in the US, resorting to smartphones to settle the matter. When Tove walked in I saw them clock her immediately. It was hard not to, given her striking half-Faroese, half-Danish looks and her white-blond cropped hair. She had a canvas satchel over the shoulder of a leather jacket and she was wearing skinny blue jeans with ripped knees. She also had more flat confidence than a twenty-two-year-old had a right to, if it *was* just self-assurance.

I hadn't known Tove very long but the few times we'd met I'd had a sense that some of her social skills were rehearsed.

She was very smart and very focused, but not necessarily very savvy when it came to personal interactions, so I suspected she might be somewhere on the autistic spectrum. I liked her quite a bit; not least for the fact that she never shied away from saying what she thought.

I picked up my beer and went over to greet her. I was expecting her usual businesslike handshake, but instead she made a brief air-kiss by my cheek – still slightly formal – which I returned before asking if she wanted a drink. She opted for coffee and once that was sorted we went to sit at a table away from discussions about flight times and conference hotels. The rest of the place was quiet.

"So, is there something else to translate?" Tove asked, straight to the point and with a nod at the envelope I'd brought.

"If you've got time. Are you busy?"

"No, it's not a problem. This is my final year for my Master's degree, so I can work when it suits me. I have very good time management skills."

It was the first even semi-personal thing she'd told me about herself.

"Okay, if you're sure," I said. "But there's something else I should tell you first: it's a police file for a death, so if you'd prefer not to do it I'd understand."

"This is your mother's death?"

"Her suicide, yes."

She thought that over, as if making sure she'd understood what I'd said. "Are there photographs?" she asked.

"No, just the report."

"Okay, so it's not a problem," she said, matter-of-factly. "It's just words."

The barman came with her espresso and a second beer for me, which I hadn't really wanted but had ordered anyway. When he'd gone I took the sheaf of papers from the envelope. They were copies of the photos I'd taken of the police file and printed in the hotel's business suite at an inflated cost.

"I've got this on a flash drive you can take with you," I said. "But can I get you to look at something now?"

"Sure, of course."

One of the first pages in the file seemed to be a summary of the incident and I turned to it now. "I think it's the start of a statement. Can you tell me what it says?"

Tove gave the page a quick, appraising scan, then focused in on the section I'd indicated. "It says he – the police officer – came to the apartment because of a call from the ambulance service. When he arrived he and his partner were shown to the dead person in the bathroom. In the bath."

"*Tak*. That's what I thought. It doesn't say who made the first call to the emergency services, though?"

"No, not here."

"It may be somewhere else then," I said. "So you'd still be okay about translating the rest?"

"Sure. It's interesting. I'm studying the history of commercial law, so this is a different thing, but still history."

"Thanks. You just made me feel old," I said, not very seriously.

She gave me a puzzled frown. "Why? Because you were there?"

"Yeah, I guess so."

She shook her head, rejecting my premise. "History can be from a few minutes ago to thousands of years; it makes no difference. The past can't be changed, only learned about more until you find the whole truth. That's why I like it."

She had a habit of making flat statements like that, without requiring a response, so I let it go when she picked up her espresso and knocked half of it back.

"There's one other thing you might be able to help me with," I said. "If you've got time. It's research rather than translation, but there'd have to be some of that, too."

"Wait a moment. Recording is easier than making notes." She took her iPhone from her pocket, tapped an app, then inclined it towards me, interview style. "Okay, go ahead."

Feeling slightly put on the spot, I regrouped my thoughts through a sip of my beer, then said, "In the mid 1970s there was a place called Vesborggård House near Skanderborg. Lýdia, my mother, worked there for a while and I'd like to know more about it. I think it was some kind of institution for young people with behavioural problems."

"So you only want general information?"

"Well, I'd like to know what information there is. If there's anything specific I'd be interested in that as well."

"For what reason? It will help me to know what to look for."

I still hadn't fully made up my mind whether my half-formed idea was worth pursuing, but one thing about Tove was that she made you decide, so I said, "After Lýdia died my adoptive father went to her flat in Christiania to collect her personal possessions. While he was there he met a teenage girl who was living with Lýdia and me, and from talking to a friend of Lýdia's today I think this girl may also have been at Vesborggård House."

"So if you can find her you want to ask questions about your mother's suicide."

"Yes, in a nutshell."

"But you don't know her name."

"No, but if there are any records from Vesborggård House in 1976 it might be possible to find out who she was."

She thought about that, but not for long. "Okay, I'll see what I can discover," she said, then tapped the app on her phone to stop recording. "It's the same rate of pay, 120 kr an hour, yes?"

"If you're happy with that."

"Yes, it's fair," she said with a nod. "How long are you here?"

I shrugged. "I don't know yet. As long as it takes – or until I run out of leads."

"Okay, then. I will do it as a priority." She cast a look at the room. "I don't think this hotel is so cheap."

"Not so much, no. Speaking of which, you'd better let me settle what I owe you for the other stuff you did and finding Rasmus Matzen's address. How much is it?"

She referred to her phone with the deft finger strokes of the e-generation. "It was one and a half hours, but I think we can leave it on your account until I've done this work too. I trust you."

For a moment I couldn't tell if she was making a joke, but when she didn't look to see if I'd got it I knew that she wasn't. "*Takk fyri*," I said.

"You're welcome. Is there anything else?"

"Not unless you want another coffee."

"No, one is enough." She knocked back the last half of her espresso and stood up. "I'll call you tomorrow. Have a good night."

And with that she was on her way out.

The last of the light had left the sky when Hentze emerged from the tunnel between Streymoy and Vágar. He'd already called Sóleyg to say he'd be late, yet again. He tried not to dwell on the fact that over the last two – no, three – weeks, his work had taken precedence over – well, most things. It was more than a month since he'd sung in the choir and nearly as long since he and Sóleyg had settled in for an evening in front of a movie. Half the time when he was supposed to be relaxed and off duty he knew his mind hadn't really left work and he felt guilty for that. Not that there was much he could have done about it, but even so…

The one consolation was that recently Sóleyg had regained some of her old social network, as was the case this evening. Karin Jensen had asked her to come over and help her with planning the menu for Bjarta's wedding, she told Hentze. She was going out now but wouldn't be late.

"Okay, but just don't let her talk you into making the cake," Hentze said, suspecting Sóleyg's reputation for good baking had not been forgotten by their neighbour.

"Oh, no, of course not," Sóleyg said, sounding bright. "She wouldn't want that. I haven't made one for ages."

"Yeh, well, just remember that's no reason to do it for free when she *does* ask."

"Oh, you're so – so *distrustful*," Sóleyg chided.

"Am I?" Hentze asked, genuinely surprised that she had this view of him.

"Well, no, not always," Sóleyg conceded. "Only where Karin's concerned."

"And with good reason," Hentze said. "Just remember the christening two years ago."

Of course she wouldn't, he knew. Sóleyg was too kind-hearted by half, and after an evening of gossip and chatter she'd come away having promised to produce the cake for the wedding, no doubt about it.

Ten minutes later he drew the car to a halt on a side street in Miðvágur, outside the red house where Uni Per Heinesen lived. Kass Haraldsen had called to tell his brother-in-law that Hentze was coming and Uni Per greeted him at the door, waving him in. He was a tall man, as bald as a rock, wearing a sweater and corduroy trousers that looked to be two sizes too large, cinched in at the waist by a broad leather belt.

Inside, the house smelled of cooking – a meal recently eaten – and Hentze accepted Lise Heinesen's offer of coffee, then followed Uni Per through to his study; a shed, more or less, tacked on to the back of the house. As Kass Haraldsen had described, it was a room stacked floor to ceiling with files, papers and books.

"Well, I don't know anything about Astrid Dam," Heinesen said when he and Hentze were seated and Hentze had described briefly why he was there. "I don't think

I've ever heard of her, but there were a lot of people at the commune – especially the first year. When I visited there might have been thirty or forty."

"As many as that?" Hentze said, surprised.

"Oh, yes. That was part of the problem," Uni Per said. "Well, part of what people *thought* was a problem. You're old enough to remember how it was back then, right? So I'm sure you can imagine what people thought when a bunch of long-haired young Danes arrived and all started living together. Some of the older people didn't like the idea at all. There were some wild ideas about what they got up to, and because no one was willing to visit the place, the stories got wilder. The paper got letters saying all sorts of ridiculous things, so in the end I asked my editor if I could go out there and do a story about what the commune was really like and what they were trying to achieve. I didn't expect him to say yes, but he did, so I spent a couple of days there and wrote an article. It was quite a big piece," he added, as if he still remembered it with pride.

"And what *were* they trying to achieve?" Hentze asked.

"Oh, the usual stuff for the time: self-sufficiency; a fairer society; life without regulations except those they made for themselves. I'll admit, I rather liked their ideas but of course, it was all pretty naïve, especially because they had no real idea of what it was like to live out there. I think that's what finished them off in the end."

"Right, I see," Hentze said. He sipped his coffee, using the moment to think about that. On the face of it there was nothing in what Uni Per Heinesen had said that would explain Gunnar Berthelsen's reaction to Annika's enquiry about Astrid Dam. But maybe there had been a connection between Astrid and something else.

"While the commune was at Múli do you remember any sort of incident that might have involved the police?" Hentze asked then. "I'm not sure what sort of incident it would have been, but something that might not reflect well on people now."

"*People?*" Uni Per queried.

"Police officers at the time."

"Ah, you mean Gunnar Berthelsen, right?" Uni Per said. "Kass told me he'd stuck his oar in."

"It could have been Gunnar, or someone else," Hentze said diplomatically.

Uni Per frowned as he trawled through his memory. "Well, the only thing I can think of is Sunnvør Isaksen – no: Iversen," he corrected himself. "Sunnvør Iversen."

"Oh? Who is she?"

"She was a young girl at the time – about eleven, I think. She went missing from home in Norðdepil one afternoon. Her parents called the police and search parties were sent out but there was nothing until the next morning when she was found wandering on a hillside. From what I was told she was suffering from exposure and had no idea where she was – as if she'd been drugged. I was also told that she'd been raped, but she couldn't remember anything about it; nothing at all from the time she disappeared until she was found."

Hentze had his notebook out now and he wrote some of this down. "When did it happen, do you remember?"

Uni Per worked it out. "It must have been April or May of 1974," he said after a moment. "It was kept out of the papers to spare the girl, but you know how things are. Pretty soon people knew that something had happened – something more than the fact that she'd just gone missing overnight – and that's when the rumours started." He made a gesture. "You can guess, right? The commune was only a few kilometres away from Norðdepil, so who did suspicion fall on? The police went there and asked questions, of course, but I don't think there was ever any evidence that anyone from the Colony *had* been involved."

"So there were no firm suspects at all?" Hentze asked.

Uni Per drew a dissatisfied breath. "I did hear that at one point they had someone in for questioning. They were excited about that, but then – suddenly – it all went away."

"Do you know who the suspect was?"

"No." Heinesen shook his head definitely. "You have to understand that most of what I know about this is – was – unofficial. At the time there was a strict embargo on anyone from the police department talking to the press. It came from the top – from Gunnar Berthelsen, I guess. Anyone who talked out of turn would lose their job, and they took it seriously."

"So no one was charged for the attack on the girl."

"No. As a reporter I kept asking about progress, but as time went on Gunnar Berthelsen made every effort to play down the whole thing. Of course, he did it on the pretext of protecting Sunnvør, but in reality that was just a good cover for the fact that they didn't find out who was responsible."

"So the case was just put aside?" Hentze asked.

"In the end, yes, as far as I know. But by then there were other stories going round about the Colony and what went on there: all sorts of things from satanic rituals to... Well, you name it. And it all fed into the prejudices that were already there, so from then on the Colonists were frozen out. No one would give them work, the shops inexplicably ran out of the supplies they wanted to buy, and so on and so on. By that autumn – 1974 – the place was finished. A lot of people had already left because of the hostility and in the end the last few diehards packed it in as well. It was a shame really, at least I thought so at the time. I thought they got a rough deal and I wrote a couple of articles to put a more balanced view, but my editor wouldn't publish them. The articles were spiked and when I complained I was told not to argue with editorial decisions. What can you do?"

Hentze considered. "What about Boas Justesen, the owner of the houses at Múli?" he asked in the end. "Did he feature in any of this?"

Uni Per shook his head. "I don't think so. Some people thought he should tell the Colonists to leave and he didn't make many friends when he wouldn't, but he always was an awkward bastard. I only ever met him in passing, but that was enough."

Hentze nodded at the familiar description. "And do you know what happened to Sunnvør Iversen?" he asked.

Heinesen thought back. "I think she and her parents moved away – maybe to Denmark, I'm not sure. As far away as they could get, I suppose." He shrugged and shifted his tall frame in the chair. "So, do you have a suspect for Astrid Dam's death, or is this just a fishing trip?"

"Are you asking as a reporter?"

Heinesen laughed. "No, no, not any more. Still, you don't stop being curious."

"Well at the moment I'm still a long way from looking at suspects," Hentze said. "After so long, even getting information about the commune isn't so easy, so I appreciate your help."

He put his coffee mug aside and made to stand up. "I'd also be grateful if you'd keep our conversation to yourself."

"Sure, of course," Uni Per said. "These days I only write poetry anyway. It's not very good but at least I don't have to check any facts."

18

Thursday/hósdagur

IN THE PRE-SUNRISE GLOOM HENTZE TOOK THE FIRST FERRY OF the morning to Nólsoy. It was too soon to tell yet what sort of day it might turn out to be, but the clear sky in the east seemed reasonably promising, he thought as he walked up the hill from the harbour.

At Gunnar Berthelsen's house there were lights on inside despite the fact it wasn't yet seven thirty, but even so Hentze tempered his knock on the door. He didn't want it to seem that he thought anyone needed to be roused from their bed.

Gunnar Berthelsen opened the door dressed in jeans and an old sweater. He had slippers on his feet and from his freshly shaved cheeks Hentze guessed that he'd been up for some time.

"Good morning, Gunnar," Hentze said.

Berthelsen scowled at him for a moment, until he put a name to the face. "Hjalti Hentze, right?"

"That's right. Do you have a few minutes to talk to me?"

"At this hour? What's the idea: to get a person out of bed and catch him off guard?"

"Were you in bed?" Hentze enquired mildly, but didn't pursue it as the answer was obvious. "May I come in?"

"Well you're here aren't you?" Berthelsen said and walked away from the door.

Hentze followed him through to the kitchen where Hildur Berthelsen was washing the dishes from breakfast.

"Good morning," Hentze said when she looked round from the sink.

"Will you leave us alone?" Berthelsen said to his wife, without any explanation for Hentze's presence. "We need to talk."

"Oh. Yes, all right," Hildur Berthelsen said, obviously at a loss. She looked to Hentze. "Would you like coffee? There's some brewing."

"Yes, thank you," Hentze said with a polite nod.

"I'll do it," Berthelsen told his wife. "You go and get on."

"Oh, well, if you're sure." She still seemed a little uncertain but made her way to the door.

"So, why *are* you here at this time of the morning?" Berthelsen said, his back turned as he tended to the coffee pot. "What couldn't wait for a more civilised hour?"

"Actually it was just a matter of practicality," Hentze told him. "So I can get the next ferry back and not have to hang around half the day."

Gunnar Berthelsen grunted. "Well, that was your first mistake, right there," he said, bringing the coffee pot to the table. "You should always let your suspect think you'll spend as long as it takes to get answers, otherwise all they have to do is spin out the time."

"You could be right," Hentze acknowledged. "I don't

think that sort of tactic is needed here, though. Either you'll tell me what I want to know straight away or you won't tell me at all. Whichever way it goes, I'll be on the ferry."

Berthelsen grunted again, as if he couldn't be bothered to contest the logic of that any further. Instead he waved Hentze to a seat at the cloth-covered table, then poured two mugs of coffee, both black.

Hentze accepted the drink. "Thanks."

"So come on, spit it out," Berthelsen said. "What's this about? More to do with the missing Norwegian woman at Múli, is that it?" He shook his head. "I didn't know anything about it yesterday, and today I still don't."

"Actually, that's not what I wanted to talk about," Hentze said. "Or, at least, only indirectly. The reason I'm here is another historical case: Sunnvør Iversen. I don't know if you'll remember, but in 1974 she was abducted from near her home in Norðdepil and raped. She—"

"Yes, yes, you don't need to list all the details," Berthelsen said, cutting him off. "What about her? If you've read the case records you know everything there is to know."

"Yes, that's what I'd hoped, too," Hentze said. "But last night when I went to look for the file I found it was missing, along with some others from the same period."

"What are you saying – that I'm a suspect for that?" Berthelsen asked with a frown.

"I hadn't thought about it," Hentze said with no trace of the lie. "Should you be?"

Berthelsen didn't answer immediately. Instead he reached for his coffee mug and took a thoughtful sip. Finally he looked back at Hentze. "So you want to know what was in the file, is that right?"

"It would help if you could tell me what you remember, yes," Hentze said, taking out his notebook and a pen.

"Well, I can tell you this much," Berthelsen said. "It was one of the most shocking cases of my time as a police officer: the worst I saw here, that's certainly true. I leave aside what they do to each other in Denmark. That much you expect."

"Shocking in what way?" Hentze asked.

Berthelsen drew a slow, considering breath. "Because of what had been done to her," he said then, his voice flat. "She was covered in bruises and there were marks from a rope on her wrists. She'd also been brutally raped. The doctors who looked after her when she was found… They said the only good thing about it was that she had no memory of what had happened. She had been drugged – although with what they couldn't tell us – and they kept her sedated for more than a week afterwards so she would have time to heal."

Hentze made a couple of notes. "When was this?" he asked.

"April 1974, the first week."

"And how long was she missing?"

"From the Friday afternoon to Saturday morning. A search party found her at about nine o'clock on the hillside near Depil at Húsadalur. She was wearing just her dress, barefoot and wandering."

"And she had no idea at all what had happened to her?"

"No. As I said, it was the only good thing."

"So how did the investigation progress?"

"It didn't, not for a while," Berthelsen said. "We had

nothing to go on. Of course, we interviewed people in the area to find out if they had seen anything odd or suspicious, but there was nothing."

"Did the interviews include the people at the Colony commune at Múli?"

"Yes, of course. I think we talked to everyone on the north end of Borðoy, and Viðoy, too. There was nothing."

"But eventually you did have a suspect, didn't you?" Hentze said.

Berthelsen gave him a sharp look, but then nodded.

"Who was that?"

"His name was Hans Jákup Olsen: lived in Leirvík. A carpenter."

"And why was he a suspect?"

"Because he owned a car similar to one which had been seen near Norðdepil on the day Sunnvør went missing. He also lied to give himself an alibi, which then fell through. So we brought him in, ran tests on his car and questioned him for two days, but in the end the Prosecutor said we didn't have enough evidence to make a charge, so he was released."

Hentze looked up from his writing. "Did you think he was guilty?"

Berthelsen shook his head. "That wasn't for me to say, was it? The Prosecutor didn't think so, so that was that."

Hentze heard the lie in this because of Berthelsen's apparent acceptance of the decision. In his experience, men like the ex-superintendent did not simply kowtow to a prosecutor's negative assessment, especially if they thought they had a good suspect for an offence such as this.

"So you never found the man who did it?" he asked.

"No."

"There were no other suspects – at the Colony commune, for example?"

"No."

"So, six months later, when there was an enquiry about Astrid Dam and her daughter, Else, what did you think? Had you any reason to link their disappearance with what had been done to Sunnvør Iversen?"

Shifting his weight, Gunnar Berthelsen set his jaw. "As I told Officer Mortensen, I don't remember *any* enquiry about them. It would have been dealt with by a sergeant or inspector."

"Yes, it was," Hentze confirmed. "It was Kass Haraldsen."

"Well, there you go, then."

"Yes," Hentze acknowledged. "But what I'm curious about is why you rang Kass yesterday and told him he *shouldn't* remember it."

Berthelsen snorted. "Isn't it obvious?"

"Not to me, no."

"Because we missed it, didn't we?" Berthelsen said, as if Hentze must be dense. "At the time, in 1974, there were two murders and we knew nothing about them. We were obviously *told* that this Astrid Dam and her daughter were missing, but we failed to realise they were dead, and as a result whoever killed them has been walking around free ever since."

"And that's the only reason you wanted the missing person report forgotten?" Hentze said with a frown. "Because you didn't want anyone to think you'd slipped up?"

"Your reputation may not mean anything to you,"

Berthelsen said stiffly. "But as far as I'm concerned I still take pride in the job I did for forty-two years. Did it well, too. So, no, I don't relish the idea that now some people will take the opportunity to say that, whatever else I achieved, we overlooked two murders."

Hentze noted the fact that even in admitting this, Berthelsen had said *we* and not *I* in respect of who might be held responsible for the omission. Still, it made sense now and he had the answers he needed. He closed his notebook.

"So what are you thinking? Do you have a suspect?" Berthelsen asked, as if he took Hentze's action as a sign that the questioning was over.

Hentze shook his head. "I'm afraid I can't discuss ongoing cases," he said. "But of course, if I need more information, I'll be in touch. Thanks for your help, Gunnar. And for the coffee. Don't get up; I can find my way out."

Outside Hentze started back to the harbour. *Pride*, he thought as he let the downhill slope of the road quicken his steps. It was rightly listed as a sin, and it was something he was as prey to as the next man. It was the reason he had not asked Gunnar Berthelsen the obvious question, which was whether – knowing what he now knew – the ex-superintendent could think of any common factors between Sunnvør Iversen's rape and the probable murder of Else Dam.

Hentze had not asked because he, too, had his pride and he would rather see things for himself than give the old man any possible opportunity to salve his reputation at this late date. Not that he really thought Gunnar Berthelsen would have had any insight, then or now, but it had been petty not to ask, all the same.

* * *

First thing on Thursdays there was a team meeting in CID. It was something Ári Niclasen had instigated and Hentze saw no reason to change it. Unlike most of Ári's other meetings it actually served a useful purpose, giving the detectives an opportunity to air cases and share problems or frustrations. People spoke freely, which was something Hentze liked, and as acting inspector it was a much easier way to keep tabs on what everyone was doing, rather than monitoring dozens of emails and reports.

A good portion of the department's work was still concerned with the events of the previous week, but slowly the more usual business was returning to the fore. Dánjal Michelsen was looking into the dumping of several chemical barrels; Sonja and Oddur were working on a series of break-ins; and there was also a potential fraud case, a theft from a boat and a domestic abuse. The case of Astrid Dam's murder was there, too, but as he'd promised Remi, Hentze didn't involve the others beyond giving them a brief summary of where things stood.

Afterwards, though, he called Annika aside and told her what Berthelsen had said regarding Sunnvør Iversen. As he did so he wrote up the most salient details on the whiteboards in Ári's office.

"So, let's assess this for a minute," he said, standing back. "Astrid is dead. She was almost certainly murdered and Boas Justesen had some involvement in that. Right?"

"Yes."

"Okay. Then are we still happy to believe that Else was also attacked and killed at about the same time as Astrid, given that she hasn't been seen since?"

"I don't see any real alternative," Annika said.

"Okay, in that case we now have *two* attacks on young girls in the space of six months," Hentze said. "First Sunnvør Iversen in April, and then Else in October 1974. Could it be coincidence that two girls of about the same age were attacked within ten kilometres of each other a few months apart?"

Annika scanned the board. "It could, but I don't think so," she said. "Violent crimes against children are still very rare, right? And the same would've been true forty years ago, so it doesn't seem likely to me that there would have been *two* attacks so close together unless they were connected. What does the case file on Sunnvør say, do you know?"

"It doesn't," Hentze said flatly. "It doesn't exist – at least not that I've been able to find."

Annika frowned. "How's that possible?"

"I don't know." Hentze shook his head. "It's not the only file missing. There seems to have been a clear-out of records from that period, possibly when we moved offices from Jónas Bronks gøta. However, Gunnar said they *did* have a suspect for Sunnvør's rape, although in the end no charges were brought. His name's Hans Jákup Olsen: he lives at Kunoy now."

"So if he and Boas committed the attacks in 1974 and they got away with it, that would have given Olsen a motive to silence Boas now," Annika said. "And Kunoy's what, twenty kilometres from Múli?"

"About that," Hentze said with a nod. "Not so far that you couldn't get there, set a fire and be home again in under an hour, that's for sure."

19

AN HOUR'S DRIVE FROM COPENHAGEN I CAUGHT THE SEVEN o'clock ferry from Sjællands Odde. The ship was a squat, twin-hulled affair, which pulled out of the harbour just as a weak sun started to rise across the water. Even at that time of day the ferry was busy, but I found a pair of high-backed seats by a window away from the main lounges and let myself doze, cut off from the people around me by the dull noise of the engines and – like as not – by the general mien of a man who didn't want company.

I'd been awake since just after four, disturbed by the trains passing six floors below the hotel window. The sound of their wheels was clanking and hollow, like someone slowly and deliberately rolling an oil drum down the road with a loose brick inside, but it wasn't just the trains that kept me from sleep, or brought me out of it.

Down in the place where there should have been rest there was an undertow now: strong and insistent and hard to resist. I didn't remember what I saw there, but the underlying restiveness made sleep less reassuring, and when I woke up I usually felt more exhausted than before: as if I'd spent the time swimming hard against currents and tides.

So in the small hours I'd given up on sleep and made coffee instead, reassessing whether the decision I'd made to go and look for Vesborggård House was still sound. I'd used Google Maps to find the address from Lýdia's letters to Elna Eskildsen, but the Street View images hadn't shown anything more than the entrance to some kind of estate, the rest obscured by trees. If I went and looked for myself I could get there and back before evening. That was the plan, but the reason for going was less definite.

From Elna's description of the last time she saw Lýdia it sounded as if she'd left her job at Vesborggård House on the spur of the moment, and by now it was fairly obvious that that was Lýdia's way. She would leave one place without warning and alight in another for a few months, then move on again. I remembered nothing about it even though I'd been with her, so I couldn't help wondering whether this behaviour was simply down to periods of mania, or if it was more symptomatic of a deeper unrest or dissatisfaction.

There was no way to know and by now I no longer expected that visiting the places we'd been would trigger a memory or even a dim recollection from childhood. Going to look at Vesborggård House would only be an exercise in curiosity; a way to kill time while I waited for Tove's translation of the police report into Lýdia's death. It was sightseeing, then, nothing more – like visiting the Little Mermaid or the Tivoli Gardens. The only difference was that I'd be the only one looking.

* * *

The entrance to Vesborggård House that I'd examined on Street View had changed. The beech hedges on either side were still there, but there were no gates now, and what had once been a gravel drive was a deeply rutted track made by the comings and goings of heavy, large-wheeled vehicles. I didn't need to be able to read Danish to understand that a temporary signboard just inside the entrance was announcing a new development of apartments. The artist's impression of the place left no room for doubt.

From the road it wasn't possible to see more, so I backed the car up a short way, then pulled on to the verge and went in on foot. The ground was fairly dry on the edge of the track and in the distance I could hear some kind of construction work, but until I came to the brow of a low rise I couldn't see its source. Another hundred yards or so further on, I got a view of a scarred landscape where one building had been demolished and another was in the process of construction, not yet risen much above the foundations. Surrounded by churned earth and littered with building materials, it looked a long way from the idealised picture on the sign at the entrance.

But whatever the state of the place, you couldn't argue with the location. Beyond the site where the original house must have stood there was an open view to a large, spreading lake, its grey-green waters glistening and its shores lined with trees to the east and west. On the far side there were fields of lush grass, some dotted with cows, others scattered with round bales of straw on cut stubble.

I followed the track down towards the construction site until it levelled out, then cast around for someone who looked as if they might be in charge. There were five or six men at work and a JCB was digging a trench but no one paid me any attention until a guy of about forty emerged from a Portakabin. He was dressed for the office, except for a pair of muddy safety boots and a hard hat bearing a company logo.

"*Hi, kan jeg hjælpe dig med noget?*" he asked, looking my way.

"*Taler du engelsk?*" I asked. "Are you in charge?"

The shift of language didn't faze him by much. "Yeh, can I help?"

"If it's okay I'd like to look around," I told him. "I lived here for a while when I was young."

That made him frown a little. "At the house?" he asked with a gesture.

I shook my head. "No, in the grounds somewhere, I think. My mother worked here."

"Oh, okay," he said. "I understand." Then he chuckled. "You know this was a place for people, er… sent because they did the wrong things, yeh? So I thought maybe…"

"Yeh – an easy mistake," I agreed, matching his smile. "I'm Jan Reyna."

"Henning Skov. I'm the architect here."

We shook hands and I nodded to the building works. "So is there anything left or has it all been knocked down?"

"You're looking for memories?"

"I suppose so," I said. "I might have left it a bit late by the look of it."

"Yes, for the big house," he agreed. "But it was very ugly. The staff houses are still here, though." He turned and pointed towards a narrow road going into the woods. "If you follow the road it's about five minutes to walk. The guy who built the big house didn't want them in his sight when he admires his view."

"Just the way it should be," I said, making sure he heard the irony. "So it's okay if I look?"

"Sure, why not? But maybe don't go inside. A lot of the roofs are *rådne* – rotted. It isn't safe."

"*Tak*. I'll stay out."

"If you don't come back in one hour I'll send someone to the rescue."

With that he moved off and I went the way he'd indicated, following an old tarmac track round a bend and then through the woods, more or less on the level. Now that the sun had come out it wasn't an unpleasant place for a stroll; easy walking and quiet away from the building work.

As Henning Skov had said, it was a five-minute walk and near the end of it the track rounded a protective hummock of land. Beyond that I found a cracked concrete yard, surrounded on two sides by cheaply built chalet units and on the third by an older, more utilitarian-looking brick building. Near the centre of the yard a burned-out car sat on its rims and between it and me there were rusted oil drums and various pieces of decaying furniture scattered around.

I walked a few paces on to the yard and looked in through glassless windows and past broken doors, making an unhurried circuit of the place in all its decay. The weeds and young trees growing from the concrete reminded me a little of pictures I'd seen of Chernobyl – nature reclaiming concrete and brick. Despite the dilapidation it wasn't so hard to imagine what the place would have looked like forty years ago, but if Lýdia and I *had* lived in one of the chalets – which seemed at least possible – there was nothing to tell me which one. Of course not. I wasn't even sure what difference it would have made if there'd been a plaque on the wall. If I was looking for memories there weren't any here, but I'd guessed that from the start. And last night Tove had been wrong, I decided, giving the place one final look. The past isn't fixed; it decays and crumbles away the further you leave it behind. History is only its bones.

Heading back I smoked my first cigarette of the day and when I got to the main building site I spotted Henning Skov standing with an older guy – a workman who talked with a cigarette in the corner of his mouth. Just out of politeness I went across to say thanks and that I was leaving.

My arrival interrupted their conversation and Henning Skov looked mildly expectant. "Did you find anything you remember?"

"Not really," I said. "But I was pretty young. I just thought I'd take a look as I was passing."

The older man said something, which made the ash fall from his cigarette.

"This is Jeppe," Henning Skov said. "I told him you used to live here and he says he's sorry for you."

"Because he thinks I'd done something wrong?"

"*Nej*, not so much." Skov gestured back towards the main road. "Jeppe lives in Hårby, the village that way, and he says everyone knew this was a bad place. Nobody wanted it here."

"He means when it was a clinic?"

"Yeh, I think so."

"So why was it bad?"

Skov turned and put the question to the man called Jeppe who took the cigarette from his mouth and tossed it away before answering. It wasn't the short reply I'd expected, but went on for more than a minute, supplemented by gestures.

"He says that before it was closed there were stories about what happened here," Henning Skov translated for me. "And one time the police made an, er... *investigation*. They were looking for a girl who was lost from Brørup, another village about five kilometres away. It's an old story in this area," he added, not a translation this time. "No one knows what happened to her. What's the word? Yeh, a *mystery*, right?"

"What year was that, does he remember?" I asked casually. More translation.

"He says it was 1976," Henning Skov said in the end.

"*Inge-Lise*," the older man said then, this time speaking directly to me. "*Inge-Lise Hoffmann. Hun var en ven af min søster. Den samme alder.*"

"Her name was Inge-Lise Hoffmann," Henning Skov said. "She was a friend of Jeppe's sister. The same age."

"She come. Here," Jeppe said with a definite gesture at the ground so there'd be no mistake, then spoke to Skov in Danish again, still with the determined note in his voice.

"He says the girl told her mother she was coming here to see her brother who worked in the garden. Then, after that, she was not seen again. But it's only a story – gossip, yeh? Nobody knows. The girl wasn't found so..." He shrugged expressively.

I could guess what he meant. Out here in the sticks an old house used as some kind of clinic or rehabilitation centre was bound to have provoked suspicion from the locals, especially if one of their number went missing.

Jeppe said something else and I heard the word *politi*, but this time Henning Skov gave the impression that he'd gone as far with this distraction as he wanted to go.

"*Ja, ja*," he said to the older man, then made an apologetic gesture to me. "I'm sorry, we have to do some work now."

"Sure, of course," I said. "Thanks for your time." I nodded to Jeppe. "*Tak. Hi.*"

He gave me a vaguely dissatisfied look, but returned the nod.

I started back up the track towards the road and the car. I was almost there when Tove called.

"You don't reply to your emails," she said, straight to the point. "I sent you the translation of the report at six thirty this morning."

"Sorry," I said. "But thanks. I'll look at it."

"I also said in the email that I had found some information about Vesborggård House," Tove said, still sounding reproving.

"Don't you sleep?" I asked.

"Sleep? Yeh, of course, four or five hours a night when I have nothing better to do."

"Really? You must be a riot to live with."

"A riot?" she queried, flat but clearly perplexed.

"A lot of fun."

"Oh." There was silence, as if she was assessing that as seriously as she might if I'd asked her the square root of fifteen, then she said, "Because I don't sleep very much you don't think I would be easy to live with?"

She sounded genuinely puzzled and perhaps a little surprised by the idea and I knew the joke had misfired, which made me feel bad. "Listen, no one could be worse to live with than a police officer," I told her. "And I have an ex-wife to prove it. What did you find on Vesborggård House?"

The shift back to something more concrete refocused her again. "It's as you thought," she said. "It was a place for people with behavioural problems but it was closed in 1977. Just the same, I think you have found something, too."

"I don't follow," I said. "Found what?"

There was a second's pause, as if she was readjusting her explanation for the mentally deficient. "Because it closed so long ago there is nothing to find out about it from public record websites, but a search for the name brings up results from 2004. There was a legal case that was reported in the newspapers – that's how I found it. Fourteen people who had been treated at Vesborggård House claimed they had been injured – harmed – by the treatment they received there, but before the case went to court it was stopped."

"What sort of treatment?" I asked.

"I don't know that yet. I'm still finding out."

"But you think there was something dodgy – suspicious – about the place?"

"No, I don't know that either," she said. "I still have more reading to do, but if you come here I can show you what I have. It will be easier than talking on the phone. You can come either now or this evening. This afternoon I have a tutorial meeting."

"Let's make it this evening," I said, deciding not to tell her where I was in case that led to more questions.

"Okay, I'll send you my address," Tove said. "It will be an email," she added, as if she still had doubts about my trustworthiness in that area. "So, I'll see you this evening. *Hi.*"

She rang off.

In the car I dug out my notebook. Old habits die hard: the habit of looking for patterns or commonality, for example; the muscle memory that sometimes intuits a possible connection between one thing and another without any real substance, but still prompts the most basic question, *What if?* But however you try to answer that *what if?* you need caution as well. Guessing and supposing are toxic; they taint whatever they touch. *If you don't know enough for a theory, don't make up a story instead.*

All the same, I considered the name I'd just written down in my notebook, and beside it the date: 1976. I had nothing that even came close to a theory, just a loose bag of facts, but when I put the notebook away and started the car I still had *What if?* in my head. Just enough.

20

IT WAS AN HOUR'S DRIVE FROM TÓRSHAVN AND BY THE TIME
Hentze navigated the narrow, boulder-lined causeway
between the islands of Borðoy and Kunoy there was a flat, grey
drizzle from the low-hanging clouds over the sound. He met
no other cars in the unlit tunnel beneath Galvsskorafjall, and
in fact saw no other vehicles once he emerged into daylight
again and followed the straight road along the western coast
of the island to Kunoy village.

The place was made up of three discrete settlements, the
first comprised of a dozen or so houses set back above the
road, the second clustered around the church and the road
down to the small, concrete quay. Here the road narrowed to a
single car's width and Hentze drove on more slowly between
the buildings. He emerged on the far side and ascended the
incline until, a couple of minutes later, the tarmac came to an
end at the third settlement.

He left the car by the verge and walked the last few metres
to a red-roofed, white-walled house, which bore a date stone
over its door: 1918. There were net curtains inside the windows
of the undercroft and no sign of life, but from a stone shed

attached to the house at the far end Hentze heard the sound of sawing and followed it as far as a pair of open doors.

Inside the shed, under two strip lights, a man dressed in overalls and with a woollen hat on his head was cutting a long section of wood with a handsaw. His movements were practised and deft and around him the workshop was tidily laid out with a variety of woodworking machines and a long bench down one wall. At the far end of the space there were several shelf units holding hand-crafted wooden toys and puzzles of the sort you could find in the upmarket design shops in Copenhagen.

Hentze didn't speak until the man finished sawing the plank, but when he made the last cut Hentze scuffed his foot on the gravel. The man looked up.

"Hans Jákup Olsen?" Hentze asked.

"That's me," Olsen said. "What can I do for you?"

He put the wood aside and dusted his hands down as he came towards the entrance, as if visitors weren't exactly unknown, but not entirely expected either. He had a roughly trimmed beard and light grey eyes, which gave Hentze a briefly appraising look.

"My name's Hentze. I'm a police officer," Hentze said. "Do you think I could ask you a couple of questions?"

Olsen stopped in his tracks. "No. You can fuck off," he said with a gesture. "I don't talk to the police." With that he turned on his heel and strode briskly back to his bench.

Hentze gave it a moment, then entered through the open doorway, coming to a halt a few paces from Olsen. "Listen, I can appreciate that you might not have had the best of experiences with the police in the past," he said. "But nevertheless I *do* need to talk to you."

"*The best of experiences?*" Olsen repeated contemptuously. He took a step forward, baring his teeth and pointing to where one was missing. "Here. You see that gap? That was your mates at the station. So, yeh, you're right, it wasn't *the best of experiences.*"

"Did you lodge a complaint?"

"A complaint? Pah! A long way that would've got. You all look after each other, I know. It'll be the same now as it was forty years ago."

He turned away and moved back to the bench where he picked up a length of planed timber.

"Okay, listen to me, Harra Olsen," Hentze said. "I wasn't in the police at the time you're talking about, but things are different now. And I'll be straight with you: the reason I'm here is to do with the case you were questioned about then. I believe the rape of Sunnvør Iversen may be linked to another crime at the time. I don't know for certain, but if you weren't involved in what happened to Sunnvør, wouldn't it help clear the cloud you've been under if we found out who was?"

Olsen made a dismissive snort. "It's too late for that now. I've had to live with the black looks and the behind-the-hand comments. I barely made a living after it happened, no one'd hire me. Mud sticks, I'll tell you that for free. No smoke without fire, is there?" He picked up a pencil and started marking up the wood using a set-square.

"As I understand it, your car was seen at Norðdepil about the time that Sunnvør went missing," Hentze said. "And I was told that you lied about where you were."

"*I* didn't lie," Olsen said without turning his head.

"Then who did?"

Olsen made a hard, definite mark on the wood, then looked up as if he wanted to settle this once and for all. "All right, listen," he said. "I was having an affair with a woman called Anna in Norðdepil, okay? That's where I was when the girl went missing, and that's why my car was there. I lived in Leirvík back then, so I drove out to Norðdepil, but I always parked on the road and walked down the hill to Anna's house. That way I thought none of the local busybodies would notice the car."

"And that's what you told the police officers at the time?" Hentze asked.

"Of course. But when they went to see Anna she denied the whole thing. Her husband was there – just got back from a spell out at sea – so she lied. She said I'd been to the house once, two months before, to hang a door and she'd never seen me again. And then my wife – cow that she was – she said I'd been acting suspiciously when I got back to the house that evening. She said that because she knew I'd been shagging somebody else and she was mad about it. So that was me fucked, right?"

Olsen hefted the wood in his hand, then crossed to a circular saw. He switched it on and while he fed the wood through the machine Hentze considered what he'd said. With hindsight it was easy to see that Olsen's apparent lack of an alibi would have made him suspicious to the police at the time, but even so it was hardly an overwhelming indication of guilt.

The keening of the saw didn't last very long and when Olsen switched it off again Hentze said, "Did the police officers at the time have any other evidence against you?"

Olsen tossed an offcut of wood into a barrel. "They *said* they could match some ropes in my car with marks on the girl's wrists," he told Hentze. "And they *said* that because there was an empty bottle of vodka in my shed that I must've got her drunk." His voice was bitter. "It was all shit. The ropes were for tying wood to my trailer, and I used that bottle to keep linseed oil in, but they didn't care. They hadn't found anyone else, so they thought they could pin it on me."

"And you were arrested?"

"Yeh." Olsen turned the sawn wood in his hands, then looked away. "They called me a monster and said I'd done horrible things. They showed me photographs… They were the worst things I've ever seen." He shook his head, then stiffened resolutely. "But I didn't do it. I told them over and over again but they wouldn't listen. They shouted, calling me names. It went on and on, but I still wouldn't admit it because it wasn't true. Then, in the end, the big boss came in – the superintendent. He told the other two to go away and gave me a coffee and a cigarette. He talked for a bit and he seemed okay; friendly, you know? He says they're just trying to do their job, and I say, yeh, I know that. So why won't I admit it, he says and slams his hand on the table. He knows I did it and he's had enough pissing about, so just tell him or I'll really be in for it. He grabbed my wrist so I chucked the coffee at him and said he could fuck off: I wasn't saying another word."

Olsen put the wood aside now and looked directly at Hentze. "After that they took me back to a cell, but on the way across the courtyard this one bloke, he pushed me down the steps and I went sprawling. I hit my mouth on the concrete and while I'm still lying there one of them kicked me two or three times for good measure. Then they dragged me up and dumped me in the cell and left me there overnight. Next morning they take me back in to be interviewed again, but this time there's a lawyer there – someone from the Prosecutor's office. He takes one look at the state of my face and the blood on my shirt and he walks out. A couple of hours later they let me go. That was it. I never heard anything from them again. No apology, nothing. But it ruined my life. My wife left me – not that I was so bothered about that – and I couldn't get work. People shunned me. For years."

"I'm sorry about that," Hentze said.

Olsen waved that away. "I don't want sympathy, and I don't care whether you believe me or not. That's what happened."

"Okay," Hentze said. "So let me ask you about a couple more things and then I'll leave you alone, all right? Did you know Boas Justesen from Fuglafjørður?"

Olsen considered for a second or two, then shook his head. "I know who he was, but that's all. I didn't *know* him."

"And did you ever go to Múli when the Colony commune was there between 1973 and 1974?"

"That place? No."

"Did you know anyone who lived there or meet any of them while you were visiting Norðdepil?"

Olsen shook his head. "You'd see them sometimes,

in Klaksvík and other places, but I never talked to them. Why would I? Some of them tried to get odd-job work that might've come my way. Not many people wanted to deal with them, though."

"So I've heard," Hentze said. "Finally, then, where were you on Thursday evening last week?"

"Here."

"On your own?"

"No. I was with Bogi and Kirstin Arge. On Thursdays we have a few beers together and play music." He gave Hentze a sour look. "I can show you my violin if you want."

"No, that's not necessary," Hentze said, ignoring the sarcasm. He was satisfied now. "Thank you. You've been a great help."

"Huh," Olsen said and turned back to his bench.

Hentze left him alone and walked back to his car. Across Kalsoyarfjørður the cloud was almost so low that it reached the coast road on the opposite island a couple of kilometres away. If Olsen was to be believed there had never been any real evidence against him regarding Sunnvør's rape, although lying about his whereabouts in the first instance wouldn't have gone in his favour. And with no other suspects coming to light it could certainly have been a temptation for Gunnar and his team to try and fit a square peg into a round hole, until it all went too far and the Prosecutor's office stepped in.

From his attitude earlier that morning Hentze wasn't sure that even now Gunnar Berthelsen would ever accept that they'd had the wrong man, but Hentze did. Which would be of no consolation to Olsen, of course; and nor was it of any real help to Hentze. It left him precisely where he'd been at the start of the day: there was no link between Olsen and Sunnvør and therefore no link to anything else.

He'd just twisted the key in the car's ignition when his phone rang.

"Hjalti? It's Sophie. I think you should come back to Múli," she said.

21

THE WIND WAS COLD ON THE HILLSIDE AT MÚLI; THE SKY overcast and heavy as Hentze left the car. The sloping field on the higher side of the track was edged by a hay-drying fence and Hentze followed it up to where Sophie Krogh and Emil Kejser, the technician who'd brought the survey equipment from Denmark, were both on their knees, scraping at earth in the bottom of a trench.

Sophie stood up when she saw Hentze approaching. She took a couple of steps down the hill, took out a cigarette and lit it with her back to the wind.

"You made good time," she said by way of greeting.

"Not really: I was on Kunoy," Hentze said. Now he was here he could also guess why. "What is it you wanted to show me?"

Sophie turned and gestured back up the slope. "Emil spotted an anomaly on the GPR trace from yesterday," she said. "It looked like a pit about fifty or sixty centimetres deep and a metre square, so we put in a trench first thing this morning. In the surface layer there's a lot of ash and charcoal, mixed with a number of rocks, but when we got down about thirty centimetres we found bones." She took a drag on her cigarette, then crushed it under her boot. "I wanted to have a clear idea what we'd got before I called you, but there's really no doubt. It's a child."

"Right," Hentze said flatly. "Well, I'd better look then."

Together they moved closer to the rectangular hole in the ground. To one side there was a groundsheet where topsoil had been dumped and Emil stood up to let Hentze see better. Sophie tossed him her cigarettes and he moved away.

Hentze took in the outlined form in the bottom of the hole. The skeleton was half excavated, reminding him not so much of a body but of a sculpture, as if it was being delicately etched out of the soil. The fact that the visible bones were nested together in foetal form made it more abstract somehow.

"Can you tell the sex yet?" he asked.

"Not yet, but given everything else I'd be surprised if she isn't the girl you're looking for."

Hentze considered the grave for a few seconds longer, then turned to cast a look back down the slope to the spot where the sheepfold had been. It was a good hundred metres. "I don't get it," he said. "Why bury one body here and the other down there? Surely it would have been easier to put them together."

"Doesn't it depend on when they died?" Sophie said. "If they were killed at different times…"

"Yeh, possibly," Hentze said, not fully convinced. He looked at the pile of earth on the plastic sheeting, and then at Sophie. "Are there *any* similarities between the two burials?"

"Apart from the fact that both grave sites were disguised in some way, no."

"So it was either one person who did it differently each time, or two different people with different approaches."

"I guess," Sophie said. "But if it helps I'd say that this burial was more considered than the other – as much as these things ever are."

"Oh?" Hentze frowned. "In what way?"

"Well, the first grave – Astrid's – had the feeling of something done in a hurry," Sophie said. "As if the most important thing was to get the body hidden from sight. But this grave would have taken some time and effort to dig, and it's more or less square. To my mind that indicates that whoever dug it had put some thought into how they were going to position the body and the foetal position makes it more compact so you don't need to dig such a big hole – unless rigor mortis has set in, of course; then you're screwed. They call them 'stiffs' for a reason."

She made this last comment deliberately upbeat, as if she'd decided they'd been sombre for long enough.

"You are the bloody limit, do you know that?" Hentze said, but mildly. He didn't really mind – even appreciated in a way – the fact that Sophie Krogh wouldn't give in to the inherent solemnity of her job for very long.

He took a last look into the grave, then turned away. "So, is there anything else you can tell me?" he asked. "What about this ash and charcoal you mentioned – is that significant?"

"Yeh, I think it could be," Sophie said. She moved aside and picked up a plastic container with several pieces of charcoal inside it. "To me it looks like the remains of a bonfire. It's hard to be certain yet – we'll need to see how much there is and how far it extends – but my guess is that something was burned here after the body was put in the ground, possibly as a way of disguising the fact that a grave had been dug."

Hentze considered the lumps of black material. "I don't suppose there's any way to tell how long after the burial the fire was lit, is there?"

"No, I can't tell you," Sophie said. "I don't think anyone could with any degree of accuracy. Logically, though – if it *was* to disguise newly turned earth – it wouldn't have been very long, would it?"

"No, I guess not," Hentze said, just as his phone started to ring. "Excuse me a minute."

He stepped away and answered Annika's call. "Hey."

"Hey. Can you talk?" Annika asked.

"Yeh, go ahead. What's up?"

"Well, I've been doing some background checks on Boas Justesen's personal life – his bank balances and so on. I also got his phone records and when I looked through the ones for the last month one number stood out. It's a local cellphone registered to Mikkjal Tausen. Justesen called it twenty-three times in the two weeks before he died, and also on the night of his death at 17:54… Hello? Hjalti? Are you there?"

"Yeh, yeh, I'm here," Hentze said. He pulled his attention back from the misty view towards Viðareiði. "You're sure the phone number belongs to Mikkjal Tausen?"

"Yeh, absolutely. Because the number appeared so often I called the phone company to find out who it belonged to. Tausen bought a contract SIM card three weeks ago."

"Okay, send the number to my phone, will you?" Hentze

said. "I'll give Tausen a call and see if he's at home. If he is I'll stop in and have a chat on my way back."

"Right," Annika said. "Where are you now?"

"At Múli. Sophie's found a second set of remains."

There was a pause and then Annika said, "Is it Else?"

"I think so." Hentze glanced towards the excavated ground. "Listen, will you tell Remi about the find? I think we'll need a case conference when I get back, and in the meantime can you also find out if Justesen left a will? If he did I'd like to know who the beneficiaries are."

"Sure. I'll get on to it now," Annika said.

"Thanks."

Hentze rang off and cast a look at the hillside down to the sea before walking back towards Sophie. "So, how long will it take to finish here, do you think?" he asked.

"It should be done by the end of the day."

"Do you need anything?"

"No, I think we've got it covered."

"Okay, I'll leave you to it, then. See you later."

He took a step down the hill.

"Hjalti?"

"Yeh?" He turned back.

Sophie hesitated, then shook her head. "No. Nothing. But a flask of fresh coffee'd be nice, if someone's passing."

"Sure, of course. I'll sort it out."

I'd driven through Ry on my way out to Vesborggård House: a small, quiet town, with high-gabled Victorian buildings along some of the side streets and a subdued but varied high street. The police station was on a residential road of neat, red-brick houses, but it was only a two-room affair in a shared municipal building with a young uniformed officer on duty. His nametag said *Hans Schou* and he was getting ready to leave.

What I'd hoped for was an "old rat", as Hentze had described himself once: an old hand who'd worked in the area since the Creation and would know about the case even if he hadn't been on it. But Officer Schou was too young to even have been born in 1976 and when I told him what I wanted to know he could hardly be bothered to exhibit any curiosity: I'd have to go to Aarhus for something like that.

"You can ask for Kriminalassistent Thomas Friis in CID," he told me, almost certainly seeing it as the most expedient way to pass the buck. "I know him a little. He knows things from the old days – old files, yeh? Maybe he can find out about Inge-Lise Hoffmann."

It was as much help as I'd get but it was probably enough. Having a name always makes it easier to get past the door, even if it's just the first one.

Forty minutes later I found the modern, red-brick police station in Aarhus beside a main road lined with leafy trees turning yellow. It was a place that definitely didn't share its facilities with the fire service or local authority: four storeys of windowless wall facing the road with the air of a place built to withstand a siege.

I couldn't park anywhere close to the station, but eventually found a multi-storey five minutes' walk away, which gave me time to assess how much I'd need – or would want – to tell Kriminalassistent Thomas Friis, or anyone else I managed to speak to. It would have been a lot easier if I'd still had a warrant card to show and without it I knew there was a danger that I'd come across as one of the walk-in nutters all coppers occasionally meet, ranging from the sad to the seriously deluded. To avoid it I'd just have to rely on talking a good game.

In the reception area, which was more like a ticket office in a train station, I spoke to a uniformed officer behind one of the screens. I told him my name, flashed a business card as if that was the accepted British way, and asked for Thomas Friis by name. The guy made a couple of phone calls, located Friis on the second, and after a brief conversation hung up.

"He says he will come. You can wait."

"Okay, *tak*."

I waited twenty minutes on an uncomfortable plastic seat before Thomas Friis appeared. He was in his early to mid-thirties, stocky and compact with unruly and very dark hair. Apart from a well-tailored suit – which looked as if he'd put it on for the first time about an hour ago – he seemed fairly laid back. We exchanged the usual greetings but he held off from asking the obvious question until he'd led me along a corridor to a small interview room. It was tatty and worn, as they usually are.

"So how can I help you?" Friis asked as we took a seat. "You asked for me by my name, is that right?"

"Hans Schou thought you might be able to get me some details on a missing person," I said. "Her name's Inge-Lise

Hoffmann and as far as I know she disappeared from a village called Brørup in 1976."

"Okay," Friis said noncommittally. "And is this an official enquiry – a case you're working on in the UK?"

"Actually it's personal research," I said. "I was told that when Inge-Lise went missing there was some connection to a place called Vesborggård House near Ry. It was some kind of centre for young people with criminal or behavioural problems, I think. My mother worked there, so I'm trying to find out more about the place. It's just background really, but you know how it is: you get curious."

I was trying to give him a sense that even if I was somewhere on the walk-in nutter spectrum I was pretty harmless, eccentric at worst. He didn't seem to notice the smokescreen, though.

"So was this girl, Inge-Lise, known to your mother?" he asked.

"I don't know. I just hoped I could get a look at the missing persons report – find out when she went missing, who her family were, what she looked like."

"Just because you're curious," he said flatly.

"Yeah, pretty much." I nodded as if I hadn't picked up his tone.

He took a moment, then shifted a little. "Well, I think you should probably contact the Missing Persons Department directly," he said. "I can find the contact details for you and if you send them an email to say what you want to know…"

I still hadn't got a clear read on the sort of copper Friis was, but I was pretty sure that if I tried any more bullshit I'd be insulting his intelligence, so it was a choice of leave it at that or take a risk and play it straight.

There wasn't much to lose so I said, "Okay, listen, I won't take up your time with a long story. One of the reasons I want to look at Inge-Lise's file is because I have a photograph of an unidentified girl taken around 1976 and I'd like to see if they're the same person."

That gave him pause for thought, but not long. "And if they *are* the same, what does that mean?"

"I don't know yet. I don't have enough information, that's why I'm here."

"Do you have the photograph with you – of the girl you want to identify?"

I hesitated for a second, then opened my phone and brought up the picture. It was a version I'd heavily cropped, but even so there was no mistaking that there was something unnatural about it, especially if you were a copper. I turned the phone to show Friis.

"Where did this photo come from?" he asked after a moment.

"Like I said, it's a long story, and if she isn't Inge-Lise it doesn't matter."

He looked at the screen again. "Can you show the whole picture?"

"I don't think you'd want to see it."

He took another look at the phone, then back at me and his tone became slightly harder. "Perhaps if you want my help you should let me decide," he said. "Perhaps you should tell me how you have this."

I lowered the phone. "Listen," I said, hoping to make it conciliatory. "I'm not trying to be difficult, but like I said, if this girl isn't Inge-Lise Hoffmann there's no point in wasting your time. But if she is I'll tell you what I know, okay?"

He rubbed his nose, as if his instinct was pressing him to walk away now, before this went any further. But I could also tell that the photo had got him, which was what I'd hoped it would do.

"Are you sure your picture was taken in 1976?" he asked then, as if it would be a confirmation of something.

"No, it could have been earlier," I said. "But it definitely wasn't later than that."

"Okay." Friis looked at his watch. "Are you staying in Aarhus?"

"No, I just came for the day. I was going to head back to Copenhagen after seeing you."

That didn't seem to be what he'd hoped for, but he made up his mind. "I have a case meeting in a few minutes," he said. "So I won't be able to look for anything until afterwards. It may take some time, but if you want to wait…"

I nodded. "How about I go for a walk and you call me when you get free?" I suggested.

That seemed to satisfy him. "Okay, tell me your number."

I gave him my business card instead and a couple of minutes later I was back on the street with Friis's promise that he'd call me within an hour or two.

22

AT RITUVÍK HENTZE PARKED IN FRONT OF THE NEW HOUSE Mikkjal Tausen was renting. There was a heavy rain now, so Hentze put on his waterproof jacket as he got out of the car but only held it closed as he made his way up the paved path to the side door. The sound of the doorbell was shortly followed by the quick thud of feet on stairs as Tausen came down to open the door.

Because Hentze had called ahead Mikkjal Tausen was expecting him, and his greeting was therefore welcoming and without question. "*Hey*, come in," he said, holding the door wide. "You can leave your boots and coat there. Would you like coffee?"

"That would be good, thanks," Hentze said.

He left his damp coat and boots by the door and then followed Tausen up the bare wooden stairs to the second floor and into a long, open-plan living room stretching across the entire width of the house. It had a hard wooden floor and a splendid view over the bay. At one end of the room there was a smart, glass-topped desk holding a computer; at the other there was a large leather sofa and matching armchairs.

Tausen went into the kitchen at the back to make coffee and Hentze went over to the large windows. The rain did nothing to detract from the panorama of sea, mist-sky and grey-green land. Idly, he tried to estimate what this view might cost on a weekly basis. It wouldn't be cheap, he was sure.

Hentze turned away from the window when Tausen reappeared carrying a cafetière and glass cups on a tray, which he placed on the low oak table in front of the sofa.

"In Arizona it can be really beautiful, too," Tausen said, gesturing at the window. "But there's never much change from one day to the next. Here? Give it an hour and you're looking at a different landscape. I'm still getting used to it again. Please, have a seat."

Hentze took an armchair opposite Tausen. "How long do you think you'll stay?" he asked conversationally.

Tausen shrugged. "At the moment I'm trying to decide whether I want to make the move back here a semi-permanent one," he said, pouring coffee and offering the first cup to Hentze. "In terms of business, I can do almost everything I need to from here, but it's a long way to go when I *do* need to be in the States."

"So you're not completely retired?"

Tausen shook his head. "I don't want to be. But the great advantage of being in my position is that you can work on your own terms. I do enough to keep up my interests, but not so much that I can't enjoy life." He sat back on the sofa, as if to illustrate the point. "So, what can I tell you?" he asked.

"Well, it's as I said on the phone, I just wanted to go into a little more detail about Boas," Hentze said. "You'll understand that because of the woman's body we found at Múli we've had to take a closer look at the circumstances around Boas's death than we might otherwise do for a suicide."

"Yeh, I can understand that," Tausen said. "Do you know who it was yet? The body, I mean?"

"Yes, she was a Norwegian woman called Astrid Dam," Hentze said, watching for any trace of recognition in Tausen's expression. There was none.

"And you think she was murdered?"

"We strongly suspect it," Hentze said. "Although I'd be grateful if you didn't spread that around. She'd been living at the Colony commune and simply disappeared in 1974." He reached for his phone and swiped the screen to bring up the missing persons photograph of Astrid, then held it out. "I don't suppose you ever saw her?"

Tausen studied the photo for a few seconds. "No, I don't think so: I mean, not that I remember after this long. I only ever went to the Colony once; I think I told you the other day. At the time I was working in Denmark – from 1972 to '76. I was doing research in the chemical industry so I only came back here a couple of times every year to visit my parents."

"I see," Hentze said. "Well, it was a long shot, but still…" He put the phone aside. "Maybe I can ask you something more up to date, though. At the funeral you said you'd seen Boas a few times before his death, is that right?"

"Yeh, a few times," Tausen said. "Once he knew I was here he sort of latched on to me. He'd call me on the phone and ramble on, saying he didn't feel well, how his life was shit, things like that. In the beginning I tried to cheer him up but to be honest, he got to be a bit of a pain. I don't want to sound unsympathetic, but you know how drunks are. It didn't matter what time of the day or night it was, if it came into his head that he wanted to talk to someone…" He shrugged helplessly. "And there wasn't really anything I could do. I mean, he'd been told he only had a few months to live and when you know that there isn't much of a bright side to life, is there?"

"No, I suppose not," Hentze said, giving it sombre consideration. "So when was the last time you saw or spoke to him, do you remember?"

"Yeh, sure," Tausen said. "I spoke to him the day he died. He called me around five or six in the afternoon but he wasn't making much sense: stuff about his pain medication not working and being punished. That was the phrase he used: 'I'm being punished,' he said."

"Punished for what?"

Tausen shrugged. "I don't know. Like I said, he was rambling. He was obviously drunk and I was waiting for a call from the States: the time difference makes it easier to get in touch in the evening. Also, Sigi was coming over – you remember her, from the funeral? – and we were going to have dinner, so perhaps I wasn't as sympathetic as I should have been. I feel bad about that now, but I had no reason to think… He didn't give me any hint that he might have been thinking of killing himself. If he had, well, obviously I'd have done something."

"Did he say *where* he was calling from?" Hentze asked. "I'm trying to work out when he went out to Múli before he died."

"No, I don't think he said," Tausen said. "I just assumed he was at home. I'm pretty sure he didn't say he was at Múli or I'd remember."

"Yeh, I can see that," Hentze said and the subject appeared to prompt a thought. "Just as a matter of interest, had you had much contact with Boas *before* you came back to the Faroes – while you were in America?"

"No." The answer came quickly, but almost immediately Mikkjal Tausen retracted it. "Well, not directly," he said. "A couple of months ago someone rang the company office and asked to speak to me. I wasn't there so they left a message to say they were calling on behalf of a relative and asked if I'd call back. At the time I was busy, and because the only relatives I have here now are all distant ones – no one I'd seen since I'd left – I didn't see how it could be important, so I didn't do anything. But then there was another call and another message, maybe a week later. They said they were calling for Boas – I guess because he didn't speak English – and asked again if I'd call back because Boas was ill."

"So you came all this way because of that?" Hentze asked, allowing a slight trace of scepticism.

"Well, no," Tausen admitted. "I mean, I suppose it would make me seem like a better person if I said that *was* the reason, but it wasn't like Boas and I had kept in touch. No, the truth is, I'd been thinking about making a return visit for a while, and I guess when I got the messages it firmed up the idea. So in the end I booked flights and I came. I thought I'd spend a week or so looking around, visit Boas, go down memory lane and that would be it. But when I got here…

Well, I met Sigi for one thing but another was— Well, I don't really know how to describe it. Have you ever lived away?"

"No, not for long," Hentze said. "A few years in Denmark."

"Well, maybe you felt the same thing. For me, as soon as I got off the plane it was just coming *home*. After nearly forty years away, and in a place like Arizona, I'd forgotten – I mean, *really* forgotten – what it was like here." He shook his head. "I don't want to sound like one of those New Age people, but I just had the strongest feeling that I'd come back to my roots: that I *belonged* here, you know? It was like—" He looked for a simile but couldn't seem to find one. "I don't know. I suppose it's just my time of life," he added with a trace of self-deprecating amusement.

"No, I understand." Hentze nodded. It hadn't passed his notice that Tausen had a tendency to turn his answers into personalised insights into his life. Perhaps it was the result of spending so long amongst Americans, who never seemed to mind telling strangers the most intimate details of their lives, Hentze thought. Or perhaps not.

"Just as a matter of interest, did you ever give Boas any money?" he asked.

"Money? No. Why?"

"Oh, just curiosity. I wondered whether that might have been a reason for him getting in touch with you after so long. As far as I can tell he wasn't so well off, and if he knew you were successful…"

"No, the subject never came up," Tausen said. "Although, to be honest, I had thought that it might, especially when I saw the state he was in. And if it had, well, I'd have done my best to help him of course. If he'd needed some private treatment for his cancer… But that was obviously not the case and, as I say, he never asked. I think he really just wanted to know there was someone there, you know? That he wasn't entirely alone."

"Yes I see," Hentze said. He finished his coffee and put the cup back on the table. "Well, I think that's everything I needed to ask," he said then. "Thanks for your time. I appreciate it."

"No problem," Tausen said.

Hentze stood up and Tausen did the same, accompanying him down to the side door where Hentze retrieved his coat and boots. "I suppose you'll be even more connected to home once Boas's affairs are sorted out," he said conversationally as he put his arms in the coat sleeves. "Perhaps that will help you decide whether to stay now."

Tausen frowned. "Sorry, I don't follow."

Feigning a slight misapprehension, Hentze said, "Oh. I was just thinking about his property: the house and the land at Múli. I assume that you and Selma Lützen will inherit them."

"I don't know. I hadn't thought about it," Tausen said, but for the first time Hentze heard a slightly false, slightly forced note in the man's voice. "But to tell you the truth I'm not sure I'd really want either place," he said.

"No? Well, I can understand that, I suppose." Hentze nodded, but left the reason for his understanding unspoken. "Well, thanks for the coffee. It was nice to see you again."

23

AARHUS WAS A BUSTLING PLACE, ON A PAR WITH WHAT I'D seen of Copenhagen. The main shopping streets were mostly pedestrianised, populated by brand shops and places where the goods were expensive and highly designed. The simpler it could be made the greater the price tag, so it seemed, but I guess someone had to spend a lot of time removing any fripperies.

I got as far as Åboulevarden and the elevated bridge crossing the river. It should have been pretty but it was cast into gloomy shadow by the tall buildings alongside it. By then I'd had enough of wandering and disengaged window-gazing, so I left the main street and found a quiet café where I parked myself under its canopy with a coffee, cigarette and Tove's translation of the police report into Lýdia's death downloaded on to my phone.

I'd already guessed most of what the papers would say. It stood to reason that if there had been anything out of the ordinary or suspicious the conclusion of suicide wouldn't have been drawn, so I had little expectation that anything odd would stand out, and nor did it. This was a run-of-the-mill task for the *politiassistent* – a sergeant named Bidstrup who'd been called in to assess things and make his report.

That said, though, he wasn't slipshod; his descriptions were detailed and thorough when that was required, but he also confined himself to the most salient points, as if he knew from experience which questions he needed to address. For no reason other than that, I pictured him as being middle-aged and possibly with other reports to fill out after this one.

His account started with a list of bald timings. At 18:07 on 13 November 1976 the emergency services received an anonymous report of a seriously injured woman in the bathroom of apartment 3, Nordrområdet 37 in Christiania. At 18:18 the ambulance crew arrived and got no response at the door of the flat, so they let themselves in through the unsecured door and in the bathroom they discovered the naked body of a woman in a bath of water.

According to the ambulance men's statements, Bidstrup recorded, the victim – later identified as Lýdia Tove Reyná, aged twenty-three – had cuts to both wrists and showed no signs of life. As a result, they didn't attempt resuscitation or disturb the scene any further but withdrew and called the police. However, when they checked the rest of the apartment, they discovered a boy of approximately five years – later identified as the victim's son, Jan Reyná Ravnsfjall – in a subdued state in one of the bedrooms. A police constable called Søndergaard arrived at the apartment at 18:32 and Bidstrup himself arrived at 19:03.

For a couple of paragraphs Bidstrup gave a physical description of the flat in general and the bathroom in particular. He noted there was no blood outside the bathtub itself; that a razor blade was recovered from the water when it was drained, and that there was no evidence of disturbance, forced entry (other than by the ambulance men) or of a suicide note. He noted, too, that when found in the bedroom, Jan Reyná Ravnsfjall was dressed only in underwear and a tee shirt and, although unharmed, could not answer questions. The boy said nothing in the time before a social worker arrived to take him away, nor during a subsequent interview at the Rønne Allé care home.

It was an odd feeling, to read what had been written about me with dispassion and distance; about something that had obviously taken place but of which I had absolutely no recall. It was a little like the time Fríða had shown me a photograph of myself before I left the Faroes. It was me, I knew that, but I saw nothing at all familiar in that boy's face.

Now, though, in the context of Lýdia's death and the discovery of her body, I felt as if I'd taken a step even further out of myself, but I didn't let myself analyse that yet. Instead I read on to the end of the report, through a paragraph that outlined interviews with other residents of the building, and noted that Lýdia Reyná had only lived there for approximately two weeks with her son and an unidentified girl aged about sixteen who could not now be found.

This last point clearly made Bidstrup anticipate that it might raise a question because he noted that many of the residents in the building were transitory. Only two reported ever meeting or talking to Lýdia Reyná and that she had seemed to want privacy and kept herself to herself. None could provide any more information on the girl in the flat other than a broad general physical description.

At the end of the report there was a separate section under the heading *Investigating Officer's Conclusion*. It was dated two days after Lýdia's death and in it Bidstrup wrote:

> There is no evidence that this was a suspicious death. The post-mortem report finds that the wounds on the victim's wrists are consistent with a suicide. This is supported by the position of the body and other physical evidence from the apartment as it was found. Therefore, it is my opinion that Lýdia Tove Reyná was probably found deceased by the unidentified girl who shared the apartment, and that it was this girl who telephoned the emergency services. In my opinion the fact that the girl has not made herself known is not suspicious given the other circumstances and the known nature of Christiania and its residents.
>
> Summary conclusion: Suicide. No further action required.

The report was signed off by a couple of higher-ranking officers on different dates. The last – a *politikommissær* – summarised it even more succinctly in a box by his name: *Agreed. Closed.* It was the last word.

There was no doubt about it, it was an uplifting read and after I'd finished it I turned off the screen. I ought to make notes, but not yet. Instead I smoked a cigarette I didn't really want, watching the street but not seeing a thing until my phone rang.

"I'm sorry for the delay," Thomas Friis said. "Are you still near the station?"

I waited in the reception area again, but not for long this time. When Thomas Friis arrived he was carrying a slim cardboard folder under his arm. We went to the same room we'd used before and he placed the folder squarely on the table with my business card neatly on top.

"The Major Crime Team you work in, what is it that you deal with the most?" he asked.

"Homicide and serious sexual offences usually," I said.

"Okay, that's what I thought."

For a moment I thought he was going to tell me that he'd just been in contact with them and had found out that my status didn't match the one I'd presented. Instead, he considered the card for a second, then slid it aside as if he'd made a decision.

"I have Inge-Lise Hoffmann's missing persons record," he said. "She was reported missing in June 1976 and has never been found so her file is still open. You have your photo?"

I summoned it up on my phone as he opened the folder and took out three or four sheets of old, printed forms, filled in with typewritten details. Stapled to the first sheet was a two-by-three photograph.

I didn't need to put the two images next to each other to know that Inge-Lise Hoffmann wasn't the subject of the photo I had. Friis's picture showed a girl of about fifteen standing in a garden with a golden Labrador by her side. She was round-faced and cheerful-looking, but rather plain despite striking, copper-red hair: dairy-maid looks. By comparison the girl on my phone was more waif-like and fragile. Even allowing for the circumstances of the picture and the difference in angle I was certain these were not the same girl, and to a certain extent I realised I was relieved.

Friis compared the photos for a little longer than me but he reached the same conclusion I had. "So," he said flatly. "Not a match."

"No."

I thought I sensed a little disappointment in his voice, but then he folded the pages back to find a yellow half-sheet at the back. It wasn't a form but a typed memo.

"This note has been added to the file at a later date," he said. "It refers to two other cases. One is the victim of an unresolved homicide in 1975 named Rikke Villadsen, the other is a girl named Thea Malene Rask. I haven't had time to locate their files in the archive because they haven't been digitised."

"Is there anything to say *why* they were linked to Inge-Lise?" I asked.

"No, I don't know." He ran a finger along a couple of lines on the sheet. "The dates of the cases are within nine months of each other and I think all would have been from the same area because Thea Rask is noted to have absconded from a placement in a rehabilitation facility."

He'd guessed that would get my attention and it did. "Vesborggård House?"

"Yes, I would say so. It doesn't give the name here, but as far as I know there was no other such facility in that area."

"Can I look at the note?"

"Sure." He turned it for me to see. "You read Danish?"

"Not really, I was just curious to see how the names were spelled." I looked at the memo for a moment longer, then turned the paper back towards him as if I'd satisfied my curiosity.

"So, forty years ago someone thought the disappearance of the two girls, Inge-Lise Hoffmann and Thea Rask, might have been linked to the murder of Rikke Villadsen," I said, stating the obvious.

He nodded. "Yeh, it would appear that way."

"And there's nothing in Inge-Lise's missing person report to say why?"

"No, it's just the standard personal details. If there is a case file from the time – if it was thought necessary to investigate further – the file will be in the archive."

He picked up the papers, turning them back to their correct order before putting them back in the folder. I knew he was using the time to decide how he wanted to proceed. He had something on his mind – that much was obvious – but he still wasn't sure about me.

"So, although the girl in your photo is not Inge-Lise Hoffmann, will you tell me where the photo is from?" he asked. He glanced at my phone. "Is it what I think?"

I didn't know what he was thinking but I could guess. "She was being abused," I said. "Badly. The images are pretty graphic."

"It was sexual abuse?"

"Yeah."

"How many images are there?"

"About twenty. They've been entered into evidence in the UK."

"Okay, I see." He looked away for a second, then back. "But they have a personal connection for you."

It was a statement rather than an enquiry, but I'd already worked out by then that Friis wasn't one of those people who thought they should disguise the evidence of their intelligence, so I nodded. "They were in a camera that belonged to my mother. She died in 1976 but I only got the camera the other day."

"She died at Vesborggård House?"

"No, in Copenhagen. But she'd worked at the house until a couple of weeks before she died. That's why I went there, to see what it looked like."

"Do you think that the photographs from your mother's camera were taken there?"

"I don't know where they're from," I told him truthfully. "Like I said earlier, it was only when I was at Vesborggård House that I heard about Inge-Lise Hoffmann going missing and wondered if she could be the girl in the photos. It was just a long shot."

"Okay, I see." He processed that for a moment, then said, "Do you know *why* your mother had such images?"

I shook my head. "I've no idea. To me it doesn't seem likely that she would have taken them, and if she didn't, the only thing I can come up with is that she acquired the camera with the film already inside, or that it belonged to someone else and was brought away with her things by mistake."

"You say the photographs have been entered into

evidence in the UK, so would you be prepared to give me a copy of that photograph? If I have time and if I can find them, I would like to compare it with the photos of the other two girls mentioned this file."

I'd already guessed he might ask that. It was a logical step, especially if you were as tidy as Thomas Friis appeared to be. And I had no basic objection, but before I committed I wanted time to reassess.

"Sure, I don't see why not," I told him. "I'll email it to you when I get back to my hotel. Although for obvious reasons it will have to be the cropped version."

He nodded. "Yes, I understand. Okay, thank you."

"And you'll let me know if you *do* make an identification?"

"Of course. In that case I think we would both have more questions, wouldn't we?"

"Yeah, I think so," I said.

It was the obvious place to end things, and I followed Friis out as far as the reception area where we shook hands and parted. Outside the building I dug out my notebook, writing down the date and the name I'd kept in my head from Friis's file: Thea Malene Rask, the girl who'd absconded from Vesborggård House on 27 October 1976, just over two weeks before Lýdia died.

It felt as if there was more than a *what if?* to this now, but I didn't rush to any conclusion. Instead I walked back to the car, mapping it out.

The fact that Thea Rask had absconded from Vesborggård House at around the same time Lýdia and I had also left didn't prove there was any connection between the two events, of course. But yesterday Elna Eskildsen had said that she'd seen a teenage girl with Lýdia and me when we were back in Copenhagen. Her impression had been that the girl had come to the city *with* us, and if that was true then didn't it imply that the girl had come with us from Vesborggård House? And in that case, didn't it also suggest that this same girl could be the unknown teenager referred to in Bidstrup's report on Lýdia's death – the one thought to be living with us?

While I assessed the strengths and weaknesses of that logic I navigated the concrete stairwell and echoing floors of the car park until I found my car and let myself in. If Thea Rask *was* the girl from the flat then I wanted to talk to her, if only to find out about the last few days of Lýdia's life, but I had no idea whether I'd be able to track her down forty years later. I did know that every Danish citizen has a civil personal registration number, though; and that it was linked to information like addresses and occupations – *if* you could access it. If Thea Rask was still alive she ought to be on it.

I sat for a moment, thinking it over, and then I called Hentze. I felt bad about asking him for yet another favour – not bad enough not to do it, but enough to be apologetic when he answered.

I could tell he was walking somewhere, but rather than take up more of his time I cut to the chase. "How hard would it be to find a current address for someone in Denmark?" I asked.

"Oh, not so hard. If you're in Copenhagen you can go to the city hall and make an application for the CPR entry. I think they will charge you seventy-five kroner. You get the result in a couple of days."

"Any chance of doing it more quickly – say if I give you the seventy-five kroner?"

He made a dry grunt. "No, I don't think that would be... *proper*," he said. "But tell me the name and I'll see what I can do."

"Okay, *takk*. Her name is Thea Malene Rask. I think her date of birth would have been between 1961 and '65."

There was a pause, as if he was writing it down. "Do you know *where* she was born?"

"No. Does it matter?"

"No, I don't think so, unless there is more than one person with the same name. I'll see what I can find."

"Thanks, I appreciate it, Hjalti. I won't ask for anything else."

"No, it's not a problem," he said, because he was that sort of guy. "But in exchange I'll ask you a question, okay? Hold on." In the background I heard a change in the acoustics and the sound of a car door closing, then he came back on the line. "So let me ask you: in your experience, if a man commits a sexual assault against a young girl, and then six months later he does it again to a different victim, is it likely that he would stop after that and commit no more crimes?"

"Hypothetically?"

"Yes, for the moment."

"Okay, then I'd say it's not likely he'd stop. A few do if they have a close call with the police – like being picked up for questioning – but in my experience, the longer they get away with it the bolder they become. The violence often increases as well, which is why if you get a rape/murder case you can usually work back through the perpetrator's history and see each attack getting worse."

"Okay, that's what I thought," Hentze said. "I just wanted an outside opinion. *Takk*."

"Any time," I said. "Is this connected to Múli?"

"Yeh, in a way," he said noncommittally. "But at the moment I'm only pursuing a theory."

I could tell that he didn't want to go into more detail so I said, "Well, if you need a sounding board just let me know."

"I might take you up on that. Where are you now? In Copenhagen?"

"Not yet, but heading that way."

"Then I'll speak to you later. And just remember, the Danes don't drive as well as us Faroese."

"I'll bear it in mind," I told him, and rang off.

24

ON HIS WAY BACK TO TÓRSHAVN HENTZE ATE THE SANDWICH he'd picked up in Runavík: a late lunch, except that it wasn't, he discovered; it only *seemed* late. Forty minutes later he parked at the station, let Annika know he was back and went to the toilet to sponge mayonnaise off his jeans: proof – not that he needed it – that eating while driving wasn't only bad for the digestion. He met Annika in the corridor as he went to his office. She was carrying a notepad and pen.

"I tracked down Boas's lawyer," she told him. "It's Nygaard in Klaksvík but he hadn't made a will. The last time they did any business with Boas was twenty-two years ago when he bought the house in Fuglafjørður. He paid cash, by the way: no mortgage."

"Really? I wonder where he got that sort of money," Hentze said, but it was an idle thought and he let it go as he sat down at his desk. "It sounds as if Mikkjal Tausen and Selma Lützen will have to split his assets between them, then, such as they are."

"Did you speak to Tausen?"

"Yeh, yeh, I did," Hentze said. "He confirmed that Boas

called him at around five o'clock on the 25th. He also said Boas was drunk and rambling on about being punished."

"Punished?"

Hentze shrugged. "Who knows? Maybe by God. Anyway, Tausen says they didn't speak for very long because he was waiting for a phone call from America." He searched his pockets, then located a slip of paper and handed it to Annika. "That's Tausen's car registration. Will you check the toll records and see if it went through the Leirvík tunnel on the 25th? Tausen says his girlfriend was with him that evening, so could you check that as well? Her name's Sigrun Ludvig and she works for Müller's, the letting agency, so they should be able to give you her number if she's not there. Dress it up as a general enquiry of some sort, though – just so she doesn't get the idea that we're checking up on Tausen, okay?"

"And *are* we?" Annika said. "Are you suspicious of him?"

Hentze shook his head. "No, I wouldn't say that, but given that he seems to be the last person we know of to have had contact with Boas I don't think it hurts to be sure he didn't make a trip out to Múli that night."

"Believe nothing and check everything?" Annika said.

"Exactly. Oh, and on the back of that paper there's a name: Thea Malene Rask. Will you find her address in Denmark when you get the chance? Do the other things first, though."

"Okay, I'll get on it."

Turning to leave, Annika almost bumped into Remi Syderbø as he appeared in the doorway. He stepped back to let her out, then remained on the threshold as if he refused to be confined by the broom cupboard's walls.

"Is there something you're not telling me?" he asked Hentze.

"I should think there are any number of things," Hentze said with a shrug. "Do you have something specific in mind?"

"Well, I know you've been to see Gunnar and ruffled his feathers."

"Ah," Hentze said as if it all became clear. He didn't bother to ask *how* Remi knew; a lot of birds flew between Nólsoy and Streymoy in the course of a morning.

"And Annika told me a second body's been found," Remi went on. "So, do you want to give me an update?" He gestured outside, so Hentze stood up and accompanied him down the hall.

"Is it Else?" Remi asked.

"It's a child," Hentze said flatly. "We won't know the age or the sex until Elisabet's done an exam."

"But chances are that it is?"

"That's what I assume. I don't want to say *hope*."

"No," Remi agreed.

They went into Ári Niclasen's office and as Hentze switched on the lights Remi looked at the whiteboards. Nothing much had changed except for one name.

"Who's Sunnvør Iversen?" Remi asked with a frown.

Briefly Hentze told him the story much as Gunnar Berthelsen had told it to him on Nólsoy that morning, although for the sake of simplicity he didn't bother to mention the dead end of Hans Jákup Olsen being a suspect. It was enough that Sunnvør Iversen had been brutally raped and no one had ever been brought to book for the crime.

222

"Jesus Christ, Hjalti," Remi said with some exasperation. "What are you doing, trawling through the old files to drag in as many cases as you can?"

"Believe me, it's not what I want," Hentze said with some feeling. "But Sunnvør's rape and the murder of Astrid and Else all happened within a few months of each other, and in the same area of Borðoy. On top of that both cases had young female victims."

"What about Astrid Dam? She wasn't a girl."

"No, true," Hentze acknowledged. "But I've been thinking that if Else was killed first – perhaps not even intentionally – then it may have been necessary for Astrid to die to stop her raising the alarm. Once they were both dead and buried it could have been said that they'd left the islands and gone home. No one would have been any the wiser."

Remi frowned but didn't argue the logic of that. Instead he moved away from the boards and sat down on a chair.

"You know, it's unusual for you to talk about something like this in such a... such a clinical way." He looked up at Hentze, inviting a response.

"Really?" Hentze made a face, as if he didn't recognise the description. "I'm simply trying to be logical about it."

"Yeh, I know." Remi took off his glasses and rubbed the side of his nose. "Maybe I *should* let you have someone else to work on this beside Annika. What about handing off most of the direct work to Dánjal and taking a step back?"

Hentze gave him a look. "How far back are you thinking?"

"Hjalti..." Remi started, but thought better of it. "I'm only saying that you went from the Tummas Gramm murder straight on to Erla Sivertsen and now this. So if you did want to slow down…" He let the thought hang for a moment until Hentze shook his head.

"No, there's no need – unless you're unhappy with the way things are going."

"No, of course not," Remi said. He stood up and put his glasses back on. "Listen, forget it. If you're okay let's leave that aside." He moved back to the boards, as if drawing a line. "So, what you're saying is that you believe Boas Justesen and an accomplice raped Sunnvør Iversen and then, a few months later, did the same thing to Else Dam, only that time it ended in her death. Is that right?"

Despite the rather clumsy shift of topic Hentze allowed himself to be drawn along with it. "Apparently an escalation of violence is common," he said. "But essentially, yes, I think so. We can't know whether it was one man or two who abducted and raped Sunnvør, but at Múli the differences between the two graves do suggest that two different people were involved in disposing of the bodies. We can be pretty sure that Boas Justesen was one of them now, so we need to find his accomplice – both for his part in the historical crimes *and* for Boas Justesen's murder last week."

"And if we do find him we clear the whole board, yes?" Remi asked. "Sunnvør, Astrid *and* Else."

"Yes, I would hope so."

"So how do we do that?" Remi said. "Is there anything more we can find out about Justesen's murder, any leads we can pursue that we haven't already?"

Hentze shook his head. "No, nothing substantial. The

fire at the house wiped out any trace evidence and obviously there were no witnesses, so unless someone comes forward to volunteer information I think our only way in is to look at this from the other end."

"Astrid and Else?"

"I think so. Our suspect, whoever he is, must have been at the Colony commune when they were killed – either as a resident there or as a visitor like Justesen. Which means that we need to speak to the people who were living at Múli in October 1974. They're the only ones who can tell us who Astrid knew, what she did there and how her disappearance was explained. *Something* must have been said to account for it; we just need to find out what and by whom."

"Well that'll be easier said than done after all this time," Remi said drily.

"Maybe not," Hentze said. "One of the founders of the Colony was a man called Rasmus Matzen who now lives in Denmark. Jan Reyná was going to see him so I asked him to put a few questions to Matzen about Astrid."

"Hold on," Remi said, raising a hand. "Why on earth is Jan Reyná involved in this?"

"His mother spent time at the commune so he wanted to ask Matzen about her."

From Remi's expression it was clear that he felt this explanation only went part way to an answer, but he chose not to follow the distraction. "So, *did* Reyná get any information about Astrid?" he asked.

"Yes, some," Hentze said. "Apparently Matzen remembered her from the commune, but once he realised that she'd been murdered – or that her death was suspicious at least – he didn't want to talk any more."

"So Reyná messed it up," Remi observed flatly.

"No, I wouldn't say that," Hentze said. "To be fair he had no jurisdiction to press Matzen for answers beyond a certain point… Anyway, the most important thing is that Matzen does have information that might be useful to us."

Remi Syderbø wasn't a man to dwell on might-have-beens once the damage was done. "In that case what do you want to do now then?" he asked. "Get someone from Danish CID to go and talk to Matzen on our behalf?"

"We could," Hentze acknowledged. "But we'd have to brief them over the phone and we'd also be at the mercy of whoever was assigned to the job. It might work all right, but without knowing the case it'd be easy for them to miss a hint or a coincidence that we might pick up."

"So you think it would be better to send someone who's already familiar with the case – which would be you."

"Or Annika," Hentze said.

Remi gave him a look. "She's been in CID since Tuesday," he said, shaking his head. Then: "How long would it take?"

"Three or four days, I suppose. After speaking to Matzen it'll depend how easy it is to trace the other people from the commune and interview them."

Remi made a play of considering it, but not for long. "Just tell me you really don't think there's a choice about this."

"I don't think there is," Hentze said.

"All right, go," Remi said. "But you'd better do it sooner rather than later. If Andrias Berg doesn't catch wind of it tomorrow – or even if he does – you'll get the weekend at least, but come Monday…"

"Okay," Hentze said. He looked at his watch. "I can probably make the five thirty flight if there's a seat."

In the CID office Hentze waited as Annika finished a phone call. She'd made a couple of notes on a pad.

"Mikkjal Tausen's car is a rental," she told Hentze. "It last used the Leirvík tunnel over two weeks ago. I also spoke to Sigrun Ludvig at her office. She confirms she spent the night with Tausen at his place."

"How did you play it?"

"I told her there was a report that her car had passed a traffic accident in Vestmanna on the night of 25 September and asked if she could give me a statement. She said there must be a mistake because she'd been in Rituvík that night – *overnight* was what she said."

"Okay, good," Hentze said. "We can put Tausen aside, then. Has Sophie called?"

"Not yet."

"Okay, come on; I need a lift and we can talk on the way."

"Where to?"

"My house and then the airport."

25

THE LAST OF SUNSET WAS BRIGHT ON THE DAMP TARMAC WHEN I cut across the parking area towards the building where Tove Hald lived. It was a modern building in Copenhagen's Amagerbro area, window frames, railings and stair banisters picked out in red, as were the doors on the third-floor landing where I rang the bell.

Tove opened the door with a towel round her waist, using another to dry her hair vigorously. In between she wore nothing else.

"*Hey*. I thought you'd be here before now," she said, standing back so I could enter the flat, which I did quickly.

"Sorry," I said, to cover several possible things I might need to apologise for.

"No, it doesn't matter," she said, following me into the living area. "This is Kjeld. Kjeld, this is Jan."

The man she'd referred to was just entering the room from the kitchen, a guy in his mid-twenties with Viking looks and stainless-steel spacers in his earlobes. He appeared not to notice that one of us was less than half-dressed.

"Hey, Jan," he said. "Nice to meet you."

"Are you making coffee?" Tove said. "If you are will you make one for Jan?"

"Sure."

"Okay, I'll just finish drying."

I couldn't help look at her back as she went off to her bedroom, seeing the snaking daisy head tattoos which spilled down her spine as far as the towel round her waist. I turned, looking for Kjeld, but he'd gone back to the kitchen so I followed him there.

"So are you and Tove… living together?" I asked.

"Sure, we've shared this place for two years." Then he reassessed for a second. "Oh, right, you don't mean it like that. *Nej*, we only share the bills and the rent, nothing else." He laughed. "She's too weird for me. I can't keep up." He handed me a mug of coffee, regulation black.

"Weird in a good way?" I asked, because it begged the question.

"Oh, yeh, for sure." He tapped his head. "She has too much working in here. She has a brain like— What do you say? Like a sponge, right?"

"Right," I said, glad to know I wasn't the only one who thought Tove was, at least, unconventional.

"And this thing – this research she's doing for you – it's got her very interested," Kjeld went on.

"Has it?" I asked, slightly surprised.

"Sure. Like I said, she's a sponge. When she gets into something she wants it all, right? Like one time we're talking and I tell her about this actor I saw in a film called *The Third Man* but I can't remember his name. It's nothing, you know –

just conversation – but the next day she sends me an email with a dozen attachments, about the film and the actor: where it's made, who wrote it… Because it interested her she'd watched it twice in the night and then looked for everything she can find out about it. She tells me she can send me more things to read if I want, so I have to say, 'Tove, it was only the guy's *name* I wanted to know.'" He laughed. "Still, some of the things she found were interesting to read. Who knew, right?"

"And who *was* the actor?" I asked.

He shook his head then laughed again. "You know, I don't remember. Weird, huh? Anyway, make yourself at home. I have some things to do but if Tove isn't back in five minutes knock on her door. Sometimes she forgets you're waiting for her."

"Okay. Thanks, I will."

Kjeld took his coffee and headed for his room and I wandered back into the living area, giving it a once-over. The over-large, worn sofa was angled towards a decent-sized TV; there were framed posters on the walls and some general clutter; but overall a sense that because this was shared space no one had put their own personal stamp on it too deeply.

I was looking at the view from the window, out across a main road and beyond that to a green swathe of park, when Tove padded back into the room, dressed now but still with bare feet. That much I could live with.

"You've got coffee?" she asked.

"Yeah, thanks." I held it up so that she could see that I had.

"Good, so we can start. I have some more information." She was obviously in business mode again, crossing to the sofa, sitting down and opening the MacBook she'd been holding. "Was the translation of the police report okay?" she asked as I took the seat.

"Yeah, very useful," I said.

"Good. Did you find Vesborggård House?"

"What's left of it, yes. It's being redeveloped. Only a few ancillary buildings are still there but I talked to a couple of people at the site."

"Okay, I can show you," she said. "I found a picture from 1923."

She angled the Mac a little and I saw a black-and-white photograph of an imposing three-storey brick building with an arch at its centre and tall rectangular windows. It had the look of a minor country house, but designed in a way that indicated the architect was more at home with prisons or military buildings. I could see why Henning Skov, the new architect, had said it was no loss.

"Did you learn anything else?" Tove asked.

"No, not a lot. As far as I could find out the place was what would have been called an 'approved school' in England at that time. Young offenders were sent there as an alternative to prison."

"Then that's strange," Tove said. "There isn't much information about Vesborggård House because it was closed so long ago, but in the directories from 1973 to 1977 it is listed as a private *clinic*, which isn't usual for Denmark. Here if someone needs treatment there are state hospitals and it is free."

"Maybe they called it a clinic because they thought it sounded better," I said. "It might have had less of a stigma attached."

She frowned. "What is a stigma?"

"Shame – something shameful."

"Okay. Yes, maybe." She picked up her phone and made a rapid note. "As I told you this morning," she went on, "in 2004 a group of fourteen people began a legal case regarding their treatment at Vesborggård House. They said that between 1971 and 1977 they had been sent there by the courts, or as a voluntary alternative to prosecution for minor crimes. They were all aged between sixteen to eighteen years old and in their lawsuit they claimed they had been given drugs to change their behaviour – to make them less 'anti-social'."

"What sort of drugs?"

"I don't know yet. I found this information in several newspaper reports but they didn't give many details; only that these people now claimed that the drugs they were given were not approved for medical use and that they had caused psychological damage in the following years: depression, anxiety and hallucinations."

"So what was the outcome of the court case?" I asked.

"There wasn't one. Before the case went to the court the company that operated Vesborggård House agreed to pay compensation without admitting a fault. There are no more details than that because the settlement was confidential."

Abruptly she shifted on the sofa, setting the MacBook aside, then standing up. "I need to eat. Do you want something, too?"

"No, thanks, I'm fine."

She went off to the kitchen and returned a short while later with a packet of Oreos. There was something automated about the way she pulled them from the pack and ate them mechanically one after the other, as if the taste held no interest for her; they were just fuel.

"So what's the bottom line?" I asked. "Are you thinking that something illegal went on at Vesborggård House and the owners wanted to keep it quiet?"

Tove shook her head while she finished an Oreo. She hadn't sat down again yet, which gave the impression that she had too much on her mind to be still. "No, we don't know that," she said, Oreo gone now. "But the company concerned is Juhl Pharmaceuticals. Do you know that name?"

"Should I?"

"No, maybe not," she allowed. "But it's well known in Denmark. It was founded in 1922 by Aksel Juhl and has been owned by the same family through four generations."

She took a step forward and picked up the MacBook, made a few keystrokes and then handed it to me. On screen was what I took to be a promotional photo: a conference stage with a lean, light-haired man in his fifties with his arm round a woman about twenty years younger. "The current CEO is Mette Lauridsen," Tove said. "That's her with her uncle, Oscar Juhl, who was CEO before that. He stepped down in 2004, although he is still on the board."

"The same year they were sued?"

She gave me an approving nod. "Yeh, although it may be a coincidence. But however it was, Juhl Pharma is a very prosperous company with a strong research division. In the past they have developed antibiotics, anaesthetics and others. So, you see the connection?"

She dropped down on the sofa, as if the lecture was over and now it was my turn – if I could – to catch up.

"You think the people at Vesborggård House were given experimental drugs made by Juhl."

"Yeh, of course," she said, making me feel – again – that I was three steps behind. "The people who sued for compensation said this, although of course that doesn't mean that it's true. Juhl Pharma may have thought it was better to settle with them than to have their business known in the court. We will find out, though. I have called their head office and sent an email saying I would like information about Vesborggård House. I have also spoken to a friend about Juhl. He wrote his PhD thesis on big pharmaceutical companies, so I'll see him tomorrow when he comes back from Malmö."

She crunched another Oreo then put the packet aside as if she'd reached her quota. "So, are you happy with that?"

I wasn't sure whether she was asking for my approval of her plans or if I was satisfied with what she'd already found out. But either way I had the sense that this had got a little out of control now and that maybe I should try to rein it in.

"It sounds like you've got a long way," I said. "But to be honest, I think you might have got as much as I need already."

She gave me a frown, as if that didn't make sense. "You don't want to know any more?"

"No, it's not that," I told her. "But you must have other things to do and I don't want it to take up all your time."

"Oh, for the cost," she said as if the penny had dropped. "No, that isn't a problem. This is interesting now."

I remembered Kjeld's comment that when Tove became

interested in something she wanted it all, like a sponge.

"Why?" I asked. "I mean, why is it interesting to *you*?"

She pursed her lips and frowned seriously for a moment, as if it was the first time the question had occurred to her. "Because I think it shows how people thought at that time," she said then. "And especially what their attitude was like to young people who didn't do as they were told. So, at a place like Vesborggård House, it seems that you have one part of our society trying to change another part to make them fit in; to make them *normal* whether they like it or not. They don't try to understand what the problem might be; instead they look for a cure from drugs or a pill."

It was when she said "normal" that I finally got it, and I wondered how many times in her life Tove had been compared to that and found wanting. I'd been as guilty of it as anyone else when we'd first met, just assuming that her brisk, abrupt manner meant that she wasn't aware of her idiosyncrasies. I'd been wrong, though, that much was obvious now, so I shifted.

"Listen," I said. "I'm probably only going to stay in Denmark for a couple more days. There's someone I want to see and a couple of places I want to go, but if you find anything more on Vesborggård House I'd still like to know. So how about we meet up over the weekend if you've got time – would that be okay? I'll buy you a drink or something."

"*Nej*, I don't drink," she said flatly and then she stood up. "If I have more information I'll call you, but now you should go. I have other things I need to do."

For a second I wondered if I'd hurt her feelings in some way, but there was no way to tell. I got off the sofa and by the time I was on my feet she was already working her phone.

"Okay, well, I'll see you later, then," I said.

"Yeh, I'll see you," she said, still fixed on the screen as she turned away. "*Hi, hi.*"

It was as much as I'd get.

26

BY AND LARGE, HENTZE WAS NOT A HAPPY TRAVELLER. HE didn't mind being somewhere different when he finally got there, but he found nothing exciting or glamorous in the actual *process* of travelling. So he endured the flight out of Vágar, hemmed in next to the window, and at Kastrup he had the small consolation of towing his single carry-on bag through baggage reclaim without having to wait for anything else. Even so it was gone eight o'clock by the time he'd caught a train and made the short trip to Copenhagen central station, emerging into damp air and setting off briskly to walk the fairly short distance to his hotel.

Apart from the mayonnaise-dropping sandwich, he'd eaten nothing all day and now he was hungry so he intended to check in, leave his bag and then find somewhere to eat before doing anything else. However when he caught the aroma from a red-and-white hotdog stand on Reventlowsgade his stomach made it clear that it wouldn't wait for that long and, lacking the will to defy it, Hentze gave in. He parked his bag and ordered the largest sausage on offer, then ate beside the stall, burning his mouth as the price of his weakness. It was a good hotdog, though.

Finally, with his hunger satisfied, at least for the moment, he felt rather more in control and remembered that he still hadn't called Jan Reyná about his record search. It would probably wait, but seeing a bar just over the road and rather fancying a beer after the salty hotdog he took out his phone.

"Hey. I was just calling to see where you were," he said when Reyná answered. "I'm in Copenhagen now, standing across the street from a bar on Reventlowsgade near the railway station. If you like I could meet you inside."

The first thing that struck me as I walked in to the Værtshuset bar was the smell of cigarettes and beer. It was a combination I hadn't come across for a long time, and hadn't expected here, either. As far as I knew the Danes had the same no-smoking policy as the British and Faroese, but here it was.

The place was fairly quiet: a dozen or fifteen people in total, sitting around in a cosy atmosphere that was more like a café than a pub; checked upholstery, retro posters and knick-knacks on the walls. None of the stripped-pine tables or chairs matched their neighbours and the green-painted wood panelling on the walls made it attractively gloomy. I already liked it before I was three steps inside.

The bar was halfway back and I didn't see Hentze until I reached it. He was sitting in a corner beside a glass screen into the rear of the place, just outside the pool of yellow light from a lamp on the wall. He was still wearing his coat and looked uncharacteristically sombre, I thought. Not that he was ever effervescent, but perhaps because I recognised a comparable thread to my own preoccupations I found myself sounding cheerful when I approached his table.

"You missed me so much you had to come to Copenhagen?" I asked. "Or is this the start of the invasion?"

Hentze made a dry "huh" then appeared to shake himself out of it. "We would make a poor army, I think: two Faroese guys to take on all Copenhagen."

"Oh, I don't know," I said, taking it as a compliment to be counted as his countryman. "Give it a couple of beers and anything's possible." I picked up his near-empty bottle. "Same again?"

"Yeh, I think so," he said, as if he'd given the matter some thought. "It's not bad for Danish."

I returned his bottle to the bar, asking the woman behind it for two more of the same. They came out of a tall refrigerator, satisfyingly cold, and I took them to the table and sat down on a chair that looked like it might have come from a school room.

In my short absence Hentze seemed to have come out of himself. He'd taken off his coat, as if he was sure he would stay now, and he picked up the new beer.

"*Skál.*"

"*Skál.*"

We clinked bottles and drank. He was right about the beer, it was pretty good.

"So what happened?" I said as an opening gambit. "You're here to see Rasmus Matzen, right?"

"As a beginning, yes." Hentze glanced away for a second

then he said, "Sophie Krogh found what we think is Astrid Dam's daughter this morning; in the fields at Múli. So what I hope is that Rasmus Matzen will tell me more than he told you."

"About Boas Justesen? He's still your main suspect?"

"Well, yes and no." He took a sip of beer then looked at his watch. "Do you have anywhere better to be?"

"Do you mind if I smoke?"

"No, of course not."

"Okay, so I've nowhere better to be," I told him, taking my cigarettes from my jacket. "But before you start telling me anything official, there's something you ought to know. Before I came out here I quit the job."

He frowned. "Are you joking?"

"Not really, no."

"Was it because of the allegation against you?" he asked.

"You mean was I forced out?" I shook my head. "No, it was my choice. The allegation was dropped, but by then I'd just had enough of the bullshit around it. So I told Kirkland what he could do and walked out."

"The big gesture?" Hentze asked.

"Yeah, something like that."

I tapped my cigarette on the ashtray, knowing he wouldn't ask any more because that wasn't his way. He did deserve more, though, because he'd been forbearing in the past, and because I didn't want him to have the wrong opinion of me – at least, not simply because of an absence of fact. So I told him about Donna Scott and the Paul Carney case in broad brushstrokes and I didn't put any veneer on my own actions either. I knew whatever conclusion Hentze came to would be based only on his personal standards and not anyone else's measure. It was one of the things I liked about him.

"So you knew what she'd done, this Officer Scott," he said when I'd told him everything of consequence.

I nodded. "I had a good idea at the time, yeah. And afterwards she told me. But I knew what Carney had done, too – and what he *would* do if he walked away."

Hentze considered, then made a small acknowledging gesture. "Then I think it was a small crime to prevent something worse," he said. "I don't say it's right, but I wouldn't say it was wrong either, so we'll leave it at that."

He took a drink, then looked at me again as he put it down. "So, you're unemployed now. That's a shame."

I had my verdict so I sat back. "I did hear that there was a vacancy in your office," I said.

He made a dubious face. "I'm not sure we could employ someone else who breaks the rules," he said drily. "And besides, you would need to speak more Faroese."

"You mean *skrapa* isn't enough?"

He chuckled. "*Nei*, not so much. All the same, if you want to apply maybe I should see how you do on a test: to see how you assess another case, eh?"

"Múli?" I asked.

He nodded, becoming serious again. "And Boas Justesen."

"Okay, go ahead," I told him.

The way he described it, Boas Justesen was still the pivotal element to the killings at Múli; not just as a suspect, but now as a victim as well. As far as Hentze was concerned, Justesen's blood alcohol count ruled out his death being a suicide, which inevitably meant that his murder could only be explained by someone having a motive to silence him. Logically, that brought the motive back to the bodies at Múli and meant that Justesen hadn't been alone in the killings; a theory Hentze supported by citing the differences in the locations and the ways in which the bodies of Astrid and Else Dam had been buried.

"As Sophie says, the earth burial of the child is much more considered," he told me. "As if they had time – even to think of burning a bonfire above it to hide the disturbed earth. There isn't so much wood on the islands, so it makes me wonder if they had prepared it, you know?"

"Or it could've been done later, as an afterthought," I said. "But you're right that two different types of burial is odd. So do you think Astrid was killed *after* Else, without as much time to dispose of her body?"

"It's only my theory, but yes."

"Is that why you were asking about sexual offences this afternoon? You think Else was their *intended* victim and Astrid was just collateral damage."

"Yeh, I think so, if you want to put it like that. I think there could be a paedophile part to all this. Six months before Astrid and Else were killed a young girl called Sunnvør was attacked and violently raped near Norðdepil. She and Else were similar – living in the same area and approximately the same age. Of course, we can't know what was done to Else before she was killed, but I think the two things together are enough to think that the same man or men could have attacked them both. The police at the time thought Sunnvør might have been drugged. She had no memory of what had happened to her for more than twelve hours, so my theory is that the same method was used on Else, but this time they went further, with the result that she died."

"Well, if it did happen that way, and if Astrid knew who the attackers were, it would certainly give them a motive for killing her too," I said. "But from everything you've told me it sounds as if you should be looking for someone local as Justesen's accomplice. Why come over here to see Rasmus Matzen?"

"Because I still have no suspect," Hentze said flatly. "Unless I suspect everyone in the islands who is more than sixty years old there is nowhere to start. *But* if Matzen or someone else from the commune can tell me that Boas used to go there with Bárður or Jákup, for example, maybe *then* I have a lead."

I recognised the sound of a long shot. "You haven't found anyone from the Faroes who spent time at the Colony?"

"Only one person who's said so; a cousin of Boas. They went there together one time but he doesn't remember when, or who else was there."

"So he's not a suspect?"

"No, I've no reason to think it. So, as I said, all I can hope is that Rasmus Matzen will give me a lead to someone who was with Boas in 1974 *and* on the islands to kill him last week."

"Well, Rasmus did remember Astrid," I said. "So maybe he *can* tell you something. I'm sorry I couldn't get more out of him when I was there."

Hentze waved it away. "No, I understand why. But from what I've just said you can't think of any other way to move forward?"

I thought about it, then shook my head. "On the face of it, no. I think all you can do is put in the legwork."

"Yeh, I think so, too." It wasn't a happy conclusion, but then he put it aside and drained the last of his beer.

I did the same, then pushed my chair back. "Another?" I asked.

Hentze considered and looked at his watch. "I still have to find my hotel, and in the morning I want to start early, but I don't think one more will hurt. It's my turn, however."

When he came back from the bar a couple of minutes later he had his wallet in his hand as well as new bottles. Once he'd sat down he looked through the wallet to find a slip of folded paper, which he handed to me.

"The address of Thea Malene Rask," he said. "There are two women of the same name in the CPR database, but the other one is only thirty years old, so I think this is the correct person. She lives at a place called Snestrup, part of Odense."

"Thanks, I appreciate it." I scanned the paper briefly, then put it away.

"Are you looking for spiritual advice?" Hentze asked.

"Come again?"

"Thea Rask is a pastor," he said. "You didn't know?"

"No, all I knew was her name."

He frowned slightly. "I probably should have asked you before, but why do you want to find her?"

"I think she was sharing the flat in Christiania with Lýdia and me when Lýdia died," I told him. "And before that she'd been at a place called Vesborggård House where Lýdia worked. It was a sort of rehabilitation centre for teenage offenders and Thea Rask is listed as absconding from the place at about the same time that we also left."

"So you think Thea Rask left with your mother?" he asked.

I gave a half-hearted shrug. "I don't know for sure, that's what I want to ask her: to find out."

"But you have a reason to think it."

I nodded in confirmation. "I think there's a chance that Thea was being abused there. And if she was, then I think Lýdia helped her get out of that situation."

"I see," Hentze said. He drew a breath then glanced away briefly. "Do you ever have the feeling that wherever we look as policemen we only find more people who have been victims? Sometimes I wonder if there is anyone left who is not."

"I know what you mean," I told him. "It's not something I'm going to miss."

"No, I wouldn't either," he said. For a moment he had the look of a man considering his own situation and finding it wanting, but it didn't last long. "So the reason you want to speak to Thea Rask is just for completeness – to have the whole picture – or do you suspect something else?"

I knew what he was asking: did I still have an objective perspective, or had I invented a narrative because that was what suited me better? It was something I'd asked myself, too, and my answer sounded more certain than I felt.

"I'm not trying to rewrite history," I told him. "Just understand it. I'd just like to find out what was going on in Lýdia's head before she died."

"*Ja*, I see." Hentze nodded slowly. "But have you also

thought that if things are as you say, you might be asking Thea Rask to remember things that she would rather not think of?"

I sensed his concern, not just for Thea Rask, I suspected, but also for me. "It's okay," I told him. "If she doesn't want to see me I'll leave it alone. She's the last lead I have anyway, so whatever she says I'll have gone as far as I can."

"And then you can rest?"

He might have meant "put it to rest", but that was another question. "I guess so," I said.

"Good. In that case, I hope you get what you need. Both of us, eh?"

Outside on the street about twenty minutes later the fresh air made me realise that Hentze had probably been right to decline my offer of another round. Either the beer was stronger than I'd thought or I'd smoked too much, just because I could. Either way, the damp breeze was cool and slightly heady and we stood for a moment as Hentze pulled out the handle from his case, then started along the street towards Vesterbrogade.

For several steps we walked in silence until Hentze appeared to have reached a decision about something and made a gesture at the world in general. "You know, I think there are two kinds of policeman," he said, in a way that sounded as if he'd given the matter some thought. "Some are the kind who think too little before making a conclusion; the others are the ones who believe they can never think *enough*, even after they know all the facts. Unfortunately for us, I think we are both in that second category."

I knew what he meant but I shook my head. "No, that's where you're wrong," I told him. "I'm not a policeman at all any more – remember?"

"Ah, yes, you're right," he said with a small bow to that fact. "How does that feel?"

"I'm not sure yet. I'll let you know."

"Yes, please, do that," he said seriously.

At the large junction at the corner of Vesterbrogade we halted again and waited for the lights to change.

"How long will you be here?" I asked him.

He pursed his lips. "I think if I'm not back by Monday I will have trouble."

"*Í skrapa?*"

"Yeh, that's close enough," he said with a laugh. We shook hands, and then he went his way with a wave and a "*Goða nátt*" and I headed in mine.

27

Friday/fríggjadagur

AT THE ENTRANCE TO THE CITY'S MAIN POLICE STATION ON Halmtorvet the next morning Hentze showed his ID and was allowed in. He was taken through to the back of the building and then up in the lift by a young uniformed constable, although now he came to think of it, all the *politibetjente* they had passed seemed to be under thirty. It had probably been the same in his day, Hentze thought. You just didn't notice when you were that age as well.

On the fifth floor there was another maze of corridors before they arrived at Christine Lynge's open door. The young *betjent* knocked – perhaps in case Hentze was too superannuated to do it himself – and waited just long enough to be sure that the chief inspector was there before making off.

"Hjalti, come in," Christine said with obvious pleasure, crossing to embrace Hentze. "You're looking—"

"Old," Hentze said.

"No. I was going to say *good*," Christine corrected. "You don't change at all, eh? What is it, five years since I heard from you? Then you're on the phone and a few days later you're here in person."

"Yeh, well…" Hentze said, failing to find any other ready response. "I thought I should pay my respects."

"*Pay your respects?* You make it sound like I'm dead."

"Sorry. Bad choice of words. I meant—"

"Yeh, yeh, I know what you meant. Your Danish is as rusty as everything else out there in the Atlantic. Come and sit down."

Hentze took a seat in one of the armchairs beside a potted plant under the window. "So you finally moved up," Christine said when they were settled. "It's about time."

"Up?"

"To inspector. Don't be dense. I saw it on your station report."

"Oh, that. It's only temporary," Hentze said, shrugging it off. "You don't need to worry, I'm not catching up with you."

"Pah. Why would I worry about that?" Christine said with a smile. "I reckon you've left it too late for a sprint finish."

There had been a pretence of rivalry between the two of them when they'd worked their first two years from the same station in Nørrebro and they had supposedly vied to be included in the most interesting cases. Although now he came to think of it again, Hentze wasn't entirely sure that his own pretence at rivalry had been equally mirrored by Christine's. Even then she'd had a drive for advancement that Hentze had never shared, so he'd always taken it as a foregone conclusion that one day she would be sitting in a *vicekriminalkommissær*'s office like this.

"So tell me why you're here and what I can do to help," Christine said. "Is it more to do with the anti-whaling protesters?"

"No, with any luck that's all over," Hentze said. "This is something different altogether."

He outlined the case of the burials at Múli and his intention to find and interview as many people from the commune as he could.

"Only you would chase a forty-year-old case, Hjalti," Christine said with a helpless shake of her head. "You always did have a weakness for lost causes."

"Well, I don't think it's lost yet," Hentze said, uncertain where this characterisation of him had come from. Perhaps it was just one of those things that happened when people didn't see each other for a long time; you were remembered or thought about in ways you couldn't correct or ameliorate in your absence.

"You're looking for a virgin in a brothel, but you know that, right?" Christine said. "And yet you've still come all this way. So what else do you know that you haven't said? Is it something to do with the English homicide officer, Reyná?"

"No, not at all," Hentze said, mildly surprised that she'd chosen to interpret what he'd told her as only part of the truth. "That's a personal matter for him, and I just tried to help. This case... Well, I'm not expecting any easy answers – if I get any at all – but I have to try. And who knows, after all this time someone might want to admit to the burden of guilt they've been carrying around for forty years."

"Well good luck with that," Christine said. "I've never

had any faith in people's consciences prompting them to do the right thing, especially if they've got away with something for years. Maybe things are different out there in the Faroes, though: everyone wants to come clean."

Hentze noted again that her reference to the Faroes could be seen as mildly disparaging, but he decided he was being too sensitive.

"Well it's certainly not Copenhagen," he said. "I can't complain about that."

Christine chuckled. "Are you homesick for the rain and the wind already?" she asked, gesturing to the now sunny window.

"No, no, I think I can stand it for a couple of days. Of course, if it takes longer than that…"

"I'd better get you sorted out as quickly as possible, then. What do you need?"

"Well, a car to begin with, if you have one free: I need to get to Dannemare. After I've spoken to Herre Matzen I may also need to borrow a desk so I can access the CPR records, depending on what information I get."

"Well, I think we can manage that for an overseas colleague," Christine said, standing up and moving to her desk. "Where are you staying, by the way?"

"The Euro Hotel."

"Really?" She winced. "Couldn't your department have had a whip-round and got you something better, or was the idea to make sure you didn't stay away any longer than necessary?"

"Oh, it isn't so bad," Hentze said. "It's central at least."

Christine chuckled and picked up the phone. "That's

the Hjalti I remember: always ready to see the bright side of things – even after a night in the Euro."

By the time he was on the road the rush hour had started, something Hentze was unused to, unless you counted the occasional snarl-ups at the end of Bøkjarabrekka first thing in the morning. As a result, it took him longer than he'd anticipated to leave the city behind and so it wasn't until just after ten that he pulled in at Rasmus Matzen's house, where a rack of pumpkins was displayed by the roadside beside an honesty box.

The fact that there was no car at the house and that he hadn't been able to find a phone listing for Matzen and so call ahead made Hentze fear that he might have a long wait if the man wasn't at home. The lack of response to his knock on the front door reinforced that, but going round to the back of the house he discovered a man in his sixties digging manure into a section of recently turned earth. It was sunny and the man was stripped down to a tee shirt, showing deeply tanned arms and the lean, muscled physique of someone who was used to manual work.

"Herre Matzen?" Hentze asked.

"Yes?" Matzen broke off from the digging and straightened up, wiping soil from his hands as Hentze introduced himself.

"I need to talk to you about the Colony commune at Múli," Hentze said, coming straight to the point. "The remains of two bodies have been found there. One has been identified as Astrid Hege Dam and the other, we believe, is her daughter, Else." He waited to see Matzen's reaction, although he knew that Jan Reyná's previous visit ruled out any element of surprise.

Matzen shook his head, as if to distance himself from the subject. "I didn't know anything about that until an English police officer came here the other day. His name was Reyná and he said someone on the Faroes had asked him to talk to me about Astrid."

"That was me," Hentze acknowledged. "But since then we've gathered new information so I need to ask you some more specific questions. Do you have any objection?"

"Would it matter if I did?"

"Well of course I can't force you to talk to me," Hentze said, noting Matzen's slightly prickly tone, although it was perhaps not surprising. "But – to be clear – I'm simply trying to find out what happened to Astrid and Else. There's no implication that you or anyone else is under suspicion."

"No? Well, I'm glad to hear it," Matzen said, although he didn't sound particularly convinced.

He stuck his spade in the ground and stepped off the dug-over soil, gesturing Hentze to a wrought-iron table and chairs beside a shed: a small suntrap. "You'd better sit down, I suppose. I'll tell you what I can."

"Thank you," Hentze said. "It would be a great help."

Once they were seated Matzen took out a tobacco pouch and rolled a cigarette while Hentze opened the cardboard folder he'd brought from the car. He slid out two photographs, placing them on the table so Matzen could see them.

"As I said, we know Astrid and Else were living at the Colony commune in September 1974. You do remember them, yes?"

Matzen paused in his cigarette rolling to glance at the photos, but it was clear that he didn't need them to prompt his recollection.

"Yes, I remember," he said.

"So what can you tell me about them?" Hentze asked, taking out his notebook and pen.

According to Matzen, Astrid and Else had come to the commune at a time when almost half the residents had already left. The growing passive resistance of the local population, problems with self-sufficient living and other factors had all contributed to the fall in the Colony's numbers and it was clear that unless something changed it would be hard, if not impossible, to stay through another winter. However, it wasn't their policy to turn people away, Matzen said, so Astrid and Else were welcomed in, given two rooms in the lower house on the hillside and told how they could best contribute to running the place. The fact that Astrid fell and injured her arm a few days later meant she was restricted in the help she could give for a time, but for all that she was very willing and enthusiastic.

"To tell the truth, I remember her best because she was one of those people who had an idealised idea of what we were trying to do," Matzen said. "You saw it a lot in those days: people who thought that if they joined a community like ours all the concerns of real life would be magically taken care of. They didn't realise that in many ways it was much harder to live like that. It still is."

"It doesn't sound as if you had much time for her," Hentze said.

"No, that's not true. I— To tell the truth, I was more concerned about the Colony's future. There was a lot of pressure on me by then."

Hentze noted that Matzen had used the phrase "to tell the truth" twice now but he said, "What sort of pressure?"

Matzen made a dissatisfied sigh. "All major decisions were supposed to be taken as a group, but there was a lot of factionalism and in the end someone had to take charge. I didn't want the project to fail, so I was trying to organise things so we could survive through the winter, but some of the others were only concerned with petty things: was there hot water, whose turn it was to do this thing or that."

"I get the picture," Hentze said with a nod, more interested in bringing the conversation back to specifics. "So do you remember if Astrid was friendly with anyone in particular?"

Matzen shrugged. "She was friendly with everyone. Like I said, she was very enthusiastic. She had lots of energy."

"So there were no arguments or bad feeling between Astrid and anyone else that you recall?"

"No, not at all."

"Did she have a sexual relationship with anyone while she was there, do you know?"

Matzen shook his head. "I didn't keep track of her sex life or anyone else's," he said. "Why would I?"

"So it's possible that she *did* have a relationship."

"Like I said, I don't know." Matzen made a slightly irritable gesture. "People could do what they liked."

"Okay," Hentze said, jotting a brief note, then turning the page in his notebook, as if moving on. "So what can you tell me about Astrid and Else leaving the commune? That *was* what you thought at the time – that she'd left?"

"Yes, of course," Matzen said. "I don't remember the details, though. Like I said, I had a lot of things to deal with so I don't know who told me or what they said about Astrid and Else. All I remember – all I thought until the Englishman came – was that they'd left because they'd had enough. There was nothing odd about that – only perhaps that Astrid hadn't said goodbye – but I had no reason to think anything had happened to them."

"And do you remember when that was? I mean, when you found out that Astrid and Else had left."

Matzen shook his head. "No, I've no idea. I suppose it must have been in October, but I don't know for sure."

"And when did the commune officially come to an end?"

"November, the first week," Matzen said. "We made the decision and people started to leave. There were five or six of us left at the end – the last ones. We closed things down and then the owner of the land gave us a lift to Tórshavn in an old van and we got the ferry to Denmark. It was a rough crossing and we were all seasick for most of the time, I remember that."

"The landlord – the one who gave you a lift – that was Boas Justesen?"

"Boas, yeh," Matzen said, as if the name had been eluding him for a while. "I was trying to remember what he was called. Have you talked to him, too?"

"No, that hasn't been possible. He died recently."

Hentze watched for Matzen's reaction to that, but there was hardly any. "Oh. Right. I'm sorry to hear it. He was a decent guy. Even when a lot of the local people wanted him to evict us, he wouldn't."

"Did he spend a lot of time at the commune?"

Matzen considered. "No, I wouldn't say a lot, although he came out to see how we were getting on from time to time. I think we were something different and he liked the atmosphere. And I remember he gave us some advice on the sheep – with the shearing and lambing; slaughtering, too."

"Right," Hentze said, acknowledging that this was nothing unusual. "And I was told that he attended some parties and celebrations there, too."

Matzen nodded. "Yeh, yeh, he did. There were more of those the first year, not so many in the last." And as if the significance of that fact wasn't lost on him, Matzen took a final puff on his cigarette, then dropped it and ground it out with his boot.

Sensing that the other man might be preparing to draw things to a close Hentze said, "Thank you, that's all very useful, but the other thing that I'd like to get from you now is the names of people who lived at the commune in those last few months. I need to interview them and ask the same questions I've asked you."

Matzen pursed his lips. "Well, I can probably remember a few names," he said, as if he didn't want to commit yet. "But apart from a couple of people I don't think I've seen anyone from the Colony for at least twenty years, probably thirty."

"Are there any records from that time?"

Matzen gave a sardonic laugh. "You mean like a school register? No. We went there to get away from all that."

"What about a diary or photographs – something that might jog your memory?" Hentze pressed him. "It may be forty years, but this *is* still a murder case, so I do need to know who was there."

The word "murder" brought Matzen's focus back to the present. "You think someone at the commune killed them?" he asked.

"I think it's possible, yes," Hentze said with a definite nod.

Matzen chewed that over for a moment, then made a decision. "I never kept a diary," he said. "But there are some old photos. If you want I can look them out."

"If you would, yes," Hentze said.

Matzen heaved a sigh, then stood up. "You'd better come into the house."

28

AT KORSØR, I PAID THE TOLL AND DROVE ON UP THE CONCRETE causeway incline towards the twin towers of the *Storebæltsforbindelsen* bridge, which spanned the fifteen kilometres from Zealand to Funen. But for all its high-vaulted, sweeping lines and the triumph of engineering it undoubtedly was, I was more preoccupied by the engineering of my own logic and whether that would prove able to take any weight.

It was simple enough: Thea Rask had absconded from Vesborggård House in October 1976 and Elna Eskildsen had seen Lýdia with a teenage girl in Copenhagen a week or two later. Those were separate facts – two nails in the wall – and I'd linked them together with a chain of possibilities, the coincidence of places and the presence of a girl. In the abstract the chain seemed solid enough, but in reality I also knew it was possible – even likely – that I'd allowed myself to see cause and effect where there was none. But either way, I needed to know, and if it turned out that I'd driven this distance for a five-minute stop – an enquiry, an explanation and then an apology – that was all right. Like I'd told Hentze the previous night, it was my last lead. If Thea Rask wasn't the girl who'd shared the flat in Christiania with Lýdia and me, then I had nowhere to go after this; I could rest.

I left the E20 south of Odense, following the ring road around to the west to the suburb of Snestrup where the roads became a warren of housing estates, all low-rise bungalows, neat hedges and paved pathways. The further I went the more claustrophobic it felt, but I knew that was me, not the place.

Finally, the satnav brought me to the house on Windelsvej: yellow brick, nondescript and with a car on the drive. Its rear door was open and as I approached a man in his fifties came out of the house carrying a cardboard box full of paperback books. When he caught sight of me I raised a hand.

"*Hi, goddag*, can you help me?" I asked. "I'm looking for Thea Rask. I was told she lived here."

"*Ja.* Yes, she does. I'm her husband, but she's at work now."

Hampered by the box's weight, he carried on to the car, putting it inside. "For charity," he said, as if it needed explanation.

"Right." I nodded. "Do you know when Thea will be back?"

"No, I'm not sure." He gave me an appraising look. "Can you say why you want her?"

"My name's Jan Reyna," I said. "I think Thea might have shared a flat – an apartment – in Christiania with me and my mother, Lýdia, back in the 1970s."

He raised his eyebrows. "The seventies? That's a long time ago."

"Yeah, well, I don't remember much about it, that's why I came to find Thea," I said.

He gave me another assessment, then said, "If you like I can call her and find out where she is."

"Sure. *Tak*. That would be great."

"Just a minute. Jan Reyná, yes?"

"Yes."

He took a mobile from his pocket and moved away, for privacy I assumed, although there was no need. I waited, looking out over the road and the neat, well-kept houses and a couple of minutes later he came back.

"Thea's at the church office," he said. "If you'd like to go there she says she will meet you. Just follow this road to the end and go to the left. There is a car park. You can walk from there."

"Thank you."

"You're very welcome," he said.

Back on the street I moved the car the short distance as he'd directed, finding the car park empty except for two vans with electrician's logos down their sides. Not far away the church was a square, red-brick building, somewhat imposing in the centre of neatly manicured grounds, but instead of heading towards it I followed a path which was signed *kirkekontoret*. It took me fifty yards or so to a more modern building, low-roofed and set beside a main road. It had the look of a day care centre or doctor's practice, an impression that continued beyond the double doors, in a lobby with noticeboards, posters and photographs hung on the walls. Beyond that there was a central hall with a wooden block floor but there was no one in sight so I lingered to look at the photos on the noticeboard marked *Kirkens Personale*. I hadn't got very far before my attention was distracted by the sound of brisk heels on the hard wooden floor.

She wasn't what I'd expected, although I had no real idea of what I thought she'd be like. She was tall with strong, lean features and stylish black-rimmed glasses to match crow-black hair which she wore long and straight over the shoulders of a grey wrap-around cardigan. As she approached me, raising her hand, the greatest impression I got was one of immediate energy and purpose, matched by her stride.

"Hi. Are you Jan? I'm Thea," she said.

In the final couple of paces I knew she was assessing whether she could see any familiarity in my features, but I couldn't tell whether she found some or not. For my own part I sought any similarity between her and the girl in the photos from Lýdia's camera and I thought I saw some; not enough to be certain, but enough.

And then she was in front of me, offering another smile and her hand: long fingers, two silver rings.

"It's good to meet you again," Thea said as we shook hands. She had a firm businesslike grip. "Povl told me you're here because of Lýdia, yes?"

"Yes. I hoped you might be able to tell me something about her," I said. "You *were* living with her – with us – when she died, is that right?"

"Yes, yes, I was," she confirmed, almost as if she'd expected me sooner. "So I can tell you what I remember, but let's go to my office."

We crossed the hall towards a door marked with Thea's name and a child's picture of a cross taped above it. Inside the room was modern, with exposed brick walls and the usual minimalist desk with Ikea bookshelves behind it, but the rest of the space had been deliberately softened by vibrant wall hangings, a chintz sofa and a couple of armchairs arranged in the way that chairs often are when moments of intimacy might be at hand.

Thea directed me towards these, closing the door. "I must tell you that I have to make a home communion visit later, but for a little while I think we're okay. Please, take a seat."

I recognised the tactic of establishing a limit, just in case it was needed. I'd have done the same thing in her place and I took the chair facing the window while she sat down opposite me, sitting erect but not stiff.

"I'm sorry to just come without any warning," I said as a way of framing why I was there. "I had some free time from work so I decided to try and find out a bit more about Lýdia by visiting some of the people she knew."

Thea nodded as if she understood that completely. "Yes, of course," she said. "What is it you do now?"

"Until recently I was a police officer."

If it surprised her she covered it so well that I didn't see it. "Ah, I see," she said. "Is that how you found me?"

I'd known it was a question that would inevitably come up. "Well, it did help a little," I said. "You probably won't remember, but you were with Lýdia when she met an old friend in Copenhagen in 1976. Her name's Elna and when I went to see her the other day she mentioned your name and then I was able to find your address."

It was an expedient half-truth, avoiding the questions

a full explanation would raise before I'd got an idea of how this might go, but Thea appeared to spend only a short time hunting any memory of the event before shaking her head.

"No, I don't recall it," she said. "But that doesn't matter. Lýdia was a great help to me – a good friend. I've always been grateful to her, so it's good that you came. Do you remember anything from that time? You weren't very old."

"No, not really," I said. "That's why I'm here."

"Yes, of course." She sat back a little. "So, what can I tell you?"

"Well, I suppose first and foremost, I wanted to ask if you were the person who found Lýdia and called the ambulance on the day that she died," I said. "In the police report it doesn't say who that was."

"Yes, it was me," Thea said, then glanced away as if she knew it wasn't enough and was deciding how better to frame it. "I'd been away from the flat for a few hours," she said. "When I came back – in the evening – I opened the door and called out to say *hi*, but there was no answer. Everything was very quiet and I thought maybe Lýdia was with you in the bedroom you shared, so I went and looked in but you were asleep on your own."

She paused briefly, then said, "That was when I first thought something was strange. I knew Lýdia wouldn't have left you alone and because it wasn't a large flat there was only one other place she could be. So I went to the bathroom and knocked on the door. There was still no answer so I went in and that was when I saw what had happened."

For a moment she had that look people get when you know

they're seeing the picture again: not with distress, but clearly not as something she would particularly wish to dwell on either.

"I think I just stood still for some time," Thea said then. "But I knew I should get someone, so I went out to find a telephone, and called the ambulance to come." She smoothed an invisible crease in the leg of her trousers before looking up. "I've always wished I'd come back sooner, you know? Or maybe seen signs that she was thinking that way. But I didn't. I'm sorry for that."

I made a gesture, negating the need for apology. "I don't think there was anything you could have done," I told her. "She'd attempted the same thing a few years before while she was still on the Faroe Islands, and that time it was only by luck that she was found."

"Oh. I didn't know."

"There's no reason you would have," I said. "From some of the people who've told me about her and from some of the decisions she made, I think she was always impulsive; maybe even manic at times. I don't know if it was some sort of mental illness – something like bipolar disorder – but it's too late to find out now, so all I'm trying to do is put together what she was like and what she was doing before she died."

"Yes, I understand." Thea nodded. "Sometimes in my job I have to try to give comfort to the relatives of people who have done the same thing. It's never easy, and when I do I often think of how I felt when I found Lýdia."

"It must have been pretty hard on you," I said. "What were you, sixteen?"

"Yes; sixteen and a few months."

"And you'd known Lýdia since you were at Vesborggård House?"

For the first time I saw her react, just a little and only briefly, as if I'd jumped to something she hadn't expected, or maybe not yet. "You know about that?" she asked.

"Not all the details," I said. "When I found out that Lýdia had worked there I did some research into the place and found out that you were listed as absconding at about the same time that we left, so I wondered if the two things were connected."

For a second Thea appeared to hold back from some instinctive reaction, but then she made a definite nod. "Yes. Yes, they were," she said flatly. "We all left together."

"Can I ask why – I mean, what the circumstances were?"

It was the obvious question, but I tried to leave it as open as I could, giving her room to step aside from the answer if that's what she needed to do. Instead though, she seemed to consider it dispassionately for a moment, then gathered herself slightly and clasped her hands on her lap.

"It was because I had been raped," she said then. "Lýdia found me and took us away to Christiania. I don't remember what happened, only the results, but they are enough."

"I'm sorry," I said, which is always inadequate. "Look, if you don't want to talk about it…"

But Thea was already shaking her head. "No, it's not a problem," she said. "It isn't the first time I've spoken about it. If you remain silent you let it win, and that's what I did for a long time. But many years later, when I was in rehab, I learned that it's important to talk: to be truthful and take back control. If you want to help others you have to be honest about yourself too."

I nodded to show I understood. If she'd been through rehab and counselling, this emotionally literate reaction was natural. There's a degree of protection in adopting the jargon, although I doubted she needed it as much as some. She was a strong woman – I'd seen that from the start – and now I had an idea where that resolve might have its roots.

"You say you don't remember anything – not even who did it?" I asked. It was another obvious question, but one I thought I'd been given permission to ask now.

"No, I don't know," she said, lacing her fingers. "I don't remember anything about the attack, so in that way I was lucky. I was at Vesborggård House and then there's an empty space until I woke up in Christiania with Lýdia, and with you. I knew what had happened and it was easy to see. Every part of me hurt in some way, that's how it felt. And on my throat there were red marks – scratching and bruises."

She raised a hand to show me the place on her neck, but I already knew. I'd seen the photographs.

"For several days I couldn't speak very well," Thea went on. "It hurt to eat, to move around or go to the toilet. I also had a fever, I think, but Lýdia looked after me. She got me well."

"Did she say how she found you or how you got to Christiania?"

Thea shook her head. "I asked her, of course, but she wouldn't say. All she would tell me was that we were safe now. We would stay safe, she said, but we mustn't talk about Vesborggård to anyone. 'You must believe we haven't been there,' she said."

I remembered Elna's description of her hurt feelings when she'd met Lýdia, Thea and me in Copenhagen and

Lýdia hadn't wanted to talk. This explained it, at least in part.

"So how long were we at the flat before Lýdia died?" I asked, moving to more neutral ground. "Can you remember?"

"No, not exactly. Maybe two or three weeks. I'm not sure."

"Did anyone else come there? Were there any visitors – anyone Lýdia knew?"

She thought back. "Only once: Mickey. I didn't know his last name but he worked at Vesborggård House – in an office, I think. I didn't see him very often but sometimes he would come to see Lýdia in the kitchen. He was from the Faroe Islands like her, but I don't know if she knew him from there or just from Vesborggård House."

The fact that there had been another Faroe islander at Vesborggård House caught my attention, of course, but all the more so because he'd been in Christiania as well.

"So one day Mickey just turned up at the flat in Christiania?" I asked, hoping for clarification.

"Yes, I think so," Thea said. "We hadn't been there very long: maybe two or three days. I was in bed when I heard a man's voice in the next room, so I opened the door to see who it was and when I saw Mickey I was frightened. I was afraid that if he knew where I was that others would come and I'd have to go back to the house. But Lýdia said no, it was okay. Mickey was here because he was a friend. He was going to help."

"In what way?"

She shook her head. "I'm not sure. Maybe with money, or to find somewhere better to live, but after I saw him he didn't stay very long."

"Did he come back?"

"To the flat? No, I didn't see him again."

I thought for a moment. "So what was Lýdia's mood like at the time?" I asked. "Was she worried or frightened in case someone came looking for you, do you think?"

"*Nej*, not afraid," Thea said, very sure. "She was... Her mind was made up. She was very determined and—"

She broke off at a knock on the door as it opened. A middle-aged man with a grey beard and neat collar and tie came part way into the room, already speaking before realising that Thea wasn't alone. He had a sheaf of papers in his hand and even in Danish I heard the note of apology before he started to back out again.

Thea spoke up, though, asking a question, and slightly reluctantly the man stated his case with a gesture of the papers he was holding. It was something that required Thea's input, it seemed, and after a moment she turned to me apologetically.

"Jan, I'm sorry," she said. "There are electricians working in the church and there is a problem for the fire regulations. I think I must have a look or all the work stops." She hesitated, but only briefly. "Can you wait? Perhaps half an hour, so I can see the problem."

"Yeah, of course, if you're sure that's all right."

"Yes. Please," she said as if she wanted to be sure that we didn't leave something unfinished.

"Okay," I said and stood up as she did the same. "I'll have a look round the church yard."

"Good. I'll come and find you," she said. "It's a nice place to walk."

29

THE SITTING ROOM AT THE FRONT OF RASMUS MATZEN'S HOUSE was populated by worn furniture and bookshelves filled beyond capacity. There was no television and no electronics of any sort, save for a radio on the mantelpiece over a wood-burning stove.

The door to the room was slightly ajar and beyond it Hentze could hear the sounds of Matzen's wife, Elna Eskildsen, moving around in the kitchen. She'd recently returned from the supermarket and immediately made coffee for their guest as soon as she discovered that her husband had neglected to do so. Hentze was grateful for the coffee and sipped it while he watched Matzen leaf through the thick pages of an album of photographs from the 1970s.

The pictures were set behind yellowed plastic film and once he found the first ones taken at the Colony commune, Matzen pored over them more carefully. From what Hentze could see, the photos of the early days had clearly been taken in a spirit of optimism, recording work at the commune as well as celebrations and significant moments.

Rasmus Matzen was able to identify five people with little

trouble – all founders of the commune who had gone out to the Faroes with him in 1973 and stayed until the end. A couple he'd seen in the last few years and told Hentze where they lived, but after that the identification of faces became more of a struggle. It seemed that the people who'd been attracted to the idea of entering a new society at the Colony had often taken the opportunity to cast off any formality about who they were, so when Matzen remembered a face it was often only attached to a first name and sometimes an adjective: *Tage the Swede*; *Nanna from Skagen*; *Jürgen the baker*. Last names were often little more than a guess or something in a general phonetic area: *was it Sørensen or Svendsen or Simonsen? Something like that.*

It was a time-consuming business, but despite the uncertainty, Hentze wrote it all down. Short of a miracle he knew there would be little chance of tracing most of these people, but with little else to go on he'd take what he could get.

"Oh, okay, that was midsummer, the last one," Matzen said, turning a page and tapping a group photograph of ten or twelve people clustered round a boulder. "That's Boas, the landlord, I think. Tobias, Silje, August…"

Hentze adjusted his reading glasses and looked a little closer. A blond-haired, bearded young man seemed vaguely familiar to him. "What about this man?" he asked. "Do you know who he is?"

Matzen shook his head. "No, I can't remember his name, although… Yeh, I think he may have come from the mainland. Some people did come as visitors over the summers. He could have been one of them."

"He definitely didn't live at the commune?"

"No… No, but I think he came several times. He had a friend he brought with him, I remember: a guy who wasn't short of money. I thought maybe he might make a donation, you know: buy a rotovator or something? He didn't, though."

With the possibility of further identifications ruled out, Matzen turned the page again and this time Hentze didn't have any doubt about who the woman was standing beside Rasmus Matzen outside one of the houses at Múli. She had clearly been a little older than Matzen at the time, but her fingers were entwined with his and her appearance wasn't very different to the photo in the missing persons report.

"That's Astrid, isn't it?" Hentze said.

Matzen nodded. "I'd forgotten this picture," he said.

"You seem pretty close," Hentze observed neutrally. "Were you?"

"Of course. Everyone was," Matzen said. "It was a commune."

It wasn't an answer, as they both knew, but when Matzen didn't seem prepared to go further Hentze straightened up in his seat and at that moment Elna Eskildsen opened the door.

"Would you like more coffee?" she asked Hentze as Matzen closed the photograph album.

"No, thank you," Hentze said. "Rasmus has given me a lot of names to look up, so I'd better get to it, I think."

Matzen stood up. "I'll show you out."

Outside Matzen accompanied Hentze round to the front of the house where Hentze had left the CID pool car, a decent-sized Ford.

"You know, it will save me a lot of time if you tell me the truth now," Hentze observed equably as he got out his keys. "I understand that there might be things you don't want to dwell on in front of your wife, so if you wish to deny that you and Astrid had a relationship, that's fine. But if someone from the commune tells me that you did, I'll only have to come back."

Matzen looked at the cigarette in his fingers. It had gone out. "It wasn't a relationship, as you call it," he said. "It was... It was nothing."

"But it *was* sexual?"

A brief pause, then: "Yes. But it was... We slept together a few times but then she moved on. You know what I mean."

"To somebody else."

Matzen nodded. He took out a lighter and struck a flame to the cigarette.

"And who was that?" Hentze asked. "Do you remember?"

"I think his name was Evald, but there might have been others."

"So she slept around?"

The phrase appeared distasteful to Matzen. "Yes, if you want to put it like that. Listen, it was different then. Or maybe it wasn't, I don't know." He made a dismissive gesture. "All I'm saying is that it wasn't unusual, okay? People slept around, as you say, if that's what they wanted to do. Why not? Life's short, right?"

"Were you jealous?" Hentze asked. "Of Astrid's other lovers?"

"No, of course not: we didn't *own* each other. If it made

you feel good, then you did it. If not…" He shrugged and drew on the roll-up, then shifted. "Look, I know what you're thinking. If you believe I was jealous of Astrid's other partners, you can say I must have killed her *because* I was jealous. Isn't that right?"

"*Did* you kill Astrid or Else?" Hentze asked.

"No. Absolutely not."

"Okay, then."

Matzen cast Hentze a suspicious look. "What do you mean?"

"I mean that at the moment I've no reason to doubt you," Hentze said. "If that changes I can come back, but for the time being – unless you can tell me anything else – I think we can leave it at that. Thank you, you've been a great help."

"So what will you do now?" Matzen asked, as Hentze opened the car door. "Do you think you'll be able to find him – the one who killed them, I mean?"

"That's my job," Hentze said. "So I hope so, yes."

"It's strange," Matzen said. "I hadn't thought about Astrid since the Colony came to an end, but when the other guy, Reyná, said she was dead, that she'd been murdered… I don't know." He shook his head. "It was more of a shock than I could have thought. After so long it's not something you expect, is it?"

"No," Hentze said. "No, I suppose not."

The email had come in at 9:36 and Tove followed it up with a phone call, as requested, as soon as she'd read it. The woman on the other end of the line – Rakel Poulsen – seemed oddly surprised by the immediate response, but said that if Tove could be there by eleven they could talk then, although if she preferred it could also be sometime next week. Tove told her that eleven was good.

Before she went out, Tove went into Kjeld's room, only remembering to knock when the door was half open. He was sitting at a table under the window working on a graphic tablet. The screen showed a brightly coloured advert for a discount store.

"Are these clothes good for a meeting?" Tove asked.

Kjeld looked up. "Who with?"

"A woman called Rakel Poulsen, the head of legal affairs at Juhl Pharmaceuticals."

Kjeld looked her over. "You want to go all in black?"

"Isn't that okay?"

"No, I just wondered."

"So it's fine?"

"Sure."

"Okay. See you later."

Once Tove had secured her bike in the stainless steel rack at the front of Juhl Pharmaceuticals' head office she was still five minutes early, so she waited outside, absorbed in her phone and sending a couple of texts. She was always punctual whenever she could be: neither early nor late.

She had considered briefly whether to let Jan Reyná know about the meeting, but had decided there was no need until she knew the result. In any case, he'd made it clear that his interest in Vesborggård House was limited to his mother's time there, which Tove understood. She had no expectation that other people would share her compulsion to follow the subjects that interested her, although Jan Reyná did seem to share some of her desire for detail. As with most people she met, she found him hard to assess, but she'd come to the conclusion that she would follow her vestigial instinct and allow him into the circle of people she trusted. "Vestigial" was a word she liked to apply to some areas of empathy and emotion where she didn't feel entirely lacking.

When her phone said it was 10:58 Tove stepped through the automatic glass door into the reception area of Juhl Pharmaceuticals and presented herself at the desk. She was directed to a conference room on the third floor. Inside, a woman with pale skin and half a dozen rings on her fingers introduced herself as Rakel Poulsen, the head of legal affairs for Juhl Pharmaceuticals. She shook Tove's hand and then turned to the light-haired man in a well-cut suit.

"This is Oscar Juhl, one of our directors," Rakel Poulsen said.

"I'm pleased to meet you," Oscar Juhl said, extending a hand.

Tove shook again, this time remembering that she ought to make eye contact, so she did. She recognised the man from the photographs she'd seen in her research.

"Is your website wrong?" she asked Juhl. "It says that since you stepped down from being the CEO you only have an advisory role in the company's operations."

"Well, sometimes they like me to earn my keep," Oscar Juhl said with a self-deprecating gesture. "Please, have a seat. Would you like something to drink?"

"No. Thank you."

Tove took a chair near the corner of the table, and perhaps not to make an obvious divide between sides, Oscar Juhl sat down with one chair between them. Rakel Poulsen didn't have any qualms about sitting on the opposite side of the table, however, placing a new legal pad on the table in front of her as Tove took out her phone. She swiped the screen.

"Do you mind if I record this interview?" Tove asked.

The word "interview" seemed to sit uncomfortably with Rakel Poulsen but Oscar Juhl said, "No, of course."

"Thank you." She placed the phone on the table with her list of questions facing her on the screen.

Rakel Poulsen shifted. "I'm afraid we have another meeting shortly," she said. "So if we can begin? In your email you said that you wanted to ask some questions about the clinic at Vesborggård House. Can you tell us why it's of interest to you?"

Tove looked up from the phone. "Yes. I was conducting research for a friend and when I learned more about it I became interested, too."

"Is that your profession: a researcher?"

"No, I'm a Masters degree student."

This didn't seem to resolve the issue for Rakel Poulsen. "I see. Can I ask your friend's name?"

"Yes, it's Jan Reyná."

Rakel Poulsen made a note on her pad. "And why is Herre Reyná interested in the clinic?"

"His mother worked at Vesborggård House in 1976," Tove said. "He lived there with her and he wants to know more about it. He's come here from England to find out about his past."

This additional information seemed to add another layer of uncertainty to the explanation for Rakel Poulsen. "So he's British?" she asked.

"No, he's from the Faroe Islands like me," Tove said. "But he was adopted in England. His mother died in 1976."

Rakel Poulsen seemed to become slightly more wary. "And you – he thinks her death is connected to Vesborggård House?"

"No, I didn't say that," Tove told her, momentarily reassessing the information she'd just given to see if it should have led to that conclusion. "They are two separate facts."

"Well, yes, of course." Wrong-footed by the flatness of Tove's reply, Rakel Poulsen reassessed for a second. "Well, from what you've said I think the best thing would be for you to meet someone from our public relations department. If there's any archive material about the clinic they should be able to find it for you."

"Will they also have information about the medical procedures and treatments used there in the 1970s?" Tove asked. "That's what I'm specifically interested in and what my questions relate to."

"Well, perhaps not about the medical aspect, but—"

"Then I don't think there would be any point in talking to them," Tove said. "Is there someone else you can suggest?"

In his chair Oscar Juhl shifted, sitting forward slightly, looking at Rakel Poulsen. "Perhaps if we heard what Tove's questions are we'd be able to point her in the right direction for her enquiry."

Somewhat reluctantly, Rakel Poulsen nodded and Oscar Juhl turned to Tove. "Go ahead."

"Thank you," Tove said. She looked down at her phone. "Number one. Can you tell me what sort of treatments were carried out at Vesborggård House?"

Rakel Poulsen made an indefinite gesture, as if to indicate that this wasn't her area of expertise. "I believe they were to treat certain behavioural problems in the patients at the time."

"Can you be more specific?"

"No, I'm afraid not. I don't have that information."

Tove accepted that without query. "Okay. Number two. Did any of the treatments or procedures carried out at Vesborggård House involve new drugs that had not been licensed for public use at the time?"

"Again, I don't have any information about that," Rakel Poulsen said, seemingly on firmer ground now. "However, I can say that it would be a breach of medical confidentiality between the company and the individuals concerned to divulge details of their treatment."

"Does that mean you will not be able to provide *any* details about medical procedures at Vesborggård House?"

"It might, yes," Rakel Poulsen acceded. "The issue of privacy – medical and commercial – will limit how much the company would wish or be able to say."

Tove thought about that for a moment. "In that case will

you provide me with a list of all the people employed to work at Vesborggård House while it was in operation as a clinic?"

"For what purpose?"

"I would like to interview them."

Rakel Poulsen shook her head regretfully, as if she would like to be of more service if not for the fact that Tove kept asking impossible things. "I'm sure you know that our industry is commercially sensitive," she said. "So all our employees sign a confidentiality clause in their contracts of employment. It's standard practice, so even if I *was* able to provide you with a list of former employees, they wouldn't be able to discuss the things you seem to be interested in. And after what – forty years? – I doubt there are many who would still remember anyway."

"Okay, I see," Tove said without any apparent regret. "In that case my final question is to ask what can you tell me about the claims for damages brought against Juhl Pharmaceuticals in 2004 by patients at Vesborggård House?"

"I'm afraid nothing," Rakel Poulsen said. "The case was settled without prejudice and in a mutually satisfactory manner as we announced at the time. It is also bound by confidentiality agreements for all parties."

Tove was silent for a moment, then she drew her phone towards her. "Okay. I understand."

"Would you like me to put you in touch with the public relations department?" Rakel Poulsen asked.

"No, that's not necessary," Tove said. She pushed her chair back and stood up. "Thank you for your time."

"You're welcome," Rakel Poulsen said, closing her notepad.

Outside the conference room Oscar Juhl accompanied Tove to the lift, as Rakel Poulsen headed off briskly in the opposite direction.

"You're very direct," Juhl said after they'd taken a few steps.

"Yes, I've been told so," Tove agreed. "Was that a problem?"

Juhl laughed. "No, not at all. It makes a change to hear someone say simply what they want to know. I'm sorry we couldn't be of more help."

Tove shook her head. "I understand why."

"You do?"

"Yes, of course. Your company has a reputation for confidentiality."

"Well, it's standard practice, I'm afraid," Juhl said. "Especially as far as the lawyers are concerned. For myself, well…" He made a helpless and slightly apologetic gesture. "I have to go along with them when they tell me it's in the company's best interest."

Tove considered that for a moment. She wondered if he was trying to convey something else but then the lift doors opened and took her attention. "Thank you for your time," she said again, remembering the formality.

"Not at all. It was good to meet you," Oscar Juhl said. "I'm sorry you had a wasted journey."

"No, it wasn't wasted," Tove said matter-of-factly. "I learned several things."

30

I WALKED TWICE ROUND THE CHURCHYARD AT NO MORE THAN a stroll, smoking and thinking, before sitting down on a bench looking out over granite and marble grave markers. Some had fresh flowers, but most not. It was an uncomfortable seat and the breeze was chilly despite the sunshine, but with my hands in my pockets and jacket closed for warmth it had the effect of centring my thoughts.

It seemed to me now that I had an explanation for most of the things I'd either suspected or surmised about Lýdia's last couple of weeks in Christiania, and at its most basic it was just as Thea had said: on finding her raped and abused, Lýdia had taken us both away from the clinic, back to Christiania where – presumably – she thought we could disappear.

What that didn't tell me, though, was how she'd found Thea in the first place, or how she'd taken an unconscious girl and a four-year-old boy more than two hundred miles. It would have needed a car, I assumed, but even then, I wasn't convinced Lýdia could have done it alone. More than that, though, why do it at all? Why hadn't she simply taken Thea to hospital or called the police? That should have been her instinctive reaction, and because she hadn't done either I could only conclude that there must have been some overriding reason against it.

I couldn't guess what that reason might have been, but as I sat and frowned at the gravestones I knew it must be connected to Vesborggård House; as was the Faroese man called Mickey who'd visited the Christiania flat with the promise of help. At this distance I couldn't tell how significant he might have been in or around the circumstances of Thea's rape. Whatever I came up with could only be guesswork, so I left him aside and considered the rest.

One of the things you do in any fragmented case is to look for similarities and convergences; of people, of times or of place. Vesborggård House was a convergence beyond any doubt in my mind now, but it went beyond the fact that Thea and Lýdia had lived there, and even beyond the fact that Thea had been raped and brutalised there, too. The thing that pulled at my thoughts now was the yellow memo slip in the back of the file Thomas Friis had showed me; the one with the names of two other girls: Rikke Villadsen and Inge-Lise Hoffmann – one murdered and one missing.

Statistically I knew that the chance of Inge-Lise still being alive had reached almost zero decades ago. So if she *was* dead it meant there had actually been two killings within a few miles of Vesborggård House and both less than a year before Thea was attacked. Inevitably, it seemed that there had been a very good chance that Thea would have become a third murder victim if Lýdia hadn't intervened and got her away. So, had Lýdia known that? Was that why she'd gone so far and sought anonymity in Christiania?

I chewed it over for a while, frustrated by too little substance and too many possible interpretations, none of which made even a half-decent theory unless I supported them with supposition or guesses. The whole thing was as unsatisfying as the bench was uncomfortable, so I was happy enough to give up on both when I saw Thea on the path from the church. She was an unmistakeable figure, walking towards me with brisk practicality.

"Did you sort out the electrical problem?" I asked, standing up.

"Yes, I think so – for the moment," she said. "We have power again and the place won't burn down, they assure me of that. At least no one can say that the job of a pastor is always the same." She gestured at the path. "Shall we walk or would you like to go back to the office?"

"No, walking's fine," I told her.

We moved off at an unhurried stroll, and for a couple of paces I think we were both trying to work out what to say next. In the end, and because I didn't want to push things too quickly, I said, "So how long have you been here, at this church?"

"Nearly ten years. Before that I was near Roskilde, but it was a smaller place and more in the country. I like the town better."

"Did you always want to go into the church – I mean, to become a pastor?"

She laughed and shook her head. "No, for many years I was a very long way from God. But sometimes, if you go far enough, you come back to the beginning and you have a new start."

"Well, maybe there's hope for me yet," I said, glib and

not very clever, I realised as soon as I'd said it.

"Yes, I think there's always hope," she said without any irony, and then after a pause, "Can I ask you a question?"

"Sure, go ahead."

She took a second, as if phrasing it in her head. "I wanted to ask if you think there was something wrong about Lýdia's death. Is that why you came to find me?"

I shook my head. "No. Like I said, I just wanted to fill in the blanks – to find out what she was doing before she died. I've read the police report into what happened and it seems pretty clear. There's no reason to think they got it wrong – unless you know something they weren't aware of."

I glanced at her and saw she was thinking back. "No, I don't think so," she said. "At the time – when I found her – I was very scared; from what I saw and also because I was afraid what would happen if anyone from Vesborggård or the police knew I was there. I didn't understand why she'd done it, of course, but I never thought there was anything suspicious." She looked my way. "I'm sorry. Does that make it harder for you?"

"Not really," I said, because it was true. "I never thought anyone else was responsible except Lýdia herself, so in that way it doesn't change anything."

"Okay. I see," Thea said, although I thought I heard a faint note of reserve.

"What about you?" I asked. "You said you've talked about what happened to you at Vesborggård House, but did you ever tell the police?"

"No." She shook her head. "At first I didn't think they

would believe me, and after I left Christiania I had other problems. I lived on the street in Copenhagen for some time, then in Malmö, Hamburg and other places, not always so good. In those days I was a very self-destructive person; towards myself and also in relationships with other people. I was addicted to drugs and alcohol, and to buy them – for money – well, you were a police officer, so you can guess. The police were not people I wanted to talk to at all."

I *had* already guessed from the way she used the phrases common in rehab, so I nodded. "How long have you been in recovery?"

"Twenty-three years and three months. It's almost half of my life, but it's the good half, thanks to Jesus."

We reached a corner in the path and I paused for a moment and took out my cigarettes. "Do you mind?"

"No, of course. May I have one, too?"

"Sure. Sorry."

I held out the pack so she could take one. She held it delicately while I lit it, then my own.

"So how did you come to be at Vesborggård in the first place?" I asked when we moved on again. It seemed a little more neutral.

"Oh, I was just stupid and selfish," she said matter-of-factly. "Like a lot of teenagers, I wanted attention and I didn't like the rules. My home life wasn't very good, so I got into trouble, but while I was young it was excused. In some ways it might have been better if they had been harder on me then, but instead I got worse until when I was sixteen I was sent to the court and the *dommer* – the justices – decided I was a 'delinquent'."

She used the word as if it had some amusement for her now – as if it missed the point. She flicked ash off her cigarette and glanced across the gravestones before looking back. "So, they told me they ought to send me to prison, but instead I was lucky because there was somewhere which had a new treatment for people like me. It was a clinic, they said: a place to make me a better person; a nice place."

"And was it?"

"Sure, yes, I would say so," she said with a nod, as if it didn't require any assessment. "When I arrived I was scared, but most of the people were caring and there weren't so many hard rules. We couldn't leave the grounds but there was nowhere to go anyway, and we were encouraged to work. The boys had a workshop and the girls could use sewing machines or help in the kitchen. If we did there was a small payment and there was a shop to buy chocolate and other things. That was where I met Lýdia. She came to the house when I'd been there for a few weeks and she worked in the shop and the kitchen."

"So you made friends with her?"

"Yes, I guess so," she said, although she qualified it. "Not *close* friends, not at that time because she was an adult and a member of staff. But whenever we spoke she was always friendly and cheerful. I remember she liked to have a radio so we could listen to music."

Thea's expression showed some genuine fondness for this memory so I had no reason to think she was polishing the truth, but I was still curious about the other aspect of life at Vesborggård House: more so in light of what she'd already said.

"Some of the information I've seen on Vesborggård

House says that the treatment they used was some sort of drug therapy. Is that right?"

"Yes, yes, it was," she said. "But it wasn't a big part of what we did there. Most of the time we just did usual things: working and some lessons if we wanted to pass our exams. The only part that might be called a treatment was that once every week we were called to have an 'assessment' in another part of the building away from the rest. It was always in a large, empty room with only a camping bed and some chairs. You would sit down on the bed and the nurse would give you a drink – orange juice, always. We called it our *vitaminer* – our vitamins – just as a joke because we knew it wasn't only that. A few people didn't like the taste but after you drank it no one felt bad. You felt very comfortable – very light – and the doctor would talk to you while you lay on the bed and you just had to listen and sometimes say what you felt. It lasted perhaps half an hour and then you would feel yourself coming down and a little time later things were normal again. They told us it would make us better people to be with, but we didn't think about that. We just liked the sensation, you know?"

I nodded, but it was still hard to imagine how any part of what she'd described hadn't raised questions from someone, even forty years ago. I could only suppose that the same reluctance to question authority or rock the boat by expressing any doubts must have applied in Denmark as much as it had in the UK at the time.

"Did you have any idea *what* they were giving you?" I asked.

Thea exhaled smoke over her shoulder. "No, at the time I

didn't know, but now I think it must have been something like LSD. It was faster to work, though, and to wear off."

"So not the same drug you were given the night you were attacked?"

"No, I don't think so," she said, thinking it over. "The 'vitamins' may not have made me a better person, but I don't think they could have been used for something like that. And for a long time I was a pretty good expert in that sort of thing."

Her slightly wry, self-possessed sense of humour was easy to go along with, but as she took a final draw on her cigarette and then flicked the butt expertly into a flower bed I sensed the subject was about to change. Before it did, there was one other thing I wanted to know.

"So while you were at Vesborggård House was there anything that seemed unusual or out of the ordinary?" I asked. "Even just rumours or stories, maybe about a member of the staff?"

"No… No, I don't think so," she said, casting back. "I don't think there was anything – except maybe for the time when they searched the woods. Someone was missing from a village nearby so there was a search around the lake and in the woods."

"By the police?"

"Yeh, and local people. We were told to stay away. I hadn't been at the house very long so I didn't want to do anything wrong, but some others went out through the gardens so I went with them to watch."

"Did the police find anything?" I asked.

"No, I don't think so," Thea said. "I remember they had

dogs – German shepherds – and we watched them looking around the Blue House, but then a policeman shouted at us and we ran away."

"What was the Blue House?"

"Oh, it wasn't really a house," Thea said. "It was an old building of stones near the lake. It had a blue door – a large one – so we called it the Blue House. No one was allowed in there but nearby there was a small beach where sometimes we were allowed to go for a party – if it was a birthday or something like that. We'd make a fire and sing and tell stories, you know?"

From the tone of her voice it sounded as if there was some genuine affection for the memory – in fact, for the place as a whole – and I wondered how she was capable of that, in light of what else had happened before Lýdia took her away.

Some of what I was thinking might have showed on my face because now that we were back at the corner of the church Thea stopped and turned towards me seriously. "So, now I've told you all this, can I also say something about me? I want to tell you because you're a police officer and I think you must see a lot of people who are victims and need to be helped, yes?"

"Sure, of course," I acknowledged.

"Okay," she nodded. "So I wanted to say that what was done to me in the past doesn't define who I am now. I haven't allowed it to do that. It didn't make me an alcoholic and an addict: that was my own way – my own road – and came from inside, so I don't blame other people, or even God. Taking responsibility for yourself and what you become is what we each have to do with God's help. That's how I stepped off my old path and found the new one. That's how I am here. So even if I could, I wouldn't change that. Do you understand?"

She gave me an intense, direct look to see if I got it, and I did. I knew she believed it and whether I did or not was entirely irrelevant.

"I understand," I told her.

She looked at me astutely for a second more, then nodded. "Yeh, I think you do," she said and then smiled. "The sermon is over. You're lucky; for me it was very short."

"*Tak*. I appreciate that," I told her, which made her laugh.

We moved on again, coming round to the main door of the church where she stopped. It was the natural place to part.

"So, will we see you on Sunday?" Thea asked. "Morning mass is at ten and you'd be very welcome."

"It's tempting," I said. "But maybe not."

"No? Well, okay," she said with a smile. "But you know where we are now if you change your mind."

She held out her hand and I shook it, a strange formality after the intimacy of what she'd told me, but maybe that was part of the reason she did it: to put a seal back on her story.

"Thank you," I said, and meant it.

31

LEAVING RASMUS MATZEN'S HOUSE, HENTZE DROVE AS FAR AS the next village where he found a petrol station with a minimarket and post office adjacent to it. He parked there and switched off the engine before evaluating the names and other details he'd written down in his notebook.

There was no denying that Christine Lynge had been right; trying to locate any of these people from the sketchy details Rasmus Matzen had been able to recall seemed like a very long shot. Still, Hentze went through the list, picking out the people who not only had first and last names but also a vague location. There were four – three men and a woman – and with his notebook propped on the steering wheel Hentze rang the *kriminalbetjent*, Will Snedker, whom Christine Lynge had assigned to help him should he need it. Snedker was affable enough, if not particularly sparky.

"They'll all be aged between sixty and seventy now, I suppose," Hentze told Snedker once he'd given the four individuals' names. "So you can discount anyone younger than that if you get several hits for a name. I'd also like addresses and phone numbers, too, if possible."

"Sure, I'll do it now," Snedker said. "Shall I email you the results?"

"Yeh, if you would."

With that settled, Hentze left the car and went to the minimarket to get something for lunch. He'd just returned to the car with a road atlas, a somewhat pallid sandwich and a bottle of fruit juice when Annika called.

"Hey, how's it going?" she asked.

"I'm not sure yet," Hentze said. "I think it'll depend on whether I get lucky."

He told her what Matzen had said about his relationship with Astrid, and the fact that he hadn't been the only man with whom she'd been friendly. He used the euphemism because to say that she'd been promiscuous seemed somehow prejudicial, even if it had been the case. As Matzen had said, those were different times.

"So could Rasmus Matzen be a suspect?" Annika asked. "If he was jealous…"

"Yeh, it's possible," Hentze said. "Except that he'd have to have gone to the Faroes to kill Boas Justesen last week and there's no evidence that he did. He says he hasn't been out of the country for over five years."

"I'll check to be sure," Annika said. "But if it is, and if Astrid slept around at the commune, it might put a different slant on things, don't you think? I mean, if she was killed by someone she'd had sex with, or who *wanted* to have sex with her, then Else would have been—"

"Collateral damage?" Hentze said, remembering Jan Reyná's turn of phrase the previous evening. "Yeh, that's possible I suppose, but I'm not convinced of it yet. And speaking of Else, have we got any more information on the second set of remains?"

"Yeh, we have," Annika said. "Sophie finished her excavation last night and I just spoke to Elisabet Hovgaard. She says the remains are of a child about ten years old based on the dental development, but it will need DNA tests or a forensic anthropologist to make an assessment of the sex. Apparently at that age it's very hard to tell the difference between boys and girls."

"So we still can't be sure that it is Else."

"Not sure, no, but Elisabet does think she can tell us a probable cause of death. There had been a blow to the side of the head causing a fracture that would almost certainly have been fatal."

"A deliberate blow?"

"She thinks it's likely, yes: something irregular in shape – maybe a rock. Sophie's going to take both sets of remains back to Denmark for a forensic pathologist to examine. We should know some more after the weekend."

"I hope the same will be true from this end as well," Hentze said as his phone chimed to alert him to an email from Will Snedker. "But it sounds as if you're on top of things there so let's talk again later, okay?"

Hentze rang off and opened the email. Even at first glance it was depressingly long. The first name on the list, Simon Gregersen from Horsens – *if* Matzen had remembered correctly – had five possible hits. It could be a long afternoon.

* * *

Silas and Majbritt Thygesen's apartment was in a four-storey building on a cobbled street off Magstræde. Tove left her bike in the entrance and took the stairs to the second floor two at a time.

Silas had left the door open for her when she'd buzzed the intercom and she went in without bothering to call out. It was an affluent and tastefully decorated flat, with stripped wooden floors, light blue walls and airy windows, all of which Tove was both familiar with and completely oblivious to on an aesthetic level. What she did appreciate about the place was the fact that there was no shortage of books. Every room had them and she appreciated the range of their subjects, and the fact that they were mostly non-fiction.

Silas greeted her in the corridor to the kitchen, coffee in hand. He was in his early forties; a stocky man, and a professor at the university. He'd known Tove since she was ten, part of her parents' social group before they moved to Aalborg, and he'd looked out for her in a circumspect way once she'd come to the university in Copenhagen to study. Despite her blunt manner she was not always as tough as she appeared, he knew, so he and Majbritt invited her round to the flat at least twice a month. Sometimes she came, sometimes she did not.

"Hi, Tove. How are you?" Silas asked.

"Hi. I'm good. How are you?" Tove said, because Silas was known to point out her lack of social graces and correct them.

"I'm good, thanks," he said. "Would you like coffee?"

CHRIS OULD

"No. I'd rather get on – if that's okay," Tove added when she saw Silas draw a breath.

Silas chuckled and nodded. "Okay. Come in and sit down."

They went into his study; a comfortable room with good light. "So, you want to know about Juhl Pharma, right?" Silas said. Tove had told him about her interest in Vesborggård House and its connection to the pharmaceutical company when she'd called him the previous day.

"Yeh, as I said." Tove dropped down on the sofa and took out her phone. "This morning I had a meeting with them."

"Who did you see?"

"Rakel Poulsen of their legal department who wears too many rings, and Oscar Juhl."

"Wow, that's impressive," Silas said. "When I was researching my thesis I couldn't get past their PR department. You must have touched a nerve."

"Yeh, that's what I think, too," Tove said with a definite nod. "There was no need for two senior people to meet me unless they were concerned about what I wanted to know."

"And *did* they tell you anything about Vesborggård House?"

"No. They said all information was protected for reasons of medical and commercial confidentiality. It was their default position." She pushed off her shoes and drew herself into a cross-legged position on the sofa. "So, can you please tell me what you know about Juhl Pharma? The company background would be useful. Then I'd like to look at your thesis and notes for the details."

* * *

Once he'd told Tove what he knew about Juhl Pharmaceuticals in general Silas dug out his research notes and his thesis: *Patent Medicine: The History and Ethical Challenges of Synthetic Drug Manufacture*. It was heavy reading, even he would admit that, but Tove didn't demur at its weight as he ushered her into the sitting room next door so he could work while she read.

There was no sound from the sitting room for the next couple of hours. The door was closed when Silas went to make a coffee and when he looked in Tove was sitting cross-legged in the centre of a rug surrounded by neat piles of papers. She was making notes on her phone.

"Would you like something to drink?" Silas asked.

"No. I'm still reading," Tove said without looking up.

Silas went away and closed the door but around mid-afternoon he took a break from grading his students' work to make a start on the evening meal. Majbritt, a lawyer, wouldn't be home until six but the stew he had planned needed time in the oven. He started on the onions and a few minutes later Tove padded into the kitchen on shoeless feet.

"Who is Dr Carl Sønderby?" she said. She had papers in one hand and her phone in the other.

Silas frowned. "I don't know. In what context?"

"You've written a note – *Vesborggård House* – on a medical paper and circled the name of Dr Carl Sønderby, who's listed as one of the authors." She read from the front paper. "It's called *Experimental Trial of Resolomine in Psychedelic Therapy to Modify Antisocial Behaviour and Emergent Addiction in Adolescents*."

Silas craned his neck to look. "Oh, yeh, I remember. I don't know where I came across it now, though."

"Why did you link it to Vesborggård House? The paper doesn't say where the drug trial took place."

"No, that's to avoid identification of patients," Silas said. "But I knew Dr Sønderby was employed by Juhl Pharma at Vesborggård House so I think that's why I made the connection."

"And this drug, Resolomine, was a Juhl product?"

"Yeh, but I don't think it was ever put into general production."

"Okay, I understand now." Tove nodded. "And what is psychedelic therapy? Does it have anything to do with psychedelic drugs like LSD?"

"I don't know a lot about it," Silas said, going back to the chopping board. "But in the sixties and seventies there was some interest in using LSD to modify different forms of behaviour. Until it got a bad name and was banned, then all the research was stopped."

"Was it effective as a treatment?"

"In some cases, yeh, I think so."

"I see." She thought for a second. "Did you speak to Dr Sønderby about his work?"

Silas shook his head. "No. I found his address but his wife told me he'd died. She confirmed that he'd worked at Vesborggård House, but beyond that she didn't want to talk any more. His death was quite recent so I left her alone."

"I think I should talk to her," Tove said, flat and decided. "Her husband may have kept records that could still exist."

She made a note on her phone, then turned and started away.

"Are you staying to eat later?" Silas called after her. "There'll be enough if you'd like to."

"No. I'll be finished by then," Tove said over her shoulder. Then remembered. "Thank you for asking."

"You're welcome," Silas said with a shake of his head.

32

IT WAS AN HOUR'S DRIVE, WEST AND THEN NORTH TO Vesborggård House and the traffic was light: nothing to distract me from thinking about what Thea had said.

Memory is fluid; it shifts and rearranges events and details to a greater or lesser degree, but despite that I was as sure as I could be that Thea had told me what she truly remembered. What most took up my thoughts wasn't a matter of veracity but of significance, and that was harder to judge.

Thea's confirmation of what had happened to her was simply that – confirmation and detail. It was the one piece of new information she'd given that I was having trouble with, though: the Faroese man she'd known as Mickey. From forty years' distance the problem was one of perspective, like looking half a mile ahead on the road. Had Mickey's visit to the flat in Christiania been close enough to the events around Thea's rape to make it significant, and if so had he played some part in our leaving Vesborggård House?

This was what bothered me most. Mickey had come to the Christiania flat as a friend, Lýdia had told Thea. He was going to help them, she said, and the implication was that there was a way forward, the promise of change.

So why had Lýdia killed herself then? Why had she abandoned the girl she'd already saved once and – come to that – why had she abandoned her own son as well?

In the past I'd always refused to wonder what Lýdia's suicide said about her feelings toward me. If I'd thought about it at all I'd always stuck to rigid objectivity, as if to prove that I had no "issues" with what she had done. In truth, though, I knew her feelings for me must have entered her thinking on some level, so maybe it was time to allow that into evidence now rather than ignore it.

So, what did it say about the circumstances in which Lýdia had taken her own life? She'd shown no sign of depression, Thea had said: she had a plan for the future, and she had a vulnerable girl and her son dependent on her. Could that still be a description of someone who, without warning, would fill a bath and reach for a razor blade?

If it was, then it seemed to me now that her path to that point must have started at Vesborggård House on the night Thea was raped. Everything else seemed to come from that place and that night, which meant that my only way forward was to retrace my steps there.

At Vesborggård House I drove down the rutted track this time, more confident than yesterday that I wouldn't end up in a mire. I parked to one side of the building site and headed towards the Portakabin, but changed course when I saw a guy in his thirties give me an enquiring look as he tended a small cement mixer.

"Hi," I said, over the noise. "Is Henning around? Henning Skov?"

The guy frowned briefly, then shook his head. "No, he's not here again until Monday. Do you need to see him?"

"No, not really. I was here yesterday and I just wanted to make sure it was okay to have another look around."

"Yeh, sure, it's no problem," the guy said with a shrug. "I saw you with Henning and Jeppe before so go ahead."

"Is Jeppe here?"

"Yeh, he should be. I'm not sure where he is, though."

He cast around but rather than cause a distraction I said, "That's okay, I'll find him later. Thanks for your help."

I followed the tarmac track I'd taken yesterday, but before it reached the decaying staff quarters I went off down a path through the woods and towards the lake, going downhill between straight pine trees until I reached a fork at the lake shore. The overgrown path seemed slightly more defined to the left so I went that way, prepared to come back if I found I was going in the wrong direction.

The wind was chilly off the water and the earth path roughly followed the shore line, a few yards away and divided from it by intermittent pines and occasional bushes reaching as far as the lake's edge. Then, after three or four minutes' walking, the path rose a little, following the contour of the land, and passed by a semicircular, bowl-like depression about fifteen yards across, facing a small beach and the lake. The hollow seemed too regular to be natural, but if it was man-made it had been there a long time and I thought it must be the place Thea had referred to when she said they had used it for parties and gatherings; it would lend itself to that sort of thing.

And the Blue House Thea had described was there, too: on the rise above and behind the hollow. It had the look of a functional structure, perhaps built for some kind of forestry work. Its walls were rough stone with a single arched doorway at its centre and another on the level above, like a barn. Some of its grey slates were missing, exposing the wooden rafters beneath, but as I walked up to it I could see the faintest hint of blue paint on the greyed wooden door, just enough to know I'd found the right place.

The door was secured by a corroded padlock, which wouldn't yield when I tugged it. The frame was rotten, though, and when I dug around the screws in the hasp with the blade of my pocket knife the wood came away in fibres. I worked at it for a couple of minutes, then tried tugging on the padlock again. This time the hasp pulled away and, bending it back, I used it as a handle to drag the door open, its bottom edge catching on the overgrown grass.

It took a moment for my eyes to adjust to the darkness as I stepped inside, and when they did there wasn't much to see. The place was an empty shell: a couple of rusting oil cans, a few pieces of abandoned timber and a broken ladder leading up to a loft. But I was more interested in the stone floor under my feet, still regularly paved with flat, bevel-edged stones. Surprisingly there wasn't much dirt to obscure them and when I scuffed away what there was I knew I'd seen them before. To confirm it I took out my phone and scrolled to the photograph of sixteen-year-old Thea, enlarging and dragging quickly away from the view of her body and looking instead at the floor beneath the table she'd been placed on.

Forty years ago the camera had only captured a small section of the floor in focused detail but the shapes and the texture of the flagstones in the picture left me in no doubt now. It would take an expert and a proper examination to match them exactly but I was sure this was the place where the pictures of Thea's abuse had been taken in 1976. And taken was right: taken or stolen.

I took a couple of photographs of my own, for reference, then went outside. I pushed the door closed, but as I turned away I saw Jeppe and the younger workman from the cement mixer coming my way. I met them on the path overlooking the hollow.

"Did you find anything?" the younger man asked.

"No, nothing much," I said. "It doesn't look as if anyone's been in there for years. I'm Jan, by the way."

"Steffen. And you know Jeppe, yeh?"

"Yeh."

We all exchanged handshakes but by then Jeppe was speaking in Danish and when I heard the name Inge-Lise I guessed what would come next.

"He asks if you've come back because you know more about Inge-Lise," Steffen said. "Do you know who that is? He hasn't told me."

"Yeah, we talked about her yesterday," I said, then looked at Jeppe. "I don't know, *Jeg ved ikke*. Can you tell me anything else about her, or about what happened when she went missing?"

Steffen translated that, then listened as Jeppe spoke, gesturing around him at the woods and then more specifically at the Blue House and the hollow to his right.

Finally Jeppe paused and Steffen turned to me. "He says the police searched all through this area – the wood. There were local people, also, like him. He says they didn't find anything, but the police were interested in the place there, the pit." He nodded to the hollow. "They looked because there had been a big fire: you know, when wood is piled up?"

"A bonfire?"

"Yeh, yeh, that's it. It had been made for Sankthans, the middle of summer festival, and then burned."

I thought about that, remembering something else, then looked at Jeppe. "Can you show me where the fire was?"

Steffen translated again and Jeppe nodded. "*Ja, absolut.* Come. Come."

He turned and went back down the path with brisk steps. Steffen and I followed singly until Jeppe strode over the bank surrounding the hollow and down on to the flat area below it. He cast around, then moved out a few yards towards the beach and gestured to his feet. "Here."

Whether or not that was the exact spot there was no way to know, but Jeppe seemed sure of his recollection as he spoke to Steffen again.

"He says the police looked through the dirt – the ashes – but they didn't find anything."

"Right," I said, then scuffed thoughtfully at the grass with my boot. The soil was sandy and loose and against its light colour I spotted something darker. Squatting down I picked up a flake of charcoal, rubbing it between my fingers. When Jeppe saw this he spoke again.

"He says people have used this place for years," Steffen said. "Especially in summer, they have parties, make fires. Even now people do that. They aren't supposed to because it's private land, but if they live around here they don't take any notice."

I nodded to Jeppe to show I'd understood, then straightened up and wiped my hand on my jeans. "I need to make a phone call," I told them.

I moved towards the shoreline, as far as the edge of the grass, while I waited for Hentze to answer his phone. By my feet there was a short drop to a narrow, sandy beach, littered with twigs and leaves. The grey water was running small wavelets up to the shore, lapping against the sand in short arrhythmic beats.

After the fifth or sixth ring Hentze came on the line and I cut to the chase. "I need to ask you a couple of things," I told him. "First off, do you remember me mentioning a place called Vesborggård House last night?"

"The place where your mother worked?" Hentze said.

"Right. So you hadn't heard of it before in any context – linked to the Colony commune maybe?"

"No, not at all." He sounded slightly puzzled. "I would have told you."

I turned to look back at the semicircular hollow behind me. "Okay, listen, this may be nothing," I said. "But you told me that the second grave at Múli had been disguised by a bonfire, right?"

"*Ja*, so Sophie Krogh thinks. Why?"

"Because when a girl went missing from one of the villages near Vesborggård House in 1976 the police were interested in the site of a bonfire in the grounds of the house."

I could almost hear his frown. "Did they find anything?"

"No, I don't think so, but if they didn't look underneath…" I let that speak for itself for a moment, then said, "That's not the only thing I've come across, either. I don't want to go into detail on the phone, but I've spoken to someone who was put through a similar experience to the girl you told me about – Sunnvør."

He understood immediately what I was talking about. "Where did this happen?" he said.

"Also at Vesborggård House."

"And you're *sure* the same thing was done in the same way?"

"The person I spoke to was older than Sunnvør, but what happened to her sounds very similar, yes. She also mentioned a Faroese man called Mickey. Has that name come up at your end?"

"No, no one has mentioned anyone called Mickey. It isn't a Faroese name."

"What about as a nickname for Michael?"

"Mikkjal? No, I don't think we would use it, but maybe in Denmark…" He trailed off to think about that for a second. "Do you know any more about this man?"

"Only that he was Faroese and worked at Vesborggård House in 1976."

Hentze was silent again, then he said, "I think I'd like to look at that place. Are you there now?"

"Yeah. Where are you?"

"On my way to a place called Horsens. Can you hold on for a minute? I want to stop and look at the map."

"Sure, go ahead."

While I waited I lit a cigarette. Near the centre of the hollow Jeppe and Steffen were standing together in conversation and I guessed Jeppe was probably telling the younger man the story he'd told me about Inge-Lise.

"Okay, I can get there in less than two hours, I think," Hentze said on the phone. "Will you wait for me there?"

"Yeah, I can wait," I said. "But Hjalti, listen, I want to bring the local police in on this, too. Like I said, there are some other things about this place – not just a possible link to the Faroes. I think they should be looked at, or at least talked about." I waited to see what his response to that would be, but for a second there was none. "Hjalti?"

"Yeh, I'm here. I was just thinking. Do you need me to find a contact for you in the local police?"

"No, there's someone I talked to last time I was here – a CID guy called Friis from Aarhus. He seemed okay, so I'll see if I can get hold of him."

"It sounds as if you have what you need, then. I'll be with you as soon as I can."

I wasn't sure if I'd heard a slight note of reservation in his voice after I'd mentioned Friis, but it was too late to worry about it now. "Okay, head for Skanderborg and Ry and I'll text you the address."

I rang off, took a drag on my cigarette, then pulled up Thomas Friis's number.

"It's Jan Reyna," I said when he answered. "Have you got a minute to talk?"

"Er, yes, I think so. Hold on for a moment. Okay. Go ahead."

"It's about Inge-Lise Hoffmann," I said. "When she went missing there was a police search in the grounds at Vesborggård House and according to someone who was there at the time, the police were interested in the site of a fire by the lake. I'm assuming they didn't find any evidence of Inge-Lise, but if I'm right I think they might have missed something."

"What sort of thing?"

"I'd rather show you in person. I'm at Vesborggård House now. Can you come out and meet me?"

In the silence I knew he was probably weighing up how likely this was to be a waste of his time. If I'd still been a copper I would have done the same thing, although I wouldn't necessarily have come to the same decision he did.

"Okay, I can be there in about half an hour," he said.

"*Tak*. I'll see you then."

I turned away from the lake and went back to Jeppe and Steffen.

"You called the police?" Steffen asked as I approached.

I wasn't sure how much he'd heard or understood of what I'd said on the phone, but there didn't seem much point in lying about it so I nodded. "An officer's coming to look."

"Jeppe told me the story about the girl," Steffen said before Jeppe cut him off with a question and a gesture at the ground. "He wants to know if you think Inge-Lise is here."

My interest in the location had obviously let Jeppe put

two and two together but rather than confirm it I made an open gesture. "I don't know. Maybe."

"So someone will dig?" Steffen asked.

I shrugged. "It'll depend what they think when I've talked to them."

I knew it wouldn't be an easy thing to sell, though, even to Hentze. Friis would probably be a lot harder to convince. All I could do was wait.

On the road verge Hentze's car was occasionally rocked by the wake of passing trucks. He looked at his road atlas again, considering the diversion he'd have to make to meet Reyná instead of going to Horsens. It was one or the other, given the distances and the directions. He called Annika.

"Hey, Hjalti."

"Hey. Tell me something: has anyone you've spoken to about Mikkjal Tausen ever referred to him as Mickey?"

"Mickey? Like the mouse? No."

Hentze took a second, then made up his mind. "Okay, listen," he said. "I want you to call Mikkjal Tausen and arrange to go and see him as soon as you can. Tell him I'm on holiday and that you're looking after the Boas Justesen case until I get back. You haven't met him, have you?"

"Tausen? No."

"Good, so play up the fact that I've left you holding the baby and make lots of apologies for having to bother him again. Tell him you need to check some details about Boas Justesen: it doesn't matter if we already know the answers, just think of something that means you need to see Tausen in person."

"Okay," Annika said. "So what do you *really* want to know?"

"I want to know where he lived and worked before he went to the States. The last time I saw him he told me he worked in Denmark after he left the islands, but I want more detail than that. In particular, was he ever living or working in the Skanderborg area. He's been pretty chatty with me, so if you can get him talking about living in Denmark he may open up."

"Got it," Annika said. "Do you want me to call you back when I've seen him?"

"Yes, as soon as you can. And Annika, don't go alone. Take Oddur or Dánjal."

"Won't that make it look like my visit's a bit more than just checking a few facts?"

"Maybe, but even so, not alone."

"Are you thinking that Mikkjal Tausen could be the one who killed Boas?" Annika asked.

"That depends on what you find out, but yes, I think there's a chance of that now."

"What about his alibi – his girlfriend – and the fact that his car didn't use the Leirvík tunnel that night?"

"I don't know yet. She could have been lying about when she was with him."

"Or maybe he used *her* car," Annika said. "I'll check."

"Yeh, good. And let me know when you've spoken to Tausen."

He rang off and put the phone to one side, assessing the road up ahead for a moment. Finally he made up his mind, put the car into gear and signalled that he was pulling away.

33

THOMAS FRIIS ARRIVED ABOUT FORTY MINUTES AFTER I'D called him. He was dressed in the same, immaculate suit he'd been wearing yesterday.

"You didn't go back to Copenhagen," he said, closing his car door and looking around.

"I went but then I came back again," I told him.

"Oh, I see." Whatever that told him he considered it for a moment, then shifted. "You said you had something to show me regarding Inge-Lise Hoffmann?"

He cast a slightly dubious look around at the building site. The proximity of mud and concrete may have been making him think about his suit.

"It's down there, through the woods," I told him. "If you've got boots…"

He went round to the back of his car and put on a pair of wellingtons, tucking his trousers into them. Somehow it wasn't an incongruous look on him and we set off along the path towards the lake. I expected him to start asking questions to prepare for whatever I was going to show him, but having made the decision to come this far on faith, he seemed content to wait.

Instead he examined his surroundings with interest until we turned off the tarmac track. Then he said, "After we spoke yesterday I looked in more depth at Inge-Lise's file. Because I was curious," he added, as if he expected me to ask. "Even so, there isn't much more information. She was last seen by her brother, here on 23 June 1976. He worked at the house as a gardener and she spent a few minutes with him, then left on her bicycle. When she didn't come home by that evening her parents reported her missing and there was a search. Her bicycle was found beside a road, and also her purse, but nothing more was discovered – there was no body – so the case was left open as a missing person."

"Did you find out why her disappearance was linked to the other two girls?" I asked, thinking of the appended memo on the file he'd shown me yesterday.

"Yes, I think so," he said. "Eight months before Inge-Lise went missing Rikke Villadsen's body was found in a ditch near Nørre Vissing, about five kilometres away. She was fourteen and she had been raped and then stabbed. There was a large investigation, of course, but in the end there was no good suspect so it wasn't solved."

I thought that through. "So there was a suspected link between Inge-Lise and Rikke Villadsen because of similarities in their age, sex and the geographic location."

Friis nodded. "Yes, I think that was the pattern they saw." He looked at me directly. "So, can you add something to that?"

"It's possible, yeah," I told him. "I can't make a definite link yet, but when I was in the Faroe Islands last week they were—"

I broke off when I saw Steffen jogging along the path, raising a hand. He came to a halt in front of us. "Jeppe's found something," he said, gesturing over his shoulder. "I think you should come."

I could hear the engine before we saw the machine: a small Bobcat digger down in the hollow. Twin impressions from its tracks showed where it had been driven over the low bank and its digging bucket was now resting on the ground at the end of a scraped trench, which bisected the hollow almost exactly.

Jeppe and a second man – one I didn't know – were standing on the far side of the trench and as Friis and I got closer I could see that they'd dug down about two and a half feet into the sandy soil. It had taken several passes, each progressively deeper, judging by the marks on the trench walls.

Friis didn't bother with English for my benefit, but instead spoke briskly and to the point, showing his ID and asking what they had found.

Out of instinct Jeppe and the other man had taken a step back from the trench when we arrived, but now Jeppe moved forward again, pointing into the bottom of the channel they'd dug, using a piece of twig to indicate the exact spot.

Friis and I went to the side of the trench and squatted down. There, outlined in pale off-white against the soil, was a circle of bone where the digger's bucket had sliced through the side of a skull. I could see it was a skull because someone had roughly scraped away the soil on one side and revealed the left eye socket and part of the cheekbone.

"For God's sake," Friis said in English, maybe thinking better of letting his exasperation come out in his own language. He turned to me. "Did you know they were doing this?"

I shook my head. "No. If I had…"

I didn't finish the thought because I wasn't sure where it was going. It was beside the point now anyway, which Friis seemed to realise, too. He took another look at the bottom of the trench then straightened up and told Jeppe and the other man to switch off the digger and leave everything as it was. It was a bit late for standard procedure, but at least he could stop things getting any worse.

I moved away while Friis made a couple of phone calls, lighting a cigarette and making a point of staying well clear of Jeppe's trench. When Friis finished on the phone he came over to me.

"I've sent for a technical team," he said.

"How long till they get here?"

"An hour, maybe. On a Friday afternoon…" He didn't bother to go on and I knew he was pissed off, either because he'd been pre-empted or because the excavation had been clumsy. He obviously viewed me with some suspicion now, too, and in his place I'd have felt the same.

"So, I think you had better tell me about this," he said, nodding towards the trench. "How did you know there was a body here?"

"I didn't," I said. "Not for sure, but I thought there was a chance there might be."

"Why?"

I knew that whatever I said now was bound to raise as many questions as it answered, but I had to start somewhere.

"When I was in the Faroe Islands last week they were investigating two bodies that had just been unearthed," I told him. "A woman and her ten-year-old daughter. The deaths were dated to the 1970s and the girl's grave had been disguised – covered over – by a bonfire. So, when I heard that the search team looking for Inge-Lise Hoffmann had examined a bonfire site here as well I thought the two might be connected."

"Why?" Friis said with a frown. "There are thousands of places where there have been bonfires every Sankthans. Why would you think that one here would be significant?"

"Because there are other things that might link Vesborggård House to the grave site on the Faroes," I said. "I don't know all the details of that case, but there's a Faroese officer called Hentze who does. He's on his way here now."

That threw him a little. "On his way from the Faroes?"

"No, he's already in Denmark."

This didn't help Friis a great deal. It gave him no greater understanding, and right now that was what he wanted most. "Okay," he said after a moment. "But whoever else comes, what I *still* don't understand is why you have any interest in this." He gestured again at the trench, then made it broader to encompass the whole location. "What is it that makes you come back here today?"

"You need to see something," I said. "Up there."

I led the way up the slight rise to the Blue House and pulled the door open. Friis gave the damaged wood of the frame a dubious look but then chose to ignore it as I took out my phone.

"I found the girl in the abuse photographs – the woman now," I told him. "She's Thea Rask, the girl who was supposed to have absconded from Vesborggård House in 1976."

"You know this for sure?" Friis said with a frown. "You've spoken to her?"

"Yeah. She has no memory of the actual abuse, which may be a good thing, but there's no doubt it happened to her."

I handed him the phone with the uncropped picture on its screen. The relatively small size may have helped to reduce its impact, but even so I saw his reaction. He looked for a moment longer, then away, but I knew that it wouldn't be enough to banish the image in his head.

"I think that picture was taken here," I said, gesturing into the building. "If you zoom in on the floor in the photo and compare it to the floor inside, I think they match."

He took the phone and went inside while I waited. When he came out again he handed the phone back to me.

"So you think Inge-Lise Hoffmann was also attacked here like this," he said. It wasn't a question.

"If it's her body in that hollow, then yeah, that's one theory," I said.

"And in that case the same attacker might also be responsible for the murder of Rikke Villadsen."

"It's possible, yeah."

He nodded and fell silent for a moment, probably putting it all together in roughly the same way I had. I lit another cigarette while I waited and in the end he drew a breath. "There's a question," he said.

"Only one?"

He ignored that. "If you believe the same man killed Rikke Villadsen and Inge-Lise Hoffmann, then how did Thea Rask stay alive? Has she told you?"

I shook my head. "I think she was drugged," I told him. "She doesn't remember anything until the next day, but I think she was taken away before she could be killed."

"By who?"

"My mother," I said.

There was no reply from Mikkjal Tausen's phone; it went straight to voicemail, as if it was switched off, or just possibly in a tunnel. Annika left it ten minutes, then tried again. The result was the same.

Frustrated, she went down to the control room and looked at the screen on the wall that showed the location of patrol cars from their GPS trackers. Alfred Tróndheim was closest, parked up at Skáli, probably drinking coffee at the tank station there. Alfred wasn't renowned as the most discreet or tactful of men and Annika was reluctant to entrust him with anything which might require subtlety, but it would take her almost an hour to drive to Rituvík herself on the off chance that Tausen was at home.

She gave it a moment's consideration, then called Alfred. "Can you do me a favour and drive round to Rituvík, the home of Mikkjal Tausen?" she said, giving him the full address.

"Okay, what's the problem?"

318

"He isn't answering his phone and I just want to know if he's there. If he is could you ask him to call me on this number. It's purely routine, but Hjalti Hentze has gone off and left me without half the information I should have on the Justesen suicide. He wants it signed off today so I just need to confirm a couple of things with Justesen's next of kin."

She felt slightly bad about impugning Hjalti, but thought he'd approve of the tactic.

"Okay," Alfred said. "I'll go and see if he's in. I was just leaving here anyway."

"Thanks, I owe you one. I'd really like to get this file off my desk today."

Twenty minutes later Alfred rang back. "There's no one at home," he reported. "Although there's a car here. I left a note in his mailbox."

"Thanks," Annika said. "That's a great help."

She rang off and considered her options. It wouldn't be of much use to Hjalti if she simply gave up on questioning Tausen because he wasn't at home. He could be anywhere, doing anything, Annika reasoned, but all the same, if anyone knew where he might be it was his girlfriend, so she put in a call to Müller's letting agency and asked for Sigrun Ludvig.

"Sorry, she's not here," the man on the other end said. "She's taken some leave. Until Tuesday or Wednesday, I think."

Sigrun Ludvig's address was only a five-minute drive from the station. Annika picked up her coat.

* * *

The house was quite small: a modest, modern terrace with a neatly painted picket fence delineating its tarmac parking space, a silver Skoda squarely in the centre. A stained-glass sunflower hung inside the porch window and a brass wind chime dripped water in the drizzle as Annika pressed the bell.

If the bell rang inside it was inaudible to Annika, so after waiting a few seconds she knocked instead: the police officer's rap, firm and businesslike.

"She's away, *goða*," a man's voice called.

Annika looked in the direction from which it had come. A man in his seventies was sitting on the porch next door but one.

Annika went back to the pavement and then along to the old man. He had a week's worth of white stubble and was wearing a coat, sitting in a striped camping chair smoking a cigarette. Beside him on an old table there were three empty coffee mugs and a plant pot nearly overflowing with cigarette butts.

"Hey," Annika said in greeting. "Do you know when Sigrun went out?"

"Yep." The old man nodded and flicked ash off his cigarette in the approximate direction of the plant pot.

"Would you like to tell me?" Annika asked. She showed him her warrant card.

The man wasn't overly impressed. "In trouble, is she?"

"No, not at all. I just need to ask her a couple of questions."

"Well, I reckon you missed your chance then," the man said, as if in his experience that's what most people did. "She went last night: seven o'clock. Two suitcases and a taxi. Nice one, too: Mercedes."

"I don't suppose you know where she was going?"

The old man shook his head. "We don't speak. She thinks I'm rude and I think she's stuck up. Still, she won't be living here much longer if I know anything about it, so I'll get the last laugh."

"She's moving?" Annika asked.

"I'd bet my boat on it," the man said, pursing his lips. "Got herself a rich boyfriend now, hasn't she? And her sort aren't the type to leave one like that on the line, if you know what I mean. He'll be gaffed and into the barrel before he can blink, that's my bet. You ever met her?"

"No, I haven't."

"Well if you had you'd know. She probably got him to take her to Barcelona or somewhere like that. I bet they're sitting by the pool in the sunshine right now." He cast a dubious, resigned eye at the grey cloud above. "Can't say I blame them, though."

"Maybe she went on her own," Annika suggested, but the old man shook his head.

"Nah, he was with her: took her bags to the car." He crushed out his cigarette in the plant pot and exhaled smoke. "He'd better get used to it, that's all I'll say. Her sort never carry their own bags."

Back at the station Annika used Hjalti's office to make phone calls, guessing that he wouldn't particularly want her enquiries to be general knowledge just yet. After two conversations and making some quick notes she called Hentze himself.

"Hjalti, it's me. Mikkjal Tausen isn't answering his

phone and I think he might have left the islands. He and his girlfriend went off in a taxi yesterday evening. Sigrun Ludvig had luggage, but I don't know about him."

"Have you checked with Atlantic?" Hentze asked.

"Yeh, they weren't on the last flight yesterday or any today, but the *Norröna* left last night, heading for Hirtshals. It's due in tomorrow at ten. I'm waiting for the Smyril Line to call me back when they've checked the passenger list."

On the other end of the line Hentze thought for a moment. He was leaving the outskirts of Ry.

"Okay, listen," he said. "I'm following another lead right now, but if Tausen is on the *Norröna* there's nothing we can do for a bit. If he isn't, we may need to put out an alert on the islands, so will you bring Remi up to date on this? I might have some more information fairly soon. Tell him I'll call when I know."

"Okay, will do."

Hentze rang off and refocused on the road for a moment, then glanced at the satnav. Ten minutes.

34

I HADN'T BEEN BACK TO THE BURIAL SITE SINCE I'D LEFT IT WITH Friis. Instead, when uniformed officers turned up to secure the area, I'd been directed to Henning Skov's Portakabin office and was asked – politely – to wait. So I did, for over an hour, watching the workmen being sent home and then the arrival of two more patrol cars and a forensic team's van.

Then, later again, I saw Hentze arrive and get out of his car. He showed his ID to the uniformed officer who was monitoring arrivals and after that he was directed my way. I took my feet off a desk and swivelled my chair as he opened the office door and came in.

"Hey," he said, taking a second to look around and see we were alone. "So, you found something, eh?" It was the obvious conclusion from what was outside.

"Not me personally, but yeah," I said, standing up.

My legs had got stiff so I told him the basics of what had been found while I paced a little to restore circulation. I'd got as far as describing the burial site and Jeppe's excavation when Friis opened the office door and stepped inside.

I made the introductions, but left it to them to work

out in Danish where each of them stood in terms of rank, jurisdiction and priority of cases. At a guess and from his reaction, Friis was outranked, but all the same he was on home turf and Hentze seemed content to let that hold sway.

"Okay," Friis said, getting down to business. "Before they were sent home the workmen who found the remains confirmed that it was their own idea to dig by the lake. Because you had taken an interest in the place they were suspicious about it, but they also had the belief that it would be hard to persuade anyone else to look closer."

He obviously thought I was responsible for giving them that impression, although he didn't seem inclined to debate how true it might be. Instead he made a gesture to start fresh, from the beginning.

"So, can we go back to the most basic facts now?" he said. "Can you tell me why you think there is a connection between this place and whatever was done here, and the case on the Faroes? It's not just because in both places bodies had been covered over with ashes, is it?"

I glanced at Hentze, but when he showed no sign of wanting to cut in I said, "No. That's one common element, but I think there could be another connection. A Faroese man known as Mickey worked at Vesborggård House in 1976. That's two years after the murders in the Faroes."

"So he's killed in both places? That's what you think?" Friis said.

I shook my head. "No, I'm not making any conclusions, just noting the shared elements between the two cases."

"And your mother would be another one, is that right?"

"Possibly, yes," I acknowledged. "She knew the man, Mickey. Thea Rask told me that this morning, before I came here. And of course, my mother and Mickey were both Faroese."

At some point I knew Friis would want to talk about Thea Rask in more detail, but it was too soon for that. Instead he turned to Hentze. "Can you confirm any of this?"

Hentze gave it some thought, or at least gave the impression that he was considering the full scope of the question. In reality I had the feeling he was already ahead of the game and was weighing up several factors of which neither Friis nor I were aware.

"Yes, to a certain extent," he said in the end. "We have two murder victims on the Faroes: a woman and her daughter, killed in 1974. They lived at a commune before they died, so I came to Denmark to interview people who knew them from there. However, as far as I know there is nothing to connect our victims to this place more than Jan has already said. There may be similarities in the way one of our victims was buried, but without more details..." He shrugged.

"And you haven't heard of this Faroese man called Mickey in your investigation?" Friis asked. "You don't know who he is?"

Hentze shook his head sombrely. "No, but I'll see if we can find out."

"Okay," Friis said with a nod. "In that case all we know for a fact is that there is a body here. It may be Inge-Lise Hoffmann, but until we have forensic results I don't think we can say any more, so I don't think there's any point in guessing whether one case connects to another, do you?" He was asking Hentze. I was out of the equation for the moment.

"No, I don't think so," Hentze said. "I think it's too soon."

"Okay then," Friis said, apparently satisfied. "Then I'll get a status report from the technical team. Do you want to look at the site?"

"No, I don't think that's necessary," Hentze said. "Maybe later."

With a nod Friis went to the door and when it closed behind him I stood up again. "Coffee?" I asked Hentze.

"Yeh, *takk*."

I went along to the kitchenette area at the end of the Portakabin and set the kettle to boil. When I turned back Hentze was checking his phone.

"So, what *didn't* you tell him?" I asked.

"Was it so obvious?"

"I don't think so to Friis, but he doesn't know you."

Hentze made a dry "huh" and put his phone away. "What I didn't say is that I think the man you called Mickey could be someone named Mikkjal Tausen. He was Boas Justesen's cousin, he visited the Colony commune and he lived for some time in Denmark during the seventies. He also came back to the Faroes about three weeks ago, just after Justesen had made contact with him for the first time in many years."

"So you think he fits the criteria for a suspect," I said.

"Yeh. It seems possible to me that he could have been Justesen's accomplice in killing Astrid and Else at Múli, and if he was then he also had a motive to kill Justesen last week. If Tausen was also here at Vesborggård House in 1976 then, as you say, he could have killed these other girls, too."

"Do you know where he is now?" I asked. "Could he be questioned?"

Hentze shook his head. "Unfortunately not. It's possible he left the islands yesterday on the *Norröna*."

That made me frown. The *Norröna* wasn't the obvious choice for a quick getaway if that's what Tausen was trying to make.

"Does he know he's a suspect?" I asked.

"No, I don't see how he would think so. But of course, if he *is* guilty he may not have needed to know. He could have decided to leave to be on the safe side, just in case we came looking for him."

Behind me the kettle came to a noisy boil and clicked off. I made coffees, both black, then handed one mug to Hentze.

"I don't want to throw a spanner in the works," I said. "But if Mickey *is* your man Mikkjal Tausen then I think there's a problem with your theory. Thea Rask told me that Mickey was Lýdia's friend, and from some of what she said I think he might even have helped Lýdia to get Thea away from here after she was raped."

"But you don't know this for sure?"

"No. Thea was drugged before the attack. She doesn't remember it or what happened immediately afterwards."

That made Hentze thoughtful. "You said the treatment given here at the house involved drugs as well?"

"Yeah. The clinic was run by a company called Juhl Pharmaceuticals. From what Thea told me it sounds as if they were using some sort of drug therapy to try and modify antisocial behaviour. Why?"

CHRIS OULD

"Because Mikkjal Tausen is a chemist," he said flatly. Then his phone rang and he looked at the screen. "Remi," he said.

"Mikkjal Tausen is on the *Norröna*," Remi said. He was at his desk with a passenger list in front of him, although it wasn't really necessary. "He's travelling with a woman named Sigrun Ludvig. According to the Smyril Line, Tausen booked a suite on board yesterday lunchtime. He told the booking agent it was a last-minute surprise for his girlfriend, which could be true: there were seats available on the flights to Bergen and Copenhagen yesterday, so if he'd wanted to get away in a hurry…"

"Yeh," Hentze said. "Although it was just *before* lunch that I went out to see him. Anyway, we can leave that aside for the moment. We know where he is, that's the main thing."

"Yes, that's true," Remi said. "But I think the most important question here is how strongly we believe he's a suspect, and for which crimes? Now he's left the islands we can't just invite him in for an interview, so we need to decide how to play this."

There was a pause while Hentze thought about that, but finally he said, "To prove Mikkjal Tausen was involved in the killing of Astrid and Else we still need more information about his movements in 1974. However, I also have some new information which suggests that Tausen could have been involved in a sexual assault at a place called Vesborggård House in 1976, and possibly even a death here."

"*Another* death?" Remi asked, unable to keep a note of slight dismay out of his voice.

"Possibly, yes," Hentze said. "The body has only just been found."

"By the Danish police?"

"Yes. They're here now."

There was a knock on Remi's door and Annika came in with a notebook in hand.

"Hold on, Annika's here. I'll switch to the speaker," Remi said as Annika came to the desk. "Can you hear me?"

"Yeh, that's fine," Hentze said.

Annika leaned in a little. "Hjalti, you know I said I'd check to see if Sigrun Ludvig's car had used the Leirvík tunnel? Well it hadn't, but then I remembered Tausen's Suzuki was a rental so I checked with the agency to see how long he'd had it. It turns out he didn't get it from them until last Thursday, the 26th: the day *after* Boas died. So I rang round all the other agencies and found out that he'd been using a Skoda from Avis before that, and the Skoda *had* been through the Leirvík tunnel on the evening of the 25th. It went north at 19:17 and came back at 21:56. Allowing half an hour to get from the tunnel to Múli and the same to come back, that leaves nearly two hours when Tausen could have been at the house with Boas."

There was a moment of silence while they all processed that, but Remi was keen to move on.

"Hjalti, listen," he said. "The way I see it now, if we know that Tausen lied about his whereabouts on the night Justesen died we don't need anything more. It makes him a suspect for Justesen's murder, plain and simple. Anything else – any connection to the deaths of Astrid and Else – can be dealt with around that. So, leaving aside any additional crimes and just thinking about the death of Boas Justesen, what's your opinion? Bottom line: do we have enough to treat Tausen as a prime suspect for his murder?"

"In my opinion, yes," Hentze said. "At the very least I think we need to conduct a formal interview and press him for answers."

"Fine," Remi said. "So in that case how do we tackle it? If he's actively trying to get away from us I'm concerned about the possible danger to his girlfriend. She may or may not be an accomplice."

"We could ask the captain of the *Norröna* to have Tausen detained," Annika suggested.

Remi made a moue. "Even if the captain was willing to do it I'm not sure where that would put us legally," he said. "Hjalti, what do you think?"

"No, I don't think that's necessary," Hentze said. "If Tausen believed we were actively suspicious of him I think he'd have left more quickly, on a plane. My guess is that he's simply trying to put as much distance between himself and the Faroes as he can, just in case. If that's so then he has no reason to do anything that might draw adverse attention to himself."

"So we leave him until they reach Hirtshals?"

"I think so. Unless he jumps off the ship there's nowhere he can go."

"Right," Remi said then, decided. "Can you be there to detain him when the ship docks tomorrow or shall I ask the Danes to do it?"

"No, I can be there. Given that he knows me I think that would be best anyway, but I'm pretty sure I'll have to arrest him when he realises what it's about."

"No doubt," Remi said. "So we need to decide how to play it once he has been detained. If you interview him there we'll have more time for questioning, but will the Danes try and push in because of this other case? How far have they got?"

"Not very far yet. I think any evidence against Tausen would be coming from us at the moment."

There was a short silence, then Remi made up his mind. "Okay, bring Tausen back," he said. "If he killed Justesen then that's the most recent case and as far as I'm concerned it trumps anything anyone else might have at the moment. The arrest clock will be running, but once Tausen's back here we can ask for an extension if necessary. I don't think we'll get any objections, do you?"

"No, probably not," Hentze said.

"Right. Good. Annika will sort out the transport details and be in touch later."

"Okay, that's fine."

"And, Hjalti, just remember we have enough on our plate without getting embroiled in Danish cases as well."

"I'll keep it in mind," Hentze said. "Speak to you later."

In his office Remi reached forward and hung up the phone, then turned to Annika.

"Hjalti will need a second officer for the escort, especially if he needs to bring back this woman, Sigrun Ludvig, as well. Will you go?"

Surprised but covering it quickly, Annika nodded. "Sure, of course."

"Get Oddur to help you sort out the transport, then. If

you're going to be at Hirtshals in time to meet the *Norröna* you'll need to catch the last flight tonight."

Hentze came out of the Portakabin as I trod out my cigarette. The earlier sunshine had gone and the breeze was cooler now, carrying light flecks of rain. It would be dark in a couple of hours.

"Mikkjal Tausen *is* on the *Norröna*," Hentze said. "It arrives in Hirtshals tomorrow so I'll meet it in the morning to detain him for questioning."

"Are you going to question him here or in the Faroes?" I asked.

"At home. It will make things easier, I think."

I nodded. Possession was nine-tenths of the law. "Are you going to tell Friis?"

"I think he has enough things to think about already, don't you?" Hentze said. "Of course, if Tausen tells us something in questioning that makes him a suspect here, too…" He made an open-handed gesture. "But for the moment Remi would like us to concentrate on our own most immediate case: Boas Justesen's murder."

"You think you've got enough to hold Tausen for that?"

"Yeh, I think so – at the least to answer questions and to see if we can find any forensic evidence that he was at the scene of that crime." He gave me a briefly assessing look. "So, what will you do now?"

I shrugged. "That depends on Friis. He wants a statement, but after that I don't know. Go back to Copenhagen, I suppose. There's nothing much else I can do."

Hentze looked as if he was going to say something, but then he glanced away. Thomas Friis was coming up the path from the lake shore.

"I've spoken to the technical team leader," Friis said as he approached. "Because the weather forecast is poor for tonight and tomorrow they'll excavate now, as soon as they have lights and equipment. It will probably take several hours so I don't think there's any need for you to wait here – unless you want to, of course," he added as an acknowledgement to Hentze.

Hentze seemed to consider, then shook his head. "No, I don't think I can do anything useful and I have some things to do for my own case. Perhaps we should agree to speak in the morning and see what we have then."

"Okay, of course," Friis said, without any hint that Hentze's absence would give him one less thing to worry about. They exchanged numbers and then Hentze took his leave, shaking hands before heading to his car.

"Do you know him well?" Friis asked, as if he wanted to establish a context for Hentze, although it was a bit late for that.

"I wouldn't say well," I told him. "But I trust him, and he's a good copper."

"And a friend?"

"Yeah."

Whether that altered Friis's opinion about anything wasn't clear, but he accepted the fact with a nod. "Well, as I said, I don't think the remains will be out of the ground for several hours, so unless you object, I'd like you to stay until tomorrow when we'll know better what we have. I can arrange a hotel for you in Aarhus if that would be okay – at our expense, of course."

I wondered what he'd do if I did choose to object, but I didn't. After all, I was the one who'd set this hare running and it felt only right to see where it would finish. At least if I knew that I'd have some idea of the whole.

35

WHEN THE TRAIN ARRIVED IN HUMLEBÆK, TOVE ALIGHTED WITH one other person. It was dark and she summoned a street map on her iPhone, following it closely as she left the redbrick station. The light from the screen illuminated her face within the hood of her coat, which was occasionally tugged by the breeze.

Once away from the main road and on residential streets there was little traffic and no other pedestrians, but Tove would probably not have noticed anyway. She was intent on her destination, walking briskly and with purpose, undistracted by thoughts outside her immediate goal.

The street she was looking for was lined with young trees and the houses were modest but modern and probably comfortable enough, Tove judged. It was the sort of place someone might downsize to in retirement if they were looking for easier and convenient living: Old People Land, she decided, and now that it was categorised she took no further interest, except in the house numbers.

Lene Sønderby's house was the third from the end of the row, the windows on the ground floor lit behind vertical blinds. A Japanese hatchback was parked in the bay directly outside it and the small garden was carefully tended.

Tove followed the path to the door where she rang the bell and then pushed her hood back, remembering that older people in particular could be wary of strangers after dark.

A few moments later she heard movement inside and then a voice. "Who is it?"

"Are you Lene Sønderby?" Tove asked.

"Yes. Who is that?"

"My name is Tove Hald. I would like to speak to you about your husband, Dr Carl Sønderby."

After a moment the door opened, but only as far as the chain on the inside would allow. In the gap a woman's face looked out. She was in her seventies Tove assessed, using her memory of her grandmother's appearance as a guide.

"My husband passed away," Lene Sønderby said.

"Yes, I know that," Tove said. "However, I have some questions about his work at Vesborggård House near Skanderborg."

"Vesborggård?" Lene Sønderby frowned suspiciously. "Who are you? Where are you from?"

"My name is Tove Hald," Tove repeated. "I am a student at Copenhagen University and I am conducting research into Vesborggård House and the Juhl Pharmaceutical company."

This additional information seemed to give Lene Sønderby a moment's hesitation. "How did you get my address?" she asked.

"From Silas Thygesen at the university. I believe you spoke to him some time ago."

Again Lene Sønderby appeared to weigh up this information and then – albeit reluctantly – make up her mind. "All right. Wait a moment."

The door closed while Fru Sønderby took off the chain, then reopened it wider. In the light Tove saw that she was rather formally dressed in a neat jacket, frilled blouse and a skirt. She also wore face powder and lipstick that had been applied some time ago and not renewed.

"You can come in," she allowed. "But for five minutes only. This isn't convenient. I have to go out very soon."

"Thank you," Tove said, stepping inside. "I don't think it will take very long. I have only a few questions."

Fru Sønderby led the way along the hall to a neat sitting room with a single high-backed armchair facing the TV and a two-seater sofa with precisely arranged cushions. The room was very warm, and Tove immediately took off her coat.

"I can only give you five minutes," Lene Sønderby said again, clearly interpreting Tove's disrobing as a sign that she intended being there for longer.

"Yes, you said that." Tove sat down on the edge of the sofa, set an app on her phone to record, then switched the screen to her list of questions. "Your husband was Dr Carl Johan Sønderby, is that correct?"

"Yes, that's correct."

Like a good hostess, Lene Sønderby hadn't sat down yet, but given that this rude girl seemed to have no concept of etiquette she now lowered herself on to the armchair.

"Can you tell me the dates he worked at Vesborggård House?"

Lene Sønderby frowned a little, thinking back. "It was from 1971 until 1977. Six years."

"And what was his position there?"

"He was a psychiatrist; the medical director."

"So he was responsible for the treatments of the inmates?"

The last word made Lene Sønderby bridle a little. "It wasn't a prison. It was a *clinic*, for the treatment and rehabilitation of young people."

For a second Tove was on the point of saying that the word "inmate" was valid in either case, but decided it would be an unnecessary distraction. "Can you tell me what sort of treatments were used?" she asked instead.

"No, I don't know," Lene Sønderby said. "Carl didn't talk about his work."

"Never?" Tove queried.

"No, not in detail."

"But you do know that he published two papers on experimental drug treatments for behavioural modification while he worked at Vesborggård House."

"Yes, yes, I knew that," Fru Sønderby allowed. "But as I said, I didn't know the details of the work. I've told people before. All I know is that they tried to help people: that was their job."

"*Which* people did you tell before?" Tove asked, looking up from her phone.

Lene Sønderby shook her head, as if she resented the topic. "I don't remember their names. People from a lawyer's office. They said they were representing patients who had been mistreated at the clinic but I told them the same thing I told you: Carl only tried to do good. He would never have mistreated anyone. He was a good man, a good doctor."

"Okay, I see," Tove said. "So, can you tell me why the clinic was closed?"

"Oh, yes, I can tell you that," Lene Sønderby said flatly. "It was because people are stupid."

"Who do you mean?"

Lene Sønderby made a general gesture. "All of them, out there in the sticks, but the ones who lived near the house were the worst. They made up stories – ridiculous stories – about what was done at the clinic, just because they didn't like the fact it was there. From what they said you would have thought the place was a Nazi experiment camp." She waved a hand as if batting a fly. "Ridiculous people, too stupid to know any better; too stupid to be listened to by any sensible person. Some did listen, though, of course. Gossip and falsehoods are always more interesting than the facts, aren't they?"

"Not to me," Tove said. "The facts are why I'm here."

"Yes, well, that's as may be," Lene Sønderby said, as if she realised she'd let her emotions betray her. "But even so, I can't tell you anything more."

She shifted in her seat, preparing to stand, but Tove was looking at her phone once again and didn't take the hint. "Did your husband keep any records?" she asked.

"Records? What sort of records?"

"About the treatment of the people at Vesborggård House."

"No, not at home. All that sort of thing would have gone, I don't know where." Lene Sønderby rose from her seat. "You'll have to excuse me now. I have to go out."

She took a step forward and Tove finally realised that she

was being given her cue to move. She stood up but it didn't stop her asking one final question. "Where did your husband work after Vesborggård House?"

"It was… He went into private practice," Lene Sønderby said. "Near Helsingør," she added, as if that would further bolster the fact.

"Okay, thank you," Tove said.

She followed Lene Sønderby to the front door, pausing by the hallway table to put on her coat, then going out through the front door as Fru Sønderby held it open.

"Good night," Tove said, as pleasantly as she could as she stepped on to the path.

"And to you," Lene Sønderby said closing the door.

Back on the pavement Tove retraced her steps in the direction she'd come, but at the end of the row of houses she stopped and looked at the time, then moved into the partial shelter of a tree by the roadside. From there she had a view of Lene Sønderby's car on the street and also of the front of her house.

Tove waited for twenty minutes without taking her eyes off the house before she concluded that, in fact, Lene Sønderby did not have to go out after all, but instead had only come back a short time ago, dressed as she was and with her lipstick unrefreshed after whatever function she had attended.

The lipstick was a small detail, but Tove noted such things when they took her attention or when she made a particular point of being alert. In much the same way she'd also noticed the letter on the hallway stand as she'd put on her coat. It was addressed to "Nursing Sister (Retired) Lene Sønderby" and bore the imprint of Dansk Sygeplejeråd – the Danish Nursing Council. Two small things, then, she decided as she finally left her spot and started off again towards the train station: one a lie, the other an omission, at least.

By the time she boarded the next train to Copenhagen twenty minutes later she was browsing the Dansk Sygeplejeråd website with absorbed interest, particularly the "Friends and Colleagues" pages.

36

THE CENTRUM HOTEL WAS A FIFTEEN-STOREY CONFERENCE hotel a short walk from the police station, which was probably part of the reason Thomas Friis had found me a room there; that and the fact that the place seemed as dead as only empty hotels can be. Given that Aarhus had seemed busy and thriving the previous day, it struck me as strange that the hotel wasn't more lively – not that I cared a great deal. The prospect of a night without the sound of trains through the window was enough to make up for any lack of atmosphere.

I hadn't brought an overnight bag, only a spare sweatshirt which had travelled the last few days in the car, unneeded. With a toothbrush and toothpaste bought at the reception desk it was enough, though, and after a shower I went down to eat in the hotel restaurant, deserted except for a middle-aged couple at a table right in the centre. Fifty-odd places were unfilled, the absence of customers exaggerated by the neat arrangement of tableware in front of each empty seat and the harsh echo of every hard sound.

Given a free choice of tables, I opted for one with a view of the main road, illuminated by street lamps and passing headlights. I sat with a beer thinking, rethinking and coming to no firm conclusions as I picked at olives and bread. When my phone rang it was Tove.

"I have new information on Vesborggård House," she announced when I answered. "The medical director was a doctor – a psychiatrist – named Carl Johan Sønderby. He's dead now and when I visited his wife she wasn't very helpful but I think she may know more than she wanted to tell me."

"More about what?"

"About the treatments they carried out at the clinic," Tove said. "Dr Sønderby co-authored two papers on the use of a drug called Resolomine in the treatment of behavioural disorders. The patent for Resolomine was held by Juhl Pharmaceuticals from 1970, but as far as I can find out it was never approved by the Danish department of health, so I think this explains why Juhl Pharmaceuticals were sued in 2004. Resolomine was obviously used at Vesborggård House."

"Do you know its effects?" I asked, thinking of Thea Rask's description of the *vitaminer* she and the other residents at Vesborggård House had been given.

"No, I don't know that yet," Tove said. "It's outside my frame of reference, but in the morning I'll find someone at the university to ask about it."

It was easy to get dragged under the tracks of Tove's bulldozer-like drive to know all there was about her chosen subject of interest, and to a certain extent I still felt responsible for triggering this particular fixation. I recognised the compulsion, but given what had happened at Vesborggård House a few hours ago I knew I should at least try to apply the brakes.

"Tove, listen," I said. "I was at Vesborggård House this afternoon. A body's been found there and there's a police investigation going on at the moment, so it might be better if you held off on any more research. I don't know what the police will find or who they'll want to interview, but they probably won't be very happy if you queer the pitch before they get there."

There was silence for a second and I could imagine her frown. "Okay, yes, I understand 'queer the pitch'," she said. "Do the police have a suspect?"

I debated for a second, but there didn't seem to be any good reason not to tell her at least part of what I knew. "Possibly someone who worked at Vesborggård House in 1976," I told her.

"Yeh, that would be logical," she said and when she lapsed into silence I thought that maybe the bulldozer had slowed just a little so I pressed the advantage.

"By tomorrow I might know more about the investigation," I said. "I'm staying in Aarhus tonight, then coming back to Copenhagen. Why don't we meet up and talk when I get back?"

"Yeh, okay, we can do that," she said, although it sounded as if she was thinking about something else. "Call me when you get here."

I said that I would and then she rang off, as abruptly as ever.

The smaller of the two incident rooms at the main police station in Aarhus was lit by four strip lights, but one wasn't working. Outside it was dark, and Vicekriminalkommissær Asger Markussen looked at the reflection of the room in the black glass of the window while Thomas Friis outlined the situation at Vesborggård House. Markussen had stayed late for this briefing, preferring to do that rather than go out to the site when there would be very little to see in the darkness.

There wasn't much solid information yet, but Friis was at pains to point out that – as he saw it – there were already two crimes they could look at: one the rape of Thea Rask, and the other a probable murder. In his view, he said, the most likely scenario was that the remains found today would turn out to be Inge-Lise Hofmann, whose case file showed definite links between her disappearance and Vesborggård House. He would review it again, he told Markussen, and highlight any factors which might help to make an early identification of the remains.

Despite Friis's obvious ability and intelligence, Markussen had never quite managed to dispel a small but innate misgiving about the man, and it was at times like this briefing that he felt them the most. Friis had settled at *kriminalassistent* grade 2 six years ago and since then had never applied for promotion, although he was certainly capable of more. He seemed to prefer the role of backseat driver, confident that his opinion should be noted, but abdicating any responsibility if it wasn't. Like the expensive and well-tailored suits Friis wore, it gave Markussen the suspicion that the man thought he was just that little bit superior to his colleagues, whatever their rank.

"So, what about this Faroese officer, Hentze?" Markussen

said. "Is he going to have some interest in the investigation, do we know?"

"No, I'm not sure yet," Friis said. "He's on his own case: a double murder on the islands from 1974, but beyond that he didn't say very much, only that there may be some similarities between the burials."

Markussen considered. "All right," he said in the end. "Until the remains are out of the ground and we have a forensic pathologist's report we can't do anything else. If the body *is* Inge-Lise Hoffmann then obviously we'll need to re-open that case, but until then I think we can wait."

"There is also the rape in 1976," Thomas Friis said. "We have at least some evidence of that from Jan Reyná's photograph and we can get a statement from the victim herself, Thea Rask. If the location of that crime was also at Vesborggård House—"

"Yes, we'll need her statement, of course," Markussen said with a note of forestalling. "But if she hasn't reported it for – what, forty years? – I think we should hold off until we know exactly what we have from the site. There's no point tying the two crimes together until we have a date for the burial."

"Okay, sure," Friis said, as if choosing his battles. "But while you're here there's something else I think we should also consider."

He moved to his laptop, which was hooked up to a video projector, and after a couple of keystrokes one of the whiteboards was illuminated by a projection: a horizontal timeline.

Markussen moved to look at the display, but as soon as he saw the photographs and the names on the timeline his body

language became stiffer and more resistant. "Thomas...
Again?" he said, pained.

Thomas Friis appeared not to hear as he moved the
cursor on the screen. "If we look at this timeline and work
backwards we have Helene Kruse in January this year; then
Louise Kjærsgaard in 2008." He skipped the cursor back
over the individual markers. "Then, as you know, there are
killings in 2001, 1996, 1990 and finally Nina Lodberg in
1982. Each incident or incident cluster has a gap of between
five and seven years before the next. *So*, if we were to go back
one further step on the line from Nina Lodberg in 1982, then
a killing in 1976 when Inge-Lise disappeared would fit the
pattern, as well."

On the screen projection Friis circled the cursor
around an unmarked point on the line where 1976 would be
represented and Markussen sighed.

"But it's *not* a pattern, though, is it?" Markussen
said. "We've already been through this. This theory of a
'hibernating killer'" – he made air quotes – "doesn't *have*
any consistent features. The time period varies – you said so
yourself. The incidents don't even happen at the same time
of year or in the same area. The *only* pattern is that none of
these killings fits a pattern."

"And they're also unsolved," Friis said, unabashed.
"But in at least three of the cases we know that some kind
of stupefying drug was employed, and *now* we also have that
as a feature in the case of Thea Rask when she was raped in
1976. So, if the body we've found turns out to be Inge-Lise
Hoffmann as well, I think we could reasonably add 1976 to

this timeline. That means it could be our best opportunity yet to identify the man responsible because it places him in a known location at a known point in time when there are witnesses and records we can check."

Markussen drew a heavy breath, as if he'd wished to avoid this situation but, now that it had been thrust upon him, he had no choice. "Thomas, listen—" He paused, as if deciding what he wanted to say was unexpectedly complex. "Okay, look, I know you're smarter than most of us round here, and *you* know I've given you plenty of leeway on this theory, right? And while it was only a pet project all that was okay, but at some point you've got to give it a rest. They only found this new body, what, four hours ago? It's way too soon to be jumping to any conclusions, you *know* that. And as for linking it to a theory about a dozen old cases…" He shook his head.

"Yes, but—" Friis started, until Markussen held up his hand.

"No. No, just leave it now," Markussen said, flatly resolved. "Natasja and Martin can look after things over the weekend and you should knock off."

Briefly it looked as if Thomas Friis might argue the point, but in the end he just nodded. "Okay, if that's what you want," he said fatalistically.

"It is," Markussen said, resisting the urge to rise to Friis's tone. Then, more mildly, he said, "Listen, it's Friday night, for God's sake. Just go and enjoy the weekend, all right? I'll see you on Monday." And with a last glance at the whiteboard, he turned away towards the door.

When Markussen had gone, Friis disconnected his laptop from the video projector and closed it down. He was gathering a few things together into his bag when Kasper Sandstrøm came in.

"I just had a call from the technical team at Vesborggård House," Kasper said. "They've found a bundle of clothes in the grave: some shoes and a bag, too."

For a moment Thomas Friis hesitated. "Okay, well, you'd better let Natasja know," he said, zipping the laptop into his bag. "I'm on my way out for the weekend."

"Oh. Right. Got something on?"

"No, not really," Friis said, lifting his bag. "Just family time."

37

WHEN I OPENED THE DOOR OF MY ROOM TO THE KNOCK I FOUND Thomas Friis in the corridor outside. He had a messenger bag on his shoulder, spoiling the line of his suit.

"I took a chance that you'd be here," Friis said. "Do you mind if we talk for a few minutes?"

"No, come in," I said, holding the door wider. "Have a seat." I gestured him to one of the two vinyl chairs by the window and crossed to the minibar.

"Would you like a drink?"

He looked and then nodded. "Sure, thanks. Is there a Coke? I still have to drive home."

I got him a Coke and a gin and tonic for myself. There was no ice, but I could live with that.

"So I can give you a progress report," Friis said when I sat down. "You might want to know that as I left the office the technical team at Vesborggård House had found clothing in the grave – not on the body, but in a bundle. If we're lucky they may help to identify who they belonged to. Also, I should say that Vicekriminalkommissær Markussen is now in charge of the case, so I think it will be one of his team who will take your statement tomorrow."

"So you're not staying on it?"

Friis shook his head. "Only to write the report from today. I have… other things."

I couldn't tell whether he felt hard done by at that. Like most coppers, I'd imagined he'd have a natural desire to be involved in a significant case, but he showed little sign of anything approaching frustration as he took a measured sip of his Coke.

"So," he said then, as if to acknowledge that he had moved on. "Just to have a better idea of how things have been left, can I ask about Thea Rask? You told me earlier that you'd spoken to her and she had confirmed that she was the girl in the photograph you have, yes?"

"Not exactly," I said. "She told me she'd been raped at Vesborggård House but I didn't show her the photograph, for obvious reasons."

"No, okay, I understand," Friis said with a nod. "But do you think it is her? Did you recognise her from the picture?"

I made a so-so gesture. "Well, she's forty years older so I'm not a hundred per cent sure, but she looks similar to the girl in the photo, and given everything else I'd say she is, yes."

"Okay, so in that case, does she know who was responsible for her rape?"

"No, she says not. From what she told me it's pretty obvious she was drugged before the attack, so all she remembers is coming round the next day at a flat in Christiania with my mother and me."

He thought about that for a moment. "Then do you

think it was your mother – Lýdia, yes? – who got her away from Vesborggård House?"

I nodded. "So Thea says. I can't see any other explanation."

"Does Thea know how? Did she ask your mother what happened?"

"She told me she asked, but Lýdia wouldn't say: perhaps because she didn't want to upset her any more. I don't know."

It obviously wasn't the answer he'd hoped for, but after a few seconds he seemed to put it aside. "Okay, let me ask you something else, then," he said. "What do *you* think we are dealing with here?"

"Based on today?" I shook my head. "I don't want to guess."

It was another answer he hadn't hoped for.

"But with one girl who was raped and another – perhaps two – who were killed, what would you say? If we think both incidents are from the same time, wouldn't it be logical to think that it was the same man who made both attacks?"

I got the sense that he was pressing this because he had his own agenda, and that made me slightly wary. "Hypothetically?" I asked. "Well, I suppose you could suspect it – *if* you knew that the remains we found today definitely date back to 1976 *and* that they're of Inge-Lise Hoffmann."

That seemed to satisfy him a little more. "Okay then," he said. "So say that *is* all true and that, if she hadn't been rescued, Thea Rask would have been killed and buried as well. Would you say that the man who did it was a serial killer?"

I sat back with my almost-cold gin and made a show of thinking it over. I wasn't sure how we'd jumped from considering the crimes at Vesborggård House to talking about serial killings but Friis clearly had something on his mind.

"Well, I suppose it depends on which definition of serial killer you use," I said in the end. "If it's just that there's more than one victim, then yeah, you could say it, but it wouldn't be my choice."

"You prefer the older definition?" he asked. "That between each victim there should be a return to normality for the killer – a 'cooling-off' period?"

"I think it keeps things more manageable, yeah," I told him. "If for no other reason than stopping the press going mad."

"So if there *were* other victims of the same man – later, with time in between – what would you say?"

I could tell this wasn't hypothetical now – at least, not for him. There'd already been a hint of it in the way he'd told me he wasn't staying on the Vesborggård case, and now I was pretty sure I knew the reason for that.

"*Are* there other victims?" I said.

It was his cue, and now I'd provided it I saw him relax just a little.

"Yeh, I think so," he said leaning back by a fraction. "Do you know of Samuel Hallard, from the United States?"

I did, but Hallard wasn't someone you'd have come across unless you'd studied the subject. He'd never been charged and it wasn't until after his death from a stroke that the Cleveland police had made a convincing case that Hallard had stalked and killed five people at intervals over nearly three decades. But what made Hallard exceptional – perhaps even unique – was the fact that he'd never been *prevented* from killing by imprisonment or circumstance; he simply *chose* not to kill for periods as long as ten years.

"Yeah, I've read about Hallard," I told Friis. "But he was unusual, maybe unique."

"Yes, very unusual." Friis nodded, in full agreement. "But I don't think he was the only one of his kind. I believe there is someone like Hallard killing in Denmark."

I raised an eyebrow, just a little. "Over what time frame?"

He sat forward. "Until today I believed that the earliest case was in 1982 and that the latest was in January this year. There are eight murders I'm sure of and two more that might be connected." He put a hand to the bag by his chair. "Can I show you?"

It was ironic really, given that at our first meeting I'd wanted to avoid giving Friis the impression that I was somewhere between sad and deluded. If I'd known he was one of those coppers who keeps a pet case in their desk I could probably have tackled things differently, then and now. As it was, though, I knew I was fresh meat – a virgin audience – and there was a lecture to come.

Friis had a timeline on his laptop, neatly laid out with thumbnails, locations and dates. He moved through it with a familiarity that spoke of many careful hours in its making and what he told me had a semi-rehearsed, abridged air; as if he was well versed in which elements required detail and which could be abbreviated.

"The earliest case was a fourteen-year-old girl named Nina Lodberg," he said. "She was found in a lake two days after she was reported as missing, in 1982. She had been strangled with a rope, but not quickly. The post-mortem showed it was done at least three times while she was alive."

"Was there a sexual element?"

"No, apparently not, and the investigation didn't find any suspects. In the end it was left open."

He hovered the cursor over her photograph, then moved it away.

"From then on there has been a killing every five to seven years. Twice there were two only a few weeks apart. I won't take your time with every detail, and some elements change: the method of killing, and of course where they take place – but in all the cases there are three things in common. The first is that the killer spends time watching his victims and chooses carefully when to attack. The second factor is the age and the sex of the victims."

He changed the screen to show a column of faces. "They are always female and, except in one case, less than twenty years old. Like the first case, there is never any sexual contact but the third thing in common is that in the cases where it's been possible to do a useful post-mortem, we find that each death was prolonged. There have been asphyxiations by strangling with a rope, a cloth or by hand; a stab wound; and three have died from an overdose of barbiturate. But whichever method is used there is always the impression that it has been… *prepared*. It's as if whoever is committing these crimes needs to be sure he will get what he wants and after that he is usually not worried about hiding the body more than a little, sometimes not even that."

He paused and looked up from the screen. "The only time I think his plan has gone wrong is in a case from this year, near Billund. The victims – a mother and daughter – were at an isolated farmhouse, and when the woman's ex-husband arrived unexpectedly the killer drove away in a van. Unfortunately, the husband didn't see him, but in the upstairs of the house he found his wife dead from a single stab wound – the post-mortem showed she had been drugged. His daughter was still alive, although she had been drugged, too, and placed on her bed naked, but nothing else had happened."

"What sort of drug was used, do you know?"

"No, it was nothing the technical laboratory could identify from its traces. It had broken down in their bodies too quickly."

"And there was no other forensic evidence?"

Friis shook his head. "No, very little, and nothing of use for identification."

Now that he'd laid out his stall he picked up his glass and took a drink, giving me time to assess what I thought.

"How long have you been working on this?" I asked.

"For a few years." He said it as if it was an admission of weakness he'd rather avoid.

"And you've told other people what you think?"

"Yes, when it became clear," he said with a nod. "But in Denmark we only have about forty-five murders a year, so the theory of a man who only kills when it suits him, and over so long... It's not an easy idea to accept. Killers don't hibernate for years at a time, do they? Only in the United States. Only Hallard."

For a moment his tone was sardonic, as if he was quoting what someone had said. Apart from his annoyance at Jeppe's clumsy uncovering of the remains at Vesborggård House it was the only time I'd heard him sound any kind of emotion.

"And now you think you need to go one step back even further – to 1976," I said, because it was obviously the reason he'd come.

"Yes, now I think so," he said, decided. "In my research I thought it was unusual that the first killing in 1982 was so efficiently carried out, as if he was already familiar with what he should do. But if it was *not* his first killing – if he has done others before where he made mistakes or with different techniques… You understand what I mean? If the crimes near Vesborggård House in 1976 are actually the first time – or perhaps the second or third…"

I could see him constructing the logic of that, and in a way I knew how he felt. But even so, I couldn't buy it: not sight unseen and only on the basis of what he'd said. I had no way to assess whether his theory held any water, let alone up to the brim, and even beyond that I knew there was another factor at work. Thomas Friis was clearly an obsessive, and today he'd caught sight of a light at the end of the tunnel. He saw a chance to validate his theory and wanted me to add fuel to his fire.

I took a drink, but by the time I lowered my glass I knew he'd read my thoughts because he'd stiffened a little.

"So what can *I* tell you?" I asked, because it was the obvious question.

"I'd like to know if you have any more information than you told me this afternoon," he said. "I think there must be something else for Inspector Hentze to come all the way here."

It was too late to back-pedal on what had already been said so I opted for flatness instead. "Sorry; all I know is what I told you already," I said. "The grave at the house may be similar to one in the Faroes, and there was a Faroese man at Vesborggård House in 1976."

"*Ja*. Yeh, Mickey," Friis said, slightly impatient. "But do you have any better idea *who* he is now? Does Hentze?"

I shook my head. "I haven't spoken to him since this afternoon," I said: easy because it was true. "But with only a first name to go on I wouldn't think he knows any more now than he did before. Perhaps you should ask him."

I'd closed the door by saying that and Friis knew it. "Okay, yes, maybe that would be the best way," he said with a note of acceptance.

He put his laptop away and then got to his feet. I did the same.

"You know, if this man Mickey can be seen as a suspect in the Faroes *and* at Vesborggård House, he must be more than sixty years old now," Friis said. "And Samuel Hallard was sixty-eight when he died, which was five years after his last killing. You understand what I mean? I think he should be found before he disappears forever, so if you think of anything else…"

"Sure, of course," I told him.

He nodded. "Okay. *Tak* for your help, then."

I accompanied him to the door, shook his hand and said *godnat*. I'd disappointed him, that much was clear, but he'd probably expected as much. He was smart enough for that.

As I went back to my gin I thought about calling Hentze, just to forewarn him, but decided I wouldn't. Hentze was canny enough to deal with Friis if the need arose, and if it did I couldn't imagine he'd be in any hurry to complicate his case any further. By tomorrow he'd have Mikkjal Tausen to talk to, and if Mikkjal turned out to be Mickey from Vesborggård House I'd have my own questions. Until then there was little else I could do: only wait and follow Hentze back to the Faroes. It would make or complete a full circle, I guessed.

38

Saturday/leygardagur

A SERIES OF TIME-LAPSE PHOTOGRAPHS OF TOVE HALD WOULD have shown sudden shifts in position followed by long periods of virtual stillness. She sat at the table in front of the night-dark window for a while, her only movement that of her fingers on the MacBook's keyboard and track pad. Later she spent some time in the kitchen, standing at the counter with coffee and her phone. Later still she was back on the MacBook, this time lying on the sofa with her knees drawn up.

From one web page to another, Tove followed a trail of hyperlinks to half a dozen different nursing forums, bookmarking, creating accounts for each one and then posting the same message in Danish and English: "Does anyone remember Vesborggård House? My grandmother Lene worked there in the 1970s and I would like to reunite her with her old colleagues while she can still remember them."

She'd thought quite hard about this message, trying to strike a similar tone to the one she had seen in other postings. In the end she still wasn't fully convinced she had managed to sound approachable and friendly rather than too direct, but without Kjeld around to ask for an opinion she went ahead anyway.

Once the message was posted she occupied herself with other things – there was no shortage of those – but every hour or so she went back to the websites to check for responses. She was aware that at this hour it was probably unlikely her message would be read. Normal people – at least those of an age to have been at Vesborggård House – probably didn't go online after midnight.

At just after one in the morning Kjeld came back to the flat, full of bonhomie and beer and with a girl whose pet name – Vivi – Tove thought unnecessarily childish. She didn't say so, however. She was aware that Kjeld didn't like her observations on the women he went with, so after a simple, "Hi," Tove resumed her note making, putting on headphones about ten minutes later when Vivi's climaxes proved to be as irritatingly girlish as her name.

A couple of hours later and finally feeling sleepy, Tove got ready for bed, brushing her teeth as she made a final check on the nursing message boards via her phone. On the third one she found a response, left ten minutes before in English.

Hi Tove1293. My mom, Sørine, was at Vesborggård in 1972 or 1973, I think. She was also a nurse (it runs in the family!). Unfortunately she has dementia now so her memory isn't so good. She's in a care home here in Vancouver but I have her treasured photo albums and I'm sure I've seen a picture of Vesborggård there. I will look and maybe I can send you a copy. Sylvie x

Sitting on the edge of the bathtub, Tove wrote a reply,

being careful to mimic the chatty tone, which wasn't natural to her. Once she'd posted the reply she checked the rest of the websites, found nothing and so she went to bed, switching off her mind – if not her phone – instantly.

She woke refreshed and without any prompting at five forty-five. By then Sylvie in Vancouver had sent her an email titled "Well what do you know?" with two attached photographs, which Tove examined closely on the screen of her MacBook while she ate toast and drank coffee in the kitchen.

The Kodacolor images were faded around the edges but still clear; the first had the words "*Vesborggård Hus, august '73*" written in biro in the margin beneath. The photo itself had been taken from some distance in order to accommodate approximately twenty people, standing on a lawn with part of a brick building behind them. Several of the women were dressed in nursing uniforms and most of the men were in suits or jackets and ties, but given the camera's distance from its subjects their faces blurred when Tove took the magnification over 150 per cent.

The second photograph was much clearer, however. Four smiling women filled the frame, all wearing white uniforms, arms around each other. In the margin under the picture four names were written in biro: *Me, Lene, Anne and Stine*.

In her mind Tove compared the woman second from left in the photo to her memory of Lene Sønderby from the evening before. It was the same woman, Tove concluded after a full minute of study, and therefore Lene Sønderby had not told the truth when she'd claimed to have no knowledge of medical practices at Vesborggård House. Therefore she could say more.

* * *

At that time on Saturday morning there were only a few passengers on the outward-bound train to Humlebæk. The previous night's rain and cold breeze had abated but when she turned into Lene Sønderby's road Tove observed the damp leaves it had scattered along the pavement and over Lene Sønderby's car. It didn't seem to have moved since she left, which Tove took as further confirmation that the woman had simply been trying to get rid of her last night.

At the front door Tove again pressed the bell, but this time she was prepared to wait. Both upstairs and down the curtains were still closed.

She gave it two minutes, then pressed the bell button again. This time it prompted a muffled, incomprehensible voice from within and shortly afterwards the inner door of the porch opened. Through the small, pebble-glazed window Tove saw Fru Sønderby's figure inside.

"Yes, yes, I heard you the first time," Lene Sønderby was saying irritably. "Who is it?"

"Tove Hald," Tove said. "I was here yesterday. The evening," she added for clarification.

There was a moment of silence, then Lene Sønderby spoke with a note of even firmer irritation. "What do you want at this time of the morning?"

"I have a photograph I'd like you to look at," Tove said. "I believe you are one of the people it shows at Vesborggård House. You were a nurse there, is that correct?"

There was another pause, longer this time, but eventually

there was the sound of a lock being turned and Lene Sønderby opened the door, just enough that she could look out. She wore a quilted dressing gown, tied firmly at the waist.

"What on earth are you thinking, getting people out of bed at this hour?" she demanded.

"I have a photograph I'd like you to look at," Tove repeated. "I also have some more questions to ask you. May I come in?"

"No, absolutely not. I'm not dressed, I haven't had breakfast and—" Lene Sønderby gave up on listing the reasons why she couldn't talk and instead gripped the edge of the door. "And besides, I can't tell you anything more about Vesborggård House. Now, go away and leave me in peace."

"I think—" Tove began, but before she got any further Lene Sønderby closed the door with a thud.

For a moment Tove considered the door, then raised a hand and rapped on the wood. "Fru Sønderby? I think you should know that the police have found a body at Vesborggård House – Fru Sønderby?"

When Lene Sønderby opened the door again she seemed to be struggling to maintain the annoyance in her expression against a rising frown of concern. "A body? What are you talking about?"

"I don't have any more details," Tove said. "Except that it may be a girl who disappeared in 1976."

"Well, I know nothing about it," Fru Sønderby said regaining her irritated belligerence. "Why would that have anything to do with me?"

"I didn't say that it did," Tove said matter-of-factly. "But it may have something to do with another person who was at

Vesborggård House so I'd like you to look at this photograph and tell me who you can recognise."

As she said it Tove brought up her phone, but as soon as she saw it Lene Sønderby was already waving it away.

"No, I refuse to be… to be accosted like this on my own doorstep. If you don't go away now I will call the police. Do you hear? Go away!"

"If you—"

"No! Go *away*!"

The last word was almost cut off by a second thud of the door, followed immediately afterwards by the sound of the lock being turned. A few seconds later the internal door closed, too, and now that Lene Sønderby's figure was no longer visible inside, Tove accepted that there was no more to be gained here and turned away. She wondered briefly whether five past eight in the morning could be considered early, but supposed that it could if you wanted a reason to avoid telling the truth.

Overnight, Tove had sent me an email with an attached photograph and the title "Vesborggård staff 1973". It showed thirty-odd people lined up semi-formally in front of the house. God knew where she'd found it, but from the fact that it had been sent at 05:52 that morning I guessed that my attempt to close her down hadn't been very successful. That concerned me a little because if she kept digging around, there was a good chance she'd eventually run foul of the police investigation into Vesborggård House. By and large, coppers don't like outsiders dogging their tracks, and they like it even less when they discover they're playing catch-up to an amateur's interest.

I couldn't see a way to deflect Tove any more than I had, though, so rather than risk encouraging her, I didn't respond to the email. Instead I studied the staff photo for a few moments longer. It didn't tell me a lot because it predated Lýdia's time at Vesborggård, and also Thea's. But thinking of Thea as I surveyed the faces in the picture, I did have another thought: perhaps not a good one given everything else, so I decided to let it lie – at least until I'd fulfilled my obligation at the police station.

Because I was expected I got a proper interview room this time, on the third floor of the building, with coffee and a pleasant enough man called Martin Davidsen, a balding *kriminalassistent* in his mid-thirties.

"Thomas says you're a detective inspector with a major incident team in the UK," Davidsen said, by way of a start. He was recording the interview on a small DAT machine.

"Was," I acknowledged and admitted in one. "I resigned a few days ago, so technically I'm serving my notice." It seemed better to get it out of the way so nothing was based on erroneous assumptions. They had their job to do.

"Ah. Okay," Davidsen said, choosing to leave it at that, at least for the time being. "So, perhaps you can tell me what you know about the human remains found at Vesborggård House yesterday."

I knew or could make a good guess at what he'd want to know and what would be extraneous detail, and by now I'd had chance to order things into a logical progression. There was no point in cluttering the account with any reference to the Faroes, so I started with the images in the camera Peter had found with Lýdia's possessions and went from there to Lýdia working at Vesborggård and leaving at the same time that Thea had absconded.

I was pretty sure Thomas Friis would have told Davidsen about my belief that the abuse photographs of Thea had been taken in the building overlooking the lake, but I repeated it for the sake of the record and added that Davidsen could apply to Ben Skinner for the evidence photos if his team needed to do so. Beyond that, the case history of Inge-Lise Hoffmann's disappearance and any link it might have to Thea's rape was something Thomas Friis would know better than me, I told Davidsen. That was as much as I knew.

Of course, it wasn't, but Davidsen was only interested in the direct chain of association that might or might not throw any light on the remains from the lakeside. One crime was enough to be going on with for him. He made a last note when I got to the end, then put his pen to one side.

"Well, I think that's all the questions I have at the moment," he said. "I have your phone number, so if there is anything else I can call you. Would that be all right?"

"Sure. If I can help just let me know."

Now we were finished, Davidsen accompanied me down to the lobby, but before we parted I said, "Just out of interest, do you know any more about the remains now?"

He hesitated briefly, then said, "Not very much yet. Some items – clothes – from the grave seem to have belonged to a female, but they were found in the grave, not on the body, so…"

I nodded. So they confirmed nothing just yet. I took my leave and headed out on to the main road, waiting until I'd turned off on to a quieter street before calling Thea Rask.

39

ANNIKA EMERGED FROM THE TERMINAL AT AALBORG AIRPORT from the first flight of the day out of Kastrup. She had an overnight bag on her shoulder and was pulling Hentze's case behind her. They had ninety minutes before the *Norröna* was due in at Hirtshals and, uncharacteristically, Hentze had ignored the no waiting zone at the entrance until Annika emerged. He'd already had to show his warrant card to one security man.

"I'm pretty sure I got all your stuff," Annika said as Hentze opened the boot and put their bags in.

"Thanks. You know there aren't many women I'd ask to do that."

"Oh, by most men's standards you're very neat and clean," Annika said with a grin. "Which is more than I can say for that hotel. It's *awful*, especially after midnight."

"You stayed there?" Hentze asked, surprised.

"Yeh, in your room." She saw his look. "It was Remi's idea since you wouldn't be there and we'd already paid for it. I'm pretty sure they *had* changed the sheets, but even so…" She pulled a face.

"Yeh, well, it's all glamour in CID," Hentze said. "You'll just have to get used to it."

Once they'd cleared the airport and found their way to the E39 Hentze checked the time and put his foot down, settling on 105 kph and sticking at that.

"So, have we a schedule?" he asked.

Annika nodded. "I've been in touch with the *Norröna*'s captain. When they dock they'll delay opening the doors and put out an announcement for Mikkjal Tausen to go to the purser's office. We go on board, arrest Tausen and escort him off. After that, assuming he doesn't tell us anything to change our minds, we're booked on the 13:15 flight from Aalborg to Kastrup, then the 19:45 Atlantic flight to Vágar. There's a detention cell we can use at Kastrup during the wait and the tickets have been arranged, so all we have to do is show up at the gate."

"Sounds like you've got everything covered," Hentze said approvingly.

"I hope so."

He glanced at her as she shifted in her seat a little, adjusting her posture, and saw the Heckler & Koch holstered on the belt of her jeans.

"You brought your pistol?" Hentze said.

"Remi's orders. He *thinks* you brought yours."

"Yeh, well, I might have if I'd known I'd have to arrest someone."

"You don't expect Tausen to make trouble though, right?"

Hentze shook his head. "I doubt it, but if he does I'll be right behind you."

* * *

They arrived at the Nordsøterminalen with time to spare and were met in the terminal building by two uniformed *betjente* from the local station. Remi Syderbø had requested the assistance, it transpired. They waited as the *Norröna* entered the harbour and executed its manoeuvres to come alongside. By then there was rain on the wind and the cold air whistled through the gaps in the covered gangway as it was extended out – twenty metres up – to reach the side of the ship.

Although he thought it unnecessary, Hentze didn't object when the *betjente* accompanied him and Annika to the end of the walkway, and in fact the uniforms served a useful purpose, parting a way through the passengers waiting on board until they reached one of the ship's younger officers.

"Did you locate Herre Tausen?" Hentze asked.

"Yes, he's in the office," the younger man said. "We told him there was a problem with the payment for his cabin suite."

Following the ship's officer they moved quickly through the passageways until they arrived at a varnished oak door with the sign "Purser" and the purser himself standing beside it. Hentze showed his warrant card. "Herre Tausen's inside?"

"Yes, and his girlfriend."

"Okay, thank you," Hentze said. "You can open the exits now."

As the purser went off to do so Hentze instructed the two *betjente* to wait, then opened the office door and went in with Annika.

The office wasn't very large: enough room for a desk and two armchairs but not much else. The three bags standing just inside the door – two cerise pink, one black – made the space even more cramped.

Hentze's entrance immediately drew Mikkjal Tausen to his feet from one of the chairs. He was smartly dressed in a blazer and open-necked shirt and he looked surprised and then puzzled in turn.

"Officer Hentze? I don't understand. What's going on? Are you...? The purser said there was problem with the payment for the cabin, but..."

"No, that's not the issue," Hentze said. "I'll explain in a minute." He turned to Sigrun Ludvig who was still seated. "Miss Ludvig, would you mind waiting with the two officers outside, please?"

The office door was still open and Sigrun Ludvig cast a glance in that direction before looking back at Hentze. "I don't understand. What's this about?"

"Please, if you would," Hentze said with a gesture to the door.

Sigrun shifted, but then looked towards her boyfriend for clarity.

"I guess you'd better do as he asks, love," Tausen said, still giving the impression that he was no wiser than she. "I'm sure this is... that there's a misunderstanding. Don't worry. I'll be there in a few minutes, okay?"

"Okay," Sigrun said, not entirely convinced. All the same, she rose from her seat and left the office. Hentze closed the door behind her, then turned back to Tausen.

"Do you have your passport with you?" he asked.

"Yes, of course."

Tausen patted his blazer and produced a green Faroese passport. Hentze gave it a cursory glance, then put it into his own pocket. The action caused Tausen to frown.

"Look, will you tell me what's going on here?" Tausen said. "There's obviously been some sort of mistake, so..."

"I'm afraid not," Hentze said. "And before we go any further I have to tell you that I'm arresting you on suspicion of murder. Please hold up your arms so I can search you."

Tausen didn't move, as if dazed by bright light. "Murder? You've got to be joking. That's... You must be mad. Murder of who?"

"Boas Justesen," Hentze said flatly. "Also Astrid Dam and her daughter, Else, in 1974."

"No," Tausen said, shaking his head, although the colour was already leaving his face. "No."

Hentze stepped forward. "Please hold up your arms."

Finally, in dumbfounded resignation, Mikkjal Tausen raised his arms and Hentze patted him down, making sure he did a thorough job, although he doubted that Tausen was the sort to carry any kind of offensive weapon. He did not, but Hentze found and removed the phone from his pocket and also his wallet, handing them to Annika, who put them into an evidence bag.

When he'd finished the search, Hentze straightened up. "Thank you," he said. "Now, hands in front of you, please."

As Annika stepped forward with handcuffs Tausen took half a step back. "Is that necessary? What do you think I'm going to do?"

"It's regulations," Hentze said. "They can be in front to

make things easier for you, or behind your back if we think there's a need. It's up to you."

After a moment's hesitation Tausen reluctantly raised his hands to waist height and Annika put on the cuffs.

"Thank you," Hentze said. "Please sit down. I'll be back shortly."

Outside in the corridor Hentze glanced left and right, then moved towards Sigrun Ludvig who was standing with a worried expression, distractedly fiddling with a ring on her finger. A diamond ring; third finger, left hand, Hentze noted.

"What's happening?" Sigrun asked as soon as Hentze approached, and then a little more belligerently, "This is ridiculous, to think Mikkjal has somehow avoided paying for the cabin. He has money, you know that, so why would he—"

"I'm afraid it's not about the cabin," Hentze said, interrupting. "It's a more serious matter and now I need a truthful answer from you."

"About what?"

"Two days ago – Thursday – you told officer Mortensen that you were with Mikkjal during the evening and night of 25 September; the night that Boas Justesen died. Do you remember?"

"Yes. Yes, of course."

"Was that true? Were you really with Mikkjal that night?"

"What are you— Why are you asking? Why *wouldn't* it be true?"

"I don't know," Hentze said. "But I'm investigating a very serious incident and I have to tell you that anyone attempting to interfere with that by withholding or providing false information could be treated as an accomplice."

"An accomplice? An accomplice to what for God's sake?" Despite her attempt at a no-nonsense attitude, worry now showed in Sigrun Ludvig's eyes.

"To Boas Justesen's murder," Hentze said flatly. "So, please, just tell me the truth: were you or were you not with Mikkjal Tausen on the night Boas died?"

For a moment Sigrun's face lost all expression. She was still for several seconds, then finally and with seemingly bitter realisation she shook her head. "Not all of it, no."

"Okay," Hentze said, measured. "So for how long *were* you with him, and from when?"

"I— I was supposed to be going earlier – for dinner," Sigrun said, her voice dull now. "But about six o'clock Mikkjal called me and said he had a lot of business calls to make – to the States. He said it would take a few hours, so could we postpone dinner till the following day. I said— I said we could, or I could come later and… And so I did."

"How much later?" Hentze asked.

"I don't know. About eleven, I suppose."

"So, two days ago, did Mikkjal ask you to lie about when you arrived at his house?"

"No – no, not— He just said he thought the police were looking into Boas's death as if it was suspicious. He didn't believe it, he told me, but they kept asking questions and he said it was just like Boas to still cause him problems even though he was dead."

"So why didn't you tell us the truth about this," Hentze asked. "Did you suspect Mikkjal of something?"

"No! No, of course not. He wouldn't— I know he wouldn't do something like that."

"Then what was it?"

Sigrun shook her head, as if she already knew that the reason would be too complex for anyone else to understand. "It was because— Because I just thought… I thought it wasn't fair. This was my chance for the future: to have something more." She broke off and lowered her head quickly. "He— He just asked me to marry him," she said, her voice choked by the disintegration of hope. "We were going to go to the States."

She was crying, Hentze realised. "I'm sorry," he said for want of anything better.

Sigrun searched for a tissue then dabbed her eyes, still not looking at him. "What do I do now?" she asked. "Am I… What will you do?"

"For the moment, nothing," Hentze said. "When you return home you'll need to come to the police station on Yviri við Strond to give a statement, but for the time being you're free to go."

Sigrun seemed to find no consolation in this. "But what about Mikkjal?" she said. "What's going to happen to him?"

"In a few minutes we'll be taking him to the airport and then back to Tórshavn," Hentze said. "So you might want to wait here until we leave before collecting your bags."

Sigrun Ludvig turned away so Hentze left it at that. He went back to the purser's office and as he closed the door behind him Tausen shifted in his seat.

"What's happening? Where's Sigi? Is she under arrest, too?"

"No, she's not under arrest," Hentze told him. "But I'm afraid she'll have to make her own way from here."

For a moment Tausen seemed to assess that, then he said, "Okay, listen, I want to speak to a lawyer. If I'm under arrest, that's my right." His tone was businesslike now, as if he'd made up his mind.

"Yes, it is," Hentze agreed. "And as soon as we get back to Tórshavn I can arrange that. In the meantime—"

"No, not in the meantime: *now*," Tausen said. He rose from his seat and instinctively Annika stiffened. "We just *came* from Tórshavn. We have hotels booked – a car – and this is a mistake. I keep telling you that. So I want to see a lawyer right now. I want this whole thing sorted out so we can be on our way."

Hentze didn't waver in the face of the outburst. "I'm afraid that isn't possible," he said flatly. "Nothing will happen until we go back, so in all our interests I suggest we do that with the least possible fuss. Do you agree?"

For a couple of seconds it looked as if agreeing was very far from Mikkjal Tausen's mind, but then he drew a hard, demoralised breath and gave up the protest. "All right. If there's no other way."

"Good. Thank you," Hentze said. "In that case, we can go."

40

THE RAIN SLOWED THE SATURDAY TRAFFIC ON THE E45, heading south past Horsens and Vejle. That was all right, though; I wasn't in a hurry. Few people rush to admit a deception or that they've broken a trust.

In Snestrup I rang Thea's doorbell. There was no car on the drive and I guessed she'd be alone.

"Hi," she said when she opened the door. "Come in."

She had a faintly wary, questioning air now, leading me through to the kitchen where a newspaper was spread on the table, as if she'd been filling the time waiting for me. I took the seat she offered as she cleared the paper away.

"Did you stay in Odense last night?" she asked; an ice-breaker.

"No, in Aarhus. After we talked I went to Vesborggård House," I said. "Can I ask you to look at something?"

"What is it?"

"A photograph taken at the house in 1973. I know that's before you were there but some of the same people might still have been there in 1976, so if you can identify anyone – maybe Mickey, Lýdia's friend… Would that be okay?"

"Yes, let me look."

I took the laptop out of my bag and put it on the table. Thea came to stand beside me and look at the screen as it came to life. The photo Tove had sent was already open and I let Thea take in the full picture for a moment.

"Oh, yes, I know that," she said. "That was the front of the house. We weren't supposed to walk on the grass."

"What about the people?" I asked. I enlarged the view as far as it would go without losing resolution, dragging the picture so the people on the left of the group were central on the screen.

"Yes. Yes, I recognise a few of the faces," Thea said. "I think that's the doctor – Carl, I think was his name. Sander, maybe. Something like that…" She traced a finger along the screen. "And the nurses I remember: those two." She pointed to one of the white uniformed women. "That one was nice."

"Can you see Mickey?" I asked.

She looked again. "No, I don't think so. Can you move it along?"

I did that and she leaned in a little closer to the screen, looking at the right-hand end of the row where there was a shift away from the medical staff to others.

"And him. Yes, him I remember," Thea said, pointing to a blond man in his twenties. "His name was Oliver or Osvald, I think. He was handsome. All the girls thought so. He drove a sports car, too – like a film star. Oh, yes, that was his name: Oscar. I remember because we thought it was like the movie statue, you know?"

"Do you know what he did – what his job was?" I asked.

"No, I don't know. It must have been something on the administration side because I don't think he came to the rest of the house."

"Right. But Mickey's not here?"

She leaned in again, rescanned the line. "That *might* be him," she said, but not certain.

She pointed to a man second from the end of the row with long hair, and wearing a sleeveless pullover. He was half turned away from the camera, caught in the middle of saying something to his neighbour, it seemed.

"Mickey did have long hair, I remember," Thea said. "Yes, it could be him, but I can't say so for sure."

"On a scale of one to ten, how certain would you be?" I asked, thinking of Hentze's case against Tausen.

"I don't know. Perhaps five. It's hard to know. I'm sorry."

"No, it's okay. Thank you," I said.

I closed the laptop and Thea stood back a little way, then moved to the stove. She tested the weight of a kettle and lit a gas burner beneath it. "Would you like coffee?" she asked.

"No, thanks, I'm fine, but there is something else I should tell you," I said. "It's the real reason I came. The police have found human remains at Vesborggård House, near the Blue House by the lake. I think there's a good chance they'll be from the girl who went missing in 1976 – the one the police searched for while you were there. Her name was Inge-Lise Hoffmann. The police are still working on it, but I think they'll want to talk to you, too."

"Me?" She looked puzzled. "Why?"

I shifted a little. "There's something I didn't tell you

379

yesterday. I probably should have done but…" I let it trail off, then started again. "Before I came to Denmark my adoptive father – Peter – gave me a camera he found with Lýdia's things after she died. I had the film inside it developed and I'm pretty sure the photos are of you – of when you were raped."

Her lips tightened as she absorbed that. "Are you sure?" she asked.

I nodded. "Yeah, pretty sure – I'm sorry."

She shook her head, then looked away to process her thoughts.

"Who made them?" she asked then. "Do you know?"

"No, I'm sorry, I don't. But from what I saw there yesterday I think they were taken at the Blue House, and because of the body nearby I had to tell the police. The two crimes could be connected, so they'll probably want to ask you questions at some point. You don't have to speak to them, of course, but I thought you should know – that I should tell you."

"*Tak*. Thank you," she said, although I'd done nothing to deserve it: in fact, quite the opposite.

She seemed to look inward again for a few seconds and I waited to see if there would be anything else she'd want to say, but then the kettle came to the boil and she moved to switch off the gas.

"I ought to be going," I said. "Unless you want me to stay – to talk – for a bit…?"

"No, that's okay," she said. "I think it's enough, yes?"

I thought I'd done more than enough. "Yeah," I agreed flatly. I stood up.

At the door I paused before I went out. "I am really sorry," I said. "If there'd been another way…"

"No, I understand. It's okay. Really. You are a police officer after all."

"Yeah, well, sometimes…"

I didn't bother to finish the thought but she shook her head as if I had.

"You know, it's really okay to forgive people," she said. "Anyone. Even yourself."

When she said that a phrase came to mind, but I didn't say it; because it was glib; because it was too easy and I wasn't sure I'd have meant it. Instead I nodded. "Yeah. *Tak.*"

"Okay. Just remember." She gave me a thin smile, then turned and went back inside, closing the door.

As I reached the car my phone rang and for some reason I thought it would be Thea, but when I looked at the screen it was Tove. I didn't feel like talking to her again at a distance so I let the phone keep on ringing as I got into the car. I'd decided there was one last place I wanted to go now, then that was it. Forgive and forget.

Tove read the email several times before calling the number it gave. On the fifth ring a man answered.

"This is Tove Hald. You sent me an email."

A pause, then: "Yes, I did."

"Who are you, please? How did you get my email address?"

"I'm someone who can help you if you're still interested in Juhl Pharmaceuticals and Vesborggård House."

"Yes, you said that in the email," Tove said. "What is it you wanted to tell me?"

There was a moment of silence. "I worked for the company some time ago. I think I can answer your questions but it must remain confidential. If you'd like I can meet you, but it must be today."

Tove thought about that. "If you have information I would like to meet you," she said. "But if you don't want to say who you are I think it would be better if we met somewhere public."

"Of course. Wherever you would feel comfortable," the man said.

"Do you know Café Ismael on Klosterstaede?"

"No, but I can find it. Is an hour too soon?"

"No, an hour is good."

"Okay. I'll find you there," the man said. He rang off.

"I'm going out now," Tove said, a few minutes later. She stood in front of the basketball on the TV while she checked things into her bag.

"Okay." Kjeld leaned to one side to see the screen around her. "Want to borrow the car?"

"No, I'll cycle. But if Jan Reyná comes later will you tell him to wait and to call me? I'll be at the Café Ismael."

"Sure." Kjeld nodded. "Do you want me to tell him where you are so he can meet you?"

"No, I just *told* you," Tove said, making her usual frown of irritation when someone failed to keep up. She turned to the TV and pressed the mute button. "If Jan comes before I get back, tell him to wait and to call me. I'm meeting someone who says he has information I want about Juhl Pharmaceuticals, but he'll only speak privately, so if someone else arrives that won't be private, will it?"

"No, no, I get it," Kjeld said, unabashed. "Wait and call."

"Exactly. You *will* be here, won't you?" Tove said, a tad suspicious now.

"Sure. Where else would I be? At least till tonight, then I said I'd meet Vivi."

At the mention of Vivi's name Tove frowned again. "She has very annoying orgasms."

Kjeld chuckled. "You think so?"

"Yes," Tove said, decided and shouldering her bag.

"Oh. Sorry," Kjeld said. "But a come is a come, right?"

Tove shook her head. "That makes no sense. Okay, I'm going now. *Hi*."

"Yeh, see you later," Kjeld said. He was already reaching for the remote to unmute the TV.

41

AT KASTRUP THEY WAITED ON THE PLANE UNTIL THE OTHER passengers had disembarked before moving forward through the cabin. At the exit they paused while Annika reclaimed her pistol from the steel box it had been stored in for the flight. She reloaded the clip and put the gun back in its holster, then took up position again by Mikkjal Tausen's right side, following Hentze as they moved along the jetway.

With his coat draped on the handcuffs he still wore, Tausen said nothing. Apart from declining a drink on the fifty-minute flight from Aalborg he hadn't said anything at all since they'd left the ferry terminal in Hirtshals, but that suited Hentze. He'd sat next to Tausen during the flight and knew that there was nothing that *could* be said without inevitably being trivial and pointless, or – worse than that – significant and better kept for an interview room.

When they emerged from the gate Hentze paused and looked around. As he did so he spotted the middle-aged man in a police uniform shirt with three pips on his shoulders.

"Hjalti Hentze and Annika Mortensen?" the man asked, coming towards them.

"Yeh, that's us." Hentze showed his warrant card.

"Hans Bering," the man said. "Glad to meet you. You requested a holding cell, right? Catching Atlantic 570 to Vágar?"

"That's right," Hentze said. "Can you accommodate us?"

"Sure, yes, no problem," Bering said. "Follow me."

It had always been Hentze's suspicion that the consumer goods palace within Kastrup terminal was just a veneer of style, and so it turned out. Once through a key-coded door at the back of the main departure lounge, Hans Bering led them along a maze of utilitarian corridors where the cream paint was occasionally scuffed and scratched, and function rather than gloss was obviously the order of the day.

Eventually they came to another door, this one marked discreetly with the *Politi* logo. Inside there was a small office space and a further short corridor which led to two holding cells.

Hentze removed Mikkjal Tausen's handcuffs and then asked for his belt and his shoes before leading him to the first cell, where the door stood ajar.

"We'll arrange something to eat and drink shortly," he told Tausen. "In the meantime is there anything you need?"

Tausen looked disconsolately around the bare cell. "No. Thank you. How long will it be?"

"The flight's at seven forty-five this evening. Would you like something to read?"

"Maybe a newspaper."

"Okay, I'll see what I can do."

Hentze left the cell and closed the door, twisting the handle. Cell doors all worked the same way wherever you were.

In the office Hans Bering was showing Annika the basic

facilities, which consisted of no more than a coffee machine, a phone and a printed plan of the terminal building, laminated and stuck to the desk. High up in the corner of the room there was a small TV monitor for the two cells.

"There's a key card for the doors into the departures area in case one of you wants to go for a stroll," Bering said. "Please don't lose it. You can get through to our office upstairs by dialling zero and I'll have someone come down at 19:00 to escort you to the gate. The only other thing I need is for you both to sign in." He produced a log sheet in a ring binder and Annika signed first because she was closest.

"So, what's he been arrested for?" Bering asked Hentze with a nod towards the cells.

"Murder," Hentze said.

"Really?" Bering frowned, as if he might have underestimated the situation before. "Unusual for the Faroes, isn't it?"

"Unfortunately not as much as it was," Hentze said.

Once Bering had gone Hentze finally had a chance to change his tee shirt and socks for fresh ones from his case while Annika made them coffee. As she waited for the machine to grind a third cup for Tausen she glanced up at the cell monitor screen. "Hjalti…"

Hentze looked up from fastening his boots, then at the monitor. Mikkjal Tausen was on his knees in front of the toilet, throwing up in the bowl.

"Do you want me to see if he's okay?" Annika asked.

Tausen remained bowed for a moment, then slowly straightened up.

"Let's give him a couple of minutes," Hentze said, looking away. "I think the situation he's in has just hit him."

"You're still sure he did it?"

"From that?" Hentze said with a nod at the monitor. "Yeh, I'd say so." He took out his phone. "I'd better call Remi and tell him we're here."

All I knew about Christiania was what I'd read in the guidebook, which was basic and trite. The place where I'd entered the freetown was dominated by four- and five-storey industrial buildings, surrounded by shacks and cabins selling the paraphernalia for dope and its lifestyle. Against the backdrop of cobbled plazas and streets, graffiti and anti-establishment posters, a few tourists wandered around in the grey drizzle looking lost, or as if they'd expected more from the place: parades and protests, maybe, or radical rallies. Instead, though, the real Christianistas who walked briskly through or went past on bikes just got on with their lives. The place put me in mind of a theme park, run down and well past the end of the season; well past putting on any kind of a show. I walked on. None of this was why I was here.

"*Er du okay? Leder du efter nogen?*"

I recognised the tone of concern and slight puzzlement and realised I'd been looking at the house for some time. I wasn't sure how long.

The guy who'd asked the question was in his late twenties,

dressed neatly in dark colours with a leather bag over his shoulder and holding a metallic-blue bike. He was about four yards away, about to approach the house down its path.

"Sorry," I said and tried for a disarming smile. "Do you speak English?"

I saw enlightenment. "Sure, yes," he said across the distance between us. "Are you okay?"

I nodded, then took a couple of steps towards him. "I used to live here," I said, glancing across to the house.

"Yeh?" The puzzlement was back, as if he didn't quite believe it.

"A long time ago. I was a kid."

"Ah, okay. I understand." He looked at the house, too. It was yellow brick, with red tiles on the roof.

"Is it as you remember?"

"It's hard to say. That's what I was trying to work out."

"I would say the last few years is the biggest change," he said. "In the past it was several apartments – flats, right? But now it's only two. I live on the ground floor," he added by way of explanation.

"It looks like a nice place. How long have you lived here?"

"Three, no four years. But my partner has been here much longer. Maybe twelve years."

I could sense he was back at the point of disengaging again, so I pushed it. "Listen, I know it might sound a bit strange, but would it be okay if I looked inside? Just to see if it's as I remember."

After a brief hesitation, he seemed to decide I wasn't a threat. "Sure, why not?"

"*Tak*. That's very kind," I said. "My name's Jan, by the way."

"I'm Nicklas."

We shook hands and he led the way towards the house, pushing his bike as far as the door, then propping it against the wall without bothering to lock it. And now that he'd committed to my company for a while longer Nicklas seemed to relax a little. "When you lived here was it on the ground floor or upstairs?" he asked as he worked his key in the door.

"Upstairs, I think. Apartment 3."

"Yeh, that was upstairs," Nicklas said. "Anna or David might be there now. We can see. Come in." He held the door open for me.

It was a communal hall and when I saw the tiled floor and the curved, banistered stairs leading up to the first floor I thought there was the faintest of memories, but I couldn't be certain.

Nicklas went ahead up the stairs and I followed. By the time I reached the first-floor landing he was knocking on a polished, dark wooden door which looked slightly too grand for the place. There was no answer and after a moment Nicklas turned away looking disappointed.

"Nobody's home," he said, then assessed me briefly. "But I have a key – to water the plants and feed their cat when they are away. I don't think they would mind. Can you wait?"

"Yeah, of course, if you think it's okay."

He shrugged. "To come from England. It would be sad – a shame – not to see it. I won't be long."

He took the stairs again briskly, then I heard a key in the lock downstairs and a called greeting to someone inside. A couple of minutes later he was back, carrying a single key on

389

a piece of red string, presumably so it couldn't be mislaid. He opened the door and called out again as he went a few steps inside, but there was still no reply,

Inside it was airy and light and open plan. I suppose I'd expected something more in line with my idea of Christiania as a bohemian, alternative place, but while there was a slightly unconventional style going on, with painted wooden furniture and Indian cushions, there was also a sense that any avant-garde tendencies were being kept under control in line with the more modern Danish approach.

I looked round, still only a few feet in from the door, searching for features that wouldn't have been changed, but I didn't recognise or remember anything about it: not even a faint glimmering like I'd had in the hall.

My new friend Nicklas waited expectantly, and partly so he wouldn't think he'd gone to this trouble for nothing I took a couple of paces, looking round the L-shape of the sitting area and then to the kitchen past a pale wooden dining table with four chairs. Beyond that there was a corridor, presumably leading to the bedrooms and the bathroom.

"Do you remember?" Nicklas asked.

"It's very different," I said. "I think a lot's changed."

"Yeh, yeh, for sure," Nicklas said. "But if you rub under the surface a little, some of the old stuff is still there. We just make it more modern on top."

With the distraction of talking I'd moved along to the corridor a short way. "Do you think it'd be okay?" I asked, gesturing on.

Nicklas gave a theatrical shrug. "Sure, go for it," he said.

"What do you say, 'In for a penny'?"

The first room was a small study with a desk and computer, and next to that was the bathroom. It was larger than the previous room, but not by much and the position of a low-silled window and the door dictated that the layout was probably the same as it had been forty years ago. Nothing else was the same. The basin, toilet and shower were modern and the tiles on the floor were almost new.

This was where Lýdia had been – where she'd died – but there was no memory. Nothing. I couldn't picture it; or rather, I knew not to trust the image my mind tried to superimpose: white enamel, brass taps and water, black and white tiles. And there was red. What my mind's eye wanted to see – to remember – was coloured by that. But it was all an illusion. I didn't know this place and there was nothing to see.

After a moment I stepped backwards and closed the door tight.

On the way out I managed pleasantries, noncommittal and general, but with enough appreciation that Nicklas wouldn't think he'd wasted his time. He locked the apartment door behind us and seemed happy enough that I'd got what I wanted when I told him that it had brought a few memories back and that it was good to see it again.

By the front door we shook hands. "Thanks. I appreciate it," I said. "You've been very kind."

He motioned it away. "No problem," he said. "It was good to meet you."

The kindness of strangers.

Outside I didn't go back the way I had come because I knew what was there. Instead I walked in the opposite direction, until the houses and cottage gardens grew fewer, and eventually I turned off the road on to a damp, sandy footpath. It led into sparse woodland, climbing a bank, then emerging on the far side alongside a wide, flat expanse of water; too still to be a river and more like a lake. There were rushes along the shore and areas of gravel and sand, like small beaches. I stopped beside one of these, where a log had been placed for a seat overlooking the water, and because it was there I sat down to smoke.

I suppose I'd hoped that by going into the apartment there would be some kind of jolt, to jumpstart any recollection I might have buried away. Memory doesn't work that way, though. We see and remember what we choose to recall: maybe only what we believe will not hurt us, or what will allow us to live with ourselves. I knew that better than most.

So the memories hadn't come, either because they weren't there or because self-preservation was still stronger than any intellectual desire to know. But if the past really is another country, then our past selves are different, too. We're no longer the person we once were; either by choice or through attrition, the result is the same.

I knew at first hand what it was like to rebuild myself, to slough off the past and grow a new skin, and I knew how I'd felt when events had lifted that skin just a little and exposed the raw flesh underneath.

Leave it alone; don't pick at the scab. I'd come this far

and still didn't know why Lýdia had chosen to die. The mute suicide is never really explained, but how somebody deals with that isn't about the deceased, it's about themself. It always is, and my own way had been never to ask.

But now I had and now I knew – as much as I would ever know – and the only decision I had to make was whether I could simply accept that, for whatever reason, I hadn't been enough to keep Lýdia from taking her life: accept and move on. Forgive, as Thea had said. My mother; myself.

I dropped my cigarette butt in the grass and trod it out. If there had been a stone within reach I might have tossed it into the water, which was rippled and disturbed by the breeze: bright light catching grey facets of waves which disappeared a second later. On the far bank the windows of a couple of houses looked back at me from the cover of trees, as if waiting passively for a decision.

Enough.

I stood up.

Enough.

42

"MIKKJAL, WOULD YOU LIKE A COFFEE?" HENTZE ASKED FROM the doorway of the cell.

Tausen shook his head. He was sitting on a thin green mattress with his back to the wall, knees drawn up in front of him. He hadn't moved from this position since he'd thrown up in the toilet. Beside him a copy of *Weekendavisen* lay untouched, along with the packet of sandwiches Hentze had brought in an hour ago. The bottle of water was still three quarters full.

"Okay," Hentze said. "Let me know if you change your mind."

He took a step back and put a hand to the door, but as he did so Tausen looked up. "Wait. Please," he said.

"Yes?" Hentze asked.

For a second Tausen seemed to rethink his request, but then he rose stiffly to his feet. "I need to see a lawyer," he said. "Here, before we go back. Then I'll tell you… I'll give you information about Astrid and Else. I had nothing to do with their deaths but I know who did. I know what really happened, and other things, too. I can tell you the whole thing, but it has to be agreed now. My lawyer needs to speak to the Prosecutor's office."

"I can't speak for the Prosecutor," Hentze said. "But if you do have information I think it would be better to wait until we're back in the Faroes with a lawyer who can—"

"No. It has to be done now," Tausen said, cutting in. "Before people know. Otherwise... Otherwise things that would prove it could be changed or destroyed." He stiffened his shoulders. "Do you want to be responsible for that? For losing a case; for letting the *real* murderer escape?"

There was some authority in Tausen's speech now, as if he'd hit his stride, but Hentze had already drawn up the police officer's resolutely impassive aspect. "I think it would take too long to do what you ask before our flight leaves," he told Tausen. "But as soon as we're in Tórshavn I'll make sure there's a lawyer available. That's the best I can do."

Without waiting for a response he moved again to close the cell door, but now Tausen took an urgent step forward.

"Wait. Just a minute." He paused briefly. "Okay, listen. To prove I'm not... to prove that I mean this, let me ask you: do you know about a little girl being raped? It was some time between 1973 and 1974, I don't know when exactly, but she was taken from somewhere on Borðoy: Hvannasund, somewhere like that. It must be in your files. You can check."

Hentze studied the other man for a second, then took his hand off the door and slid it into his pocket. "What was this little girl's name?" he asked.

"I don't know," Tausen said, shaking his head. "But it was Boas who did it, I know that. He gave her a drink – a spiked drink – then he took her somewhere and he raped her."

"Did Boas admit this to you?" Hentze asked.

"No, it was—" Tausen broke off for a second, as if judging how much to give away. "It was someone else; someone worse. But that's as much as I'll say now. Nothing else. If you want to know the whole picture I must have a lawyer. I must have assurances, and it has to be now."

Hentze let the silence hang for a moment, then he gestured back at the mattress. "Okay, why don't you sit down again, Mikkjal? Let me see if I can verify what you say."

"And if you can, you'll bring a lawyer?"

"Let's see what I can find out first."

Hentze left the cell, closed the door, then turned to see Annika standing at the end of the corridor. Hentze didn't speak until they were both back in the office and the door to the corridor was closed behind them.

"I wondered what was keeping you," Annika said, half in apology for her eavesdropping.

Hentze waved it away. "How much did you hear?"

"That Boas Justesen raped Sunnvør Iversen. And that he drugged her to do it."

Hentze nodded. "Which matches what Gunnar Berthelsen told me about the state she was in."

"So you think Tausen's telling the truth?"

Hentze pursed his lips. "A small part of it, maybe – or maybe nothing at all. I don't think it matters. He's obviously hoping that if he volunteers information about other crimes – other people – he can make some sort of deal with the Prosecutor over Boas's murder."

Annika frowned. "But in that case, wouldn't he have to have something really significant to offer?"

"Well, if he's blaming Boas he can concoct any story he likes. Boas can't answer back now."

"Yes, I suppose so," Annika said, not entirely convinced. "But if he *was* going to make up a story why would he mention Sunnvør? I mean, as far as he knows we've never even heard of her, so why would he link what happened to her with Astrid or Else's deaths unless he does know more than he's said?"

Hentze drew a dissatisfied breath and rubbed his unshaven chin. "Yes, well, you might have a point there."

"So if he *wants* to talk, couldn't we get him a lawyer?"

"Sure, we *could*," Hentze said. "The only thing is, if we start down that road we don't know how long it might take, or even if it'll turn out to be anything more than a delaying tactic so we miss our flight."

His dissatisfaction hadn't abated – in fact it had got worse. He could ignore it, of course, but the obvious vehemence of Tausen's assertions hadn't been lost on him either and the nagging *what if* wouldn't be silenced.

"I think I'd better see what Remi thinks," Hentze said, taking out his phone.

"Hjalti, it's not up to suspects to dictate the terms under which they'll talk," Remi Syderbø said, speaking up over the noise of his car when Hentze reached him a few moments later. "You *know* that. Besides, if he starts talking to lawyers the next thing we know they could be challenging our right to bring him back here at all. That's probably what all this is about. Tausen's not stupid, is he? *And* he's got money, so he probably hopes he can get an expensive lawyer to hold things up while the arrest clock is running."

"Yeh, I've thought about that, of course," Hentze said. "And you could well be right. Even so, Tausen definitely knows more than he's said so far – especially about Múli. He's also indicating that there are other crimes, too."

"You think that's genuine?" Remi asked.

Not wanting to muddy the waters of the case – not at a distance – Hentze still hadn't told Remi about the human remains found at Vesborggård House and their possible connection to the man known as Mickey. He thought of doing so now – briefly – before dismissing it again.

"I think there could be something in it, yes," he said. "So if getting a lawyer in now makes the difference between getting him to open up now and refusing to comment once we get him back there…"

"Yeh, I follow," Remi said. "Hold on for a second, I need to park."

Hentze heard the engine note change in the background. He also suspected that Remi was using the delay to consider his stance.

Remi came back on the line. "Listen, I'm not standing where you are, so I can't properly judge what Tausen's saying. I'd still prefer it if he was questioned here, but if you can satisfy yourself that he's for real, then give him what he wants. And just remember that if he spins it out we'll have to go through the Danes if we need to extend his detention."

"I'll keep it in mind," Hentze said. "Thanks."

"And let me know what you get," Remi said, punctuated by the sound of his car door closing.

"Will do."

Hentze rang off, looked at his phone for a moment, then made a decision.

"I'm going to give Tausen the chance to stretch his legs," he told Annika. "Just as far as here. Okay?"

"Okay," Annika said. "Do you want me to do anything?"

"No, but if anyone comes in shoo them away."

He glanced round the room, a quick check of potential hazards, then went along the corridor and opened Tausen's cell.

Immediately he heard the locks turn Tausen stood up and faced Hentze expectantly.

"I've been able to verify some of what you said," Hentze told him. "A young girl *was* abducted and raped in April of 1974."

"Right. So—"

Hentze held up his hand. "But I'm afraid that changes nothing," he said. "We'll look into it, of course – and any other details you want to give us – but when I spoke to him the Prosecutor was adamant that there couldn't be any deals. You can't trade one crime off against information on another; that's not how things work."

Tausen looked crestfallen, but then stiffened, defiant. "Suit yourself then. You'll never know. Give it a day and there'll be nothing. I told you, he has money, resources; you'll never get to the truth."

Hentze nodded sombrely. "Well, then," he said. "I suppose you have the choice of spending your króna today or finding it's worthless tomorrow. The only thing I *can* say is that if you choose to tell me something and I think it requires immediate action then I'll take it directly to Vicekriminalkommissær Christine Lynge in Copenhagen. I'll tell her exactly where the information has come from and ask her to act on it. That's as much as I can do."

He considered Tausen for a second, then turned away. "I'll leave the door open for now. You can have five minutes' exercise in the corridor if you like."

Annika looked up when Hentze came back to the office. He shrugged in answer to her unspoken question and moved to the coffee maker, inserting a capsule and standing over the machine as it ground away. When the flow of liquid ceased he picked up the cup and turned in time to see the door to the corridor open tentatively. Mikkjal Tausen took half a step into the room, his water bottle held in one hand.

He glanced at Annika, then at Hentze.

"I'll make a statement," he said. "But I won't talk about Boas – about his death – without a lawyer. I'm saying – admitting – nothing about that, is that understood?"

"If you'd like to make a statement, what you say is entirely up to you," Hentze replied. "Do you want to sit down?"

Tausen moved to the table and drew out the chair facing away from the door.

"I want it recorded as well, the whole thing," he said. "I want it on the record that I've helped you with this."

"Of course. That's procedure."

Taking her cue, Annika took out her phone and set it to record. When Hentze sat down she placed it on the table between the two men, then stood by the wall out of Tausen's sight line.

"Are you ready?" Hentze asked.

"Yes," Tausen said.

"Okay. This is a recorded interview with Mikkjal Tausen taking place at Kastrup airport holding cells. The time is 16:13 hours and those present are Mikkjal Tausen, Officer Annika Mortensen and Acting Inspector Hjalti Hentze of Tórshavn station." He paused and looked at Mikkjal Tausen. "You wish to make a statement, is that correct?"

"Yes."

"Okay, go ahead."

Now that he had the floor Tausen seemed uncertain of the best place to start, but then he drew himself up squarely and said, "I'm making this statement in order to help the police with their investigation into the deaths at Múli on the Faroe Islands in 1974. The men responsible were Boas Justesen and Oscar Juhl. Oscar Juhl is also responsible for other crimes, including murder, and the rape of a girl at Vesborggård House near Skanderborg in 1976. I was a witness to some of those crimes."

As if he had got this far on a single thrust, like a swimmer pushing off from the side of the pool, Tausen paused, then picked up and drank from his bottle of water.

Sensing that Tausen might be searching for the best way forward again, Hentze said, "Can I ask a question?"

Tausen nodded.

"Who is this man, Oscar Juhl, and how did you know him?" Hentze asked.

"I worked with him at Vesborggård House," Tausen said. "It was a clinic, here in Denmark – a facility to rehabilitate young offenders. Oscar was in charge of research and development – the administrative side – but his family company, Juhl Pharmaceuticals, owned the clinic as well. I was part of the research team, assessing the effect of different drugs. We were—" He hesitated briefly. "We were friends. At least I thought so, until I found out what he'd done."

"And what was that exactly?" Hentze asked.

"I told you: he raped a girl, one of the patients at the clinic. I found her and when I saw what he'd done – what he was going to do – I knew I couldn't do nothing so I— I helped her. I got her away. But then, when Oscar found out, he admitted that he'd done it before. He told me about Múli – what he and Boas had done to a little girl there – and how they'd killed her mother as well and buried their bodies so no one would know." Tausen leaned forward, pressing his point. "You have to understand, he wasn't trying to hide it; he was *boasting* about it. He was proud of how clever they'd been. He admitted it all, I'll swear to that in court."

On the edge of his vision, Hentze saw Annika shift, just a little, but he kept his attention fully focused on Tausen, timing his next question neither too fast nor too slow. He straightened slightly, as if for the crux of the matter.

"When we spoke earlier, you said that if the person who'd committed these crimes found out that we were questioning you, he would destroy evidence of what he'd done. Is that right?"

"Yes." Tausen nodded. "He will. He's bound to. He'll

know what I can tell you, so he'll try to cover it up."

"And – to be clear – we're still talking about Oscar Juhl here?"

"Yes."

Hentze nodded. "So what sort of evidence is it you think he could destroy or cover up?"

"His history," Tausen said. "His— Whatever traces there are. After Vesborggård he was locked up – confined – by Ulrik, his father. Ulrik knew what Oscar was; he told me as much. He said Oscar would be – must be – locked up. He'd be treated, he said, to keep everyone safe."

There was no doubting the passion behind Tausen's words; it burned, Hentze thought, like a glimpse into hell. He let nothing show on his face, though. Instead, he took a sip of his coffee, then put the cup down with precision.

"What year was this, do you remember?" he asked.

"Of course. It was 1976."

"And why didn't you report these crimes at the time? If things were as you say why didn't you tell the police?"

But even as he said it he could see the shift in Mikkjal Tausen. "No, I'm not saying any more without seeing a lawyer. I agreed to tell you who to look for, who to go to, and that's what I've done. I want it on the record that I've told you what Oscar did, and that I'll tell you as much as I know, but I won't say any more now without a lawyer being here."

Hentze gave it a moment, then nodded. "In that case, this interview is concluded," he said. "The time is 16:19."

He drew Annika's phone towards him and stopped the recording.

403

"So what will you do now?" Tausen asked.

Hentze stood up. "Annika will take you back to the cell and I'll make some calls," he said, businesslike.

"To bring in a lawyer?"

"I'll check what you've said," Hentze said without committing himself. "Then I'll let you know what's decided."

Hentze was still standing and obviously thinking when Annika came back to the office from Tausen's cell.

"What do you think?" she asked. "You believe him?"

"All of that? No," Hentze said. He dropped his empty cup into the bin. "I think he's left out large bits of the truth, not least his own part in it all. There must have been more, but if he can distract us with a bigger, better story…"

He shook his head as if he was seeing the mess of Tausen's assertions spilled on the floor at his feet. "How long till the plane?"

"Just under four hours."

"All right," Hentze said, deciding. "Let's see if Hans Bering knows a lawyer who won't take all day to get here."

43

IN THE HOTEL I SHOWERED AND CHANGED OUT OF THE CLOTHES I'd worn for two days, then I stood by the window and watched the trains going in and out of the central station. Occasionally the pedestrians walking around the balustraded edge of the space caught my eye, but only briefly. The trains and the people had destinations; I didn't. I was stopped; brought to a halt. I just stood there and looked until my phone rang.

"*Hey*," Hentze said. "Can you talk?"

"*Hey*. Yeah. Did you find Mikkjal Tausen?"

"*Ja*, he's arrested. We're at Kastrup, for tonight's flight."

"Any trouble?" I asked.

"No, not so much."

"Okay, well, I was going to call you when you got home," I told him. "I thought you should know that I saw Thea Rask on my way back to Copenhagen. I showed her a photo of people at Vesborggård House in 1973 and she thought she recognised the man they called Mickey as a member of staff."

"Was she sure it was him?"

"About fifty-fifty."

"Okay, I see," Hentze said, sounding pensive. "Did she recognise anyone else?"

"A few people, yeah: nurses and doctors."

"What about someone named Oscar Juhl?" Hentze asked. "That was why I called you: to ask if Thea Rask had mentioned his name when you spoke before."

"Do you mean Oscar Juhl of Juhl Pharmaceuticals?"

"Yes. You know about him?"

"I know his family owned or ran Vesborggård House," I said. "And Thea recognised someone called Oscar who worked there. She didn't know his last name, but I suppose it would be logical if he was Oscar Juhl. Why – what's your interest in him?"

There was silence for a few seconds, then Hentze said, "Mikkjal Tausen has made a statement that Oscar Juhl was responsible for the rape of a girl at Vesborggård House in 1976. He also claims that Juhl was with Boas Justesen when Astrid and Else were killed at Múli."

"You believe him?"

"No, not everything he's said, but at the same time I don't think he could have made up some of these things from nothing at all, so I think he may be telling some part of the truth."

I thought that through for a few seconds. "Hjalti, listen," I said. "It may have some bearing or not, but when Tove Hald wanted information from Juhl Pharmaceuticals, one of the people she met with was Oscar Juhl. At the time I thought he was in the meeting because there'd been a lawsuit over treatments at Vesborggård House, but if it wasn't just that – if he was worried she might be looking for something else…"

"*Ja*. Yeh, I see." Hentze sounded troubled. "Do you have any other information on Oscar Juhl: his background, anything else?"

"Not much myself, but Tove probably has reams of it, knowing her. Do you want me to find out?"

"Yes, please. How quickly can you do it?"

"Now if you want. I'll call her and ask what she has. Let me put you on hold."

"Okay."

I did that, bringing up Tove's number under missed calls. After five seconds it went to voicemail. I rang off and went back to Hentze.

"Hjalti?"

"Yeh, I'm here."

"Tove's not answering but I missed a call from her earlier today, so she may be busy."

"Okay, in that case will you do me a favour and try her again later? Tausen says he will give more information about Oscar Juhl when he has a lawyer, but I need to decide whether what he says is credible enough to delay taking him back to the Faroes. There is only one flight tonight and by the morning my time to hold him will have run out. I don't know for sure that I can get an extension."

I could see the dilemma. "What's Remi think?" I asked.

"He says we should get on the plane."

"You didn't want your promotion anyway, did you?"

He laughed drily. "No, but keeping my old job would also be good."

"What time's your flight?"

"Seven forty-five."

I looked at my watch. "Okay, give me an hour. I'll try to talk to Tove and see what she knows about Oscar Juhl. If it's anything that could back up Tausen's accusations I'll let you know and you can decide how much you want to piss Remi off." As I said it I picked up my jacket from the bed and went to the door.

"You're sure that's okay?" Hentze asked.

"I'm sure. I'll call you back."

Twenty minutes later I tried Tove's number again as I climbed the stairs to her flat and got no response. I left a message this time then knocked on her door, half expecting she'd open it. Instead it was Kjeld in jeans and a tee shirt.

"Hi Kjeld," I said. "Is Tove here?"

"Hi. *Nej*, she went out. She said you might come, though. *Kom ind.*"

He held the door wide and I went through to the living room. The TV was on, showing sports, muted, and there was a late-afternoon beer on the coffee table.

"Tove said you should call her if she wasn't here," Kjeld said following me in to the room.

"I've been trying," I said. "It goes straight to voicemail so I think it's switched off."

Kjeld laughed and shook his head. "Tove's phone? *Nej*, never, not even at night. She has spare power packs, too. Maybe it's just a bad signal."

He dropped down heavily in an armchair and reached for his

beer while I tried Tove again. The result was the same, though.

"What time did she go out, do you know?"

"Around midday, I guess. She said she was going to see a guy about something she's researching for you. A drugs company, yeh?"

"Juhl Pharmaceuticals?"

"Yeh, I think so."

His attention went back to the TV and I looked at my watch. Midday was nearly five hours ago. "Where were they meeting, did she say?" I asked Kjeld.

"A place called Café Ismael. It's near the university."

"And it was definitely a man she was meeting?"

"Yeh, she said he had information and wanted to talk off the record, you know? That's what she said."

That could be as straightforward as it sounded, I supposed: Tove could have set her phone to divert so they weren't disturbed. But I also knew Tove well enough by now to know that if she'd left an instruction to call her that's what she wanted me to do. There'd be that irritated frown if I failed to comply; which meant she should be answering her phone, and she wasn't.

"Listen, could you do me a favour?" I asked, turning back to Kjeld. "Will you call the café and see if Tove's still there? It'll probably be easier if you do it rather than me."

"Sure, okay," he said, good-natured enough. "Let me find the number."

I stared out of the window while Kjeld talked on the phone. There was some back and forth, an explanation and then another couple of questions before Kjeld said my name.

I turned and he was still holding the phone.

"The guy at the café says Tove *was* there. I told him what she looks like and he remembers her because she was drunk: like, *really* drunk, yeh? Do you want to talk to him? His name's Robert. He speaks English."

"Yeh, thanks." I took the phone. In the background I could hear café sounds: crockery and voices. "Hi, Robert? Listen, I'm sorry to take up your time but I'm a bit worried because my friend's not answering her phone. Can you tell me when she left?"

"Maybe one o'clock or one thirty. We were busy so I'm not sure."

"Do you remember who she was with?"

"Yeh, he was an older guy, maybe sixty years or a little more. He has to help her stand up and carries her bag."

"Had she been drinking a lot?"

"*Nej*, I don't know," Robert said. "They weren't in my section so I don't know what they ordered."

There didn't seem to be any more I could get from this so I said, "Okay, thanks for your help. I appreciate it."

"No problem. I hope you can find her."

I rang off and handed the phone back to Kjeld who had obviously been following the conversation.

"You think Tove's in trouble?" he asked. "You know she doesn't drink, right? I've known her for three years and she's never even had a piss beer."

"Yeah, I know."

"So what do you think has happened?"

He was looking to me for some kind of insight or

explanation. There could be several, but now that my concern had risen a notch, the one that loomed largest wouldn't make him feel better. I was still resisting it, too, so instead of a direct answer I moved to Tove's MacBook, which was charging on the table in front of the window. When I opened it the screen came to life.

"Do you know if Tove has any location apps set up on her phone – anything to find it if it's lost?" I asked Kjeld.

"Yeh, maybe," he said. "She has hundreds of apps, but…" He paused for a second, then made up his mind. "If you think she's in trouble we should call the police."

"Yeh, maybe," I said. "Just give me a minute."

I pulled out a chair and sat down at the MacBook. There was no log-in password and because I knew my way around my own Mac it wasn't hard to locate Tove's internet browser and then her iCloud homepage. That did want a password but it had been saved as an anonymised string and when I tapped that I was in.

I chose not to dwell on what that might say about Tove's general safety awareness but instead clicked through various options in the Find My iPhone page, then waited as the software did its thing. It brought up a map screen which quickly narrowed itself down to Copenhagen, showing more detail until the grey dot on the screen was focused on the corner of Klosterstraede. Beside it there was the word "offline" and the time it had last been online, 13:37.

Behind me Kjeld came closer to look at the screen. I didn't bother to tell him what he could see for himself, but after a second I went back to the list of devices at the top of the page and chose "all".

Almost immediately the screen map pulled out to show a broader view of the city and I got two more dots on the screen, both green this time. One was named as "Toves iPad" and it only took me a moment to realise that it must be here in the flat, but the second was located about ten kilometres south, marked simply as "2nd iPod". The last updated time was a couple of minutes ago.

I zoomed in on the second location and changed the view to a hybrid of satellite and map. "Do you know where this is?" I asked Kjeld. The view now showed the red-tiled roof of a building, which stood out against the grey ones nearby. It was the last building on a short road at the edge of a neatly gridded enclave that ran up close to the shore of the sea.

"No, I don't know it," Kjeld said. "It's past the airport. I've never been there."

There was probably some clever way to transfer the map to my phone but I didn't know it and rather than waste time I took a photo of the screen instead. I zoomed in again on the name of the road – Strandvey – and took another, then I stood up.

"You're going there?" Kjeld said.

"Yeah, to make sure she's all right."

He drew himself up. "I think we should call the police now."

"Yeah, do that," I said. "Call them and tell them you're worried and explain why, but it could take some time so I'm still going to go." I found a pen and wrote quickly on a stray piece of paper. "This is my number and this one is for a police officer called Hentze. If you don't get anywhere with the Copenhagen police call him instead, okay?"

He frowned at the paper, then at me, caught by indecision. "Maybe I should come with you," he said.

For a second I was tempted to agree because he was a decent-sized guy, and because it might have been useful to have someone who spoke Danish. But if my worst fears weren't baseless, I wanted to cover my back.

"It'd be more use if you stayed here, talked to the police and kept an eye on that," I said, gesturing to the MacBook. "If the location changes call me."

And with that I started for the door.

44

FROM THE FLAT IT WASN'T A DIFFICULT ROUTE: ONE STRAIGHT road due south – Englandsvej – but until it broke free of the urban streets, car lots and industrial units alongside it I upset the well-mannered Danes by running several lights on amber and overtaking on cross-hatches and turn lanes. I was being pushed by my instinct, by the ideas I was putting together, and by an almost certain sense that too much time had already gone by; certainly too much to waste any more making phone calls.

Hentze would get it as soon as I told him, I didn't doubt that, but this wasn't his patch and even for him I knew it would take time to convince anyone else to take notice. A young woman goes out for a drink, has a good time and goes home with a man she's only just met. Has anyone said that something looked wrong? Was there coercion? No, not at all. So she'd switched off her phone; there was no law against that: she was over eighteen and entitled to do what she liked.

That was what I hoped I would find. I'd live with the embarrassment if that was the case, but what I didn't want to live with was the alternative version: that Mikkjal Tausen was telling at least some of the truth from his cell; that Thomas Friis had been right when he saw a link between Vesborggård House and his hibernating killer; and that Tove had unwittingly disturbed the one person who *could* satisfy her desire to know what had been done; because he'd been there; because he'd had full run of a place for vulnerable people and access to drugs to make them even more so. Then and now, with periods of inactivity between, Oscar Juhl was the one common thread. Oscar Juhl was the one man who knew enough to draw Tove in.

When the road broadened into a dual carriageway I sped up even more. There was farmland beside me and the traffic ran faster, thinning out once I'd passed the E20 and gone through the tunnel under the airport. Half a mile beyond that I braked hard for the turn on to a side road signed to Søvang. Although it was a narrower road it was dead straight and fast for two or three minutes until I braked again, entering a residential plot where the houses were yellow and white and bounded by neatly kept hedges.

I was looking for a turn, alongside but not part of the neatly gridded streets up ahead, and I almost missed it, set back as it was and screened by the house on the corner. There was a sign, though – Strandvej – and once I'd hauled the car round I was on a single-track lane with an open field on one side and a few high-angled houses widely spaced on the other.

I kept my speed down now, peering forward. It wasn't dark yet, but the half-light was greyed out by a soft drizzle which foreshortened how far I could see. Then, thirty yards short of the lane's end, I came to a field gateway and pulled in on the small margin of grass there. I switched off the engine and picked up my phone to look at the photo I'd taken of Tove's laptop screen. It wasn't great quality, but I knew where I was now and I matched it up to what I could see. A house just behind me and off to the right was the last one directly fronting the lane; the one before me – red roofed – was down a short private drive beyond the point where the lane's tarmac ran out.

I got out of the car and started towards the house, but then changed my mind after a couple of steps and went back to the car. Opening the boot I lifted the carpet over the spare wheel and searched for a moment until I found the tyre lever: a foot long with a socket head at one end and a flattened point at the other. I pulled it free of its clip; it was reassuringly solid in my jacket pocket as I set off briskly towards the house once again.

When I reached the entrance to the short drive I stopped to assess. On the neatly paved brickwork there was a new-looking silver-grey Audi. Rainwater stood in droplets on the waxed roof and on its glass, but the bricks beneath it were dry. Beyond that the house wasn't particularly grand, but I guessed from its location that it wouldn't have come cheap. The tall upstairs windows in the gable end were dark and the ones below them were obscured by closed vertical blinds, but as far as I could tell there was no light behind these either.

I moved up the drive watchfully, approaching the Audi from the passenger side. Inside it was tidy and clean: nothing to show ownership other than a chamois cloth by the gear stick and a pair of sunglasses on top of the dash; nothing else except part of a canvas shoulder bag, half visible as if it had been pushed back some way under the passenger seat. I wasn't certain I recognised it, but I thought so, enough to try the door handle and find it was locked.

Some things just don't sit right, don't *feel* right. The dark house, the car on the drive and the bag. They could all be explained innocently enough, but added to what else I knew, my instinct said it was wrong and I didn't need more than that to move on along the rest of the drive, taking a good look at the house, weighing it up.

Beside the front door there was a mailbox, but there was no name on it. I tried the lid and found it was locked.

Decide.

I pressed the doorbell and held it: a last chance for normality to reassert itself if it could. I heard the bell ringing inside – hollow and echoing – and when I let up the silence after it was unbroken. All the same I waited a few seconds, but by then I knew no one was coming so I tried the handle. It turned, but the door didn't give and it was too solidly built to yield easily to force. I left it and made my way around the house to the right, following a paved path. I passed two more windows, still showing no signs of life behind the closed blinds and double glazing. I didn't expect any now, though. Instead I was looking for a way in.

The path ended at a faux-rustic stable door in the wall of a single-storey extension, which blocked the way to any further prowling. I could have retraced my steps and gone the other way, but I was well hidden from view by the tall hedge surrounding the grounds so I moved to the door and cupped my hand against the small window in its upper half.

Unlike all the other windows I'd passed, the glass in the door was only a single thickness, but beyond it I couldn't see very much in the greyness: some kind of utility space, that was all. I stood back after a moment, then tried the handle. Like the front door, it was locked, and I paused, assessing how far I was prepared to go.

More than ever, the place seemed deserted but I couldn't be sure. Just because Tove's bag was in a car on the drive it didn't mean she was inside, I told myself. But she *could* be, and when I weighed that against the idea – more of a certainty now – that the man she'd gone to meet was Oscar Juhl, I didn't feel like debating with myself any more.

Instead I took the tyre lever out of my jacket pocket then shrugged off the jacket itself, folding it roughly and holding it against the glass in the door. I struck it twice and hard with the heavy end of the tyre lever, and felt the window give with a muffled crack, followed by the sound of the glass hitting a tiled floor inside.

I put the jacket aside, then looked at the jagged triangular hole in the glass. It was large enough – just – so I pulled down my sleeve for protection and inserted my hand, reaching awkwardly inside until I found the thumbturn and was able to twist it. The door gave a little as the dead bolt retracted and I pulled my arm out carefully, then opened the door further and listened.

There was nothing to hear – stillness and silence – but I was committed now so I opened the door enough to step through. I couldn't avoid crunching glass on the tile floor, but once I'd stepped beyond it I stopped to look round.

Even with the open door there wasn't much light. The room was some sort of storage area: slatted wooden shelves on the walls, most of them empty; a freezer and some sealed plastic storage boxes stacked up in threes. Beyond was a short corridor going off to the right, which ended in darkness. It had to lead somewhere – probably into the rest of the house – so I went a couple of paces, letting my eyes adjust to the deeper darkness until I could just make out the shape of a door at the end. In the greyness there was nothing else: no stray bar of light from beneath it and absolutely no sound, only dead air.

I went forward again, another couple of steps, moving with care. When I got to the door I paused, listening hard for sounds from the other side and picking up a faint, regular bleep, as if something inside was on standby.

I felt for the door handle and turned it slowly; it opened towards me, bringing with it warm, humid air and a watery, mineral smell. Beyond the threshold there was a very faint background glow of light; the sort you get from a digital display of some kind. It gave me the impression that the room was quite large, something confirmed by the sound of the electronic bleep, which echoed faintly.

After a second of listening I took a single step forward but couldn't see or hear anything more so I reached for my phone. The screen light was bright for a moment as I looked for the torch symbol and then I thought I heard the faint sound of something moving. But even as I started to register that my left shin exploded in pain. I saw dazzlingly bright lights in my head and knew I'd shouted out even before I fell like a bag of rocks to the floor.

The intense, stunning pain blanked out everything else for a time. I don't know how long. It was an involuntary thing, like being submerged by a wave you didn't see coming. Instinctively I'd curled up on the hard floor, grasping my incandescent leg at the knee, as if a tourniquet pressure could stem the screaming nerve impulses. It didn't, not really, but after a few seconds the jagged high notes couldn't rise any further and then the pain fell back to a loud, insistent shout and finally I was able to open my eyes, only to be dazzled again by a dozen lights drilling down from the ceiling.

A voice was speaking – a question – but it took me a moment to focus. It was a man's voice, but I couldn't see him until I raised my head a little and looked to the side.

I knew how old he must be, but he was fit and lean enough for somebody younger, although at that moment he wasn't as poised or relaxed as he was in the photo Tove had shown me on the Juhl company website. He was just as well groomed, though, in tan trousers and a pressed denim-blue shirt. A pair of long bolt cutters hung incongruously in his left hand and I knew without question that they were what had smashed into my shin. The Glock pistol he held in his right hand was only for show. He could see I was no kind of threat.

Because I hadn't responded to what he'd been saying he spoke again, more aggressively now. "*Hvem er du? Hvad vil du her?*"

I shook my head, still trying to regain full focus. "English."

When he heard that he made a contemptuous sound. "I

asked who you are, but now I can guess. Your name is Jan Reyná, yes?"

I nodded, but at the same time I'd shifted my weight and the pain that washed up my left side took me out of things again for a few seconds. When it was over I looked back at him, seeing him straighten up from putting the bolt cutters down on the floor.

"Do you know who I am?" he asked then.

I shifted again, more cautious this time. "Oscar Juhl."

"Good, yes, you're right," he said with a small, polite nod of acknowledgement. "So, now that we know each other, do you think you can stand up?"

"Where's Tove?" I said.

"She's here," he said matter-of-factly. "If you can get up you can see her."

I gritted my teeth against the jagged pain as I levered myself up into a sitting position. Beyond that I wasn't sure how much further I could get. Juhl watched me dispassionately. "I think you need help," he said, and for a moment I thought he might volunteer it, but then he cast around and strode briskly to the back corner of the room.

He was searching for something but I didn't watch what he was doing. Instead I tried to figure out what sort of place I was in. It seemed like some kind of spa room, about the size of a double garage, with a tiled floor and pine-clad walls, except for the longest one, which was faced with layers of black slate. There was a massage table to my right and various fitness machines by the slate wall, but around and between them the place was untidy, scattered haphazardly with various tools, rolls of black plastic, and discarded pieces of metal and wood. It looked as if alterations were being made, or that the room's original function had been subverted to another purpose.

My brief appraisal was interrupted by Juhl coming back. He brought a length of aluminium pole about four feet long – perhaps the handle for a mop or a brush – and held it out towards me.

"You can use this to help you. Come now."

There was a peremptory note, as if I'd wasted enough time, but I took the pole anyway and as soon as I did he stepped away, levelling the Glock in my general direction again.

I'd fallen close to the wall by the door and by using the pole to lever myself up I was finally able to stand, panting and sweating with the exertion, balanced on my right foot. The wall took most of my weight.

"Good," Juhl said. Now I was upright he seemed a little more satisfied that he was getting what he wanted. "Go over there."

Then, on the floor where I'd dropped it, my phone rang. Juhl looked at it sharply, took a quick step towards it and picked it up. He looked at the screen, then stopped the ringing and put the phone in his back pocket.

"Okay, move now," he said, more businesslike; as if there'd already been too many distractions from our true purpose.

"Hold on, just listen," I said, trying to pitch my tone somewhere neutral; somewhere reasonable and controlled despite all factors to the contrary. And then I saw Tove.

Six feet from where I was standing there was a raised area: a couple of tiled steps leading up to the lip of a round spa pool. It was large enough to hold six if you were friendly, but now only Tove.

She was naked as far as I could tell, but below the flat of her chest the water was redly opaque. Her head was cushioned by a towel on the edge of the pool – eyes closed, skin the colour of paper. She was half sitting, half floating, supported by two rough lengths of wood, which had been lashed to the pool's stainless steel steps with tangled blue rope. Her arms were draped over these battens, held in place by lengths of white bandage, and from the crook of her left arm a thin plastic tube trailed up to an IV bag of clear liquid tied to the handrail of the steps. The only sign that she was alive was the bleep of a heart monitor balanced on a plastic box, connected by a wire to a pad on her chest.

The crude, makeshift quality of the whole thing would have been – should have been – weirdly pathetic, but somehow its improvised nature only served to make it all the more malign. I fought to make sense of it as I pulled my gaze back to Juhl. He was watching me closely – candidly – as if he was hungry for any trace of reaction.

"Get her out," I said; not demanding or pleading, just flat. "You don't have to do this."

He took no notice, as if he was deaf. "Go to the chair," he told me, gesturing to a plastic lawn chair beside the pool. "I won't ask you again."

I held his gaze for a moment, then grasping the top of the pole with both hands I took a small, experimental step forward, no more than a foot. It was as much as I could manage without putting weight on my left leg but even so the movement was enough to start hot fires in its nerves all over again and I clenched my teeth very hard.

Juhl watched this dispassionately until I repeated the process. Then he rounded the pool briskly from the other side and slid the chair to within a few inches of me, as if he'd decided this was the most expedient way to hasten the process.

"Sit now," he said, gesturing brusquely.

There was no point in arguing. I lowered myself awkwardly on to the chair; just on the edge, though. I heaved several short breaths as my leg subsided again into duller, throbbing pain.

"Put the stick on the ground, please," Juhl directed, and I let it fall with a clatter.

"Listen, just get her out," I said again. "You can stop this."

Now I was seated Juhl had relaxed just a little, but what I thought about anything was of exactly no interest to him.

"Did you tell anyone you were coming here?" he asked.

"Listen—"

"Did you *tell* anyone?" His voice hardened.

I shook my head. "No. I came to find Tove and—"

"How did you know where to come?"

"I was at her flat and I was worried about her, so I tried tracing her phone to—"

"Don't lie," he said sharply, cutting me off. "Her phone isn't here."

"I'm not lying," I said. "Her phone was switched off but I traced her iPod. I think it's in her bag, outside in the car."

That threw him, but only a little. "*Skødesløs*," he said to himself.

It was a small opening, but I took it. "Listen, it's still not too late to do something about this," I said. I glanced back at Tove. "If you help her now, or let me help her—"

"Then we'll forget anything happened?" He laid the sarcasm on thickly. "Is that part of the training for police officers in England: to be reassuring, to make friends and gain trust?"

He must have seen the question cross my face because he made a sardonic noise, then gestured to Tove. "She was very talkative – very open – while we were still at the café. In the first stages it's one of the effects of the drug I gave her. So, now tell me the truth: who else knows you are here?"

"No one. I came on my own."

"I know that. I saw you outside. But who else did you *tell*?"

"No one," I repeated, letting exasperation sound in my voice now.

In response Juhl shifted and took a couple of steps to a small steel trolley, where he picked up a syringe.

"Do I have to be boring and make threats?" he asked me, gesturing towards Tove. "It's obvious what I can do, so tell me the truth: who else knows you came here?"

I drew a hard breath but knew I had to give something. "Her flatmate, Kjeld," I said bleakly. "He was there when I looked at Tove's computer, but he was half stoned so I just told him I'd come and make sure she was all right."

"What about your police colleagues? If you thought you needed to come here, did you tell them as well?"

"No! For Christ's sake," I said, more angrily now. "What do you think I'd have said? 'She's not answering her phone so

425

I think she's in trouble'? Jesus." I gave him a contemptuous look. "Besides, if you *were* here I wanted to find you myself."

It was a bluff, and I thought he might call it, but then his eyes narrowed and he pursed his lips with a nod, as if something finally made sense.

"So you remember what happened. Is that it?" he asked.

"Some of it, yeah," I said flatly, deliberately vague to cover the lie. "Not everything. You were there, though. I remember that."

"Ah, okay," he said, and I thought I heard a note of satisfaction as well. He put the syringe back on the trolley, then looked me over again, gesturing to my leg. "You know that is certainly broken," he said conversationally. "Would you like me to give you something for the pain?"

I couldn't help glancing down to where the blue of my jeans was turning a rich latigo red as blood seeped through. "I don't think so," I said, looking away.

Juhl gave a sardonic laugh then glanced at his watch. "So tell me *what* you remember," he said, still conversational. "I sometimes wondered about that. I thought I'd given you the right amount of sedation for your size, but after a while there you were, in the doorway of the bathroom. Do you remember?"

I knew what he was talking about; it couldn't be anything else.

"The bathroom, yes," I said. "Just snapshots."

Juhl nodded. "You looked very cute," he said, almost indulgent. "Rubbing your eyes and talking to your mama as she lay in the bath. I don't think you looked at me once, even when I took you back to your room afterwards."

There was no memory, but that didn't matter. If I needed a picture I only needed to look towards Tove, which I did now.

"Does she remind you?" Juhl asked, sounding genuinely curious. Then, almost apologetic, he gestured to our surroundings. "Of course, it's not the same. Not at all. Very hurried. But, nevertheless, I think there is some… Some kind of symmetry now."

"Symmetry?" I tried to keep any scorn out of my voice but it was hard.

"Yes, yes, of course," he said, as if I'd provided my own proof. "You were there then and you're here now."

He came a little closer and I could see he was taken by the thoughts in his head. It showed in a brightness behind his eyes: the spark of madness.

"And with Lýdia it was the first time I saw the real beauty of that moment: *the* moment, you know? Before that, I will tell you the truth, there had always been a sexual element. But Lýdia was…" Briefly he sought the air for a word. "*Graceful*. Yes. Yes, I would say that. And it was then that I realised I wasn't even aroused in my body; only in my mind; in my *soul*. When you see that moment – the one that you have created – you see the *truth* of the person you are; the truth inside." As he said it he touched his hand lightly to his chest, as naturally as if he'd genuflected on entering a church. "There's nothing more… *pure*. Each time I've seen it I've known that is true."

He looked me over intently now, studying my face to see if I'd understood the significance of this epiphany. He was hungry for that.

"How many times?" I said. It was all I could manage

to drag from the tumbling fog of my thoughts: that and the pressing knowledge that I had to keep him distracted from Tove, and from any suspicion that time might be short. But the disappointment showed in his eyes, like a shutter coming down.

"For the record?" he asked, not hiding his scorn. I was too blind to see. Then he looked again at his watch. "I don't think we'll wait any longer," he said. "Just to be safe."

He crossed to an aluminium flight case on the tiled floor, then squatted and put the pistol aside while he took out a new syringe and a small bottle of liquid from the foam padding.

"Oscar, listen," I said, aware how false it sounded to use his first name. "I meant what I said before. You don't have to take this any further, okay? If you're going to leave, do it now. Leave her alone. I can't stop you. Just go."

He didn't look away or bother to reply as he inserted the needle into the bottle and drew down the clear liquid. I was too stupid to bother with any more, and as he filled the syringe I made the only decision I could.

I pressed my hands down on the arms of the chair, then stood up carefully, balancing my weight on my good leg, trying to ignore the angry protest of the other as the bones shifted again. I was dizzy and my face felt waxen and clammy, but once I was upright I remained standing.

The movement had taken Juhl's attention away from what he was doing. "Sit down," he snapped.

"I won't watch her die," I told him, and before he could reply I forced myself to take a step towards the door. I felt bone grate against splintered bone and my head swam.

"Do you want to die also?" Juhl's voice rose at being defied.

He left the syringe and reached for the pistol instead as he straightened up. "If you force me to do it I *will* shoot you now."

"Fuck you," I said, and with all the determination I could muster I dragged my useless leg forward again, ready to take another step for the door.

My whole body was tensed for the shot, but it didn't come. Instead I heard Juhl stride towards me and I knew then what he'd do. He didn't want me dead – not yet anyway – but it would be easy to barge an off-balance man to the ground, so as he raised a hand to push me I shifted my weight and threw myself sideways and towards him in a desperate lunge.

It was the only move I could make and as we thudded together I grabbed for his arms, hoping to pin them and drag or wrestle him down. A split second later the pistol went off, deafening in the small, hard space; burning the side of my ribs. But with the shock of the noise I felt Juhl instinctively pull back and when I realised I had my good leg beneath me again I forced the advantage, punching his body and at the same time pushing against him as hard as I could.

He clawed at the back of my head, but I hit him again and was rewarded by the sensation of toppling as he lost his balance and was propelled backwards beneath me.

He broke my fall with a thud when he hit the floor. The gun clattered on the tiles and I heard the dull, expelled sound of air from his lungs. His struggling stopped and if he was winded or stunned I knew I had a momentary opening, so I pushed myself up to a half-kneeling position over his torso, ready to pin him down if I could.

There was no need, though, because there wouldn't be

any more fight. His head lolled to one side. He was either unconscious or dead and I didn't care which. I just knelt there, heaving breath until I heard the heart monitor bleep and came to my senses. Tove.

I went backwards, crawling on all fours, and heaved Juhl's dead weight roughly on to his side and then further, so he slumped on his face. When I did that he moaned and made a half-conscious movement, but I ignored it and pulled my phone from his back pocket. The screen was cracked from corner to corner but it still came to life and I swiped it quickly, seeking out Hentze's number, then pressing it hard.

It only rang once and then his voice was urgent and troubled. "Jan, where are you? I had a call from—"

"I need an ambulance now," I said, cutting him off. "I'm in Brodby..." I struggled to recall the address. "Strandvey, the last house."

"*Ja*, I have the address. I'm coming there now. Are you hurt?"

"Yes, no, it's not me. It's Tove. Get an ambulance, Hjalti. I need—"

There was a split second between the sensation of impact, the blazing pain and the yell I couldn't stop when Juhl's foot raked down my broken leg. And then for several seconds I lost all sense of anything beyond the surge of blackness that washed up through my head in thick, Indian ink waves.

When they finally started to ebb I was still for a moment, then jolted back to alertness by a movement beside me. I pulled my head round and saw Juhl hunched over, struggling to stand. He swayed dizzily, but then he seemed to shake his head clear. I saw him cast round and when his eyes fixed on something just beyond my left shoulder I knew what he'd seen.

He took a staggering lurch forward, attempting to get past me and the most I could do was throw myself on to my side, scrabbling for and then grabbing the gun on the floor. I felt Juhl's foot kick my thigh as I rolled onto my back. He was standing over me, stooped, and at that moment I fired the pistol, braced for its recoil, then fired again.

In the small space the noise was deafeningly, stunningly painful and both rounds struck his belly. He was so close I couldn't have missed, and I saw his mouth and eyes gape at the impact and shock before his legs started to buckle and he crashed down to his knees.

And then he just knelt there, not looking at me. He'd clasped his hands to his belly, and that's what he stared at for two or three seconds before light seemed to dawn.

"*Hvad har du gjort?*" he asked, looking up.

His expression seemed hurt, as if I'd broken some trust, and when I saw that I felt a water-cold upwelling of hatred and disgust rise in my chest. I shifted the aim of the pistol, but not very much, and then I fired again.

45

"JESUS CHRIST."

Despite himself, Hentze was stopped short. He'd stepped around the body on the floor with hardly more than a look. The man was so obviously dead that he warranted no further attention, but what stopped Hentze now was the almost motionless tableau of Jan Reyná cradling the naked young woman in a spa pool of bloody water. Against the dirty red of the liquid her skin was a marbled, blued white, and Reyná himself looked almost as pale, almost as deathly.

"Get her out," Reyná said, his voice defeated and hoarse, as if any hope had been drained out of him into the water and all that was left were the hollow reeds of the words.

"*Ja*, it's okay. Hold on," Hentze said, galvanised again.

He was still holding Annika's pistol, he realised, and immediately put it away, turning to Boel and Ipsen, the two PBs from the airport security unit.

"Go and bring the paramedics in as soon as they arrive," Hentze ordered as he quickly stripped off his coat, and to Boel: "Come on, man, help me."

Stepping up to the poolside Hentze experienced a split

second of unbidden, instinctive revulsion as he sat down and swung his legs into the opaque water, not knowing what was beneath. He allowed himself no hesitation, though, and he dropped down into the waist-deep water and waded two steps to where Jan Reyná was standing. The man still hadn't moved and Hentze realised now that he was frozen in shock.

"Jan? Jan, it's okay, I'll take her," he said.

Hentze put an arm under the girl's shoulders. She weighed almost nothing and might even have floated unaided, Hentze thought, but even so Reyná still held tight to her wrist.

"Jan, you need to let go," Hentze said, more forcefully now, putting a hand on to Reyná's. "I have her."

Dully, Reyná seemed to drag himself back to some slight awareness. "Yeah. Take her." He loosened his grip on her arm, revealing a narrow plastic tube, which emerged from a surgically straight slit in her wrist. Now it was released from compression, Hentze saw a slow globule of blood squeeze its way out of the tube.

Quickly Hentze covered the tube with his own hand and reapplied pressure, then he glanced up to locate Boel on the poolside, wading forward and taking Tove with him to the edge.

"Take her under the shoulders and lift," he instructed Boel. "I'll raise her legs. Then as soon as she's out we need—" He broke off as two paramedics arrived, each carrying medical packs. "Here," he called urgently, seeing the first paramedic pause beside the body on the floor. "He's dead. This is where we need help."

It all went more quickly then. Between them Hentze, Boel

and the paramedics raised Tove Hald easily out of the pool and on to the tiles at its edge. The paramedics immediately started a calm, rapid assessment and with his responsibility for the girl lifted, Hentze turned back to Jan Reyná, who still hadn't moved, although his bleak gaze was directed towards the activity on the side of the pool around Tove.

Hentze waded back to him two cloying steps. "Jan? It's okay, they've got her now. Are you hurt?"

After a second Reyná seemed to refocus and nodded. "My leg. It's broken."

"Okay, then," Hentze said, adopting the calm, practical tone he used for victims. "Here, lean on me, yes?" He positioned himself alongside Reyná, putting a supporting arm round his back. "Come now. I think we both need to be out of this, eh?"

Christine Lynge arrived fifteen minutes after the second ambulance had left carrying Reyná. It was fully dark now and Hentze was sitting damply on the back seat of a patrol car, speaking to Annika on his phone, but when he saw Christine approach he ended the call and stood up to meet her.

"So you decided to stay here and ruin my Saturday night," Christine said, but there was next to no humour in the remark.

"It wasn't what I had planned," Hentze said. "Do you want to look?" He gestured towards the house.

"How many people have been through?" Christine asked.

"Me, two *politibetjente* and two ambulance crews – one

for the victim, one for Jan Reyná."

"Bloody hell," Christine said. "Well, we're not going to do any more damage after that, I suppose. All the same…"

She handed Hentze a pair of plastic overshoes and they moved down the side of the house to the door, which was propped open. "Have you searched the rest of the place?" Christine asked as they pulled on the overshoes.

"Not myself, no." Hentze gestured vaguely to his soaked lower half. "I thought it was better not to. One of the *politibetjente* took a look, though. He says it's more or less empty; doesn't look as if anyone was living here."

"Okay, well, Technical can go over it properly later then."

They entered the house and went along the short corridor to the spa room at the end. Lynge paused there for a moment then stepped inside, watching where she put her feet.

Oscar Juhl's body hadn't been moved. It lay on the tiled floor in an irregular, congealing puddle of blood. There were two gunshot wounds in his lower abdomen, but clearly it was the third which had killed him, the bullet entering his face just below his left eye.

Christine Lynge assessed all this for a moment, then glanced at Hentze. "Jan Reyná did this?"

Hentze nodded. "So he told me: in self-defence."

Lynge gave the body one further glance, then looked away. "How badly was he injured himself?"

"A broken leg – a compound fracture – and a possible gunshot wound to his ribs, but it's more of a graze. He's also in shock."

"And there was only one weapon?"

"Yeh, a Glock pistol. I photographed it where it was, then moved it for safety."

Christine turned to look at the pool. The water was a shade of mud red now and the tiles round its edge were streaked and stained the same colour where the water had dried. "So what was the situation when you got here?" she asked.

"Jan Reyná was in the water with the young woman, Tove Hald," Hentze said. "He was holding her up and keeping pressure on a wound in her arm. Oscar Juhl had put a tube into a vein in her arm so it allowed the blood to flow into the water. Her heart stopped just after we got her out of the water but the paramedics managed to revive her. Even so, she has critical blood loss, so…" He let the rest speak for itself.

Christine nodded. "Do we have any idea how long she was in there?"

"Not yet, no. I would say for some time, though."

"Right."

Christine was still assessing the untidy mess of clinical equipment, DIY materials and the medical packaging left by the paramedics, but then she seemed to have looked at it enough and turned away.

"So what else did Jan Reyná tell you?"

"Not very much. As far as I can tell he broke into the house because he thought Tove was in danger and when he came into this room Oscar Juhl attacked him and broke his leg. After that…" Hentze shrugged. "Obviously there was a fight – a struggle – and Juhl was shot."

"Three times," Lynge said flatly, and then her phone rang. She answered it, listened, then said, "Okay," and rang off. "Technical are here," she told Hentze and cast a final look round the room. "What a fucking mess."

Hentze opened the cell door without knocking to signal his presence. Inside, two chairs had been brought in for Tausen and the lawyer, a smartly dressed man in his forties named Timmermann. There was no table so Timmermann was making notes on a legal pad, which he was resting on an attaché case across his knees.

"Excuse me, this is a private consultation," Timmermann said. "Who are you, please?"

"Vicekriminalkommissær Hentze, Tórshavn CID," Hentze said, momentarily searching for his warrant card before deciding the hell with it.

"Okay, well, we're in the process of writing a statement so you'll have to wait for a while," Timmermann said. "We've barely got started."

"Good," Hentze said flatly. "In that case you won't have to cross out so many things when you start again."

"Again?" Timmermann frowned up at Hentze, then glanced to the open doorway as Annika arrived and stood on the threshold. "What do you mean?"

Hentze ignored the lawyer's question and looked at Tausen instead. "You might want to know that Oscar Juhl has been found," he told him. "Because of that development you'll be kept here until the morning and then we'll make a decision about whether we take you back to the Faroes or hold you in Denmark while we assess additional charges relating to Oscar Juhl's crimes."

"Additional charges? What do you mean?" Tausen said, looking shaken. "How can you think...? For God's sake, I haven't seen him since 1976, so whatever he's done, it's nothing to do with me, is it?"

From the doorway Annika could see Hentze stiffen, and when he spoke again his words were more tightly angry than she'd heard him utter before.

"Nothing to do with you? Is that what you said?" Hentze asked coldly. "Well, if that's what you think perhaps you should know that before he was stopped, Oscar Juhl had drugged a young woman into unconsciousness, then he'd tied her to the railings of a spa pool and opened a vein in her arm so he could watch her bleed slowly to death."

"Now wait just a moment," Timmermann said, starting to rise. "This is—"

"Sit down and be quiet or I'll have you removed," Hentze snapped at him with barely a glance. He took a step closer to Tausen, and pulled up his sweater to reveal the stains on the white tee shirt beneath. "Can you see this?" he demanded. "This is that young woman's blood. From me it will wash off, but not from you, I think."

Tausen recoiled, open-mouthed, as if he was afraid that somehow Hentze might rip off the shirt and hurl it at him.

"I have to protest—" Timmermann started.

"Don't bother," Hentze said. He let his sweater fall damply back into place and turned to the lawyer. "I'm done here. In fact, to tell you the truth, I'm not sure I can stand to be in the same room as your client any longer, so I'll leave you to continue your consultation. Maybe you'll be able to come up with an explanation for why Herre Tausen chose to keep silent about a psychopath like Juhl for the last forty years. I hope you can, because very soon there will be a lot of people asking the same question."

He gave Tausen one final glance, then turned on his heel and stalked out of the cell as Annika stood quickly aside.

On the hard plastic chair Mikkjal Tausen looked ashen and his shoulders had slumped, but as Hentze disappeared something galvanised him again and he rose to his feet.

"It's not true!" he called after Hentze. "I helped the girl! Thea. I saved her! Ask her. She'll tell you!"

There was no response but after a moment the door at the end of the corridor closed with a soft thud.

In the silence Tausen looked from Annika to Timmermann and then back to Annika again. "It's not true," he repeated, but now it was a flat, lifeless statement with no expectation of being believed.

Annika turned to the lawyer. "Let us know when you've finished," she said and stepped out of the cell.

In the small office she found Hentze removing clothes from his case on the table.

"Want a coffee?" she asked.

"What I want is a *drink*," Hentze said tersely. He tugged a clean tee shirt from the case, then looked in Annika's direction. "Sorry," he said.

Annika waved it away.

"I shouldn't have shouted at the lawyer, either," Hentze said, dispiritedly. "That wasn't professional."

"Oh, I reckon he'll live," Annika said. She studied his face. "Was it… very bad?"

"Bad enough," Hentze said. He took a moment to consider. "I think it was just the sheer *deliberateness* of it. You'd kill a ram or a ewe more… more *humanely* than that."

"Will she live, do you think?"

Hentze shook his head. "I don't know." He closed the case and put it down on the floor. "Listen, call what's-his-name – Hans Bering – upstairs. Get him to send someone down to give you a break while I find a shower and change. I need to get rid of the smell of that place. After that— Oh, I don't know. We'll sort it out later, okay?"

"Okay," Annika nodded.

Hentze picked up his dry clothes and went to the door before turning back. "And make sure no one tells Tausen or his lawyer that Juhl is dead. The longer they think Juhl can give us his side of the story the more likely it is that Tausen will tell us at least part of the truth." He tugged on the door. "Not that I care much one way or the other right now, but still."

I

IN THE MORNING, HAVING PRESENTED HIS WRITTEN STATEMENT to Hentze, Mikkjal Tausen declined to make any comment regarding the death of Boas Justesen and Hentze didn't press it. By then Remi had secured an extension to the arrest, which gave them enough time to put him on a plane and return him to the Faroes for more detailed questioning. After that, in all probability, he would be charged with Boas Justesen's murder. Even now Tausen's house was being searched and various items of clothing had already been seized for analysis. There was a decent chance that at least a few of these things would provide physical evidence to show that Tausen had been with Boas Justesen on the night of his death and the ensuing fire.

Once he'd seen Annika and Tausen on to the plane – accompanied by a *politibetjent* from the airport unit – Hentze took the train into Copenhagen, using the time to re-read Tausen's statement. In it, Mikkjal Tausen repeated and elaborated on the same basic story he'd told the previous evening, claiming that Oscar Juhl had accompanied him on two visits to the Faroes in 1973 and 1974. Tausen had introduced him to Boas Justesen there, who in turn took Juhl to two or three parties at the Colony commune at Múli.

According to his statement, Tausen had no knowledge of any crimes being committed on the Faroes until 1976, when he'd discovered Thea Rask, drugged and unconscious at the hut by the lake at Vesborggård House. Confronting Juhl and appalled by the crime, Tausen then claimed he had enlisted Lýdia Reyná's help to get Thea safely away.

Of course, Tausen or his lawyer must have realised that this inevitably led to the question of why he had not immediately gone to the police, but this was partially addressed by Tausen's admission that he had been wrong not to do that. However, at the time he'd been young and impressionable, he said, and when Oscar's father, Ulrik Juhl, had arrived at Vesborggård House he had allowed himself to be swayed by the older man's pleadings. Ulrik had said he would take care of everything; that Oscar was sick and needed treatment so he would do no further harm. And surely it was far better for that treatment to be given in a caring, confined environment at home rather than prison, Ulrik had said. He had the money to provide all the security and therapy needed for Oscar, so wasn't that the humane thing to do?

And so he had allowed himself to be convinced, Tausen admitted in his statement. That had been a mistake, he saw now, but at the time he fully believed that Ulrik Juhl was a man of his word, acting only out of love and concern for his son.

Hentze didn't believe it for a moment, of course. His own, more cynical and simpler interpretation was that

Mikkjal Tausen had not gone to the police because he knew that his own part in Oscar Juhl's crimes would come to light if he did. Instead, offered a handsome incentive to keep his mouth shut and leave the country to start a new life, Tausen had taken Ulrik Juhl's money and gone to the United States without looking back.

At the Halmtorvet station Hentze attended a case meeting with Christine Lynge and several senior staff. There he outlined the case against Mikkjal Tausen for the murder of Boas Justesen ten days earlier, and also for his involvement in the deaths of Astrid and Else Dam in 1974. This time Hentze was more candid than he had been with Thomas Friis on Friday, but the bottom line was the same: apart from the connection between Tausen and Juhl in the 1970s there was no reason to think there had been any contact between them since, which meant the investigation into Justesen's murder could be dealt with as a discrete case.

In light of the previous night's events Christine and her colleagues were happy enough to agree that the charge against Tausen was one for the Faroese to pursue on their own. Overnight a document had come in which indicated that Oscar Juhl could be a suspect for multiple killings over the last forty years. It still had to be properly assessed, Christine Lynge said, but the officer who'd compiled the report – a *kriminalassistent* from Aarhus called Thomas Friis – had made a strong case and if there was any substance to it they'd be looking at a major, nationwide investigation, which would only be complicated by dragging Mikkjal Tausen into the equation.

With that much decided the meeting broke up and Hentze accompanied Christine back to her office.

"Have you read his statement?" she asked, closing the door and waving Hentze to a chair.

"Whose statement?"

"Jan Reyná's."

"No," Hentze said, sitting down. "I didn't know he'd made one. Was it last night?"

"Yeh, before he went into surgery. It's only a preliminary account but we needed something." She lifted a single sheet of paper from her desk. "Basically he says he thought Juhl was going to kill him or the girl so he acted in self-defence. Which of course is exactly what any experienced police officer *would* say in those circumstances."

Hentze frowned. "You don't believe him?"

Christine gave him a look. "Hjalti, he shot the man twice in the belly and then *again* in the face. It's hard not to interpret that as a deliberate act." She dropped the sheet of paper on the desk and sat down.

"Even though we know what Juhl was capable of?" Hentze said. "Christine, you *saw* that place. The man was a psychopath and the only reason Tove Hald is still alive is because of Jan Reyná."

"So you're his advocate now?" Christine asked.

"No, no more than I would be for anyone else in the same position," Hentze said neutrally. "What does the Prosecutor think?"

"Too soon to say. Given the circumstances and depending

on Reyná's full statement I think they'll probably go along with self-defence for the time being – at least until the full investigation's complete and the inquest's been held." She looked at him levelly. "Unless you know of any other reason Reyná might have had to kill Juhl. I'm thinking about his interest in his mother's suicide. Because if he thought – rightly or wrongly – that Oscar Juhl had had a hand in that..."

Hentze shook his head. "He hasn't said anything about that to me. And as far as I know he's never had any reason to question the original inquest verdict on her death."

Still not seeming fully convinced, Christine gave it a second, then put it aside. "All right, well I guess we'll just have to wait and see what comes out at the end of all this," she said. "God knows, there'll be enough to deal with for the next few weeks. So what are you going to do now – go back to your islands?"

"Not yet," Hentze said. "I still have interviews to conduct relating to the deaths in 1974."

"What you already have isn't enough?"

"No, I want to be sure," Hentze said flatly. "I want as much as I can possibly get."

II

Thomas Friis knew his secondment to Copenhagen CID hadn't gone down well with Asger Markussen. It wasn't only because Friis had contacted the senior investigating officer in the Oscar Juhl case without authorisation, but also because it now looked as if his serial killer theory would be vindicated. However, whether he liked it or not, Markussen had made no attempt to block Friis's temporary transfer to the capital and so, on the following Monday, Friis was in Copenhagen, visiting Tove Hald in Amager hospital.

Tove had already been interviewed a few hours after she'd regained consciousness the previous day but she remembered almost nothing about events leading up to her abduction by Juhl; only leaving her flat for the Café Ismael to meet a whistleblower from Juhl Pharmaceuticals. Beyond that she had no memory until she regained consciousness in hospital.

Having read her statement, Friis was certain that Juhl must have spiked Tove's drink – or perhaps an item of food – in the café when they'd met. He also believed it was probably the same drug Juhl had used on Helene and Maja Kruse in January, so the technical lab was investigating dozens of samples seized from Juhl's various properties, trying to identify the substance. However, that wasn't Friis's area of interest at the moment and instead he restricted his questioning of Tove to her research into Vesborggård House.

He found her responses – in fact her whole attitude – vaguely disconcerting. She had recovered well enough to be bossy and abrupt – even bad-tempered – and she often responded to his questions as if the answer should have been obvious to anyone with any intelligence. Nevertheless, she was a victim and Friis made allowances for that, especially when she told him about her visits to Lene Sønderby in Humlebæk.

* * *

The following day Thomas Friis knocked on the door of Lene Sønderby's house, accompanied by a female *kriminalassistent*.

"I believe you spoke to a young woman called Tove Hald last week," he said when Lene Sønderby admitted them to her sitting room. "Did you tell anyone else that she'd been to see you and why?"

"No. Why would I do that?" Lene Sønderby said, the denial overly aggressive, rather like the woman herself. "Who would I tell?"

Friis ignored the question and said instead, "You may have seen in the news that Tove Hald was assaulted at a house in Brodby last Saturday, and that a man called Oscar Juhl of the Juhl Pharmaceutical family was shot and killed there."

"No, I don't watch the news," Lene Sønderby said, a very poor lie. "Besides, what's that to do with me?"

"Your husband, Dr Carl Sønderby, worked for Juhl Pharmaceuticals, didn't he? As a psychiatrist."

"Yes."

"And when he retired, he had a company pension, which you still receive. From what I can tell it seems very generous: well above the norm, especially as he'd been in private practice for more than thirty years."

"I don't see what business that is of yours," Lene Sønderby said. "The pension is no more than I'm entitled to. Are you a tax inspector as well as a policeman? I don't understand what any of this is about."

"All right, let me ask you a direct question then," Friis said. "When your husband went into private practice, did he continue to have professional contact with any members of the Juhl family?"

Lene Sønderby took a moment, then gave a terse nod.

"And who was that?"

"I... I don't know." She shifted in her chair, then more defiantly she said, "If you want to know look in the roof space. They're all there: Carl's records. He was always very clear that they had to be kept to make sure that the Juhls didn't try to wriggle out of their responsibilities – their obligation."

"The obligation to pay your husband's pension?"

"Yes."

Friis nodded and stood up. "Could you show us, please?"

In all there were seven plastic storage boxes in the roof space, containing papers, files and audio cassettes. Friis and the female *kriminalassistent* carried the boxes out to the car, filling the trunk and the back seat as Lene Sønderby watched silently from the sitting-room doorway.

It took over a week for Thomas Friis to work his way steadily through the contents of the boxes, and as he did so he discovered that they all related to Dr Sønderby's treatment of Oscar Juhl, which had started in December 1976. It was clear from the papers and tapes that Oscar Juhl's father, Ulrik, had placed his son in private confinement on the family estate near Helsingør at that time, and had then employed Sønderby to cure Oscar of his psychopathic urges.

The treatment – in the form of drug therapy and analysis – had continued until March 1982, when Oscar Juhl had managed to leave his confinement without much apparent difficulty. However, two weeks later Juhl had returned and in their next session he calmly described to Dr Sønderby how he had strangled and killed Nina Lodberg. From Sønderby's notes it seemed that at least part of the reason Juhl had returned home after the murder was to talk about what he had done. He appeared to be fascinated by the moment of death and wanted nothing more than to analyse and deconstruct it from every angle, presumably safe in the knowledge that Dr Sønderby was the one person in the world with whom it was safe to do so.

From Sønderby's files it wasn't possible to tell whether Oscar Juhl was more securely confined after killing Nina Lodberg, but in 1990 Juhl repeated the pattern of absconding and returning, this time after a month and having murdered two girls aged sixteen and eighteen near Vejle and Esbjerg. Again Sønderby's therapy notes recorded the details beyond doubt, and – hardly a coincidence – the psychiatrist's financial records also showed that he received a substantial increase in his consultation fees from Juhl Pharmaceuticals.

By then it must have been obvious to Sønderby that Oscar Juhl was beyond treatment, much less a cure, but his notes continued to take an optimistic view of their regular sessions until, in May 1995, they ceased abruptly. Public records revealed that Ulrik Juhl had died from a stroke at that time and after several months and some litigation, Oscar Juhl inherited the majority share in Juhl Pharmaceuticals. Clearly, despite knowing of his son's crimes, Ulrik Juhl had valued commercial continuity more highly than human life when he'd made his will.

Public and financial records also showed that in September 1995 Dr Carl Sønderby gave up his psychiatric practice and took early retirement on a generous and regular pension from Juhl Pharmaceuticals. On his death nearly twenty years later, the payments had transferred to his wife and Lene Sønderby had continued to keep her late husband's files safe in the roof space of her house.

During further questioning Fru Sønderby steadfastly denied any knowledge of what her husband's files contained, but to Thomas Friis whether she had known or not was a small issue. From what he'd already discovered and from the evidence he accrued later, Friis had the far greater satisfaction of seeing his theory about the serial killer vindicated beyond doubt. Oscar Juhl had killed fifteen people over more than four decades and no one had even suspected it except Thomas Friis.

III

A month after his arrest, Mikkjal Tausen was interviewed by a member of the Danish team investigating Oscar Juhl's crimes, but refused to answer any questions. However, a few days later and at Tausen's request, Hentze visited the prison at Mjørkadalur where he met with Tausen in an interview room. The man looked sunken and hollowed out, Hentze thought: the Arizona tan had long faded and his voice was dulled as they exchanged a few pleasantries. Tausen then handed Hentze a three-page handwritten statement.

"I have nothing else I want to say," he told Hentze. "I admit it. That's all. Now I'd like to go back to my cell."

Hentze didn't demur, but after Tausen had gone he sat in

the interview room and read the document twice. In it Tausen stated that while he had worked for Juhl Pharmaceuticals he had helped to develop a drug called Resolomine which he had then provided to Oscar Juhl for "recreational purposes" while they were both at Vesborggård House. Tausen also admitted that following the murders of Astrid and Else during a visit to the Colony, he had been summoned by Boas Justesen and Oscar Juhl to help hide the bodies, doing so only under the threat that he would be implicated for providing the Resolomine the other two had used on their victims.

This, so Tausen claimed, was the reason Boas had been able to blackmail him forty years later, threatening to uncover the bodies and admit to his guilt if Tausen didn't help him find a treatment for his cancer. Unable to persuade a drunken Boas that there was no treatment on earth that could save his life, there had been an argument and a fight at the house at Múli, during which Tausen had strangled Boas to death, and then tried to cover his crime with a staged suicide.

The confession was a ploy, Hentze was certain of that. By admitting to killing Boas – for which there was mounting forensic proof now anyway – Tausen was hoping to prevent the addition of Astrid and Else's killings to his charges. Hentze's interviews with the residents at the Colony commune in 1974 hadn't yielded any firm statements or evidence about Astrid and Else's disappearance, so Tausen was probably gambling that the Faroes' Prosecutor would have little appetite for a trial with no physical evidence and where the only two direct witnesses – Boas and Juhl – were both dead.

And in that respect, Tausen's gamble paid off. Three days

after he received Tausen's statement, the Prosecutor accepted the confession to killing Boas Justesen, and in December Tausen was sentenced to the maximum term: sixteen years. He would be nearly eighty before he was freed.

The murders of Astrid and Else Dam were not officially laid at Tausen's door, and although Hentze saw the practicality of that decision it didn't sit right with him either. In his more cynical moments – which were more frequent these days – he was fully convinced that Tausen had not only been closely involved in the events at Múli, but also in those at Vesborggård House.

But of course, there was no way to prove it, nor to fully make sense of all the conflicting evidence. It was possible that, as Tausen claimed, he had indeed suffered an attack of conscience when he saw what had been done to Thea Rask at Vesborggård House; maybe even enough that he'd helped Lýdia Reyná get Thea away, taking Oscar Juhl's camera at the same time as some sort of insurance for their safety.

However, in his private moments of dark storytelling, Hentze believed it was even more likely that Tausen had done nothing at all to help Lýdia or Thea – nothing except use his friendship with Lýdia to track her down in Christiania at Oscar Juhl's behest; to reassure her, perhaps, and to find out how much of a danger she posed.

But whichever way it had been – even as a mixture of the two scenarios – when the records of Juhl's "therapy" sessions with Dr Sønderby had come to light, there was no longer any question that it *was* Oscar Juhl who had murdered Lýdia Reyná in Christiania. Juhl had described the killing calmly and in exultant detail to the psychiatrist over several sessions, each time marking it out as a moment of epiphany in his own warped view of his actions. It was his *enlightenment*, as he described it, but to Hentze it seemed that nothing short of an utter darkness could have descended over the man.

So then Hentze lived with and revisited the last question that arose from all that, which was whether Jan Reyná himself had known this truth about Lýdia's death. Had Reyná worked it out before he went to the house at Strandvej, or had Juhl himself confessed it in that foetid spa room before he was shot dead?

There had been three shots; Hentze knew that because he'd heard them over the phone. One-two, and then three. But how long had the gap been before the last shot? How long was enough to make one interpretation of events more likely than the other?

He didn't know, and part way through the darkest month of December he made up his mind and finally chose to give Reyná the benefit of the doubt. After what he'd seen and what he now knew about Oscar Juhl, Hentze didn't want Juhl's black, corrosive evil to eat away at anyone else any more. Enough, he decided; let there be an end to it all now. Just let it end.

IV

There was snow on the mountains half circling Tjørnuvík, and on the slopes of Eiðiskollur across Sundini sound. From the bedroom window I could see both over and between the roofs of the houses on the flat crescent of land behind the black beach. It was a good view but it wouldn't last much longer in the January afternoon. I turned away from the window and went downstairs.

The house Signar had left me in his will had turned out to be on the old side of Tjørnuvík, to the west of the church: not overly large, but recently remodelled. Finishing it off had given me something to do for the last few months and the sense of camping in the space had maintained the feeling that my occupancy was only a temporary arrangement. Inevitably I'd accumulated some things, just to make life slightly more pleasant, but since the start of the week I'd been divesting myself of the surplus and now I was back to what would fit in a couple of bags. They sat on the living-room floor, almost ready to go.

I'd been waiting for the knock on the door and when it came I let Fríða in. We hadn't seen each other for more than a month, although we had spoken on the phone. I was glad she'd come.

It was cold and damp outside and she came in wearing a parka, which she immediately ditched in the warmth of the heating. That was one thing I didn't skimp on. My left leg was a lot better than it had been and I was only using a stick about half of the time but the bone still ached in the cold.

"Hjalti's here too," Fríða told me after we'd exchanged kisses. "He's gone for a walk."

"He thought you needed an escort?"

"*Nei*. No, of course not."

"I didn't mean—" I shook my head. "Bad joke."

She nodded because she'd already figured that out.

In the kitchen I set the kettle to boil.

"Have you spoken to Tove?" Fríða asked, spotting the single postcard stuck to the fridge: a view of the Tivoli Gardens.

"Yeah, about a week ago. It wasn't for long: she was busy. You know what she's like. But I'll see her in Copenhagen if she's got time."

"When you see her will you give her my love? Tell her to come and see us."

"Sure, of course."

Despite what she'd been through – none of which she remembered – Tove had recovered in a couple of days, although she complained of headaches and sleeping too much for a while. She'd even come to see me in hospital and thanked me, which I said missed the point.

"What point?" she'd said with a frown. "If you hadn't come I would be dead. Everyone says so."

"Yeah, but if I hadn't got you involved in the first place…"

"No, that logic is faulty," she'd said with her usual frown at stupidity. "It implies that any event has only one causal effect, which is never true."

"Okay, if you say so," I'd told her, just so she'd be quiet. I thought of this approach as Tove-management now.

When the kettle boiled I made coffee, then gave Fríða a tour of the house, pointing out the things she might need to know when it came to letting the place. I'd intended to sell it, but Fríða held the opinion that it was still too hasty a decision to sever all my ties to the islands. She knew better than to fully rely on that argument, though, and added the pragmatic truth that a small but regular income might also be useful, given my lack of employment.

I wasn't convinced on either front but in the end it made no real difference to me so I'd gone along with it, on the understanding that Fríða had charge of the place, took an agent's fee and kept me out of it. I don't know why she agreed, but she did; a day after the Danish Prosecutor's office had officially accepted that I'd shot Oscar Juhl in self-defence and to protect Tove.

I suspected the Prosecutor's decision had finally been as much a matter of politics as of legal distinctions. The more information that surfaced about Oscar Juhl's past, the harder it would be to convince anyone that it hadn't been a justifiable killing, so why drag it out? There's a Faroese saying: *galnir hundar fáa rivið skinn* – mad dogs get their skin torn – and there was no doubt that Juhl had been a mad dog.

So now I was formally, officially blameless; free to leave Danish jurisdiction, and that's what I was going to do.

"You still have no definite plan?" Fríða asked when we'd finished the tour and I'd given her a set of keys.

"Just to drive on a straight road for more than two or three miles," I said. "I've been cooped up too long."

She wasn't the sort who approved of aimlessness but she also knew the futility of arguing the point.

I collected my stick and a coat and we left the house and walked towards the sea. When we emerged on to Teigagøta I saw Hentze opening the gate to the churchyard and started that way until I realised Fríða hadn't moved to go with me. I stopped and turned back.

"Tell Hjalti I'll wait in the car," she said. She gave me a wan smile. "Travel safely, okay?"

"*Ja*, I will. *Takk*," I said.

Inside the church I found Hentze sitting straight-backed in a pew. The seats weren't designed for comfort but they could certainly focus your mind, which was undoubtedly the intention.

"Have you taken up praying?" I asked. I didn't sit down but leaned on a rail.

"No, not so much."

"Good."

He frowned. "Why do you say that?"

I shrugged. "I never saw you as the praying type, that's all. It would upset my view of the world if I found out you were."

"Well, I wouldn't want that," Hentze said and I thought I heard a slight edge in his voice, as if I'd come close to a line. But maybe not.

"Thomas Friis called me a couple of days ago," I told him. "He has a book deal. They want to publish as soon as the official investigation's concluded."

"Yeh, I heard that," he said. I knew he didn't approve. "I'm not so sure he will get official consent, though."

"He seems to think he can get round that one way or the other."

Hentze still didn't look convinced. "Has he reached his own conclusion, then?" he asked.

I shrugged. "His theory is that when Juhl realised an investigation into Inge-Lise's murder would eventually get round to him, he decided to take one more victim while he still could. He'd already met Tove so he knew what she was like, and it wasn't hard to come up with a ploy to abduct her."

Hentze wrinkled his nose.

"You don't like it?" I said.

"Not very much. I don't say that it's wrong, but if it is true it means Juhl is easily dismissed. We just say he was evil and then we don't have to think about it any more: to look for a better explanation; to know why. That's the thing I don't like." He considered that for a brief moment longer, then shifted focus. "So why did Friis call you?" he asked. "For more information?"

"Partly," I said. "He was trying to reel me in. He wants me to tell my side for the book. It'll be a bestseller, he reckons. It's got all the right elements: Ulrik Juhl locking up his son on the family estate; the private psychiatric treatment; the escapes and then Oscar taking over the company when Ulrik died."

"So, did you agree?"

I shook my head. "I don't like the idea, and Friis is a bit too pleased with himself. Anyway, he's only really interested in getting a description of what happened at the Strandvej house."

"Well, I suppose some people would like to read about that."

"Yeah, and life's full of disappointments," I said.

"Yes, yes, that's true," he said with a nod, then glanced at my stick. "How is your leg now?"

"Doesn't like the cold and the damp, which is a good excuse to go somewhere warmer for a while."

"And then what will you do? Do you know yet?"

I shrugged. "Maybe some consultancy work. I don't know. I'm not good at networking."

"No, I've noticed that," he said drily. "Maybe you should try harder."

I gave him a look. "Yeah, well, the truth is – with very few exceptions – I don't like most people that much."

"You are hard work, do you know that?"

"Sorry."

He shook his head. "No, I don't think you are."

I drew a breath and looked up at the roof of the church, smelling the wood-resin smell. "No, you're right," I said in the end. "But like I say, there are a few exceptions."

"Well, I suppose that's something," he said, and I could tell that was an end to it now. He stood up. "I should find Fríða."

Outside we walked the short gravel path, and Hentze closed the black iron gate behind us. "Will you come back?" he asked.

"No, I don't think so."

He nodded and then we shook hands.

"*Farvæl og takk, ja?*"

"*Ja. Somuleiðes,*" I said.

V

There was bright sunshine, made sharper and more dazzling by the recent rain and the cold wind across the car park at the back of the station on Yviri við Strond. Annika Mortensen was coming down the grey fire-escape steps with a box in her arms as Hentze approached from his car.

"So, your things are all gone now?" he asked with a nod at the box.

"Yeh. And I've stolen six pencils and a packet of envelopes."

"That's a coincidence: that's exactly what we were going to give you as a leaving present."

"Yeh, yeh." Annika grinned and then put the box aside on the step to give him a hug, which Hentze stiffly accepted, a little embarrassed.

"Listen, I know you won't come," Annika said when she stood back. "But all the same there's a small party at my place tomorrow night to say goodbye."

Hentze frowned. "Why do you think I won't come? What time shall I be there?"

"It's from eight, but you can be late. We won't go out to the town until midnight."

"That's okay; midnight's my bed time. Will Heri be there?"

"Sure, of course. You heard his attachment came through as well?"

"No, I didn't know that. No one tells me anything."

She gave him a look. "Maybe you don't listen. Anyway, he has six months at the station in Indre By so by the end of that we should be able to decide what to do next."

"Good," Hentze said, and meant it. "So, I'll see you tomorrow night, then."

"Okay." She picked up her box and started away. "And bring Sóleyg," she called back over her shoulder.

"Of course."

Although he knew there was no *of course* about it.

But as Hentze climbed the steps he decided he *would* ask Sóleyg if she wanted to go. Why not? Things were different all round after the last two or three months. And as he unlocked the door to Ári Niclasen's old office he wondered if he should finally buy a coffee machine to replace the one Ári had reclaimed. He knew how Remi would interpret that move, though: give it a few hours and there would be no more *acting* inspector about it.

For helviti, he thought, shaking his head at the idea of selling his soul for a morning espresso. What had he come to? Still, a new coffee machine *would* be nice.

AUTHOR'S NOTE

BY AND LARGE THE GEOGRAPHY OF THE FAROES IS AS IT'S described in the book. However, I have used some licence with the descriptions of individual buildings and locations, some of which are transposed from other places. I should also point out that, as far as I know, there has never been a commune at Múli or a clinic known as Vesborggård House. I would also like to emphasise that this is a work of fiction and that none of the characters or incidents portrayed here are based on real people or events.

ACKNOWLEDGEMENTS

I CONTINUE TO BE INDEBTED TO THE OFFICERS AND STAFF OF the Faroe Islands Police Department for their hospitality and invaluable assistance with the Faroes trilogy – I hope they know who they are by now. I must also thank their Danish counterparts, Kristian Bruun Jensen on Samsø and Kim Bolø in Copenhagen. I'm especially grateful to Henning Munk Plum for his insights into Danish police work.

In civilian life I'd like to thank Dr Nick Leather for his continued medical advice; Jasmine Kilby for her knowledge of pharmaceuticals; and Anne Birgitte Beyer for her help on Samsø. As always, any mistakes are mine alone.

Finally, to my long-suffering editors, Miranda Jewess and Sam Matthews, *gott er at svimja, tá ið annar heldur høvdinum uppi. Takk.*

ABOUT THE AUTHOR

CHRIS OULD IS A BAFTA AWARD-WINNING SCREENWRITER WHO has worked on many TV shows including *The Bill*, *Soldier Soldier*, *Casualty* and *Hornblower*. Chris has previously published two adult novels, and two Young Adult crime novels. He lives in Dorset.